I0721876

Hotel Impala

Copyright© 2024 Pat Spears
All Rights Reserved

ISBN # 978-1-940189-35-2

This is a work of fiction. Names, characters, businesses, places, events, locales, and incidents are either the products of the author's imagination or used in a fictitious manner.

Excerpt from *Bastard Out of Carolina* reprinted with permission from Penguin Random House

Cover design by Babski Creative Studios
Cover photograph by Bob O'Lary

Printed in United States

Twisted Road Publications

Hotel Impala

a novel by

Pat Spears

Things come apart so easily when they have been held together with lies.

Dorothy Allison, *Bastard Out of Carolina*

Prologue

Leah

Washed in blood, her spent body was lifted onto a cold slab. Overhead, a burst of brilliance like a dying star blinded her to the ghostly forms crouched above her. Their heavy breathing pushed through masked lips that moved without sound. And she was delivered into a state of nothingness.

The Pathway to Rapturous Bliss
Fall 2015

— 1 —

Grace

The school bus pulled away and Grace glanced back toward home. She sometimes still imagined their mom standing in front of the purple door, waving long after the bus had rounded the corner and vanished from sight. Zoey dared not as much as a backward glance but hugged her backpack to her chest as though a substitute for all she needed.

"Mom waved. Didn't she?" Zoey's eyes were focused elsewhere.

"You tell me." Her sister's improbable optimism, too early, wore on Grace's own resilience. The glimmer of hope slid from Zoey's face, replaced by a pinched expression, and she squeezed her backpack even tighter.

Regretting her harshness, Grace leaned and whispered, "Dad said she'll be well enough to volunteer at the animal shelter again soon. That's good, right?" But she knew Dad, too, often chose hope when there was little else to offer.

Zoey chewed on a bleeding cuticle, and Grace knew only one of her better stories, drawn from her earliest memories of their mom and baby Zoey, would satisfy her sister. Zoey never stopped begging for more of Grace's stories; peppered with plenty of Grace's sweetest lies. The worst part of living in stories that were never completely true was Grace's fear of someday running dry of stories, leaving her and Zoey to live fully inside their mother's tilted realities.

— 2 —

Leah

Leah woke from what must have been a long absence. Through the scarlet-edged pain that was the heavily medicated workings of her mind, she struggled to salvage bits and pieces of what was once familiar. To make whole again scattered remnants of faded memories and surrendered sensations. She traced the tender pink scars on her wrists, and heat from her shame rose before she remembered she no longer cut herself.

Bad memories must be sealed away in the deepest recesses of her mind if she were to wake to the good of the here and now. Had she heard or only dreamed: two sets of hurried feet. Twenty toes, one set bigger, the other smaller, treading lightly across the floor. The wiser voice repeating the family mantra: *Our Mom is fine. It's just that she sometimes lives inside her head.*

Her Grace was kind, though stoic in her denial of the harshest truths. Zoey was beautiful and sweet, and yet a fully selfish child. Impulsive yet timid and lacking in proper deference. Their father, while compassionate, was a sad man who had yet to find his true voice.

In the dream, the sucking sounds of a rubber seal yielding; cold milk sloshed into two shallow bowls. Milk dribbling from the corners of Zoey's overstuffed mouth, wiped onto the back of her perfectly shaped diminutive hand. Bowls half full. Raised voices. Chairs scraped across worn tiles; hurried feet, door swung wide, and stale air escaping.

The roar of the yellow dragon, belching toxic poisons, carried her daughters away, and she had done nothing to save them.

— 3 —

Grace

The afternoon school bus slowed at the corner of McDaniel and Avenue C, and Grace squinted against the sun's glare toward home while Zoey looked no farther than her double-knotted shoelaces. Theirs was the house painted canary yellow with a purple door. Windows that faced the street were covered in sheets of plywood like those seen in advance of a hurricane.

Grace studied the old Impala parked in their driveway. Mom often referred to it as her *sweet chariot*. She sometime sat alone in the car for hours, as if she had forgotten her intended destination. Grace was relieved on days when the rear tires showed the chalk marks she had drawn on the driveway.

Grace scanned the patchy lawn for other clues as to what might await her and her sister on the opposite side of the purple door, adorned with hundreds of white, hand-painted stars. Mom had painted the door a shade she called *passionate purple*, pointing to an empty paint can with a label that read nothing of the sort. After painting the door, Mom had painted each joint of their walkway in a rainbow color, declaring her artistry a gift to the neighborhood's enlightenment, akin to a Picasso marvel.

At the time, Grace had not understood what their mom meant when she announced their walk was a *pathway to rapturous bliss*. It was only after Dad's repeated early arrivals home from his job that Grace understood the association of purple with their parents' loud sex.

On reaching the point where the public sidewalk joined their rainbow walkway, Zoey squatted and stared at the star-studded door as though she was seeing it for the first time. Grace took the hidden key from beneath a pot of dead geraniums, inserted it into the deadbolt, and quietly pushed open the door.

The house reeked of the ammonia scent of urine, and it reminded Grace of trips taken to visit Granny Sybil on Christmas Eves and her birthdays; the two times a year Dad had insisted on family visits.

Sometimes, before Dad left for work, Mom permitted him to strip her of her soiled pajamas and bathe her. Grace had asked that he load and start up the washer and leave everything for her to dry and fold, rather than pile urine-soaked bed linen and pajamas outside their bedroom door. That way, the house would stink far less. He had agreed, but did not always remember if he was running late for work. When she had reminded him, he said now that she was twelve, she would need to help out more with her mom. He blushed when she told him that she would not turn twelve for another six months. *Flare-up* was the word Dad had instructed her and Zoey to use when speaking of Mom's illness within the family, while forcefully, though needlessly, cautioning that they were never to speak of her illness outside the family.

Mom's flare-ups sometimes occurred around the time of Zoey's birthday, and Grace wondered if her sister recently turning five may have triggered her current episode. Zoey had yet to have a birthday cake Mom baked, though Aunt Josey always came through with what she called a make-do cake. Grace believed Zoey understood the pretty cakes had not come from Mom after she turned four.

Grace sometimes secretly wished Mom's illness was noble, like cancer. She and Zoey would wear pink tee shirts and march in parades, chanting *Save our Moms*. She would feel hopeful for a cure and never need to feel ashamed.

Grace stepped through the door onto the carpet, still blood-stained after multiple scrubbings, a reminder of an earlier flare-up. She was careful not to tread on the one thousand puzzle pieces scattered about on the dining room floor. They were pieces of a puzzle she and Zoey had worked to finish, hoping to surprise Mom, only to have her scream that they were never again to touch her artwork.

Gardening books and magazines were stacked in exact counts of twelve on the floor against one wall. Bags of unopened potting soil were propped against a second. Grace sometimes felt guilty that she had allowed Mom's rule to keep her from rescuing the two dozen pots of dead mums which were once stars of an imagined gardening project. Their home and attic were filled with reminders of Mom's once-grand ideas, abandoned after she moved eagerly to an even grander undertaking.

Grace tiptoed into the hallway and stood holding her breath outside her parents' bedroom door, listening for any movement. Mom's silent recoveries were more predictable, but they were also lonelier. Grace remembered overhearing Dad refer to the emptiness that was sometimes in Mom's dark eyes as the dead-eyed stare of a ghost. She thought her sister's reluctance to enter the house was her fear that in their absence, Mom had vanished to wherever ghosts resided.

Grace went back to the front door and waved Zoey inside, tempting her sister with a cup of hot cocoa and a saucer of warm milk for Jimmie, a stray tabby who had shown up at their back door and now spent school days sleeping on Zoey's pillow when he was not enraging their nearest neighbor by stalking birds she claimed as her own.

Zoey came through the door into the darkened living room and peered along the hallway but did not advance toward the closed bedroom door. But on her way into the kitchen, Zoey attempted to match Mom's longer stride of purple footprints dried into the carpet. Other colors of paint partially covered the dining room walls, leaving the only clues as to how Mom might have imagined them.

When Grace had filled a pot with water and set it on a burner to heat, she retrieved the pile of soiled laundry and put it on to wash. Had Mom allowed Dad to bathe her, and he was running late? Was this a sign that she was better? Though a pee-stained gown could simply mean yesterday's folded pajamas didn't suit her. Everything about Mom, even at her best, made it hard to know what was to come.

— 4 —

Leah

Leah opened her eyes to a labyrinth of locked doors for which she had no keys, her consciousness passing through a tunnel of fogged mirrors. Yet, an array of familiar sounds beckoned her to come closer. She pushed back the weighty bedcovers and stood in a narrow strip of light from the window. She flexed her toes in the rug's thick pile and a sensation pulsed through her bare soles with such intensity, tears spilled down her pale cheeks. She stared at her feet, signaling the first and then the second to move forward, until they had carried her beyond the contours of the rug and toward the familiar voices.

At Zoey's frantic screams, Grace turned from the bubbling pot of pasta, her surprise so complete she felt faint.

"Mommy, Mommy, you're back," Zoey called, her arms encircling Mom's thighs.

Leah leaned heavily on the door frame and blinked as though she had awakened among strangers in an unfamiliar place. Palms flat, fingers spread, she stroked Zoey's springy curls in the cautious way one might an unfamiliar dog, though Grace chose to believe Mom would have spoken warm mother-to-daughter speech if only she had remembered the right words.

Leah pushed Zoey off, covered her mouth with her fingertips, and took an awkward step backward. She stared at Grace and maybe she had seen her for the first time. She reached a tentative hand toward Grace but withdrew, and

Grace stood awkwardly, her hands jammed inside the pockets of her jeans.

"I remember…. It's you… you dislike… cooking."

Was Mom asking, or actually remembering? Still, Grace answered.

"Oh, no, and you've got to be starving. Food is nearly ready." For weeks, Grace had been placing trays of food and pitchers of fresh water on the small table outside Mom's door each morning, only to return to find the food largely untouched.

Leah did not respond but stared at her bare feet as though the kitchen tiles were covered in broken glass, and she took hesitant steps in retreat.

"No, Mommy, you can't go back. You've got to sign my smiley faces." Zoey grabbed Mom's wrist in an attempt to hold her back.

"No, Zoey, stop." Grace pried Zoey's locked fingers apart, breaking her grip, and Mom stumbled out of the kitchen, back along the hallway and into her bedroom.

"Oh, no. See what you did?" Zoey cried, and gathering her scattered school papers, she began ripping them into shreds. When Zoey had exhausted her rage, she ran from the kitchen, wailing in hurt and disappointment.

Grace did not follow but set the drained pot of pasta aside and took her cell phone from the back pocket of her jeans.

"Grace, what's happened? You girls okay?" Dad always answered the same whenever she and Zoey were alone with Mom.

"We're good, but Dad… just now Mom came into the kitchen."

He reassured her that he was on his way, but his voice was thick with wariness. "And Grace, remember, you two need to stay calm and not push her."

"I know, Dad. I know." She feared Zoey's selfish fit had driven Mom back into more weeks of absence.

Mary and Beauty
Fall 2015

– 5 –

Grace

Mom did not relapse as Grace had feared. Instead, she continued to improve. Within six weeks, as Dad had predicted, she was able to return to volunteering at a local animal shelter. Despite Mom's many failings with past employers, co-workers, teachers, prying neighbors, and random strangers, she knew secrets about the pain of abandonment suffered by shelter animals, especially dogs, and they trusted her.

Most days, Mom seemed content to clean pens and feed and walk those dogs deemed unadoptable, whom she referred to as unjustly doomed, but spoke sadly of her two favorites. Mary was a Lab mix who Mom had said was dumped at the shelter under the cover of darkness, her right eye nothing but a cavity, the eye socket hollow. Starved, Mary's body was covered in infected lacerations, the result of sharp teeth. Gentle Mary's recent history was one of brutal assaults by gangs of young pit bulls in training. Mom had learned nothing of the comatose dog she had named Beauty. Grace felt the name was unkind, but in a loving way, so she said nothing.

Mom took photos of Mary and Beauty and created a flyer to be passed among potential adopters. Grace wanted to help find forever homes for the dogs, but worried that their effort to find good Samaritans was certain to fail.

Mom selected the day of the animal shelter's monthly puppy adoption event to distribute her fliers, mindful that the event drew large numbers of adopters. By mid-afternoon, as rejections of Mary and Beauty mounted, Mom became verbally aggressive toward would-be puppy adopters, and when they continued to rush past her, her desperation turned physical: she blocked the entry with her body, thrusting fliers into their hands.

A stout man, his face flushed crimson, rushed from the building, shouting at Mom with threats of trespassing and inciting public disorder.

"You and… they…", he pointed toward her and Zoey, "must leave immediately. If you don't, I'll call the police and have you removed."

Mom spewed a stream of profanities, declaring she would never forsake Mary and Beauty. Further incensed, the man stepped away, his phone pressed to his ear.

"Oh no, can they arrest kids?" Zoey questioned, her face pale.

"Mom, please, we've gotta go," Grace insisted, but Mom only became more agitated.

A woman in a white lab coat, who Grace decided was one of the shelter vets, must have overheard Mom's pleas for the two dogs and the man's escalating threats.

When the woman approached, Mom turned to her, and Grace believed Mom and the woman may have recognized each other. Grace did not hear what passed between them, but Mom walked away, and the woman followed.

After a further exchange, Mom hurried her and Zoey into the Impala and drove them away. Grace glanced back at the man, who walked smartly back into the building. He likely thought that he was rid of Leah Killian and her mad crusade, but the arrogant man had clearly misjudged the fiery resolve that burned in Mom's eyes.

— 6 —

Ellie

Ellie drove away from the animal shelter, where she volunteered half a day each week to care for animals who needed treatment before they were medically cleared for adoption. She exited the interstate onto the beach highway toward an area known locally as Bailey Cove and felt the release of the city's tensions. But she was unable to set aside the scene with the woman and her fervent appeal on behalf of the two animals, or the pleas of her daughters that they leave before the police arrived. Ellie sensed that this was not the first incident in which the daughters had feared an encounter with law enforcement.

Ellie knew the woman only by her reputation as an unrelenting advocate on behalf of the most physically and emotionally damaged dogs. She had told Leah that she had not examined either of the dogs pictured on the flier, but offered to review their medical records and to approach the supervisor on their behalf, should she find a reason to support their adoption. But that had not been enough to satisfy the agitated woman. It wasn't until she had made an uncharacteristically impulsive decision that, should the dogs prove to be unadoptable, she would assist in a way fraught with questions of unprofessionalism, if not legal jeopardy, that the woman agreed to leave.

Before leaving the city, Ellie had reviewed the medical recommendations of the other volunteer vet, and she agreed with his decision that the two dogs' state of health and advanced ages rendered both unsuitable for adoption. While his conclusion had oddly relieved her mind, it had not altered the fact that she would now have to keep her second promise.

After a thirty-minute drive along the coastal highway, now bordered on the windward side by a magnificent estuarial marsh, a nursery of abundant sea life, Ellie turned onto the crushed oyster shell road that led to a vintage clapboard beach cottage perched on an elevated sandscape carpeted in sea myrtle, red trumpet, chokeberry, and palmetto, reigned overhead by a stand of native longleaf pine, some one hundred feet and more in height.

All bore scars from their resistance to salt spray, battering winds, and hurricanes that had arrived long before the practice of naming storms. Beyond the house was a narrow strip of white shoreline, shaped and reshaped at the will of rising and receding tides. She shared this wild beauty with her wife, Jordan, a police officer.

She bounded through the cottage door, and thoughts of the woman and her daughters gave way to the promise of a long-awaited weekend to be shared with Jordan; a rare occasion when they each had an entire weekend free.

— 7 —

Ellie

In the distance, a single figure emerged despite the gathering darkness, and Ellie smiled at Jordan's efforts to outrun an approaching thunderstorm. Jordan ran most days, her motivation in part her training for her job as a police officer, but also pure enjoyment, stemming from her high school days as a competitive long-distance runner. In one of Jordan's darker moments, she had described her runner's endurance as a life-skill.

Their perfect weekend was coming to an end, and Ellie felt a moment of melancholy. Although she had managed to set aside tomorrow and her questionable decision, she hoped the unfurling fury of the storm was not a foretaste of what lay ahead.

Jordan yelled ahead against the gathering wind, and Ellie hurriedly kicked sand on the last of the embers and grabbed her beach bag. With the sandy blanket wrapped around her shoulders, Ellie giggled, and she answered as she made her way onto the path home. Jordan playfully overtook her and raced ahead, though neither escaped the first of the downpour. A shared hot shower was ahead.

Monday morning early, Ellie kissed Jordan good-bye, content to leave her sleeping, and drove back into the city, her thoughts fixed on her pledge to the woman whose full name she had yet to learn.

— 8 —

Leah

Leah woke fully cognizant of her impending mission, and she slipped quietly out of bed, leaving Daniel snoring lightly. She gathered jeans, a light jacket, boots, and socks, and stepped quietly toward the door, pausing to glance back at Daniel, who had continued to sleep undisturbed.

Leah made her way into the kitchen, where she changed out of her nightgown and into her choice of purposefully masculine clothes. She twisted her long hair into a knot and stuffed it beneath one of Daniel's hats. She stepped through the back door and set out for the nearest bus stop, walking along a row of mostly deteriorating homes on small lots, flanked by litter-strewn streets. A single discolored yard sign stood alone among a citizenry Leah believed had largely washed their hands of politics.

Streetlights cut through the fading darkness and dense fog rolling in from the coast with air that felt like squeezed raindrops. As far as she could see, the streets were empty of those who might have preyed upon a lone woman. Still, she kept with her hard-earned vigilance, and had stuffed the loose bills she would need for bus fare inside her boot.

Reaching the bus stop, she walked past the bench and stood in the greater safety of deep shadows. The welcome headlights of the five-forty bus, the first of the day, soon appeared in the distance, and Leah stepped into the circle of light.

One hour and two bus changes delivered Leah within four blocks of the animal shelter. She circled through the adjacent vacant lot and approached the building from the rear. Using a duplicate key she had made in secret, Leah entered the building and called a greeting to the alarmed dogs as she approached the pen Mary and Beauty shared. Mary stood ready at the kennel gate while Beauty remained huddled in a far corner.

Leah slipped a soft collar over Mary's head and injected into the old dog's trembling right shoulder the last of the pain meds she had stolen from the vets' cabinet. She wrapped a trembling Beauty in her jacket, settled the dog on her hip, and Mary followed through the gate. Mary's energy seemed to have stirred and their journey began with a slow walk at a nearby park.

The sights, sounds, and scents of freedom had always made Mary happy. At the greetings of songbirds, she turned to watch their flight. Delighted by the scent of freshly cut grass, she stopped to roll in its early morning dampness. Leah was certain that Mary had once known a good life before brutality, and the loneliness of her confinement at the end of a length of chain.

Nature had peeled back the outer edges of darkness, and tall pines stood distinguishable, one from the other, and when Mary had tired, Leah took a seat on a park bench. She placed Beauty next to her on the bench and Mary lay at her feet.

A shift in Leah's mindfulness, like the lifting of the morning fog, embraced from afar the playful sounds of children's laughter, spilling forth as an unspooling of colorful ribbon. A girl, swift-of-foot, wearing scuffed sneakers, her pigtails trailing like bright streamers, pumped her sturdy legs, propelling herself higher and higher as though she intended to touch the sun's rays.

An old man approached, wearing baggy jeans caught up on narrow hips. She reimagined him as a young boy in hand-me-downs from an older sibling or from a pile of cast-offs. The boy had a thatch of unwashed hair, black as a slick tar road in rain. His grey eyes were set wide in his pale face, and they bore a measured weight of rejection. The boy looked first at Leah, and then at Mary.

The wise dog studied the boy, and maybe she dreamed of a boy from another time.

"She yours?" He asked.

"No, she's my friend." Leah believed Mary smiled.

The boy's scowl deepened. "But she's ugly. Who'd want her?"

The dog turned her head, showing the boy her good eye, and his pain was reflected there. The boy's scowl disappeared, and he asked, "What's she called?"

"Mary. Mary is her name."

"That's a dumb name for a dog."

"I think Mary likes her name."

"I'm called... Homer." There was a trace of melancholy in his tone, and he whispered, "I hate my name." He glanced over his right shoulder as though bad memories followed him.

"Then I will remember you as David, the brave young boy-slayer of giants."

Homer looked a bit puzzled, though pleased.

Mary continued to watch the boy.

"She's mean, right? All of them scars and that cloudy eye?" He winced and momentarily looked away, as though wishing to hide his own secrets.

"Those were never her fault but were wrongly inflicted."

The boy blinked hard. He risked two fingers toward Mary, and she moved into his touch. The boy stroked her, his fingers tracing the ragged edges of her torn ears. Then, stepping back, he jammed his hands deep within his pockets, as though he meant to savor the scent of Mary's kindness so that he might draw upon it in times to come.

"Will you bring Mary back tomorrow?"

"No, my time with her is now."

"What will happen to her?"

"From now on, only good."

The boy looked away and then back at Mary. "She knows, doesn't she?" There was finality in his tone.

 Leah nodded. "I believe she does."

The boy's thin shoulders sagged, and then he lifted his craggy face; no longer a boy, but the broken man he had become. He turned and limped back in the direction from whence he had come.

Leah called, "David, why are you sad?"

He answered back over his shoulder, "Mary knows. Bring her to me."

Mary softly barked.

Leah had never before heard Mary's voice. Yet it was as she expected: kind and, more than anything else, forgiving. Leah led Mary to the rear of the building and rang the doorbell labelled Emergency Only. Mary sat patiently watching a male cardinal, its brilliance reflected in a small puddle of last evening's rain. Ellie, the shelter' volunteer veterinarian, opened the door, glanced anxiously toward the parking lot, and ushered Leah and Mary inside. She led the way along a narrow hallway into one of three exam rooms. Sitting on a tray next to the steel table were four syringes and vials of pentobarbital and a second drug.

"Beauty first, do you think?" Ellie asked. Her tone was both sad and anxious, Leah thought.

Leah looked at Mary and back at Ellie.

"Yes, I think Beauty would want Mary with her."

Beauty trembled against Leah's chest the way she had since the day they met. Her fear had lessened only after she and Mary had shared a kennel. Leah placed Beauty, still wrapped in her jacket, on the table.

Mary stood quietly.

"Given her extreme poor health, the drug should take only a few minutes to take effect." Ellie slipped the needle into a vein and injected the tranquilizer. Moments later, Beauty opened her eyes in complete recognition. Her trembling subsided: her twisted muscles relaxed, and Ellie administered the second drug. Beauty's demise came as a silent gift, and she was unafraid. Her eyes now closed, her twisted body uncurled, she was at peace.

Mary's big brown eye showed sadness in the presence of loss, and she whimpered. Leah knelt next to Mary, waiting for her to signal her readiness. Ellie lowered the hydraulic table and Mary stepped onto the platform and lay on her side without being told. Ellie raised the table and turned to Leah.

"Do either of you need more time?" Her voice was heavy with emotion.

Leah took Mary's paw in her hand and Mary lifted her head, touching Leah's hand with her wet nose, and lay back on the table. Leah's heart pounding with the roar of her loss, she nodded in response, acknowledging what she understood as Mary's acceptance.

Ellie administered the first drug and Mary closed her good eye, and shortly thereafter she was unconscious. She administered the second injection, and as Leah touched Mary's once crippled shoulder, she experienced the sensation of Mary's spirit separating from her body, her soul ascending into that space where goodness alone resides.

Leah and Ellie were met at the park by a man who limped to the car and asked if he might carry Mary to a grave site he had prepared in a secluded spot, away from walkers and bikers.

With Mary gathered tightly in his arms and Beauty in Leah's, the three entered the park, the man leading the way.

He and Leah lowered first Mary and then Beauty into their shared grave. When the man had backfilled the grave and raked leaves and small branches onto the site to conceal the freshly disturbed earth, he disappeared into the thick foliage.

"The kind man, did you know him before today?" Ellie asked.

"David, yes, maybe elementary school, I remember he was always a sad boy." Leah turned and glanced in the direction the man had gone as if she expected to see him there.

The two women walked on and from a nearby elementary school the bright sounds of children at play resonated across the park. Leah's loss reshaped itself into images of an engaging Beauty no longer afraid and a spirited Mary who leaped into the air while retrieving a bright red ball tossed by a cheering boy with black hair. Dog and boy romped freely beneath a brilliant sky.

— 9 —

Ellie

In the week after the euthanasia of Mary and Beauty, Ellie overheard comments among staff about the weird volunteer and her dismissal following aggressiveness toward potential adopters. Others spoke admiringly of Leah's exceptional skills and kindness for those animals deemed unsuitable for adoption and scheduled for euthanasia. But oddly, Ellie heard no mention of Mary and Beauty or their fate. It was important for her to know what the shelter's computer records might tell her before she decided what, if anything, she would say to Jordan about her decision to aid Leah in her determination to give the dogs peaceful deaths.

Ellie entered the lobby and was greeted by Jason, an able intern enrolled in a local community college vet tech program. She knew him as an exacting follower of rules and would have preferred a young defendant with a chip on his shoulder, doing community service hours under a court order.

"Hi Doc." Jason glanced up from a clipboard, his gaze narrowing.

"Yes, you're right. I'm a day early." She smiled. "I forgot a recording task on my last visit."

"May I help you find the records you need?" The eager young intern came from behind the counter and stood ready.

"That's sweet, but it's a minor correction and I'll only be a minute." Ellie wished she had not mentioned records. She was bad at lies, the basics of keeping secrets.

Ellie opened the door to the small records room and Raymond, one of the court mandated volunteers looked up from the computer monitor.

"Ah, do you mind if I check something there before you close those records? I never remember the password and I'm really in a hurry."

He shrugged, offered her the chair, and closed the door behind him.

Ellie sorted through the records for the date Mary and Beauty were scheduled for euthanasia. Scanning the identification numbers assigned to each animal at the time of its intake, she noted that both dogs were listed among those animals euthanized on the same date Leah had delivered the dogs to her office.

What she was seeing was either poor recordkeeping or an act of intentionally falsifying records. If the latter, was it motivated by the administration's wish to avoid any future confrontation around the suitability of the two animals for euthanasia? But additional questioning of the records might raise suspicion about the disappearance of the dogs.

In addition to poor recordkeeping, Ellie also discovered that the shelter's standard protocol omitted the use of a pre-euthanasia tranquilizer. Without the benefit of such a drug, both animals, especially Beauty, would have suffered terrifying moments before their demise. While she took comfort in knowing that she had given the two dogs a far less traumatic death, she would need to find another way to lobby the shelter administrator for a kinder practice.

Tupelo Honey
Spring 2016

— 10 —

Grace

Grace woke to the hushed voices of her parents; Mom's giggles and Dad's deeper voice coming from their bedroom across the narrow hallway. Jimmie rose on stiff legs, arched his back in a leisurely stretch, and resettled next to a sleeping Zoey. Grace still cringed at her childish notion that the otherwise jittery cat's newly found ease around Mom was somehow an indication of Mom's well-being. Neither could Grace accept at face value her mom's insistence that the daily doses of her prescribed drug cocktail was the miracle she had long sought. Still, Mom's steadiness over the past nine months had persuaded Grace that she no longer needed to secretly monitor her mom's daily drug intake.

Grace closed her eyes and dozed, for how long she was not sure, but the loud roar of the Impala's engine startled her awake. She hurried out of bed and to the bedroom window, only to catch a glimpse of Mom's car as she sped away. Grace's thoughts spun in an anxious rush, and she asked herself where her mom was going in such a hurry. Had her parents had an argument she had slept through?

Grace stood outside her parents' bedroom door, but the room was silent. Holding her breath, she quietly pushed open the door and peered inside the room. Her dad lay sprawled full length across the bed on his stomach. A muscled arm hung from the edge of the bed, and he was naked. He moaned and turned to his back, fully exposed. Shocked, Grace was struck by a rush of both shame and curiosity. She stood staring while fear of being caught turned her blood icy cold in her veins. She backed away and eased the door shut, retreating into her and Zoey's bedroom.

"Where'd you go?" Zoey spoke from beneath the covers. "And where's Jimmie?"

"Nowhere. Been right here, and why should I care where that weird cat is off to?" The cat was hiding beneath the bed, only the tip of his tail showing. Grace mentally scolded herself for considering what, if anything, explained Jimmie's sudden change?

Dressed, Grace went into the brightly lit kitchen where a pot of coffee was brewing, and the kitchen table, cleared of its usual clutter, was neatly set for four. A large bowl of pancake mix sat on the counter and Grace checked for milk in the nearly empty fridge. Pressing her hand to her heart, she felt relief well up inside her. Mom has simply gone to the market for milk.Otherwise, how could there be the family ritual of Saturday morning pancakes; a thing Mom did when she was Mom.

Grace waited at the front window and at her first glimpse of the Impala approaching, she rushed outside to help with whatever Mom might need.

Mom got out of the Impala, clutching a large brown bag, and called Grace.

"Good morning, my sleeping beauty. Wouldn't you know that with your dad doing the shopping the pantry was nearly bare. What would my breakfast surprise be without your father's Florida Tupelo honey?" She hurried past Grace, calling back that she should bring in the rest of the shopping bags while she got breakfast properly underway.

The ten bags of groceries nearly filled the pantry shelves and there remained little space in the fridge. Dad's weekly shopping, on the day he was paid, had been barely enough to replace the essentials for the coming week.

"That's a lot of food." Grace sighed.

"Yes, thanks to my new low-interest, cash-back credit card." Mom giggled. "Your dad is going to think it's Christmas morning." Mom had unpacked six jars of honey and placed them alongside the four she had purchased earlier. Grace stole glances at her mom in an attempt at judging her mood, remembering that Granny Sybil had given Dad a jar of the same honey on each of their Christmas visits to the nursing home. She had smiled and patted Dad's blushing cheeks, calling him her sweeter-than-honey baby boy.

Dad had thanked Granny Sybil and smiled in a way that brought tears to his mother's pale eyes. In exchange, he had given her yet another Bible study book that she declared was the very one she had wanted. After Granny Sybil's death, a battered shipping box had arrived from the nursing home. A brief enclosed note stated that the contents of the box were the entirety of what Granny Sybil had left behind. It held a collection of Bible study books, and among them Grace discovered duplicate titles. Nothing had ever been said about Dad passing along the annual jars of honey to Aunt Josey. The realization that neither Granny Sybil nor Dad had really known each other well had saddened Grace. Dad had remarked that a well-intended lie was often kinder than the truth.

The same box had also contained a single, framed photo. Daniel, son, age fourteen, and Joe, father, age forty-two, was scribbled on the back of the photo. Dad sat poised on the front fender of a car he called a 1955 classic Studebaker Silver Hawk, an arm draped across his dad's shoulders. He smiled proudly and said that he and his dad had completely rebuilt the Hawk's engine.

Grace had felt there was something sad in her granddad's eyes, and his loose stance reminded her of her dad. Dad had carefully removed the small photo from its tarnished frame and slipped it into his wallet behind her and Zoey's last school pictures. The photo and her dad's pride were all Grace knew about her paternal grandfather.

"My God Grace. You haven't heard a word I've said." Mom turned from her task at the stove. Her flash of irritation rekindled bits of Grace's earlier alarm.

"Uh... sorry Mom. I was just thinking how much Dad's going to love that you remembered his favorite honey." Grace thought of her lie as yet another link in her family's preferred version of what was now a near truth.

"Oh, your father appreciates whatever I put before him. But I asked what you wanted." Mom stepped to the fridge and took out a family-size package of wieners, suggesting she could make slaw, baked beans, and French fries for lunch. "And your favorite lemon pie for dessert."

"That'd be great, Mom. Thanks." There were no beans or cabbage among the items Grace had unpacked, only an economy-sized package of frozen French fries.

"Great, and we'll... eat at the picnic table out back. That will be festive, don't you think? Use the red and white checked tablecloth and matching napkins. You girls can wear your swimsuits and play in the wading pool."

Grace shivered at her mom's notion that she and Zoey should play in the kiddy pool they had long ago outgrown and disposed of as garbage.

"And, yes, yes, of course, your father must clean the nasty firepit so we might roast hotdogs. Yes, that's what we'll do." Mom giggled as she sometimes did in her confusion and uncertainty as to how best to untangle her jumbled thoughts while concealing her anxiety.

Still, Grace forced a tight nod.

"And you must invite your friend Alice to join us. Yes, and her poor father... but you are not to invite her ridiculous mother." Smoke from overheating oil billowed and Mom swore, frantically waving her hands, but just as quickly she turned back to Grace. "But first, my darling girl, we have breakfast to prepare."

Grace stepped around her mom to the stove and turned on the hood fan.

Mom raved about her pancakes as an art form while she searched for the one skillet she insisted turned out perfectly shaped and sized pancakes. Grace busied herself pouring fresh orange juice into small glasses while searching for the right response to deflect any further talk about Alice and her mom.

"Grace? Did I not say you are to call Alice? And why has she stopped coming over? Are you two no longer science project partners?" Mom stared blankly, as if she had forgotten her public argument with Alice's mother that had enticed startled neighbors to come onto their porches and stare in disgust.

Her hand unsteady, Grace overran the glass, spilling orange juice onto the counter.

Mom slid the hot pan of breakfast sausage off the flame and Grace sensed the onset of a conversation she had wanted to avoid.

"Uh, about that... Alice and I don't have the same science class anymore."

"And why is that?"

"Uh," Grace shrugged. "A scheduling mess up." Grace was counting on her mom to have missed the fact that Mrs. Patrick was now driving Alice to and from school to prevent her and Alice from sharing the same bus ride.

"Are you sure it isn't Madeline Patrick's misguided obsession with the cat's natural instinct to stalk birds? Or her ludicrous claim of ownership of wild birds?"

"No, Mom, it's like I said."

Mom smiled and opened her arms. Grace stepped into her warmth, depending on her mom to forget about the craziness of a picnic and to move on to anything that did not include Alice's attendance.

Dad stumbled into the kitchen in his sock feet, though the day was cool. He wore no shirt and his jeans hung loosely on his spare hips, a patch of dark curly hair below his navel exposed. Grace looked away, hoping no one, especially her dad, noticed.

Eyeing a stack of perfectly round pancakes smothered in honey, Dad kept his dislike of honey to himself and gave Mom a cheering thumbs-up.

"No, sir, mister." Mom stood with her fists on her hips, in mock disapproval. "Find yourself a clean shirt or lose your place at my table." Mom spanked Dad playfully on his butt and he played the obedient kid. But he stopped near Grace, tilted his head to one side and winked.

"Hey, tough girl. What's up with those rosy cheeks?" He leaned and kissed Grace atop her head. Despite Grace and her dad's customary ease with acts of affection, she stiffened.

"Whoa now. Don't tell me you've gotten too big for your old man's hugs?"

"No, Dad, you just surprised me, that's all." Grace's self-consciousness stung like a swarm of bees, though knowing that he had not seen her earlier made her feel slightly better.

Dad eased into the laundry room and emerged wearing a wrinkled shirt, his knotty wrists laid bare. Grace swore that today was the day she would fold and put away the over-stuffed baskets of laundry.

Zoey ran into the kitchen, the hem of one of Grace's hand-me-down tee shirts nearly dragging the floor. She wrapped her arms around Mom's thighs and stared up at her like a newly rescued pup. Mom enfolded Zoey in a tight squeeze before turning and ceremonially presenting her special surprise.

Zoey squealed with a little girl's delight as Mom set before her a single, plate-sized pancake with a smiley face made with plump blueberry eyes, a strawberry mouth and whipped cream eyebrows. Everyone cheered Mom's artistry and she beamed with pleasure. It was as though Mom wanted to make up for all the mornings she and Zoey went off to school after a cold breakfast and nights when they slept hungry.

They settled into eating. Dad smiled at Mom and asked for more of the second sweetest honey in the entire world. Mom blushed. Their exchange comforted Grace, and she set aside her earlier anxiety, choosing to believe that Mom was fine, at least for now.

Jimmie stretched full length on the kitchen floor in a patch of warm sunlight, and contentedly licked his paws.

— 11 —

Leah

Leah's morning routine had her rising early to prepare a breakfast she and Daniel shared. She had pinched his smooth, freshly shaven face between her palms and though she understood that their good moments would always be stolen by her illness, their closeness had aroused her. Their lovemaking was more impassioned, more intense than she remembered, though from their beginning, they were an improbable match.

At the sound of Daniel's truck speeding away, Leah had only minutes to spare for herself before waking her beautiful daughters to a hot breakfast. Afterwards, she stood in the open door and waved until the bus had rounded the corner and disappeared.

With the Impala sidelined until Daniel had a free evening to complete a brake repair job, Leah took the number fifty-one bus to the city's high-end downtown commercial area. There she exited the bus and wedged her way through the jostling crowds for the remaining two blocks to the building that housed her employer. She entered the towering granite and glass lobby and went directly to the Red Eye kiosk, where she purchased her first-of-the-day large cup of dark roast coffee, though she barely tolerated its bitter taste of burnt beans. Now that she had begun ingesting her daily cocktail of anti-psychotic drugs at half-strength, she needed the hefty load of caffeine the coffee delivered.

Before her last "flare-up", she had held a promising position with AMI Data Corp. Having returned as a new hire made it imperative that she continue demonstrating her excellent performance.

The gradual reduction of her medications without altering her behavior was akin to walking a mental tightrope. But as she approached her one-year performance evaluation, doing so was an essential part of her effort to mitigate the drugs' debilitating side-effects. Just last week, she noticed a slight hand tremor that threatened to slow her pace and was certain to limit her data output if it continued.

If she was to support Grace's dream of attending a first-rate college and afford Zoey's tuition at an expensive private school for gifted children, she would need to earn her way onto a middle management team, with its sizable increase in job security, salary, and benefits.

Daniel was a good father, but a poor provider. He had inherited his father's dream of owning his own mechanic shop, even though the iconic one-man, fix-all shop had become an historic relic. Still, Daniel kept his father's tool chest, and now the dream was Daniel's, with the same predictable failure.

Donuts with Sprinkles
Fall 2017

— 12 —

Grace

Mom had increasingly referred to sleep as a cruel stranger. Grace was routinely awakened by the sounds of her mom's harried pacing through the house. Mornings, Grace frequently found Mom collapsed face down on the couch and Grace worried that she had slept no more than three or four hours. Still, most evenings she stayed late at work. Cleaning, cooking, and laundry were left to Grace, who had fallen behind in her Language Arts reading program. Grace worried that her A grade in one of her favorite classes was in jeopardy.

Dad had taken time from a repair job to help with chores. He and Grace stripped the couch of its cover, which reeked of dirty feet, animal odors, and a full range of what Mom criticized as their disgusting habits of careless living. When Grace had washed and dried the cover, and the two had returned it to the couch, she folded a week's worth of laundry. Zoey picked up the clutter in their bedroom and dusted every piece of scratched furniture. Dad vacuumed the stained carpet throughout the house.

Dad walked through the house surveying the surprising results and teased, "Danged if I couldn't quit fixing junk cars and open up our own cleaning services."

"Go ahead, but count me out. I'll settle for just one lazy Saturday sleep-in."

At the sound of Mom's arrival, the three stood grinning, waiting as she came through the door. At the sight of them, she stopped short and stared.

"What's this?" She looked around the room and appeared confused.

"Can't you see? The girls and I cleaned." Grace felt his struggle to keep disappointment from his tone.

"Everything. And smell." Zoey took Mom's hand and led her to the couch.

"Oh yes. I see. And it's... good. I'm... I'm so proud of you three." Mom smiled and though her response felt less than genuine, it was good enough for Dad. He declared a long over-due celebration of Mom's hard work and their good effort. They went out for Mexican food and Dad paid with money he had earned from a side job.

A loud noise awakened Grace from a sound sleep, and she sat, rubbing sleep from her eyes. She got out of bed, walked into the living room, and called over the roar of the vacuum cleaner.

"Mom, what're you doing? Remember, Dad did that already." Grace failed to contain the exasperation she felt.

"Grace, thank God, you're up. You need to get dressed."

"Now? But, Mom, it's still dark outside. And remember, we cleaned already."

Mom ran her fingers through her hair, and she looked as if she meant to pull her hair out by the roots.

"Yes, now!" Mom screamed. "Oh, Grace, how can I trust you when you break promises? I fear your word is becoming no better than your father's."

Mom's sudden irritation frightened Grace.

"Okay, Mom. Please, I'm sorry and I'll start as soon as I'm dressed." As Grace retreated to her room, Mom shouted specific instructions for what she was to do.

"Zoey, wake up. Mom's freaking out and she won't be put off."

Zoey whimpered. "But she means you, not me."

"Yeah, but you've gotta hold the damn flashlight."

Dad staggered into the hallway and called, "What the hell's with all the noise? And where are the two of you going at this hour?"

"It's Mom... and... she's cleaning." Grace moaned.

"What? Just how fucking clean does a worn-out carpet gotta be?" He called Mom, but she did not heed. He put a palm to his brow and muttered that he had a job across town in less than three hours.

"Right, Dad, we've got this." He went back into the bedroom, likely searching for his military grade ear plugs. And why not, Grace thought. There was nothing weird in her and Zoey digging a trench by moonlight. Murderers did it all the time.

Zoey followed Grace into the backyard, and as Mom had instructed, Grace set about digging a six-inch deep, one-foot wide, six-foot long trench along the decaying wood fence. When it was ready, Grace removed each of twelve tiny dead plants from their crumbling peat pots and placed them in the trench.

With the first light of day, Grace backfilled the trench and tamped down the loose soil. Zoey stood over the trench, fingers laced, her head bowed. "Jesus, I'm supposed to tell you that Leah Killian is sorry she killed these babies. Amen." She lifted her cherub-like face, and a cunning smile shaped the corners of her mouth.

"You're... you're just pathetic."

Mom came onto the patio and called. "Girls, what's taking you so long? There are gardening books to return to the attic." She abruptly turned and hurried back through the door. The scent of scorching oatmeal leached forth from the kitchen.

— 13 —

Grace

Saturday morning, Mom, dressed for work, stood in front of the open fridge searching for half and half for her coffee. An empty carton in her hand, she turned to Grace for an explanation for why half and half had not gone on the shopping list.

Dad came in from the garage, wiping grease from his hands. He asked Mom to take at least one weekend day off from work, but she brushed past him, and he wisely conceded the argument, walking Mom to the Impala instead. He stood watching as she sped away, then walked back into the house, offering a playful tease.

"Don't know about you ladies, but I'm just not feeling another breakfast featuring burnt oatmeal. How 'bout I scramble us a pan of eggs and you two make up a batch of cheese toast?"

Each set about their individual task in strained silence, as though they each searched for the right explanation. Mom was simply reacting normally to stresses at work. She was surely taking her meds; Dad had faithfully called the pharmacy for her refills each month.

Shortly after noon, the satisfied owner of a repaired Jeep drove away, and Dad went into the kitchen to make peanut butter and jelly sandwiches, which signaled a trip to the nearby park.

Dad pushed Zoey in one of the kiddy swings, but before she had gained attitude, the toes of her shoes dragged the ground. Dad had somehow missed that Zoey was no longer the squealing little girl he remembered. Nor was she the little sister who was comforted by Grace's magical stories of Mom and baby Zoey.

They sat at a picnic table and ate the sandwiches Dad had made with more strawberry jam than those he called Mom's *skimpy* jam and peanut butter sandwiches. Jam ran down Zoey's wrist and she giggled, licked it away.

"Dang, Zoey, that jam was mine." Dad reached and captured a bit of jam before it dropped from her elbow, and he got the playful giggles he'd wanted earlier.

"Good grief, Dad. Mom would've freaked out at you two."

"But Mom's not here," Zoey said, swiping at Dad's unfinished sandwich.

Grace wished that Mom had wanted to spend the day with them, but time spent with Dad was easier; relaxed and more fun.

He gathered the loose wrappers from their sandwiches, and on returning from a trip to the trash container, he winked at Zoey, and taunted Grace.

"Ok, tough gal, you up for a butt kicking?" He smiled in the playful way Grace most loved.

"Oh, yeah, old man," she quipped, striking a bold pose. "I guess your new best friend, LeBron, stood you up and you're daring to take me on alone."

He tossed her the basketball and one of their do-or-die, one-on-one games was on full tilt.

Zoey danced along the sideline, cheering first for Grace and then Dad.

He challenged Grace hard, and she fought back, believing he did it to remind her of this slogan: wit, grit, sweat, and nothing less would earn her what she wanted from life. It was a lesson she took into the classroom, while he readily admitted to having failed to do the same.

Throughout the afternoon and well into the evening, Mom had not returned home or responded to Dad's several texts and phone messages, prompting him to drive into the city. Grace dozed on the couch, awaiting word of his search, and was awakened by the familiar sound of the Impala pulling into the driveway. She listened for the welcome sound of her mom's key in the door lock.

"Grace? What on earth? You startled me. Why aren't you in bed? And where is your father?"

"He went into the city, looking for you."

Mom's face flushed red. "Why? Am I not capable of looking after myself?"

"Yes, but we were worried. You didn't return his calls."

"God, I detest his... your damn smothering. I am not a child." She rushed past Grace and into her and Dad's bedroom, slamming the door behind her.

Grace wished that she had said something honest about how good it would feel to have a mom who didn't throw temper tantrums. Instead, she called her dad and told him Mom was home.

He let out a deep sigh before asking, "And how... does she seem?"

"Angry, mostly."

He agreed that a slower drive home would be smart. Grace left a pillow and blanket on the couch and went to bed, but she did not sleep soundly until she heard his quiet entry.

— 14 —

Grace

Grace heard the door to the patio open and close. She lay awake, waiting for her mom to smoke her last cigarette of the night and to return to bed. When Leah remained on the patio, Grace worried that her insomnia might mean her horrid headaches had returned; headaches that forced her into her darkened bedroom for days on end without relief.

Wishing to satisfy herself that her mom's restlessness was due only to normal concerns about her increased workload, Grace left her bed and went onto the small patio.

Leah sat in her treasured wicker rocker, the air heavy with the odor of nicotine that overpowered the sweet scent of the Rose of Sharon. Crushed, half-smoked cigarettes overflowed the seashell ashtray, as though Leah had wished to chasten herself with each light-up.

Grace called softly to her mother.

"Oh, Grace, sweetheart, it's so late. You have school. You must return to bed."

"It's okay. It's Saturday, and I had to pee."

Mom's tone was solemn, but her comment was ironic, even laughable. There were no rules about bedtime, meals, homework, tv ratings, violent video games, or even school attendance. Rules would mean their parents needed to monitor her and her sister's compliance. Instead, their household ran on what Grace had labeled R & R; meaning a rapid response to whatever Mom's newest demands required.

Grace moved to sit on the floor next to Mom's chair and to Grace's surprise, her mom ran her fingers through the thickness of Grace's dark hair.

"And, yes, you do have your father's nice hair." Leah's tone was one of having answered an unasked question and Grace remembered an earlier time when Mom had compared her hair to her sister's and declared Zoey's blond curls a genetic anomaly. Grace had not understood and when she asked, Mom had laughed, claiming yet another of her family's many secrets.

"There, my darling, is your birth star." Mom pointed to the brightest star in the sky, and a warm glow brightened her face. Grace felt her tears well up, that a memory of her had gifted her mother with such a smile.

"I remember it as the time your father and I were at our very best." Leah stared toward the lone streetlight visible from the patio and abruptly leaned forward, fingertips pressed to her temples, and she moaned. Grace recognized the behavior as signaling the onset of one of her mom's blinding headaches; the ones that came with such vengeance she screamed in agony at the slightest sound or flash of light filtered through the heavy bedroom drapes.

"Is it... umm... a bad one? Want me to get your headache meds?"

Leah sat erect and asked Grace to listen quietly.

"Oh, I do love nights when the scent of salt air arrives on the wings of gentle breezes. Sometimes it hushes the loudest noises inside my head."

"Then we should go to the beach. Would you like that?" Grace so wanted the return of the earlier moment of her mother's brief happiness.

"Oh, no, you've forgotten that I'm afraid of water. That once I nearly drowned." She paused and reached for Grace's hand.

"I'm sorry... and no, you never told me that story."

"I remember I was innocent… a toddler tossed about in turbulent waters, and with me was my heroic John Wayne, who struggled mightily. But a wee rubber ducky was no match for the rising waters." She stared off into the cover of darkness.

"Mom, what happened?"

"Umm, yes. Father. I believe… he must have been lured away… by some voluptuous mermaid, or perhaps he chased a beautiful poetic line before it could evaporate from his muddled thoughts?"

"Mom, do you mean grandfather?"

Leah felt Grace's strong presence and she would tell her daughter what she dared.

"Oh, my darling, your grandfather came with arms spread like a magnificently winged bird, and I was lifted upward onto a warm cushion of air. And I was to know no fear."

Dad came onto the patio and lifted Mom into his arms as easily as if she were Zoey. Mom whispered his name, and rested her head against his broad shoulder. He spoke softly, words intended for Mom alone, and carried her to their bed. When he had settled her, he took his pillow from the bed and quietly pulled the door closed behind him. The clock read 3:33, and Grace shivered beneath her covers, for all she knew, and for that she could not know.

— 15 —

Leah

Leah sat behind the steering wheel of the Impala, captive to the deafening roar of frantic motorists surrounding the car as she navigated mid-afternoon traffic. Her cheeks twitched as though angry ants crawled the length of her body. Her throat tightened as she tasted oily exhaust from the mushroom cloud billowing overhead, and she felt as if her last breath had rushed from her lungs.

She stood next to the Impala gulping warm humid air into her deflated lungs and struggled to sort her scrambled thoughts. She had left work for home, but where had she expected this unfamiliar route to deliver her? Surely not here, to a pathetic strip mall. She took the folded paper from her pocket and wondered if there was a use-by date. She had felt no urgency to fill yet another prescription for the latest miracle drug touted as having a remarkable history of reducing psychotic breaks among a high percentage of patients. Leah knew she was not now, nor had she ever been, among those of good fortune, and her disappointment was best delayed.

Returning the prescription to her pocket, Leah started the Impala and drove back into an entanglement of speeding vehicles. A sudden onset of blaring horns further shattered her fragile nerves and she braked hard, sending the Impala into a tailspin. Its engine stalled, leaving the vehicle to straddle two lanes of traffic. Leah restarted the engine, accelerated through a caution light, and made a hard left, crossing lanes of oncoming traffic. She escaped into the parking lot of Granny's Donut and Coffee Shop.

Leah ignored the blaring horns, dismissing her near disaster as merely an act of patronizing a local business. Her choice of Granny's wasn't entirely deliberate, but she nevertheless approached the drive-through window. A plump woman stuffed into an unflattering uniform featuring a bib apron looked first at Leah, and then back toward the outraged drivers who were working to disentangle their vehicles.

"My gracious, Ma'am…," the woman stammered. "That was some more crazy… I mean… welcome to Granny's. May I take your order?"

Leah had no idea what she was referring to. She ordered an extra-large coffee with five yellow packages of slow-killing chemicals, and a dozen chocolate-covered donuts without sprinkles.

"Don't kids just love it when Mom shows up with after school donuts?" The woman popped grape-favored bubble gum.

Leah dug through her purse for loose change, then took the balance from the nicotine-smelling coins in the overflowing ashtray.

"Sorry for the nasty smell." Leah imagined forgiveness, and she offered the woman a donut. The woman declined, explaining that she got plenty of discounted two-day-old donuts.

Leah parked in an out of the way space near an overflowing dumpster that was swarming with flies. Still, she cranked down the windows in an effort at catching a cross breeze and opened the box. She began eating right to left across three rows of four donuts; a deliberate pattern to prove she had control over a stronger random impulse. It was small but encouraging.

When she had consumed the entire dozen, she licked her sugary fingertips and although she had quit cigarettes for a second time that week, she dug through the clutter that was the contents of her purse for the crumpled half-pack she carried for just such an occasion.

Leah was unsure when she had decided to surprise her girls by picking them up from school, saving them from a long bus ride and guaranteeing their arrival home in time for her to drive Grace and Alice to a wildly popular concert. Leah had purchased two tickets with her newest credit card, and both girls were elated.

Her sweet Grace was not to be disappointed, but first her mother would enjoy a cigarette. Afterwards, she would close her eyes for a much-needed nap. She lit up, turned the radio to the sexy sound of Springsteen's *I'm on Fire*, and leaned her head back against the headrest. But she could not escape the image of a clogged river of pure sugar slugging its way through her gut.

A sudden convulsion rose in her throat, and she flung open the door. The aftermath of her gorging was a sickening burst of sourness, and she vomited onto the greasy asphalt. It felt odd to have had such a thought, but she was surprised that regurgitated sugar tasted sour and not sweet; then she decided that if good sex could turn violent, then why not sugar?

Leah caught sight of a yellow school bus. Panicked, she sped onto the street in reckless pursuit. Overtaking the bus, she pulled alongside and repeatedly sounded the horn, waving and shouting for the startled driver to pull over.

Excited kids, their foreheads pressed against the windows, stared down at her. They laughed and twirled their fingers at their temples, mouthing chants of Cuckoo. Leah did not recognize the driver, and she saw neither Grace nor Zoey.

Swearing, Leah tightened her grip on the steering wheel and maneuvered the Impala across two lanes and into a left turn lane. If her beautiful daughters were not to have a pleasant ride home, then she would have donuts and glasses of cold milk waiting.

"Grace... was that Mom?" Zoey whispered, emerging from where she had hidden.

"No way. There's a zillion old black Impalas in the city. Right?"

Zoey squinted. Her doubts remained, but she took her seat and said nothing more.

— 16 —

Leah

Leah bargained for a discount on a second dozen donuts and approached the intersection that would take her home. Suddenly, she remembered that her father had delighted in all things sweet. She would first stop off for a quick visit with Father before continuing home.

She passed beneath the arched gateway to Eternal Rest Cemetery, remembering it fondly as a pastoral haven, surrounded by a meadow and a bubbling brook. Now, it lay between a trailer park and a strip mall anchored by a cheap retail outlet with a nail salon, liquor store, and a payday lender. A narrow patch of overgrown weeds and roadside debris served as a thin barrier between the deceased and those defying death.

Remembering that her father had detested sprinkles, Leah stopped the car and plucked the last bit of brightly colored sugar crystals from the melting frosting. Donuts remade, Leah parked the car and approached her father on foot.

"Hello, dear Father," she called ahead. "It's your favorite daughter, Leah. I've come for a brief visit, and I've brought sweets."

"Thank you, my darling Leah. How loving of you to remember," she heard him say in his richly lyrical poet's voice. She removed a weather-tattered box from a prior visit and replaced it with the box of newly defrocked donuts.

The memory of his warm, fleshy hand in hers, Leah read from his favorite book of poetry well into the gloaming hour. Tombstones leaned toward the retreating light and the ground, warmed earlier by the day's heat, had begun to cool. Having wrung out the last of the emotion that had delivered her to the cemetery, Leah closed the book and returned it to the safe keeping of its rusting tin. She came stiffly to her feet and wrapped her arms tightly about herself in a memory embrace.

"Goodbye, my dear Father." Leah spoke gently, turning away his lonely plea that she stay. "Oh, but Father, you no longer need to be afraid of the dark. And I must go."

Leah drove back through the arched gateway, a rising moon appearing on her right shoulder. Before her, a brilliant light unfurled and in its glorious realm she drove a glittering pathway cut between two universes; a kinder space where gravity was but a tether to be broken, and beyond lay the gift of silence and its deliverance. Leah closed her eyes, granting an angel of mercy its will.

— 17 —

Grace

Grace worried that Mom's wild attempt to overtake the school bus foreshadowed the demise of an elaborate plan she and Alice had made to attend a popular concert, in defiance of Mrs. Patrick's decree that the two were never to be friends again. They had spent the month planning every detail; the risk was both exciting and scary.

The entire plan hinged on Mom's promise to leave work early so that they could collect Alice from her friend Ashley's. From there, Mom would drive her and Alice to the concert. Afterwards, they were to take the cross-city bus back, and because neither dared risk a sleepover, Mom would drive Alice back to Ashley's, where Mrs. Patrick was to collect her the following morning.

Nearing the time for Mom's arrival home, Grace changed into her newest skinny jeans and one of the cool concert tees Mom had ordered online. She combed her thick dark hair back from her forehead and studied herself in the mirror. Satisfied with her overall appearance, she neatly folded the second tee Alice would later change into and placed it, along with the two coveted tickets and money for bus fare and refreshments at the concert, into her backpack. She went into the living room and sat where she had a full view of the driveway.

When Mom was an hour late and had not responded to any of her text messages or returned her calls, Grace, against her exploding disappointment, considered that her mother's failure to keep her promise might be more serious than poor memory or an act of selfishness.

Dad answered right away, his words only slightly slurred, and explained without her asking that he was helping his friend Sam tune his Harley. Grace recognized his go-to response as truth for a false reason. Had he meant to hide that he sometimes drank too much, or that a chain of half-truths and omissions served him well in a family with much bigger secrets? She told him only that Mom had promised her and a friend a ride and she was late, without giving away the bigger conspiracy.

"Uh, maybe she... just... failed to note the time. Forgot. We know how she is.... So, do you need me to come and drive you and your friend?"

"No, Dad, that's not... why I'm calling."

Grace told him where she had last seen her mom. There were muffled voices and then he came back with Sam's offer to come for her and Zoey, take them to supper, and then to their Aunt Josey's to stay overnight while he went to look for Leah. Grace refused, preferring to stay in case Mom came home on her own. Aunt Josey would have come for her and Zoey, but Mom resented her older sister, claiming Josey meddled in their lives, and Grace was unwilling to risk her anger should Mom actually show.

Grace sat alone on the patio in the rain-soaked wicker until the call came that she had dreaded.

"Hey, Alice, I'm sorry. I meant to call earlier to say everything here has gone shit side up. And...." Grace's truth wadded in her throat, and she was, in that horrible moment, speechless.

"What happened? Is it your mom?" Alice's voice broke. "Please tell me, Grace. Am I uninvited?"

"Uh, no... it's... nothing like that. I'm sorry, but I don't know what to tell you."

"Oh Grace, for once can't you just tell me the truth?" Alice's voice was tense.

Grace mumbled something she knew was meaningless, and before she could say something even more dishonest, she silenced her phone.

Grace grabbed the wicker rocker and flung it as far as she could into the yard. She later returned the rocker to its rightful place, her anger having risen in fury and fallen in equal regret.

— 18 —

Officer Jordan McCall

Jordan pulled the patrol car to a stop at a dodgy package store where she could make a quick bathroom stop and grab her drug of choice, a steaming cup of high-octane caffeine. The remaining three hours of her eleven-to-seven-shift included a hot-spot zone of declining neighborhoods on the outermost edge of the city. Once a cluster of small communities surrounding thriving orange groves and a prosperous juice concentration plant, these neighborhoods had been populated by first and second generations of Irish and Italian immigrants and white hillbillies who had brought their dreams of access to the middle class in exchange for their manual labor.

Jordan had spent her first eleven years in such a neighborhood as the only child of Officer Jamie McCall, a sixteen-year veteran who was shot and killed by a fourteen-year-old boy he had once coached in Little League. The boy was hyped up on crystal meth and the mystical powers of what was known as a Saturday night special, purchased from a car-trunk street merchant.

At the sound of the store's door opening, an old woman raised her head and rubbed sleep from her bloodshot eyes. She emitted a deep grunt, which Jordan accepted as the woman's brand of customer greeting. Jordan scanned the empty store.

"Had yourself a slow evening, did you?" she teased. She figured Miss Joyce Ann was eighty or older, and that she'd lived a black and blue life.

"Every pitiful loser still able to stagger through that door's been and long gone. Poor sonsabitches bought what couldn't do them one bit of good. Then, you can bet your sweet ass I was tickled pink to separate them from their ill-gotten means."

Hers was the pot-licker-smooth drawl of the crackers Jordan had grown up hearing. Right or wrong, there was something in the old woman's crude honesty Jordan found appealing. The woman slid her ample behind off the stool, planted a hand-carved hickory cane firmly, and slow-walked toward the coffee machine on what she jokingly referred to as a perfectly matched set of worthless knees.

A sudden squeal of tires from the direction of the road redirected Jordan's attention, and she watched a late model F-150 skid to a rough stop next to the patrol car. A heavily bearded young man exited the truck and rushed toward the door. The sight of a patrol car was usually enough to discourage a would-be robber, but a dude hopped up on crank might overlook the obvious.

Her hand on her revolver, Jordan stood alert.

"Oh, girl, that ain't no damn robber. That's Noah Nance. Damned if his hypocrite daddy didn't name all seven of his half-wits after men in the Bible."

Young Nance pushed open the door, nodded a hurried greeting to the proprietor, and turned to Jordan. "Ma'am. Officer, you'd be...?" He sucked air and stared about as if he had forgotten the reason he had rushed through the door.

"Yep, that would be me." Jordan stood erect, staring down at the shorter boy.

"Yes Ma'am. Officer, Sir... Ma'am."

"Young man, if you need time to remember why you're here, I think I'll go ahead and pee."

"Um, you see, it's just now that I saw it."

"All right. And how 'bout you get to the point and tell me what you saw."

"Uh, a big-ass Chevy Impala." He tilted his head to one side. "Don't think they even make them models no more." He squinted hard, like the answer was suddenly more important than whatever he'd come to say.

"And where exactly will I find this marvelous vehicle?"

"Oh, yeah, my daddy's nursery business. A mile or so back up the road. Did I say the driver slammed that old car over a ditch and right through an eight-foot chain link fence? And still plowed under a double row of fruit trees before it ground to a stop? Damned if 'em old fuckers weren't built like tanks."

"Language boy. You're talking to a lady cop."

Noah looked at the old woman and mumbled an apology to Jordan.

"I know the place." Just her luck to catch a single-car accident located a good twenty minutes from the closest EMT satellite station. Jordan's vision of a hot shower and breakfast with Ellie had come undone. It was unlikely she would make it home before Ellie left for her morning office hours.

Jordan notified the dispatcher that she was enroute to a single car accident and the boy followed her to the scene. She pulled the patrol car onto the shoulder and waved the excited boy on his way. The last thing she needed was an eager kid sticking his nose in her business and slowing her down.

She grabbed her flashlight and took a pry bar from the trunk. At the break in the fence, she jumped the narrow ditch and made her way along a car-wide swath of flattened trees. The Impala was buried to its axles, like the boy had said.

Approaching the car, Jordan made out the figure of a woman slumped across the front seat like a rag doll. She forced open the locked door and leaned in.

"Ma'am, I'm Officer Jordan McCall. If you can hear my voice, please tell me where you're hurt."

The woman was unresponsive. Jordan could see a nasty slash over her right eye and a large lump at her right temple, alerting her to the possibility of a concussion. Stepping away from the car, Jordan called for emergency medical response.

The woman stirred and attempted to push herself upright. She stared up at Jordan, her eyes vacant, as though sorting through random thoughts for an answer she did not seem to have.

Again, Jordan identified herself and asked the woman her name while cautioning her against movement and informing her that a paramedic unit was in route.

"No, no, I must go." She looked anxiously around the car. "I have after-school treats and I must get home before my daughters' bus runs."

Jordan reached for the empty donut box on the floor. "This what your mean?"

"Oh yes, and please, what I'm about to tell you... is... a secret." She glanced about as though she expected intruders. "My... gift... his exquisite madness." She sank back against the seat, tears filling her eyes.

Jordan retrieved a purse from the floor and requested permission to search for identification. She located a driver's license issued to Leah Killian: height 5'7", brown hair, brown eyes, and a photograph matching the driver. A hand-written note identified Leah Killian's next of kin, a woman, and listed a phone number. A further search for the vehicle registration led to the name Daniel Killian as the owner of the Impala. Leah Killian leaned heavily against the seat, her breathing labored, all the while declaring herself fit to drive.

"First, let's get you checked out. Then, I'll contact Josey...."

"No, no, weren't you listening. You're to notify my father."

Her voice was shrill, and she had clearly become more agitated. Jordan wondered if her distress with the mention of Josey Pierce meant the two women had had a falling out. Jordan pulled her notepad from her pocket and asked for the best number to reach Killian's father.

"Please, no phone call. He loathes any means that limits the use of beautiful written language. Father writes exquisite notes in perfect cursive."

"Okay, can you give me a name and physical address? I'll request that a local officer be dispatched."

"Eternal Rest." Leah paused. "It's beautiful there. And father has many admirers who regularly visit in search of inspiration. And, yes, of course, he'll be displeased, but never angered." She smiled shyly in the winning way of a pampered child. "You know I'm his favorite. The inspiration for his most beautiful verses."

Jordan closed her notepad and slipped it back into her pocket. Her earlier notion of a concussion now gave way to something more troubling. Her training in identifying and responding to a psychotic episode had been a fifteen-minute video.

The driver of the approaching ambulance parked behind the patrol car. Two paramedics—a male driver and Anna, a medic Jordan knew—hurried to the rear of the vehicle and unloaded a stretcher and a bag of medical equipment.

Jordan stepped away from the Impala and quickly relayed what she suspected. Anna nodded and approached Killian, who insisted that she must arrive home before her daughters returned from school. When she was not allowed to drive away, Killian became more agitated. Anna administered a mild sedative and together the EMTs and Jordan transported Killian across the open field and placed her in the ambulance. Anna informed Jordan that they would take Killian to County General.

"Her hyper-anxiety, rambling and incoherent speech do, as you suggest, indicate a possible psychotic episode. We'll let the experts in the psyche unit figure it out."

At the station, Jordan placed a call to Josey Pierce, the woman identified as Killian's next of kin. Their exchange was brief, and after completing the resulting paperwork, Jordan changed out of her uniform into jeans and a tee. Ahead, an hour drive home, where she would catch a few minutes with Ellie and maybe a quick breakfast before Ellie left for her office. Afterwards, Jordan would finally get the sleep she desperately needed.

— 19 —

Jordan

Jordan eased the truck onto the oyster shell driveway next to Ellie's Jeep, exited the cab, and quietly pushed the door closed. The salty scent of the nearby marshes rose to meet her, and she felt a sensation of safety that she experienced in no other place like here. She paused at the uppermost height of a sand dune at the head of the beach pathway to watch sea gulls skimming the water's surface in search of a wide variety of food sources: small fish, mollusks, plankton. She had seen wintering birds behave as scavengers, eating junk foods like corn chips.

She turned back to the house and after taking the deck steps two at a time, eased the door open and stepped inside. She locked her badge and service weapon away before turning to greet Ellie, who had come into the kitchen and now stood, leaning on the counter, rubbing her right eye.

"Morning stranger." Ellie said, her voice groggy with sleep.

"I'm sorry, sweetheart. I didn't want to wake you. I'll grab a quick bite and join you back in bed."

"You didn't wake me. I never sleep soundly until you're home. And don't you even think about eating that two-day-old meatloaf I meant to toss earlier."

"Yeah, you're right. It does look a bit like roadkill."

"Why don't you get a hot shower while I scramble some eggs and make buttered toast? That will be quick."

Jordan kissed Ellie and whispered, "Thank you. I guess I do smell like the inside of a patrol car. I'll only be a minute."

Jordan showered, dressed in an old tee and shorts, and returned to a plate of warm food with gratitude the size of her appetite. Ellie sat next to Jordan, cradling a hot cup of coffee between her palms.

"Why so late this time?"

"Caught a late one-person accident. A woman drove a big Impala through a fence and into Nance's nursery."

"Good grief, that's awful. Was she hurt?"

"Maybe a slight concussion, so I called for EMTs. Oddly enough, she was more concerned about getting donuts to her kids for an after-school treat, despite the fact that it was midnight. That was a bit worrisome, but when she directed me to contact her dead father about the accident, it was clearly something I'm not trained to assess. So, I called for those who are."

"What decision was made for the poor woman? And were her kids alone all that time?"

"Anna packed her off to County General. And your question about the daughters, I can't say. I think there may be a dad in the picture. The driver was not the owner listed on the registration."

Jordan carried the dishes to the sink, rinsed and placed them in the dishwasher. She looked up at an obviously troubled Ellie, who still sat across the counter from her.

"I get you're concerned. But please remember, I'm a cop, not a social worker. So, I'm going to bed. I need the sleep."

— 20 —

Grace

When Grace's phone finally rang shortly after midnight, the number on the screen was her aunt's. Why was Aunt Josey calling and not dad?

"Oh, Grace, sweetheart, it's me. Thank God you girls are okay." Aunt Josey paused. "Hated to wake you... but your dad's not answering his cell."

"Um, he's not here just now. And I don't know where... think he talked about... working late, helping his friend, Sam. Is there something wrong?" Grace felt wedged between her loyalty to her mother's secrecy and lying to her aunt. She worried she had grown too good at side-stepping, half-truths, and straight up lies.

"Lord, honey, I'm sorry, but I can't explain just now. If you hear from him, tell him to call me right away."

"Yes, ma'am. I expect him back any minute now. He'll call you."

Grace had made a promise she was unsure she could keep. Dad had called hours ago, asking if she and Zoey were okay. He'd had no luck locating Mom, but he assured her that she and Zoey were not to worry; he would find Mom and bring her home.

Grace returned to the bed she and Zoey now shared, quietly slipping in next to her sister.

"Was that Dad? And is Mom with him?"

"No, it was Aunt Josey. But I just called Dad. He's still looking."

"Is Mom in big trouble?" Zoey whimpered.

"Maybe, I don't know."

Why had Aunt Josey called so late, asking to speak to Dad? Did she know something about Mom's disappearance that Dad didn't? If so, why hadn't she told her? Grace hated that they kept her in the dark. After all, she was hardly a child.

— 21 —

Daniel

Daniel returned Josey's call but heard little of her blistering rant until the words *Leah* and *accident*. He interrupted her long enough to ask *how bad*? She answered she wasn't sure, but from the little revealed by the officer, she had decided Leah's physical injuries were not serious. Yet he found little solace in her directive to meet her at County General, apart from the fact that the staff on the twelfth floor knew Leah from previous admissions.

Daniel parked illegally and rushed into the main lobby. He approached the pink-clad volunteer behind the visitor information desk and inquired about his wife. The tidy, blue-haired woman smiled and asked his wife's name. When he answered, the woman instructed him in a hushed voice to take the elevator to the twelfth-floor lounge and wait for the attending physician.

"Twelfth floor? Are you sure? She was in an auto accident." He felt as if his scalp lifted from his skull, but he worked at fighting off an all too familiar bout of denial. He wanted Leah to have sustained minor bruises and scratches, even a broken bone; injuries that with proper care would heal, resulting in no discernable scars.

The woman stiffened and repeated her instructions in a firm voice. Daniel imagined he heard judgment in her tone, and in his desperation to deny what he most dreaded, he was robbed of reason. He wanted to call out the woman; punish her for all the anguish he felt. Instead, he thanked her and hurried along the labyrinth of intersecting corridors to a bank of elevators.

He nodded a greeting to the lone occupant of the elevator, and the young woman, dressed in scrubs, moved to the rear. Self-conscious, he rubbed a quick palm over his unshaven face and along the front of his oil-stained tee shirt, his body odor noticeably foul.

"Uh, pulled a night shift. Wife was in an auto accident." The young woman did not look at him but muttered an impersonal regret. Yet, he experienced a sense of relief, even gratitude.

The doors opened and he immediately spotted Josey standing in the corridor. His instinct was to retreat, but he stepped from the elevator into what he dreaded would be her lecture on how he must never again leave the girls alone. She would be right, but just now he wanted her to cut him some slack.

At the sound of the elevator, Josey turned and faced Daniel. Despite her long-standing grievance that his repeated acquiescence to Leah's demands overrode the welfare of her nieces, she appeared relieved at the sight of him, for she, too, was no longer alone.

Together they had shared repeated emotional bruises, as though Leah's relapses were their personal failings.

"Sorry I took so long. But I can explain about the girls."

"God, Daniel... the time for that has passed. We're here now."

They took seats in a corner of the waiting room, and Josey told Daniel what little she had gleaned from the rushed hospital staff.

"The nurse said her cuts and bruises were minor, but she sustained a pretty nasty concussion."

Daniel commented it was likely uncertainty about the concussion that had worried the police and EMTs. "And... what about the other? Did they say?" He asked.

"Only that Leah demanded the officer notify Father as her next of kin. And that the accident occurred off Tower Road."

"And you're sure the officer said *accident*?" He asked.

"Yes, I'm sure. Her injuries were nothing like what happened before."

He squeezed his eyes shut and slumped back in the chair, relieved that Leah had not intentionally harmed herself.

"Would've sworn she was taking her meds. Me and Grace had always checked behind her. But maybe we slacked off because she talked a lot about her determination to stay on them."

"Right, but why didn't you call me? You know I would've gone for the girls while you looked for her."

"I thought maybe it was a drinking binge, and if I could just find her, bring her home, she'd let me take care of her and I wouldn't need to worry you."

"I care far more that you left those babies alone. And that our Grace felt she had to lie. Just promise me you won't do that to her again."

"I'm sorry. And I'm to blame, not Grace."

"Did you call Grace?"

"Not yet, but I will."

Josey frowned, but she did not push harder.

He would call Grace. Let her and Zoey know that he had located their mom. But he would do so only after he had spoken with Leah's doctor, and was sure that it was an accident, and nothing more.

– 22 –

Leah

Leah had raged hopelessly against the python-like restraints that had rendered her powerless to escape the hot needle thrust into her quivering flesh. Its effect had been rapid, stealing the last of her flagging will to resist and severing her from her roaring river of pain; the loss of consciousness her single victory.

At the first sound of his perfect intonation, Leah opened her eyes to the voice calling her name. She touched the cold steel bed railing that imprisoned her. She was naked beneath the pastel smock, and she covered her breasts. The room reeked of his repulsive smell, and she knew she must withhold secrets the voice wasn't to learn. She glanced at her intruder's pale, oblong face and remembered her father's laughter as he had placed her atop a sad brown pony. The animal, its head hung, had walked in a tight figure-eight, the empty, cheerless, tinny sound of carnival music in the background.

"Good morning, Leah." He smiled. "The good news from your physician is that the bump on your head is of no medical consequence. And you have been released into my care."

While he fooled others, he with his trained smoothness, he did not fool her. His smile possessed all the warmth of a lizard, though his tone was deceptively gentle; kindness weaponized as control.

"I trust you've had a restful sleep." He spoke, but he was not real in the same sense she was real. Yet, from her earliest memory, the scent of his cologne was real.

She heard his attempts to win her trust as empty jabber. Her silence was her only weapon, and she did not look at him but toward the adjacent rooftops; tall buildings constructed of bright Lego pieces and pliable pipe cleaners.

"Would you like me to go first?" he asked, clearing his throat, and she imagined his prominent Adam's apple rising and falling. "My name is Dr. Nathan Ehrenreich, and our records show that you and I have spoken before. Is that correct?"

Leah easily ignored the one who called himself Nathan.

"Leah," he repeated, and she still refused to look his way. Her strategy was to deny him authority over her thoughts. She would expose his preposterous claim of descendance from King David, a boy brave in childhood who grew to be a beautiful poet and great lover with a clever murderous soul. But this Nathan was a fraud; cowardly and impotent.

"Leah, can you tell me why you are here?"

She had made no decision to be here. What was he blathering about?

He waited for her answer, and she giggled inside her head, where his presence was nothing but a tease, and like the lioness she was, she pounced on his ego.

"Descendent of King David, can you tell me your noble ancestor's weapon of choice?"

"Yes, I do recall your admirable sense of humor."

Gratified, she closed her eyes to his resolve.

"Very well then. I recommend you stay with us for a time, so that you and I may get reacquainted." He stood, bid her a good day, and walked from the room.

— 23 —

Daniel

Dr. Ehrenreich entered the waiting room and was coolly professional but mercifully brief. He explained that Leah was experiencing a psychotic episode and he had ordered a mood stabilizer and sedative and that she was currently resting comfortably.

"Your wife will, of course, be with us overnight and I recommend she remain here under my care for an extended stay so that I might perform a more thorough evaluation. Unfortunately, she is uncooperative, and her further retention would require her permission." His impatience showed in the sharpness of his tone.

"May we see her?" Daniel asked. His stance rocked slightly as he leaned away from the messenger. Leah was terrified of confinement and would never willingly agree.

"Visitors at this time would be unwise and I could not agree to an exception." As he turned to leave, he wished them an improbable *good day*.

When they reached the hospital lobby, Daniel failed to find words to express the kinship he had felt earlier with Josey and managed only a weak *thank you*. The two parted, Josey for the visitor's garage and Daniel to collect the parking ticket pinned beneath the wiper blade. He felt an abundance of relief that his truck had not been towed.

He texted Grace: **Your mom had an accident and is in the hospital, where she's resting. Home early-will explain then. Supper is on me.**

It would be better to deliver the rest of what little he had learned in person.

Daniel clocked in to work three hours late, counting on Josey to have broken the news to Robert. Though family was rarely a consideration, Daniel wished to avoid a hassle over his late arrival.

Leah was right that he needed to find a job with decent pay and a boss who was not her damn brother-in-law. But he had yet to find just the right time. Even when Leah was well enough to work full time, they barely broke even. Now that she could no longer continue her present job, he needed to do much better at finding work after hours and on weekends. Working for Robert remained his best shot at offering his services to customers unable or unwilling to pay Robert's higher charges. Daniel's ethical qualms were long ago overridden by his need to care for his family.

Daniel went to Robert an hour before quitting time and told him that the repairs on the Buick were taking longer than he had counted on, but with what was going on with Leah, he needed to leave work early. Robert's reaction was what Daniel had expected and he was squeezed between his promise to the girls and his future paychecks. Kissing Robert's fat ass meant he would continue to hand off overtime to him rather than pass it on to one of the other mechanics. The loss of Leah's income would shoot their monthly budget to hell and back. He'd need all the overtime he could get. Still, Daniel thought about just how sweet it would be to tell her brother-in-law to shove his cheap job where the sun didn't shine.

Unwilling to create more delay, Daniel decided against calling Grace and Zoey to tell them about their mom. He further reasoned it was a conversation best had face to face.

A large pizza box balanced on his forearm, Daniel unlocked the door and stepped into an unusual silence. No music blaring and no Zoey rushing to greet him. He called out what he was certain would result in Zoey's loud approval.

"Pizza delivery!" He went into the kitchen and placed the pizza box on the kitchen table and considered the possibility that Grace had somehow confused his earlier text and that she and Zoey had ridden the school bus to Josey's place.

"No, no, stop, let me go!"

"Traitor. Go ahead." Grace called after Zoey, who ran into Daniel's outstretched arms. The feel of Zoey's arms around his neck helped only briefly to lessen his concern for Grace's rightful anger.

Still, he called out to Grace. "I brought your favorite and if you don't get in here. Zoey and I are going to start without you."

"Go ahead. I don't want your damn pizza!" Grace shouted.

Daniel left Zoey to start eating alone and went to stand outside the girls' locked bedroom door.

"Grace, I get that you're pissed, and God knows you've got a right to be. And I'm sorry I didn't take time to talk to you about your mom. The other's not entirely my doing. But I should've called. Let you know I'd be late. I'm sorry."

"Yeah, Dad. But it was what you didn't say. I'm thirteen and not a child. Why's that so hard to understand?"

"I get that you're no child. But we couldn't have the conversation you wanted through a text message. And for sure not through a locked door. Let's eat, and when you're ready to listen like an adult, I'll tell you everything I learned."

Daniel returned to the kitchen where Zoey sat, content for the moment to stuff pizza into her mouth. His thoughts lingered with Grace, aware that his sarcasm was sterner than he had intended.

In Grace's unlikely outburst, he had heard an echo of his own ire. Nothing he had attempted had overridden Leah's clever deceptions in cutting back her medications or stopping them altogether. With each new episode, he was faced with the same haunting question, lodged in his brain like a hot spike: how could he keep Leah on her meds? The spike only cooled when Leah was able to renew her resolve that the drugs were needed to help managed her illness.

The aroma of pizza wafted from the kitchen and maybe it was Grace's hunger that finally brought her in to join them. She took a seat across from Daniel and glared, though he thought her heart no longer supported her earlier anger. Rather, what he now sensed was her sadness.

He spun the pizza box around to her and when she had eaten, he pushed back from the table and clumsily took a stab at the conversation. But how did a father tell his children that their mother suffered from an illness that had no timetable other than its recurring cycle of pain? Instead, he began with what he had learned of the physical injuries she sustained in her accident. He paused and, rubbing the heels of his hands across his chest, told what little he had learned from Dr. Ehrenreich.

"For now, your mom will stay in the hospital. She's medicated... and resting."

"Oh, no, Daddy, she can't stay there. It'll make her sad again." He knew Zoey required a more promising story, but he did not have Grace's gift. Still, he smiled and said what he always promised. "It's okay, baby, your mom will be home soon. She's there just long enough for... um, a test to find the best way to help her."

Zoey's forehead wrinkled. "And will that fix her?" In that moment, Zoey's face was not that of a seven-year-old but of someone much older.

"Yes, something like that."

Zoey seemed somewhat relieved. Grace's frown had intensified, though she did not choose to confront his ambivalence.

"Are we allowed to visit her?"

He answered in the way he was told.

"Did you tell 'em that's wrong? And that they can't keep us from seeing her."

"Grace, please, it's more complicated than that."

"No, Dad, it's not just complicated, it's fucking hard. And why can't you for once do something?"

Grace stood and walked from the kitchen and Zoey followed her sister.

Daniel took the overflowing kitchen trash to the cans and rolled them to the street, then folded a load of laundry. When Zoey had prepared for bed, he scooped her up into his arms and carried her giggling to bed.

"You want me to read from one of your books?"

"No, Daddy, what I want is to dream." She put her warm hand into his large rough one, and he leaned and kissed her.

Grace lay with her back to him, pretending to sleep. He dimmed the night light and reached back to pull the door closed behind him.

"Dad." Grace called softly, and he turned back expectantly. "Do you swear, no matter how bad Mom gets, we'll always bring her home?" Grace choked back what he thought were fresh tears.

"Yes, baby, I swear."

He crossed the narrow hall to the bedroom he shared with Leah and sat on her side of the bed. The scent of her was on the pillow he squeezed to his chest. He was desperate to always find within himself the strength to keep his promise to his daughters, though he remained godless and alone.

Old Woman
Spring 2018

— 24 —

Daniel

Leah was out of the hospital but once again unable to work. During the first two months of her convalescence, Daniel had struggled to keep the mortgage payments current while purchasing food, maintaining household expenses, and paying for Leah's costly prescriptions on his income alone.

He and the girls ate a diet of eggs, dried beans, potatoes, canned meats, cereal, two-day-old bread, peanut butter, jelly, and sometimes fresh milk. He now drank his first, last, and for the road coffee on the job. The girls packed school lunches of pb & j. He bought just enough gas to drive to and from work and once, when his money ran out at the end of the month, he stole a roll of toilet paper from the work bathroom. Rather than spend grocery money to replace light bulbs, he moved the good ones around from room to room as needed.

There were far too few options for raising additional cash, forcing him to set aside his pride and accept Sam's offer of a short-term loan. Sam lived with his mom, allowing him to put a little aside, and was thus the one person Daniel knew who did not live from paycheck to paycheck. Still, Sam would rightly expect his money returned. But before he could come up with any amount of cash for Sam, despite the familiar adage that a debtor cannot borrow themselves out of debt, he gritted his teeth and surrendered the title to his pickup in exchange for a short-term, loan-shark style loan. Afterwards, he figured he had cash enough to pay for another round of refills of Leah's meds and to hire an undocumented woman willing to work cheap to stay with Leah while he worked and the girls attended school.

On his and the woman's first meeting, he asked her name, and she handed him a note with the words *Old Woman enough* scribbled on the paper. Her one condition was that he pay her in cash daily, reminding him of yet another old adage: here today, gone tomorrow. He understood her need to move silently, like a puff of smoke, and he did as she asked.

Old Woman came and went unnoticed, avoiding encounters with noisy neighbors. She understood more English than she spoke and was kind to Leah. On Fridays, when he had remembered to buy Rice Krispies and marshmallows, she made after school treats for the girls. Their name for her was *Miss Nice*, and he fell back on his upbringing, referring to her as *Ma'am*. He quickly developed an affinity for her, and when he could, he drove her to the bus stop nearest where she stayed with those he believed to be a large extended family.

Daniel could only afford half days, which left Grace alone to care for herself, her sister, and their mom after school, and late into evenings whenever he was lucky enough to have extra work. Grace no longer had time for her friends. When he remembered to ask her about school, she shrugged and said only that she was okay.

Unbeknownst to Robert, Daniel was picking off as many customers as he could from those who rejected or simply could not afford Robert's prices, which included additional markups on parts. But like the old woman, he worked cheap. He demanded payment up front for parts ordered directly from wholesalers at no markup to *his customers*. He assuaged his nagging guilt with the satisfaction that he was helping strapped guys like himself, mostly self-employed grunt laborers. Their ratty-assed vehicles were essential to their getting to their jobs and keeping their families afloat.

Daniel was shocked the first time Tampons had appeared on Friday's grocery shopping list. He glanced at the box in Grace's hand and stammered.

"About those... I'd expected your mom would be the one... you know... a talk between you two. But... if there's anything...." He felt as though he'd swallowed an entire hippo in one gulp.

"Jesus, Dad, you can be so basic. I've got this. And before you decide it's time for the sex talk, I'm not having unprotected sex with boys. I'm not having sex, period. So, lighten up, won't you?"

He was not entirely sure, but he thought *basic* meant *wholly uncool.*

All expectations Daniel had of staying minimally afloat died when the cashier at the bank refused his deposit. A thirteen-hundred-dollar check for a major repair job had bounced clear to Venus.

He and Sam drove to the address the thief had given him, only to learn from the raging landlord that the man, his knocked-up wife, and three kids had skipped out in the middle of the night, owing two months of back rent.

"One look at that fucking loser and his heap of a car should have been warning enough." Daniel was pissed at himself for having extended credit to a con artist. But there was nothing to do now but drive away, leaving the landlord howling at the moon.

Sam shrugged. "So, what if you'd caught up to this guy and his family? What then?"

"I'd beat the living shit out of him and rip the fucking radiator I replaced right out that piece of junk."

"Oh yeah, tough guy. Right there in front of those three half-starved kids?"

Daniel had groaned. "Are you just fucking with me or is that some kind of bullshit philosophy straight out of your ass?"

"Ah, my friend. You have posed a rebuttal to what was merely a question of self-examination."

"You're one crazy bastard — no offense to your dear, sweet momma."

Sam laughed. "Let's face it, bro, we're dinosaurs destined for Amazon fodder." They laughed and Daniel momentarily felt a weight lift. How could he stay pissed, hanging with Samuel Gandhi?

Daniel dropped Sam off at his mom's place and headed home empty-handed. Leah's regular argument that he should retrain for an occupation with better wages and a promising career ladder rang in his ears. She never said anything about job satisfaction and a man acquiring something of his own. Then, she was right that he would never win the lottery. Nor would he realize his boyhood dream of opening his own shop where he could do the work he had grown up doing. Admittedly, he was barely holding his own in servicing the newer, computer driven vehicles. He had learned a little, but felt he was being called upon to reinvent himself as a lightweight electrical engineer. He would never get used to thinking about himself as a technician. He was a mechanic, and a damn good one.

The worthless check meant that the bills Daniel had paid, believing they would be covered with his deposit, were now delinquent plus late fees. Included among the bounced checks was last month's mortgage payment, and the current mortgage payment was due within ten days. A third month's delinquency was bound to trigger a foreclosure warning.

He was forced to sell his recently reclaimed truck for half its value to a guy who wanted it for his over-indulged teenage son. He handed over the title and keys in exchange for barely enough cash to cover the delinquent payments and fees.

— 25 —

Leah

Leah woke to the scent of her own urine, sweat, and lingering despair. She sat on the side of the bed until the room stopped spinning before pushing onto her feet. She took a measured first step, a second, and a third. Emboldened, she straightened her back and stood erect. In that moment, her weakened legs betrayed her, and she cried out as she slid down the wall to sit, weeping, in her own stench.

"Oh God, Leah, why didn't you call me?" Daniel called for Grace to come clean up the floor and bring her mom a clean gown while he guided Leah into the bathroom and onto the toilet.

"Dad, remember, they're all in the wash."

"Then bring me one of my tee shirts without grease stains." He was not sure he had such a shirt.

He drew a warm bath for Leah while she remained sitting slumped on the toilet. Maybe she would allow him to wash her oily hair, though she complained that his strong fingers were too rough. He thought she was waiting for *old woman*, but he had let her go because he could no longer afford to pay her.

"Daniel, my legs don't work." Leah placed a trembling hand on his arm.

"I know it must feel that way. But let's get you out of that gown and cleaned up."

"But, Daniel," she moaned. "My legs? What's wrong with my legs? They don't work."

"I promise your legs are fine. It's just the new drugs. Your system needs time before you'll start to feel... right again." He thought to say *normal*, but the truth was she would always need to commit herself to a daily regimen of drugs.

"But I'm afraid."

"I'm here, Baby. You don't need to be afraid."

He removed her gown and lifted her into the tub of warm water. Kneeling, he gently washed her in the sweet-scented body wash she liked. Before the water cooled, he helped her out of the tub, toweled her dry, and slipped his shirt over her head. He dried her hair while she sat on the toilet. Grace had changed the bed linen and he helped Leah into a clean bed, pulling the covers under her chin the way she liked. She spoke his name, but whatever else she had intended, the words were lost to her fatigue. She closed her eyes, and he believed she was sleeping.

He whispered. "I love you, too." Leaned, and lightly kissed her cool lips. Was he selfish to want to hear his wife say she loved him? He thought not.

He took a seat across from her and watched as she slept, believing that she rested better with him watching over her.

— 26 —

Daniel

Daniel slipped the dolly from beneath the F-150 and stood for a moment, arching his back. It was midnight, but still he considered starting on the Chevy sedan parked in the driveway. The truck had been a quick job better suited to a rookie mechanic, worth no more than a C-Note. It was barely enough to buy the groceries they needed, with nothing left to add to the small amount of money he had set aside to catch up with the mortgage payment. He would do what he could now and get an early start on her before heading into the shop.

Daniel cleaned up at the garage sink and went into the kitchen. He stood before the open fridge and finding nothing appetizing, he ate cold baked beans. Behind him, he heard scuffing feet, and he turned.

"Grace, what're you doing up at this hour?" The stove clock read two-sixteen.

"Uh… had to pee."

He nodded. "You want some of this?"

"No, thanks. I was thinking a big slice of chocolate pie."

"Nah, beans are healthier." He finished the beans and washed the container.

Grace leaned against the counter. Her question, as yet unspoken, hung in the air.

"Nearly three full months now, but I think she's coming around," Daniel offered.

"Yeah, me too. Yesterday she watched part of a kid movie with Zoey, and afterwards she sat outside in her chair for a time."

"Did you go out with her?"

"No, I couldn't tell if Mom wanted company then."

"It's a crap shoot, all right."

"But Dad, earlier Mom asked where you kept the unpaid bills."

"And what'd you tell her?" He swore under his breath.

Grace hesitated.

"Grace?"

"How could I tell her what I don't know?"

"Right, let's me and you turn in. Nothing's getting fixed with us standing here. We could get a few hours of sleep. You've got school. And I've got a fix waiting on me in the garage." He'd catch about three hours of sleep before rising to start on the Chevy. He had less time than he thought to square things before Leah would demand to know the details of their financial snake pit.

"Yeah, I've got a big-ass test in algebra."

"How's all that smart kid stuff going?"

"It's school, Dad." She grinned. "You know, slates, chalk, and dusty erasers. Teachers with their hair up in a bun." He gave her a smirk and they shared a hushed laugh. "But Dad... never mind." Grace turned to leave.

"Okay, what're you holding back?" He leaned against the kitchen sink.

"There's this school science competition with prize money." She paused, and he encouraged her to go on. "But there's a fifty-dollar entry fee and travel cost involved. And I know money's hard to come by. And the deadline is next Friday."

He worried that his Adam's apple had surely betrayed his lack of confidence, but he consented after questions about travel and teacher chaperons.

"Sure, why not? You're the smartest kid I know."

"Right, Dad, I'm the one brainy person you know."

He reached an arm around her shoulders and drew her in close. She was his rock, and no father could be prouder.

— 27 —

Daniel

For three nights, Daniel worked late, putting time in on an ancient Oldsmobile the size of a boxcar. The owner, an elderly gentleman named Mr. George, suffered from an overload of sentimentality, and had the financial means to make whole again the vehicle his deceased wife had driven and loved. Now that Daniel had made the car road ready, bumper to bumper, it was unlikely the car would ever leave the old man's garage.

As agreed, Mr. George handed Daniel twenty-five hundred dollars in cash, then the old man got into the passenger seat of the Oldsmobile, turned, and waved. Daniel tipped the bill of his cap and returned Mr. George's wave, believing the lonely man sat next to his wife, and they were off on an imaginary trip.

Daniel's route home took him past O'Lary's, the neighborhood bar where he and the boys of summer had gathered after city league games, whether games were won or lost. His better judgement told him to continue on home, but his stronger impulse was to join the comradery he had missed since leaving the team. He took two twenties from the envelope and placed the bills in his shirt pocket. The balance he returned to his locked toolbox. He had no plans to spend both twenties, but he just liked showing up with a little extra.

Daniel's entrance raised a welcome burst of friendly taunts and Tiny, the three-hundred-pound, cross-dressing owner and barkeep who got nothing but respect, slid a cold one across the counter, announcing it was on the house. Daniel had just wrapped his hot hand around the cold longneck and taken a seat among the loud drinkers when his cell blared *I'm So Excited.* A gnawing reminder of just how long he had gone without sex. He imagined getting drunk enough to proposition the very next woman who looked his way, but a sense of rejection came with the realization that Leah would likely not care that he had sex with another woman.

Daniel pulled his phone from his pocket and stepped away from the noisy drinkers. Leah was much better now, and he decided that if there was a real problem, the caller would be Grace and not Leah. He would stay awhile in the company of his friends. He let Leah's call go to voice mail and chose not to listen to her message.

After several rounds of beer and more laughter, Daniel joined the other guys heading home, joking about jealous wives and early schedules. Daniel declared himself fit to drive, though he owned a tornado-size buzz. He drove slowly, though fast enough to avoid attracting the attention of a bored night cop. He cut the headlights, eased into the driveway and shut down the engine. As he stared into the unlit house for clues to what might lie ahead, an all too familiar sense of wariness settled about him. He quietly closed the car door and approached the house. Slipped his key into the deadbolt and pushed open the door.

— 28 —

Daniel

As though blinded by a glaring light, Daniel felt the heat of Leah's blistering fury, and he was rocked back onto his heels. In her hand was an envelope: not just any envelope, but the exact one he thought was well hidden. Leah got into his chest, waving the envelope, and shouted that he had destroyed their lives. Daniel glanced toward the hallway, where Grace stepped back into the shadows. Zoey was nowhere in sight.

"I can explain, but first, can we go into the kitchen to talk? Not wake the girls?" He needed time to think. Was there anything he might say to calm her?

"They are fine. They are with their mother, and why would they not be? And don't you dare try lying your way out of this. Your ineptness has lost us our home. Our innocent daughters are now homeless."

His impulse was to reject her accusation that he alone should bear the full weight of their on-going financial disaster. But past experiences had taught him that nothing he said in his defense could possibly penetrate her rage.

"I'm sorry I kept it from you. But I thought it was best. But please hear me out. I have a plan." He took the envelope of cash and held it out to her. "With this and my next paycheck, we can catch up on the mortgage." He withheld the fact that he would actually be short one hundred and ninety-three dollars plus what he had spent on four beers and the money he had promised Grace for her science competition.

"Liar! Liar!" Leah screamed, and when she slapped his outstretched hand, bills scattered onto the floor like worthless confetti.

Daniel was not just behind on the current month's mortgage, but on the two previous months as well. The third letter warning of foreclosure had arrived five days earlier. His credit was shot to hell, and he doubted he would qualify for a decent rental. If they were lucky, his family was bound for federally subsidized housing. He'd heard from other guys facing the same situation that the process could take months, but he had yet to apply. Still, he offered what little confidence he could muster.

"Look, this straight-up guy I know has talked to me about cutting his company's ties with Robert. And bringing me on to service his sizable fleet of delivery trucks. It could lead to something solid for us, maybe even getting ahead enough so that I had money to attend one of those trade schools you've talked about."

"Oh, God, Daniel. Are you even listening to yourself? You're such a hopeless failure."

"Baby, please...." His unspoken words caught in his throat. He wanted desperately to reclaim the good he had felt earlier, and for once to have his wife support him.

Leah's face flamed with fury; she began to pound Daniel wildly in the chest. He caught her wrists and managed to pin her against a wall and hold her there. He pressed his lips to her ear and over her screams of profanity, he invited her to bitch all she wanted about his failings and her loathing of him, but this time, he wouldn't give her the satisfaction of the fight she invited.

Grace, who had been barely three at the time, had witnessed the nasty fight between her parents. Neighbors from the adjoining duplex called the police, and he was arrested and taken away in cuffs. He spent the balance of the evening in jail. Leah had not pressed charges and he walked out of the county courthouse the next morning. He had promised himself he would never again follow Leah into the dark place of her unbridled rage.

Overpowered, Leah stopped struggling against his strength, and he released his grip. She slid along his body and slumped onto the floor. Desperate to break through her anger, he knelt beside her, searching for words that might change their moment of ugliness into something civil. He dared to embrace her, and in his own madness, he kissed her. She gave him her open, wet mouth, and he felt he might have reached her. She took his penis in her hand and when his arousal froze his brain against all but his desire, she angrily pushed him away. Her bitter laughter was chilling, and what he'd willingly interpreted as consent became obvious revulsion.

"Oh, how I wish I'd never let you force me into marriage. I would have preferred two bastard daughters rather than have the likes of you father my darling Grace."

Bewildered and humiliated, Daniel struggled to his feet, and he heard a tearful moan from the direction of the dimly lit hallway, though he caught only a glimpse of Grace as she turned and ran. He called to her, but there was only Leah's screaming demand that he leave and never return.

As Daniel sped away, Leah's biting words that he was *never to return* reverberated in his head, like the roar of a hurricane, and he felt his universe crashing around him. He pressed the gas petal to the floor and screamed his own rage.

— 29 —

Daniel

Daniel woke to the sound of heavy traffic moving beyond him on the interstate. His joints were stiff, and his head throbbed with the jarring assault of a jackhammer. The whiskey bottle he had emptied rattled onto the floor of the Impala.

His physical punishment was nothing compared to the greater pain of having left Grace and Zoey alone with Leah and her rage. Right or wrong, he was in an impossible situation: leave his daughters or face arrest on a charge of spousal abuse that Leah, in her fury, would almost certainly claim. His anger had subsided, though it had left him mentally exhausted and physically drained.

A man showing plenty of road wear of his own climbed down from his semi, paused, and gave Daniel a knowing nod of kinship. "Coffee ain't all that bad here. And no disrespect intended, young fella, but you look like you could use a caffeine hit."

Daniel's raw throat seized and the best he managed was *thanks, but no*. He needed coffee the way he needed air to breathe, but he dared not walk into a place where the smell of fried food was certain to make him gag.

The stranger walked on; hands jammed deep within his pockets, and he jingled loose change with the repetitive echoing of a nail gun. Daniel closed his eyes against the brightness of the early morning sun and rested his head against the seat. Leah's demand that he *never return* was throbbing inside his head. The times before, he had waited for her anger to cool, and had returned. But this time felt somehow different. The blare from his phone startled him, and he retrieved it from the floorboard.

"Dad? Are you okay?" The sound of Grace's voice brought him to tears.

"Oh, God, Grace. Are you and Zoey okay? I'm so sorry. I was wrong to leave the way I did."

"Ah, we're... okay, I guess." Her voice betrayed her anxiety.

"Right, and... your mom?"

"Sleeping, I think."

"I'm so sorry about what happened. And... uh... that I'm not there to make you girls' breakfast." There were so many ways he had failed her and Zoey. How did he even start to go about making things better?

"I know, Dad. But we've still got milk for cereal."

Breakfast together, and afterwards dropping his daughters at school on his way to work, had played its part in fostering the appearance of the four of them as a normal family, as he, Grace, and Zoey wove their own cocooned portrait of family. He thought of himself and the girls as a truth residing within the larger deception.

"Here you go, son." The old man pushed a small bag wearing the store logo and a steaming, extra-large cup of black coffee through the open window. Daniel was so grateful he was unable to speak. Still, he reached for his wallet.

"It ain't *me* you owe." The man nodded toward the phone squeezed in Daniel's hand. With that, he walked to the semi and climbed back into the tractor cab. Touching the brim of his cap, he made his slow way back onto the interstate.

"Dad, you still there?" The stress in her voice was palpable.

"Ah, yeah, baby, I'm here." He understood Grace had asked a much bigger question: what she might now expect of him.

"Grace, about...."

"Uh, it's the bus. We've gotta run." Daniel heard the distant sound of the school bus grinding to a halt, and he called out to Grace. But following his moment of hesitation there was only silence.

The emptiness he had felt last night flooded back, and he considered how it might feel to drive north and then west to the shores of the Pacific. Swim naked in the ocean under a starry sky. Have ravishing sex on a beach with a woman he pleased.

Daniel finally understood that the stories he had told himself of Leah someday becoming whole again were the desperate lies of a grieving man. The woman of his best memories was no longer; she had been cruelly taken by a monstrous disease bent on destroying her. He accepted that he no longer loved Leah as he did in those memories, and it was his abiding love for his daughters that held him to his wife's illness. He now believed that Grace and Zoey were no longer safe with their mother, and he was determined to forge his way back into their daily lives. He restarted the engine and made his way back onto the interstate.

Mandatory Minimum
Fall 2018

— 30 —

Leah

Clara Curtis' skepticism was barely veiled by her artificial expressions of sympathy as Leah detailed the heart-wrenching narrative of herself as an only child, duty bound to care for her beloved father through the last months of his horrific battle with cancer. Leah accepted Curtis' tissue, and she believed Curtis' admission that the replacement she hired in Leah's absence was a disappointment. Leah felt lifted, though she had yet to learn just how much she had lost during her extended absence.

Shaken, she walked from Curtis' office, not as a salaried employee, but as a six-month contract hire who would perform the same basic tasks as before but at reduced compensation and without health insurance and sick leave. Yet Leah was confident that her exceptional skills and talent would once again win Curtis' admiration, and that she would not only be awarded a sizable bonus for *exemplary product delivery* but be reinstated as a full-time employee, with a substantial raise in salary and full benefits. She alone would rescue her precious daughters from the dark future to which their father's ineptness would have doomed them.

At the sound of the Impala in the driveway, Grace bookmarked her science textbook, gathered her scattered notebooks, and waited to learn her mother's mood. She wanted more than anything to have her splintered family reunited, but for Dad to rejoin the family, Mom would need to drop her ongoing grudge war. This would mean she had to stop bitching about Dad being a poor provider every time Grace passed along a nasty phone call from a bill collector or another letter from the mortgage company threatening foreclosure.

Grace watched Leah get out of the Impala and struggle to balance three takeout cartons and a flimsy tray with two super-size sodas. Reaching back for her purse, she tipped the tray, and the sodas spilled onto the ground. She stared at the empty cups as though they somehow mocked her. She carried the takeout cartons into the kitchen and dropped them onto the counter.

Grace followed Leah into the kitchen and stood slouched against a kitchen counter, hands jammed deep inside her jean pockets.

"My god, Grace. I'd expected that you would have given up on your misplaced anger." Leah exhaled sharply, her shoulders slumped. "Do you even care that I planned a wonderful surprise? But now, just like your father, you've ruined everything."

What kind of celebration was so fragile that she had spoiled it so easily? Still, Grace removed her hands from her pockets, stood erect, and in an act of practiced appeasement, offered to mix a pitcher of lemonade.

"Oh my, you are right... but first drag your willful sister in here so that she, too, may hear the good news first-hand."

Grace coaxed a fussy Zoey into the kitchen. In a burst of sudden brightness, Leah stepped onto a kitchen chair and made a grand gesture, as if she imagined thunderous applause rather than a bewildered audience of two.

"My darlings, I come before you with breaking news." Leah giggled at her clever turn of phrase and weaved, close to toppling forward, but regained her balance.

"Your mother, by her own wit, will no longer suffer the disgrace of meaningless work. And did I mention financial rewards? And your worthless father is gone forever." Her eyes narrowed in anger. "He will no longer be part of our family."

Zoey glanced at Grace before slowly coming to her feet with weak applause.

"And Grace, am I to believe that you heard nothing worthy of celebration?" Leah stepped down off the chair.

"Ah, no. I mean... I'll make the lemonade."

"But I brought frosty cola for you and your sister." Mom glanced about. "Oh, silly me, of course. We'll have lemonade." She giggled.

Grace had not spoken to her dad since their short phone conversation the morning after her parents' big fight. He had said nothing then about any intention to stay away, and Grace believed if he had meant to do anything like what Mom said, he would have told her. But he had not answered her phone calls or texts since then, and she had no idea why.

What had changed between her parents? All the times before, their getting back together was somewhat predictable, even made sense in its shared weirdness. A night or two after a fight, after he had slept in his truck or at Sam's, Dad would drop all attempts at defending his notion of reality, which Mom dismissed as his stubborn defense of a false argument. Then Dad would be allowed back into the house and his behavior would be somewhere between a prisoner whose guard had the authority to shoot him without cause, and so obliging that Aunt Josey referred to it as Dad's puppy with two tails.

Grace had understood what was required for Dad to get back into Mom's good graces, though his over-indulgence of her every whim was at times humiliating. Still, Dad had slept on the lumpy couch for a time in penitence before Mom allowed him back into their shared bed.

Everyone dutifully acquiesced to Mom's distorted version of the truth, and they had always returned to presenting themselves to teachers, neighbors, and random strangers as a *normal* family. But without Dad, Mom's revised family portrait, with herself as a dutiful mom to her two happy daughters, was skewed. Because although Dad was not the parent who brought home the larger paycheck, it was he, not Mom, who was the glue that held their family together.

— 31 —

Daniel

Daniel parked the old car he had borrowed from Tiny in the alley behind O'Lary's bar, where he had crashed for most of the last two weeks, sleeping on a camping cot in the storage room and washing in its utility sink. He took the crumpled envelope from his shirt pocket and read again Leah's allegation that she feared for her own safety and for that of her young daughters. He folded the summons to appear in court tomorrow morning at ten o'clock and returned the paper to his pocket.

Sam advised that a lawyer worth his salt could counter Leah's allegation with Daniel's claim of self-defense. But Daniel worried that the slightest hint at Leah's mental incompetence might lead a judge to declare that neither he nor Leah were suitable parents, plunging the girls into the foster care system.

The back door swung open, and Tiny called that he had chased out the last drunk and had closed for the night. Daniel took his one suit, best dress shirt, and tie from the back seat and followed Tiny back through the door.

In exchange for his stay, Daniel wiped down tables and mopped the bar floors. Drunks were lousy slobs to clean up after, and he had purposely avoided the bar during business hours as a precaution against becoming one of those slobs. Before Leah and Grace, he'd had a brief history with alcohol that he was determined not to repeat. His dad was a heavy drinker, and Daniel grew up thinking an occasional drunk was all a part of manhood.

"Ham and cheese there. And grab us a couple." Tiny motioned toward the walk-in cooler as he set bread, hot mustard, and a jar of dill pickles on the counter. He dropped into his oversized recliner and lit a joint. He was a heavy user to relieve the chronic pain of arthritis, a condition aggravated by his weight and long hours behind the bar. Tiny had once commented with a shrug that he lived with what he had.

Daniel sat across from his friend and wolfed down a couple of sandwiches.

"Tomorrow's judgement day. How do you feel?"

Daniel nodded. He stepped to the cooler and brought back two more.

"You got a plan for what you'll say to the judge when it's your time to speak?"

"No, not really. Figure my word against her pretty face and clever lies ain't changing my fate. And I'm worried about showing the judge too much. I'll keep my mouth shut and take whatever the judge hands out. A guy at work said he didn't even bother to show up."

"Have you stopped to think about how that's gonna play with your girls? And don't go fooling yourself that they ain't hearing from their mom, every time your name comes up. Add to that their daddy didn't care enough to push back against being cut out of their lives."

"Don't think she'd do that to them... to me. Besides, if she did, Grace knows better."

"Damn boy, you're a bigger fool than I thought." Tiny sighed deeply and pushed up from the chair. "Did that same smart boy tell you that if you've got nothing to say in your defense, that judge is gonna figure you deserve more than the mandatory minimum five-day sentence? For sure you're gonna need a change of underwear." Tiny walked from the room, leaning heavily on his cane.

— 32 —

Daniel

Daniel texted Josey before leaving the bar through a side door. She was his one connection to Grace and Zoey, now that direct contact was a violation of the judge's temporary injunction.

"Good God, Daniel, what on earth is so urgent you gotta do it at this hour?"

"Yeah, it's late. I know. And I hope I didn't roust anyone." He had meant Robert, but it was still a foolish thing to say.

"Well, nobody but me. What do you want? Are you okay?" She was whispering and Daniel believed he'd heard the sound of a door.

"I'm sorry about everything, but I'm more likely than not to go to jail tomorrow. Uh, and I need you to tell the girls." He was unsure as to why he had hedged.

"Wait. You want me to tell the girls *what*?" She was breathing hard and for a moment, he worried that she might faint. He rushed to tell her all that he'd held back. The big fight with Leah and his choice to drive away, leaving the girls alone with Leah's fit of rage. His erroneous belief that after the fight things would go back to the way they had been like all the times before. His surprise when the officers waylaid him as he was leaving work the next day, smirking as if they shared an inside joke, and slapped a temporary injunction and summons to appear into his chest.

"I'm telling you that tomorrow at ten I'm due to appear before a judge to answer why I should not be issued a restraining order against future contact with Leah and the girls. And why

I should not serve a mandatory five-day sentence for domestic abuse."

"My God, and you've waited till now to say anything?" The sharpness in her tone stung but was well deserved.

"Like I said, I kept thinking it would blow over." The time before when Leah had sought an injunction, she withdrew her filing before the court hearing.

"And now, at this late hour, you want me to let Grace know why you've disappeared from her and Zoey's life without a word?"

"It's an awful ask, I know. But after the court appearance... well, they'll take me straight to jail." Daniel did not tell Josey, but when he had asked the officers what was so damn funny, the older cop had answered that the judge who had issued the injunction was a *bitch man-hater*.

"No, Daniel. I won't do that. That way is all wrong. Those girls have to hear it from their daddy. It's bad enough they've got to know you're in jail, but coming from me, and not you, will break their hearts. Especially Grace." He had known Josey was right all along, but he had been too cowardly.

Daniel eased the borrowed car to the curb and killed the engine. He was relieved that houses along the street were dark. He stared up and down the quiet street before taking up his phone and texting Josey to wake Grace, who would need to weigh her own rightful anger against the risk of doing as he asked. He opened the package and slipped the burner he had purchased on his way here into his pocket. He would wait for Grace in the tool shed, as arranged earlier with Josey.

He eased out of the car and quietly pushed the door shut. A neighbor's dog barked, and he waited for the curious dog to resettle before walking the alley between the rows of houses and into the yard through the back gate. The tool shed offered an unobstructed view of the patio door. He lifted the warped metal door and forced an opening wide enough to squeeze inside. He wiped sweat from his face on the sleeve of his tee and his mouth felt as if it were lined in cotton.

The moon would set soon, and fog from the coast lay like a heavy veil. He strained to make out any motion or the slightest sound coming from the direction of the patio, but there was none. He sat on an old camping stool and waited.

At two-forty, Daniel had still seen no movement from the back of the house, and he feared his nerve was slipping. His stomach churned with the thought that Leah might have somehow acquired notice of his having violated the injunction, and he could now be charged with stalking. Still, he was here, and he'd stick it out a little longer.

An hour later, Daniel decided Grace was not coming, and he had squeezed back through the narrow opening when he heard what he thought was the sound of the sliding glass patio door. He stood perfectly still, his heart racing. He was unsure who he saw, for whoever was a mere gray figure now standing on the patio. The figure drew closer, and he could not know with certainty the one approaching was Grace. In the distance, he heard the siren of an approaching law enforcement vehicle.

– 33 –

Grace

Grace crossed the yard and approached the shed. She could see Dad just inside the shed, peering out at her through the narrow opening.

"Grace, thank God, it's you." He touched her arm, and she felt his hand tremble.

"What is this? Have you lost your mind?" What would she do now that she had two insane parents?

"Let's talk in here, out of sight," he whispered. He had taken cover back inside the shed.

"No, not until you tell me what's going on. Why here, at this hour, when you haven't bothered to return any of my texts or calls?"

"God, Grace, I get you're pissed. But I was placed under a temporary restraining order the same afternoon you and I last spoke. I haven't been allowed to contact you."

"Are you saying Mom did this?" Grace glanced back over her shoulder toward the patio door. She was no longer sure Mom was taking the meds that helped her to sleep.

He nodded. "Yes, and I was caught off guard. No warning before the order was served. Left me with no time to call. And tomorrow I'm due in court. After the hearing, I'll go directly to jail to serve a mandatory five days, or maybe more. I wanted you and Zoey to hear it first from me."

"Sweet. You're going to tell me you robbed a mini market. Now I can go back to bed." The knot in her gut had only tightened and she felt she would throw up. Still, she squeezed through the opening and sat on a chair opposite where he had taken a seat on an old camping stool.

He explained what had happened in the aftermath of his fight with Mom, the part that neither of them had expected. She listened, and when he had finished, she hung her head, struggling to take it in. His fear that any counter to Mom's version of what happened could jeopardize her and Zoey made sense.

Daniel took the temporary injunction from his pocket and offered it to Grace, but she shook her head. He then took a phone from his hip pocket.

"It's a burner and I put Sam's number in the contacts. You can trust him to be available to you while I'm in jail and beyond. But use the phone only in an emergency."

He stood, and she moved into his embrace.

"Grace, I'm so sorry." He paused. "About everything. And I promise there will be no more secrets between us." She desperately wanted to believe him, but at that moment he felt dead to her.

She waited until he had closed the gate behind him, then hid the phone among a stack of discarded drapes until she could find a safe place in her and Zoey's bedroom.

— 34 —

Daniel

Judge Watkins entered the hushed courtroom, and Daniel could hear his heart pounding. He remembered the gruff warning of the officer who had served the injunction that in her courtroom, he was guaranteed a harsh result. Though the judge's slight physical stature appeared less formidable than Daniel had imagined, the strength of her voice and her clear command of the courtroom overrode any prospect of leniency he might have foolishly permitted himself.

The clerk directed him and Leah to stand, and in turn state their full names, and to swear to tell the truth. Judge Watkins turned to Leah.

"Ms. Killian, as the plaintiff you may now make any statements, present evidence relevant to your allegation against Mr. Killian, the defendant, and present witnesses to speak on your behalf."

Daniel heard a broken narrative that exposed his and Leah's shattered marriage and a litany of his personal failures as both father and husband. Yet his mood was lifted with the judge's sharp retort that Leah was to focus her remarks strictly on accusations as presented in her brief before the court.

Leah apologized and in a tearful voice she constructed a convincing fabrication of his drunken, brutal violence against her; an attack in which she had pushed back, fearing for her safety and that of their children. Afterwards, she sat quietly sobbing.

"Mr. Killian, I have heard your wife's statement of the allegations against you, and now is your opportunity to present any statement you wish to make in your defense. Present any evidence and witnesses you may wish to call."

Daniel stood awkwardly, his sweaty hands jammed into his pockets, and he felt he'd gag on his own tongue. He wished for the kind of anger that would allow him to call out Leah on her lies, but there was too much at stake to allow himself that kind of satisfaction.

"Mr. Killian, I have two teenage sons and I have no interest in tolerating similar disrespect from a defendant. Take your hands out of your pockets and find your tongue or I promise you this will be a short hearing. Do you understand?"

"Yes, Your Honor. And I do apologize. I mean no disrespect." His face burned with embarrassment, and he felt faint. His arms now hung by his sides as if they were no longer an integral part of his body. His brain was on fire with his ineptness.

"That's better Mr. Killian. Now, what do you have to say for yourself against these charges?"

"Your Honor, I've never meant to be a threat in any way. Not ever. I love my wife and our daughters. If my actions frightened either my wife or daughters, I sincerely apologize." He wanted to tell the judge that Leah's mental illness made her unfit to care for Zoey and Grace, and that he was called upon to shoulder much of the responsibility for parenting their daughters. But he was terrified of what that might mean for the girls.

"So, you are acknowledging that the allegations regarding your actions on the date specified are true?"

"Yes, Your Honor, I am. And as I said, I deeply regret any distress I caused my wife. I love my family, and it would cause me great pain to be denied the role and responsibilities of parent to our daughters."

"And those of a good husband, Mr. Killian?" The judge had clearly heard his unintended omission. Daniel understood that it had always been a matter of Leah's false testimony and who the judge would choose to believe. Still, he responded.

"Yes, Your Honor."

"Mr. Killian, the court acknowledges your forthrightness and your apology. However, I am granting the plaintiff's plea for a restraining order, enforceable for a period of twelve months. In addition, you are remanded to the county jail to serve a mandatory five-day sentence for domestic violence."

The judge stood and left the courtroom, and the clerk dismissed the proceedings. Daniel glanced across the room at Leah, searching her face for the slightest sign of remorse or even pity, but he saw neither. He felt numb to all but the pressure of the handcuffs around his wrists, and the sour breath of the escorting officer.

Shopping Spree
Winter 2018

— 35 —

Grace

Over her shoulder, Grace heard her name called and her impulse was to escape the sound of her mother's voice; to deny her presence. She pushed farther into the crush of kids, determined that she would be among the first to board the school bus. But her best effort to escape was not enough to outrun the swell of laughter that rose like a wave over the gathering of gaping kids.

Despite the day's mid-winter chill, Mom was standing on the hood of the Impala wearing her summer favorite, a pumpkin-orange sundress, with brightly beaded flip-flops and purple knee socks. Mom's choice only made sense if one considered that she had missed most of the previous summer hidden away in her room, and she now wished to reclaim one of her lost sunny days. The school cop ran toward the Impala, demanding that Mom get down from the hood while threatening her with a ticket for illegal parking and reckless endangerment of children. Grace accepted defeat and stepped out of the bus boarding line and hurried toward the Impala. Mom blew the young cop a kiss, climbed down without protest, and got behind the steering wheel. She saw Zoey hunkered down in the front seat and figured there must have been a similar scene at Zoey's elementary school. She slumped into the back seat, determined that she would leave school forever.

Grace defiantly followed Zoey and Mom into the retail store, where Mom invited her and Zoey to each take a cart and choose whatever they wanted. The shopping spree was to be their back-to-school splurge. Biting the inside of her cheek, a wary Zoey glanced at Grace, who shrugged. The girls settled for sharing a single cart, though neither was willing to further test their mother's cheerful mood. Yet Grace worried that they were about to enact yet another of Mom's failed shopping adventures.

When Grace and Zoey had loaded the shopping cart, Leah wheeled it into line at the nearest check-out station. A nervous middle-aged woman, proudly wearing a *Cashier Trainee* badge pinned to her employee's navy jacket, over-performed a scripted corporate greeting as she pretended not to notice Leah's skimpy dress. She set about scanning the mound of items. Grace's anxiety grew with the mechanical sound of the paper tape passing through the machine and curling on the floor at the cashier's swollen feet.

"My, ain't that unusual? Four hundred and four dollars even." Her round cheeks flushed as though she considered for the first time the prospect of Leah paying. Leah smiled reassuringly, selected a card from the banded stack of twenty or so she took from her oversized cloth bag, and slipped the card into the machine. The cashier squinted at the flashing light. Her brow gathered.

"Ma'am, I'm very sorry, but your account is flagged... as... inactive."

"Hmm, silly me." Mom giggled. "I must have failed to swap out the old one for the newly arrived replacement." She calmly chose a second card as if playing a game of draw poker. She sometimes juggled as many as twenty-three credit cards in what she defended as spreading the debt among predatory lenders. Dad had pleaded with her to stop applying for new credit cards, but his attempts were like arguing with a thunderstorm for rattling windows.

The baffled cashier sighed. "I'm afraid this card has also been rejected." Her cheeks glowed brighter than before.

"Afraid? There's nothing to fear. You need only to rerun the card. No doubt the machine malfunctioned." Mom placed a trembling hand atop Zoey's curls, and Zoey, much better at hanging onto hope in the face of a pending disaster, smiled sweetly at Mom. The third and fourth cards yielded the same result.

"Mom, please, let's just go. We don't really need this stuff." Grace felt sweat forming on her upper lip and what she wanted was to leave behind the hostile stares boring into her back from those who had remained in line behind them.

Without another word, Mom upended the bagged items and sorted the contents into fourteen separate stacks. She then placed a single credit card atop each stack, declaring the balance of each card was equal to the cost of the separate stacks of merchandise. She smiled brightly at the anxious cashier and demanded she get underway.

"God, Mom, let's just forget all this stuff and leave."

"No, Grace. Can't you see I'm right?"

In a nutty way, Grace got Mom's erratic reasoning, but the loud eruption of protest from frustrated shoppers had attracted the attention of a store manager who was hurrying toward them, accompanied by a uniformed security guard.

The exasperated cashier wept through her explanation of what she kindly labeled an *unpleasant situation*. Leah's loud insistence that she receive proper customer service resulted in the security guard taking hold of her upper arm and forcefully escorting her from the store.

Mom started up the Impala and shouted back at the security guard that he bore full responsibility for her having broken her promise to her daughters.

"That's okay, Mom."

I just wanted the colored pens and the drawing tablet," Zoey sniffled.

Mom reached into the oversized pocket of her sundress and took out a stolen box of pens, promising the drawing tablet, along with the jeans and sneakers Grace had chosen, on a return trip. Grace shrugged, claiming that she didn't need new jeans. Forget that last year's jeans were a full inch too short.

"I know you girls are starved," Mom said, as if nothing out of the ordinary had happened, while making a quick turn into Zoey's favorite fast-food place. Despite having eaten only a hurried bowl of cereal before school, Grace cringed at the prospect of yet another public scene. Mom parked the Impala and began searching through her bag for her wallet and what she called her surprise stash of cash. She pulled two wrinkled twenties from the wallet and laughed in a manner that suggested she, too, was surprised, as well as relieved.

Mom stepped from the car into a stiff wind and stood shivering while Grace retrieved her team sweatshirt from her backpack. Mom put on the sweatshirt over her sundress, ensuring that their entry would not go unnoticed.

When they had finished their meal, Mom flashed enough additional cash for movie tickets and a bucket of popcorn. Leah chose the movie, declaring it was the story of a brave newspaper woman who dared to publish stolen papers against a deceitful government, defeating a president and bringing home soldiers from a corrupt war.

"Is it a true story?" Zoey asked.

Mom smiled and said, "My darling girl, there are no true stories; only those we hold as secrets."

Zoey squinted at Mom, but Mom only smiled and teased that Zoey should share her popcorn.

While the movie had interested Grace, what she loved far more was sitting in the darkened theater where no one stared in judgement. It felt the way she thought of as normal: mother and daughters out for an evening.

Yet her best-loved memory of the evening came unexpectedly on their drive home. The radio played at full blast and at the first notes of an old song, Mom screamed with excitement and steered the Impala to a quick stop astride a public sidewalk. She got out of the car and invited Grace and Zoey to join her.

Grace hesitated, to which Mom responded, "Yes, my darling girl. Life's most precious gifts are lived in the sweetness of the unexpected. Joy must never be cautious."

Grace, her eyes filled with tears, danced with Mom, and to Grace's amazement, her earlier humiliation was set aside. It was as though she, Zoey, and Mom were the only three voices to be heard on the planet, and she howled with unrestrained joy. She could not have known that this moment would remain with her long after all her mother's joyful laughter had ended.

It did not matter that Mom had spent money that should have gone toward the purchase of food for the coming week.

— 36 —

Grace

Mom had promised to grocery shop on her way home from work, but like so many of her promises since starting her new job, it was one Grace could not rely on.

"I'm calling Daddy. He'll bring us pizza and Pepsi."

"Right, you do that. And we'll flag a ride on a spaceship bound for the moon, where we'll eat Moon Pies until we throw up." It was a silly thing Dad once said that had made her laugh, but out of her mouth, it just sounded stupid.

Grace had dared to use the burner phone to call Sam to set up a time for a call with Dad the day he was released from jail. He had sounded exhausted, even more than the times he took care of Mom when she was sick. When she commented about how tired he sounded, he answered that the county jail was no decent place to catch a nap. He laughed, but he sounded nothing like himself. He said he was going to the room he rented from Sam's mom and sleep for a week.

Zoey was bathed and dressed for bed but insisted on waiting up for Mom. The two sat together on the couch, Grace studying and Zoey drawing her favorite subject, a sleeping Jimmie, until she tired.

"I bet Mom isn't coming home. She's drunk again and Dad has gone to find her." Zoey looked expectantly toward the door as if she had called up one of Aunt Josey's Jesus-like miracles.

"No, she's not doing that now. She's working and has forgotten about us." Grace set aside her study notes for her class in psychology, a subject that sometimes helped her make sense of her screwed-up family.

It did not matter what time Mom came home. Whenever she did, her arms would be loaded with more work. She would pretend to scold her and Zoey for being up late on a school night but had refused to respond to Zoey's teacher's email about scheduling a conference to discuss Zoey's uncharacteristic inattention in class. Nor had she provided the money she promised Grace to ride the city bus home from basketball practice and home games.

Bus fare would mean Grace's teammates' parents would no longer need to trade off on who drove her home. While she desperately wanted to stay on the team, and appreciated their kindness, she was still embarrassed to be the subject of their unspoken pity.

Dad still came to her home games, but no longer joined other parents in the team's designated seats. Rather, he sat on the gym apron and from there he could hear the announcer call the game.

Grace was relieved that curious teammates and their parents bought whole cloth her elaborate lie that Dad's new job required him to take frequent emergency calls from stranded motorists. Grace thought it odd that Dad's unlikely behavior warranted a plausible response, but there had been no rumors about her mom's illness that reached her.

When Grace grew so tired of her family's lies, she fantasized about a moment when she would grab the mic and give her own introduction: *Welcome your Tiger's leading scorer: at 5'11, playing center forward, our very own Grace Killian! Daughter of an accused wife-beater and a loony mother!* Wild cheering would explode from the fans.

The door slammed back and Leah, her arms loaded with a stack of jumbled folders, rushed into what now served as both her bedroom and her home office. When she emerged, she exhaled sharply.

"I trust you girls have eaten. I think I'll just grab something and eat at my desk." She had recently purchased an expensive new computer, executive desk, and chair with what Grace suspected was a new credit card.

"No, we don't have food." Zoey frowned. "Can we call Dad to bring us food?"

"Grace, what on earth is your sister talking about? There has to be food. I gave Josey shopping money… just, just… days ago."

"Mom, Zoey's right. That money was for last week's shopping."

"Good God, Grace. Why do you choose to sit on your hands while your sister goes hungry? What's wrong with you that you don't understand I do what I must to provide for your futures?"

"Not fair! I'm no miracle worker. Why can't we just go now?" Shopping would take less than an hour away from her precious work.

Mom's chin quivered and a moan escaped her parted lips. She stared as though Grace was a threatening stranger before retreating to her room and locking the door behind her. Mom's screams echoed through the house and Grace, near panic, knew she and Zoey needed to leave, but where would they go? She willed her heartbeat to slow, and her resolve to act matched her terror. She would do whatever it took for her and Zoey to escape their mother's rage. She retrieved the burner from its hiding place in the bedroom closet, and she and Zoey ran from the house.

"Where are we going?" Zoey asked.

"Any place but here." Grace answered.

Zoey's hand in hers, they ran the three blocks to the neighborhood park.

— 37 —

Daniel

Daniel had idled away yet another evening at O'Lary's, where the beer had flowed. When ankle-deep bullshit had run its course, he made his way to the junk car and drove toward the basement room he now rented from Sam's mom. He was ten minutes in-route when his cell phone vibrated, and he fished it from his jacket pocket. The number displayed on his phone shook him, and at the sound of Grace's trembling voice, he was instantly sober.

"Grace, what's happened?" Daniel brought the car to a jolting stop.

"Dad, it's crazy... I just lost a big fight with Mom... and Dad... she's... flipped out. I promise I didn't mean to... argue. The right words just came out... all wrong."

"Are either of you hurt?" He had until now believed the girls were physically safe from even the worst of Leah's rage.

"No, but can you come right now?"

"Just tell me where you are."

"The neighborhood playground, near the kiddy slide. And Dad, I know it was wrong to call, but I didn't know what else to do. Mom never wants Aunt Josey to know when she flips out, and I didn't want to make it worse."

"No, no, you did the right thing. Did she follow you to the park?"

"No, I don't think she even knows we're gone."

"What's that yelling?"

"Older boys on bikes, but I don't think they've seen us."

"Stay quiet and out of sight. I'm less than ten minutes away."

"What'd he say? Is he coming for us?" Zoey whined.

"Yes, now shut up." The yells of the two boys on bikes drew nearer and Grace shifted positions to avoid being seen. Zoey scooted closer and took hold of Grace's hand.

"I'm scared."

Grace squeezed Zoey's hand to silence her. The riders circled the basketball court so close that in the dim light Grace recognized the street's biggest bully. He rode a bike he'd stolen from a younger kid who was too afraid to tell his parents. He and his posse circled a second time before laughing and riding away,

"Mom's crazy. I'm staying with Dad," Zoey leaned and whispered.

"God, Zoey give it a rest. You know why we can't do that."

"You mean because Mom needs us?"

"Right and besides, he doesn't have a real place."

"Okay, but can we ask Dad for something first? I'm hungry."

Grace nodded, praying the approaching headlights were those of his truck. But it was a car dad would never drive. It slowed and Grace got to her knees.

Daniel sped toward the park, his heart racing, and his mind pulsating with images of his vulnerable daughters, alone and frightened. His fear, coupled with his resentment toward Leah and his own guilt at not fighting the restraining order, swelled in his chest so that he thought he might stop breathing.

Approaching the park, Daniel spotted Grace and Zoey's shadowy forms huddled together beyond the reach of a security light. He slid the car to a rolling stop and caught Grace and Zoey in the glow of its headlights. He hurried out of the car, and they stood and ran to meet him. He gathered both girls in his arms, holding them fiercely against his chest, and felt their runaway hearts pounding against his own.

Zoey patted his damp cheeks. "Were you scared too, Daddy?"

"Not anymore, now that I know you two are safe." It was not until he had first held a newborn Zoey that the lingering pain of Leah's betrayal had subsided. His first love was Leah, but his pinnacle love would always be his daughters.

"Dad, I know you aren't supposed to, and I don't want to risk more trouble... and I know we've got to go back... but Zoey and I are hungry."

Daniel drove them to the all-night I-Hop. When the girls had stuffed themselves, he returned and parked half a block from the house, where they sat staring toward the brightly lit house.

The three got out of the car and stood in the shadows, holding each other. It was Grace who pulled out of Daniel's arms.

"And Dad...." Her voice was strained.

"Yeah, baby."

"Uh, never mind. It's okay." The girls walked on, and upon reaching the door, they quietly entered and eased the door shut behind them.

– 38 –

Daniel

Daniel waited until the light in the girls' bedroom window had flashed off and the house bore signs of being settled, then drove to an all-night grocery store and selected items Grace could prepare that did not require immediate refrigeration. He picked up a couple of cheap coolers to hold the food and returned, parking on the street a safe distance from the house, in compliance with the dictates of the court order. He waited for the neighborhood's last late-night dog walker. Satisfied his approach was safe, he placed the food in the two coolers and hid them where he and Grace had agreed.

Back in the car, he climbed onto the back seat, retrieved the smelly blanket and pillow he had stashed, and settled for the night, though his pain was nearly unbearable. He no longer had any faith that their daughters were safe with Leah. He would somehow find the money to hire a decent lawyer; someone who could tell him how to navigate the legal system to regain his rights as a father to protect his daughters from harm.

Just before dawn, Daniel woke to a hard tap on the window. The officer moved her hand onto her service revolver and motioned for him to lower the window while he kept both hands in sight.

Daniel glanced toward the house with its still darkened windows and did as he was told. Hundreds of explanations swirled through his mind, though he feared none would save him from a trip downtown. The cop's sternness convinced him that only the truth had a snowball's chance in hell of working.

"Sir, registration and driver's license?"

"Officer, the car ain't mine. Belongs to a friend." He felt himself begin to sweat.

"I see. And if I was to call your friend, is he gonna be surprised that you're driving his... car."

"No, ma'am. This car surely ain't worth stealing. What I mean is... he won't be surprised."

She frowned but said, "Right. I take your point."

She studied his license and the frown returned. "That your house there?"

"Yes, ma'am. It... was...."

"You got a good story as to why you're parked here and not in your own driveway?" She had asked the question he feared most, and a half-truth was all he had against jail.

"Officer McCall, ma'am, I was worried about my two girls going hungry and I left two coolers of groceries there." He pointed. "And I stayed a while longer just watching and worrying, and I fell asleep."

"Get out of the car, sir." She stepped back, a hand returning to the butt of her gun. She cuffed him and put him into the backseat cage.

She stepped away and talked to someone on the radio.

No doubt the restraining order would come up, and though he had violated the order, he was now just outside the limit.

He was surprised when she walked to where he had pointed.

She returned to the patrol car and ordered him out of the car.

"Daniel Killian, it appears you have violated your restraining order. And I should be hauling your skinny ass to jail. But delivering food to your hungry kids ain't likely against the law."

"Officer, I swear to God I've never hurt my girls or my wife. And they were going hungry." He choked on tears he was struggling to hold back.

She studied him with an intensity that he felt clear to his bones, and he prayed she knew something about hunger.

"Turn around." She uncuffed him. "Don't you ever let me catch you within two miles of this house."

He hesitated.

"Killian? Am I clear?"

"Yes, Ma'am."

"Alright. Now get the fuck off this street before I come to my senses."

He was grateful to have escaped with a stern warning and a ticket for loitering overnight on a public street. He drove away, his hands trembling with relief, though his violation was a matter of record.

– 39 –

Leah

Pain passed the length of Leah's spine, producing an incandescent fear. She lay puddled on the bedroom floor, trampled underfoot by an advancing army of nine-inch soldiers fashioned from aluminum and globs of blue bubble gum. Her daughters' blood-curling screams split Leah's skull with the precision of an executor's axe and only through sheer willpower did she rise and answer their calls. She drew forth her Brave Maiden's sword from its gold sheath, repeatedly striking the evil hordes, blow after blow, hacking through to the wicked heart of the motherboard. The killer robots were instantly vaporized. The scent of electrical sparks and blood fouled the air; her daughters were nowhere to be seen. Had they too vanished? She rose from the ashes and began to search for those she believed she had lost.

"Mom, Mom, it's Grace. We're okay. It was a bad dream." Leah felt pressure on the upper portion of her arms, and she was helpless to resist. The voice calling to her penetrated her brain fog, and she struggled to move toward its sound.

"Oh, Grace. Is that you? Please forgive me. I was so afraid. I never wanted to lose you and Zoey. I only want to be normal; a good mother... where is your sister? Did they take her?"

"No, Zoey's just fine. Sleeping. We're okay, Mom. I promise. Let's get you back into bed."

Leah crossed her arms over her exposed breasts, whimpering her humiliation as she stood naked. Her illness had been fully exposed, and her Grace would never unsee what she had shown her.

When Grace had helped her back into her nightgown and had gotten her back into bed, she asked if she should turn off the overhead light when she left.

"Oh, no, Grace, I fear your father and his army will return. Take yourself and your sister away." Leah clung to Grace and sobbed in anguish.

"No Mom, Dad would never do that."

Grace had once asked what it was like inside her head, and she had replied that explaining her illness was like explaining a bark without ever having seen a dog.

"Grace, I won't survive without you. You must promise to never leave me."

"I promise I'll never leave you."

Leah buried her face into Grace's shoulder, whispering a litany of regrets that Grace denied, but knew to be true.

Performance Evaluation
Spring 2019

— 40 —

Leah

Leah paced the cavernous executive lobby on the twelfth floor of the AMI DATA Corp building. She counted the sixty-three steps from the elevator to the first row of perfectly aligned, mauve-cushioned chairs. There, she took a seat and studied the plushness of the cathedral-like space. She ran her tongue across her upper teeth, tasting the bitterness of caffeine residue, and searched her purse for a breath mint. Finding none, she approached the chubby, apple-cheeked security guard. He hesitated before reaching into his trouser pocket and pulling out a crushed pack of white Orbit gum.

"No, no, weren't you listening? I asked you for a mint, not gum." She explained to the deaf young man she was here for an evaluation of merit with Clara Curtis. In the future, he was to come better prepared. He put the packet of gum back into his pocket and with an air of dismissal, he turned away.

In the face of his insubordination, the throbbing pain behind Leah's eyes flared with the brightness of a torch. Pain so unrelenting, she silently pled for the mercy of a forever stillness. She moved to a better seat where she was certain she would hear her name when called. She inhaled deeply, held her breath, and exhaled audibly, fighting back her exploding anxiety.

She glanced at the clock on the wall and saw the hands spinning out of control: one clockwise, the other counter, a tragic collision inevitable. Its yellow eyes winked at her. Gasping, Leah got to her feet and rushed across the room to where the security guard stood.

"You must reprimand that clock." She pointed out its gleaming yellow eyes of evil.

"Uh, Ma'am...?" He stuttered and stood so close she could smell his cheap cologne. His face flushed bright pink as he pushed onto his toes, and she imagined neurons firing sluggishly in his reptilian brain like a sadly neglected machine.

She gathered herself and leaned, whispering, "The clock, there on the wall."

He stepped back, stared at her, and had the impudence to ask if she wanted him to call a family member or friend. Surely he knew Daniel had abandoned her and his children, and that she had no friends.

"Caffeine, too much caffeine. And, you know, there are the pain meds." He placed a clammy hand on her shoulder and nodded as if he could understand. "And yes, yes, thank you. I am calmer now."

Leah retook her seat and refused to meet the clock's gaze. She rammed her fist in her mouth and chewed her knuckles, welcoming the physical pain that helped to distract from her worse pain of being discovered for who she was.

Leah removed an envelope from her purse, unfolded the single page it contained, and traced the imposing corporate logo with her forefinger. The signature of the Director of Personnel, Clara Curtis, in bold black lettering, saturated the fine linen paper. Leah held the letter to the sunlight pouring through the bank of floor to ceiling windows. Not even nature's opulence diluted the grandeur of Clara Curtis's message. Her summons could only mean that Leah's excellence had earned her an invitation to join the ranks of rising corporate stars; powerful men, and a scant number of women, would be gathered, champagne chilling, all awaiting her celebratory entry. Her talented daughters' bright futures secured.

More confident, Leah stood and walked to the receptionist's desk. The woman's greeting was too edgy for the insignificance of her position. Nevertheless, Leah asked politely to see Ms. Curtis's appointment calendar, only to be told that Director Curtis's calendar was private. Her long bangs swished like the loose twine on an old-fashioned rag mop.

"Yes, yes, of course. But I'm sure if she knew I was here, she would wish to see me right away." Leah stepped closer, where her distorted reflection was visible in the highly polished desk.

"I'm sorry, but do you have an appointment?" The woman's thin shoulders lifted, and her tone bore a snarkier edge. Leah would see to it that the woman regretted her rudeness. Leah dug again into her purse and handed the letter to *Betty Spooner*.

"Ms. Killian, I'm sorry, but it appears you have misread the letter. It is a notification that your contract has not been renewed. Your employment ended last Friday. You're supposed to be here to pick up your personal items."

No, it was Betty Spooner who was mistaken. Leah insisted she notify Director Curtis that she had arrived. Spooner's posture stiffened, and Leah sensed sudden motion behind her. She turned to face the approaching security guard, the cherry in his cheeks heightened by his consternation, and his youthful pimples flashing brightly like pinpoints of light.

Leah heard only *is there a problem here?* She struggled to recall any part of her lost morning, for she was apparently the subject of some crisis. Her desperation had robbed her of what remained of her cleverness; her charade. Yet her mind opened with the smoothness of a well-oiled hinge, and she wisely accepted her fate.

The officer took hold of her arm, his blunt fingers pressing into her fleshy underarm, and she bid Betty Spooner a polite good day, cleverly leaving open a future door. Clara Curtis would always need a mind larger than her own. A uniformed woman wearing men's black oxfords stepped from the elevator carrying a single cardboard box. Leah could see that the box contained a framed photograph of Grace and Zoey wearing Halloween costumes Leah had sewn during one of her more lucid periods, and a lone potted African violet. A single bloom hung from a limp fur-like stem.

The three exited the building, and the second officer handed Leah the box and stepped back. Perhaps the woman believed there were appropriate words to be spoken, but she remained mute. After an agonizing silence, she abruptly turned and reentered the building. The young man watched the woman, a brief disappointed expression on his broad face, as if he had counted on the female officer for some woman-to-woman response.

In her failure, he offered, "Shitty deal, if you're asking me."

Then he too reentered the building and joined the woman. Perhaps they shared words of redemption; reassurances that they had simply done their jobs, and maybe they agreed to grab a beer after work. The two entered the elevator, and they were obviously done with any regrets they may have felt.

Leah glanced up at imagined co-workers staring down at her from the pit, worrying about their own arbitrary futures. She took the photograph from the box, removed it from its frame, folded it into quarters, and placed it in her shoulder purse. She tossed the frame into a nearby garbage can, pressed the dying violet into the crook of her arm, and hurriedly walked thirteen blocks to a liquor store she knew well.

The tarnished bell above the door announced Leah's arrival, and a store clerk called a spurious greeting. She paid the devil's helper and exited the store, the uncapped bottle wrapped in a brown paper bag. She walked aimlessly and took frequent pulls from the liquor. The cheap whiskey burned its familiar path down her throat, hitting her empty gut, and she gagged. An old enemy had made its gleeful way back into the worst of her darkness.

— 41 —

Grace

Mom wasn't home by midnight and had failed to answer Grace's repeated texts. Her fear for her mom's safety overruled what she knew of the risk to Daniel. When she called, he told her to pack an overnight bag, and that he was on his way. When he arrived, he said only he would settle them in for the balance of the night before starting to look for Mom.

Dad drove into an unfamiliar neighborhood of mostly old two-story houses set back from the wide street. Homes that may have been grand in another time, but now they reminded Grace of those she had seen in the intros to horror movies, but without the scary music.

Dad parked beneath a streetlight and roused a sleeping Zoey from the backseat. Grace followed him along a dimly lit path, encroached upon by overgrown shrubs, to a set of brick steps leading to a padlocked basement door. In a far corner of the large basement, a partitioned room was what Dad sheepishly called home.

He pushed open the door to a windowless room. The air smelled like Mom's abandoned clay pots. There was an unmade double bed, a platform rocker with a ripped seat cushion, and a dimly lit floor lamp, its shade missing, standing next to the chair. The one thing Grace recognized as Dad's was a framed picture of their family on their last trip to the beach, which was sitting on a wooden crate next to the bed. She and Zoey were to sleep on the bed and Dad on an air mattress borrowed from his friend Sam.

Grace changed into her pajamas in the closet-sized bathroom and got into bed next to Zoey, who had already fallen back asleep. Except for a small night light, the room was dark, and Grace felt as if she was sealed in a tomb. She lay awake plagued by questions: If Mom came home and read the note she'd taped to the bathroom mirror, would she call the police and accuse Dad of kidnapping? Would the cops know to look here? Still, her greater fear was for Mom's safety as she imagined her wandering the city's dark streets, lost and alone.

Dad flipped onto his side on the poorly inflated air mattress and sighed. Grace wondered if he was worried about having broken the law. He would not be in jeopardy had she not called him. He moaned, and she believed he only pretended to sleep. She whispered his name.

"I'm here baby. You should try to sleep."

"But why aren't you out looking for her?"

"I'll catch a few winks and then go. But soon, I promise."

Though she wished he were out searching, she was glad that she and Zoey weren't alone in this smelly room. She pulled the covers over her and Zoey, imagining skittering roaches, their nasty whiskers twitching in the dense blackness.

Grace woke to a light knock on the door, and a man who identified himself as Dad's friend Sam invited her and Zoey to breakfast. He instructed them to get dressed, then take the outside stairs to the yellow kitchen door. Grace was surprised that she had slept through Dad's departure. A folded note stood propped on the fully deflated air mattress.

Zoey sat on the bed and rubbed her eyes, muttering, "This's not a real home. It's a shoebox"

"You're right, it's not. But it beats being homeless." At least Dad was no longer sleeping in his car and showering at work.

Zoey frowned. "You're silly. That's for ragged people and their skinny dogs."

"Stop talking and get dressed. We're going to breakfast."

"But where's Daddy?"

She read Dad's note that said they were to go with Sam while he looked for Mom. They quickly dressed and headed for the bright yellow door. They knocked and were greeted by a woman who introduced herself as Sam's mom, Miss Belle. She smiled and invited both to sit for breakfast. Her plumpness against Grace in a hug was comforting, and she smelled of the cinnamon toast she placed before them, along with eggs and breakfast sausages.

Grace thought about Granny Sybil and tried to imagine her preparing breakfast. It felt disrespectful that she couldn't swallow more of Miss Belle's tasty food with any hope of keeping it down. After breakfast, Sam invited her and Zoey to a dog agility event.

Zoey left the event pleading with Sam to take her to the animal shelter, where Grace was sure they were not welcome, so she could adopt a puppy to train. She would ask Dad to set up obstacles in their backyard and she and her puppy would practice every day. Sam told Zoey about all the responsibilities involved in taking a puppy home and gently suggested that just now might not be the best time. When he could not persuade her, he distracted her with a trip for burgers and fries. Afterwards, Sam showed all the weariness of a well-meaning but childless adult with the end in sight. He was nice, but he had tried too hard at pleasing. Zoey had him twisted into a human pretzel with a wallet by the time they returned.

Dad returned but stopped first to talk to Sam. Grace strained to hear what Sam was saying about the risk of Dad going to the police. From where Grace was eavesdropping, she saw Dad nod, seeming to agree with Sam that he should delay contacting the police. Next, Dad talked to Aunt Josey on his cell, relaying his and Sam's decision. Then he called her, only now ready to explain his decision.

"Delay? Okay, I get that, but why talk to everyone but me? Aunt Josey, okay, because she's family. But Sam, what could he possibly know? He's never even met Mom."

"I understand you're upset and for that, I'm sorry. But Sam knows a lot about the law. And we've talked before about your mom... you and Zoey... and what it can mean."

"And now if I only had a dad who understood that I'm not now, nor have I ever been, a little kid, this would be so much easier."

Grace walked deeper into the overgrown garden and onto a path that led to a swing hanging from a massive oak. She sat back in the swing and studied the light filtering through the massive cover of the trees, preparing for what she knew about long waits.

— 42 —

Leah

Leah woke in an absence of time or a sense of place. She welcomed the throbbing of a mind-bender as an antidote to her ever-greater pain. She remembered little more of last evening than his sour scent. His whimpered failure of an erection, and her emptiness. She had cupped the back of his head with her hand and given him her breast while watching the light patterns as they floated across the dingy ceiling.

She pushed up from the soiled bed and stood, leaning heavily against the washbasin. She wiped what was left of her shame on the back of her hand and scrubbed her teeth with her finger. She watered the thirsty violet and when she had tucked it into the crook of her elbow, she reentered an alien landscape of piercing lights, head-splitting noises, and swirling motion.

Desperate for relief from all she couldn't remember, Leah entered an unfamiliar liquor store and the well-heeled clerk frowned, as though he'd fouled himself while wearing his best suit trousers. She greeted him with her most diabolic smile, and she used the last of her credit to purchase the store's more expensive bottle of bourbon. She took the package off the counter and on her way out of the store, she noted the prominently displayed photograph of the store's manager.

She smiled and turned back to the clerk. "Oh yes, Malcolm dear, please give my best regards to Carl. We were once backseat sweethearts."

Leah, with her pricey bottle, bought a movie ticket, took a seat near the back, and uncorked the bottle. The scent of charred oak filled her nostrils, and the rarity of her indulgence aroused her. She squeezed her eyes tightly closed against the lewd darkness around her and pleaded for the gift of that smallest silence inside her screaming head.

Waking from her drunken slumber, Leah righted her clothing and staggered from the theater's darkness into an unforgiving brilliance. Her hands shielding her eyes against the stark jolt, she staggered forward, weaving her perilous way through the crushing maze of alien bodies with heads lowered and eyes focused elsewhere.

Leah was swept along, like so much driftwood set upon by a raging river, among those with destinations and quests for timely arrivals. Her eyes blurred with tears and when she could no longer stand on her own, she slumped onto the sidewalk amid the discordant rhythms of the stutter-stepping strangers. She became the lone ladybug scurrying along the deadly sidewalk in search of a place where she might hide.

A pair of bright red sneakers appeared alongside, and a woman leaned. Her wide girth shielded Leah. Her lips were moving but Leah made out only, *lord gal, you got anybody...?* Leah's pain swelled up so tight in her throat, she felt only his name on her lips before darkness closed in around her.

— 43 —

Daniel

Daniel accepted a call from a number he did not recognize. A kind voice identified herself as an employee of Harbor House, a service center ministering to homeless women and their children. She told him that a Good Samaritan had brought Leah Killian to the center, and that she was now sober and asking for him. His heart exploded with relief, and he shouted into the phone that she was his wife, and he was on his way.

Daniel cared for Leah through the first two days of pain that he believed was linked to acute anxiety, as well as tremors, nausea, and cold sweats; symptoms he attributed to alcohol withdrawal. However, at the dawn of day three, he was convinced that her recurring bouts were more than he had initially thought. He wondered if Leah had mixed one or more illegal street drugs with alcohol. It was clear his wife needed more help than he could provide. She needed the care only available to her at County General, where she could receive treatment and likely a recommendation for an extended hospital stay. A plan for long-term treatment was the critical missing piece in Leah's ongoing struggle with her illness.

He formulated a plan to call 911 for assistance to have her transported, but first he needed her employee health card. He searched her purse but did not find the card. Instead, he found a wrinkled envelope and an enclosed letter that stated her employer had declined to renew her service contract.

Despite the medical treatment Leah desperately needed, he could only afford the modest fees for a visit to the community health clinic.

Daniel sat with Leah in the clinic's overcrowded waiting room. Leah was exhausted from lack of sleep and an overdose of an anti-anxiety drug he'd located among the many bottles in her possession. She leaned against his shoulder, a trembling hand resting on his thigh, and whispered his name, along with something he couldn't make out.

He kissed her damp forehead, remembering a time not so long ago when his name on her lips was all he'd ever wanted. Now, his emotions were a whirlwind of contradictions: love, sadness, pity, despair, and loathing. Yet through all his vacillating, he accepted that if he was to remain in his daughters' lives, he must find an emotional space that allowed him to respond to her needs while shielding himself from his own pain.

A teenage boy, bleeding from an open wound on his right arm, burst through the door and was immediately taken to one of the examination rooms. Ahead, an anxious call for one of the two young doctors serving the clinic. In response, an audible sigh rose from those waiting. There were no appointments here; just waiting between emergencies. Yet they were all resigned to waiting for as long as it took to see a doctor.

Across from him, a teenage mother, her face prematurely aged, held a feverish infant while a toddler with dark hair like his and Grace's slept across two chairs next to her. An elderly woman, delivered by a taxi, leaned heavily on a cane as she made her slow way through the door. A bent gentleman stood and held the door open, assisting her to the chair he'd vacated.

The boy, pale and grimacing, his arm heavily bandaged, came into the lobby and exited through the door. A receptionist called for Leah, and Daniel helped her to her feet. They followed the young nurse along a narrow hallway to an examination room. It was at this point that Leah pushed him away.

He didn't argue but retreated back through the waiting room and stepped outside to call Grace and tell her that Leah was in with the doctor.

"After a stop by the pharmacy, we should be along within the hour."

"Okay, and Dad.... thanks for being... with Mom... here with us."

He choked out a weak reassurance that he'd always be there for her and Zoey. They both knew he couldn't make such a promise, but he believed Grace was comforted. He brushed a tear from his cheek and went back inside to wait.

— 44 —

Leah

Leah followed the nurse into the examination room and sat waiting for the doctor, who arrived promptly. She listened attentively as Leah struggled to explain her current condition as job stress. Leah paused, her breathing labored, and the doctor pushed back on the wheeled stool.

"Ms. Killian...." Her words were guarded. "According to our records, this is your third visit with similar symptoms. Am I correct?"

Leah stared at her but didn't know how to answer what she thought were unfair questions. No, she surely did not have a history of mental health issues. She was an occasional heavy drinker, but no, she wasn't an alcoholic, and no, she wasn't insane. Nor was she a threat to her children. It was their father who was not to be trusted. He was a criminal.

"Ms. Killian, I am sorry, but I am not qualified to further diagnose your illness, or to prescribe the treatment that you appear to need. And I think it wise that I refer you to the county mental health clinic. There are professionals there who I believe can help you."

"But I'm... you are my doctor." Leah pointed to the nametag pinned to her coat. "There. Can't you see?"

"Yes, and today, if you will agree to follow up on a referral, I'm willing to write you a fourteen-day prescription for a general anti-anxiety medication."

Leah nodded, without commenting that she knew the drug to be worthless overall, but could be of some help in calming her immediate anxiety.

Leah stopped at the nurse's station and Daniel helped to get her prescription called into the correct pharmacy. The nurse agreed to call it in right away and gave Daniel a discount coupon, commenting the drug was expensive and that there was no generic substitute. Daniel thanked the woman and paid the examination fee.

He and Leah exited through the lobby, and he noted that the young mother and her kids were no longer there. He wondered about the infant and the dark-haired toddler. The old woman still sat slumped, her chin resting on her chest.

He phoned Grace to tell her they would be home soon, and learned that Grace had washed, dried, and returned fresh linen to their bed, to prepare for her mom's arrival.

— 45 —

Grace

Mom stumbled into the house alone, carrying a small bag from the local pharmacy. When Dad didn't follow, Grace hurried to the door, only to see him driving away. In her bewilderment, Grace denied what she feared most, and followed Mom into her bedroom. Mom collapsed across the bed, fully dressed, without removing her shoes.

"Mom, where's Dad going?" She wanted to hear that he was off to do any one of several errands Mom might have asked of him.

"How do I know?" Mom turned her back to Grace, folded her arms over her chest and drew up her knees.

"But I thought Dad was back to stay." Grace moved to the opposite side of the bed to face her mother.

"He's gone away." Mom moaned, pressing her palms to her ears.

"No, he'd never agree to leaving us alone."

Mom lay still as death and Grace hurried from the room, slamming the door shut. She paced the room, anger pulsing through her brain as she dialed his number. At the sound of his voice, she screamed.

"Why didn't you tell me you were leaving us here alone with her? Zoey and I need you! Why'd you lie about staying?"

"No, Grace, I didn't lie. I argued with your mom, but you've got to know... everything between your mom and me is always going to be... complicated. I'll try talking to her again tomorrow when she's better. I'm going to sleep at Sam's."

"You'll try? God, Dad, she isn't ever going to be better! And *try* is the best you've got? Everything in my and Zoey's life is complicated!"

"Grace, please...."

"No! A *real dad* doesn't leave his kids with their weird mother... and... I hate you both!"

"Grace, please...."

Grace silenced the phone.

— 46 —

Daniel

Sarah from last night slept with her knees drawn, freckled arms crossed over her bare breasts as though she dreamed regrets. Daniel ran his fingers through his overgrown hair and attempted to untangle the slippery slope of decisions that led him to the place where he now found himself.

He swung his long legs over the side of the bed and sat with his forehead resting in his palms, struggling to fight off the alcohol sickness churning in his gut. It was his memory of Grace's anger that tortured his battered psyche. He rubbed his temples and last evening slowly came into clear focus.

It began on the drive home from the clinic with Leah's surprising rant that she no longer needed nor wanted his smothering attention, and certainly not his blundering attempts at sexual intimacy. She wanted him gone — forever out of her sight, and away from *her* daughters. He had failed in his attempts to persuade her otherwise. Finally, he had given up, and driven away in his own fit of anger. When the worst of his anger had cooled, he returned and parked near the house, where he had watched for signs of distress. He'd stayed until the lights in the girls' bedroom had gone out, though his vigil had done nothing to lessen his sense of failure as both a father and husband, then drove to O'Lary's, having no other welcoming place to get in out of the night.

He took a seat at the bar and signaled Tiny, sporting a pink hairdo, who was leaning on the bar across from a dude he was working hard.

"Hey, skinny ass, thought you were back on the wagon."

"Was, but tonight I'm chasing that wagon from afar."

Tiny sighed and poured a double shot of Wild Turkey. Sometime between drink three and four, he had signaled Tiny, who slow-walked back to where he still sat. Daniel motioned toward the image in the mirror behind the bar.

"What's she drinking? The one who's smiling."

"If you're asking about her and what I think you've got on your drunk mind," he shook his head, "I've never known her to do anything but walk out alone. Given the pathetic shape you're in, I don't give you a blind hog's chance."

Daniel remembered feeling something like relief. Still, he asked a second time.

Tiny squinted. "You sure about this?"

"Fuck no. I ain't sure about nothing." He removed his wedding band and slipped it into his pocket with the same sliminess he had accused other unfaithful men of.

"Good morning. You're up early...." Sarah squinted at the clock on the bedside table.

Maybe it was his guilt that caused him to hear ambivalence in her voice. "I thought we were both a bit nervous." Her voice seemed strained. "You're my first... since.... You weren't... disappointed?"

"No, not at all. You were good. The best, I mean." He hadn't had sex with another woman since his and Leah's marriage, and he had worried that he was too drunk to perform.

Sarah's morning blush was what he'd wanted. So much so that, even with all his guilt, he was unwilling to burn his bridge to the only sex he'd had where he felt he'd pleased a woman. Sex with Leah had depended on her mood more than his need or desire. Their sex life had been largely feast or famine.

"Uh... I wish I could stay longer but I can't be late. The boss is a genuine asshole." He retrieved his jeans from the floor, pulled them on, and slipped last night's smoky tee over his head, then went into the bathroom and turned the water faucet to full force while he plundered the medicine cabinet. He retrieved a bottle of aspirin and tossed three against the back of his throat and chased it with tap water he scooped into his palm.

He followed Sarah into the kitchen, where she offered him a steaming cup of coffee. As much as he needed coffee, he yielded to some nonsensical notion of fidelity and declined her coffee. Nothing he did or didn't do made sense to him anymore.

"Take it. It's free. You're too hungover to drive safely."

"And I thank you... for everything." He took the coffee, but his stupid remark was met with the sound of her breath caught up short. She looked past him toward the door.

"I'm sorry... I meant the coffee... had to sound to you like... It was a stupid thing to say, and I apologize. It's just that right now, everything in my life is... complicated."

"Yes, Daniel, the larger part of living is." She opened the door and stepped aside for him to pass.

Daniel crossed the parking lot, got into the old car, and drove into the early morning tangle of blue-collar workers,

Showered and dressed for work, Daniel patted down his pockets and realized that he didn't have his wallet. He searched the jeans he'd worn, then remembered that he'd started the night with the few dollars he'd stuffed into his jeans and his wallet locked in the car. It was his way of limiting what he spent and cutting back on his drinking. But last night, after approaching Sarah and she'd agreed for him to sit with her, he'd excused himself and gone to the car for his wallet.

He considered calling her and asking if he could stop off at her place later today. But showing up at her door so soon could send the wrong message, one that said he was desperate, and he thought that would scare her away. He could text her, ask her if she'd bring his wallet with her to the bank and suggest that he could stop by after work. But what if she should decide that meeting him there would be too awkward?

He had a feeling his life had just gotten even more out of control. Still, he texted Sarah. She replied that she had expected to hear from him earlier about the wallet. He suggested they meet as before, and she agreed, but said that their meeting would need to be brief.

Daniel arrived on time, parked, and went into the bar. Sarah sat at a corner table near the back. He nodded to the sleepy-eyed barkeep and ordered a glass of the red wine he remembered she drank and a beer for himself. He did so without remembering exactly how much money he had in this wallet.

He greeted Sarah, and she neither smiled nor frowned, and he pondered the best approach and decided on forthrightness, if not the total truth.

"Thank you for meeting me. I hope it isn't too much of an inconvenience." He felt like an awkward fifteen-year-old boy who had been caught with his first porn magazine.

Sarah sat quietly, twisting the wine, glass while he rattled off scattered bits of nonsense to diffuse the building tension. He finished his beer in gulps and signaled for another.

The barkeep nodded toward her half-empty glass, and she shook her head.

"I'm sorry. Did I get it wrong? Should've asked first."

"No, the wine is fine. It's just that I have a long drive across the city to have dinner with my mother. She's a resident at Golden Gardens."

"Ah, yes, I used to visit my mom. But never as much as she wanted. She's gone now." He thought Sarah would like hearing about his mom's gift of honey, and how much it had meant to him. Over the years, he told himself so many versions of the story, he was unsure how he had actually felt.

"I'm sorry."

He nodded. "Oh, she was happy there. She especially loved visits from her two granddaughters." He exhaled sharply. The pinch between his shoulders had tightened.

Sarah took his wallet from her purse and placed it on the table between them.

"I believe you came for this."

"About what I just said. I can explain." He pressed his hands tightly between his thighs.

Sarah shifted forward on the seat, and he believed she meant to leave.

"Please. Just hear me out. That's all I ask." He thought about how Grace had refuted his lame lies and he wanted something better from himself. But could he start?

Sarah glanced toward the door, but hesitated, her hard gaze holding him to the truth.

"My wife Leah and I are... separated." He struggled to find words that explained his and Leah's strange dance at marriage. His unwillingness to own Leah's assessment of him as a lover and husband prevented him from admitting any part of his failures. "We've had our ongoing disagreement... mostly about finances." He swallowed hard.

Sarah's eyes narrowed, but she didn't interrupt.

"The strange part with us is that Leah sometimes needs my help and I never know when she'll want me back. Or whether she will. And I get you might've made a different decision had I been more forthcoming." It was far more truth than he thought himself capable of.

"If you mean whether to have sex with a married man? Yes, and now neither of us can know which decision I might have made. If you think that doesn't matter to me, then you're wrong."

Sarah stood, and without a word of parting, she walked toward the door. She paused only to pay for her wine before exiting the bar. Behind her, a glaring light flooded the otherwise dark bar and, just as quickly, the door closed and the darkness returned. Daniel ordered a third beer and sat alone, entangled in his thoughts of betrayal.

− 47 −

Leah

Leah took a discarded newspaper from a vacant table, ordered a regular coffee, and selected a table apart from other customers. She hurriedly scanned the local news and was relieved that her dismissal from AMI Data had continued to escape media attention. The vindictiveness of Carla Curtis, her former supervisor, was well known, and Leah feared Curtis may have engaged in an act of unprofessional blackballing her with potential employers.

Leah turned to the section mislabeled *employment opportunities* and read the columns of mostly dead-end jobs. The few positions matching her previous experience and skills paid considerably less than she had earned as a full-time employee with benefits. She could not apply for these jobs, for they would require resumes that included an applicant's employment history and Curtis' job performance rating.

Her most recent employment had been a low paying, no questions asked, temporary service job with a local auto parts distributor. She was hired to maintain the store's computerized inventory system. Leah had found these minimal data entry tasks excruciatingly boring. It was during one such job in a string of others that Leah became a clock watcher.

She continued to sit, sipping the last of the cooled coffee, while watching those she suspected were coping with their own crushing idleness. When she had grown weary of doing so, she neatly refolded the newspaper, leaving it behind for the next desperate seeker, and exited the coffee shop to rejoin the endless flow of the rudderless in quiet desperation.

Leah sat through the arrival and departure of four city buses before deciding to save the bus fare and walk the five miles home. On her arrival, she would accept defeat, surrender to forces greater than her own, though she had none of what she would need: packing boxes, tape, and infinite courage.

Hotel Impala
Summer 2019

— 48 —

Grace

Homelessness began with the arrival of the stranger: a man as wide in the shoulders as their front door. He wore dark green work pants and a shirt with heavy sweat rings under his muscled arms. It mattered not a whit to him that Mom had lost her bitter war with the mortgage company. Nor that she swore he was an accomplice in condemning her innocent daughters to the horrors of street life: human trafficking, child-rape, and murder.

Unmoved, the man tacked an eviction notice onto the faded purple door, exactly like the one Mom had destroyed the previous day. He signaled the two younger men who were waiting in the truck. They wore the same uniform as the first man, and the three set about removing the remaining household furniture, kitchenware and appliances, and gardening tools from the garage. Those household items having even minimum value, including the television and Dad's few remaining tools, had already been sold.

Grace and Mom worked to remove the few clothes and personal items they could ahead of the men. When the three completed the job they were sent to do, the lead man ordered everyone out of the house, then locked windows and padlocked entry doors. Without another word, the three men got into the truck and drove away.

The noisy neighbor who could be counted upon to come from inside her house to pass judgement had stood on her stoop, gazing. But Grace did not care about her. Rather, she was grateful that Alice and her mother had driven away shortly after the men arrived and had not returned.

Mom had insisted that neither Dad nor Aunt Josey were to know that she had lost another job and that they had been threatened with eviction. Mom had also been unable to continue paying for a second phone line and had taken Grace's phone. The burner phone Dad had given her had run out of minutes. Although Grace had considered approaching Alice about the use of her phone after yesterday's eviction notice, she had been too proud, and she had yet to find another way.

Noon had come and gone, and Mom sat in her salvaged wicker rocker without talking while Grace and Zoey, Jimmie clutched to her chest, sat silently on the curb next to the piles of household debris.

"Mom, what do we do now? We can't just sit here!"

"Uh, yes, there is that." Mom stared into a cloudless blue sky as though it were a good omen and smiled as though their choices were as vast as the universe. She stood and declared, "My darling girls. There remains the balance of our lives, so let's fully embrace our glorious opportunities."

"But Mom, where are we going?"

"My darling, destinations are for those hobbled by needing to know. We, my pets, are bound for wherever we end up." She giggled, as though that had quieted Grace's churning gut.

Mom spent an hour picking through what they had salvaged ahead of the movers; clothing, shoes, picture albums, hardened cans of purple paint, rusted gardening tools, Zoey's busted bike, gardening books from the attic, and her prized wooden chest with its broken lock that held what Mom called her treasured documents: her college diploma, an elaborately framed certificate of merit signed by Clara Curtis, Dad's honorable discharge from the military, and a sealed envelope containing her and Zoey's birth certificates. Grace, as directed, squeezed what she could manage into the trunk of the Impala and onto the floor between the seats, leaving behind what remained of their family's ruptured lives.

Mother and daughters crowded into the front seat and without a backward glance, Leah drove them away from the only home Grace and Zoey had known. Zoey asked her mom if their leaving made her sad. Leah shrugged and said nothing. Zoey looked to Grace for an answer for her confusion, but Grace stared at the road ahead, and though she fought back tears, she said nothing.

— 49 —

Daniel

Daniel swore and scooted the dolly from beneath Sam's jeep, and as he suspected, the caller was Josey. He had intended to call her earlier. Reassure her that at the completion of this job, he'd have the balance of what he owed for Leah and the girls' share of Josey's weekly grocery shopping. He needed no reminder that Zoey had outgrown her sneakers, but relief for her pinched toes would need to wait until his next payday.

"Hey, I meant to call you earlier."

"Oh God, Daniel, tell me you've talked with Grace." Her voice was tense, high pitched, and his dread ratcheted up a notch.

"Uh, yeah, just yesterday. No, on second thought, it was Thursday morning before her first class. Why're you asking?"

"Daniel, I don't know how to say this any easier... but they're gone, cleared out." Her tone had turned frantic.

"What are you saying?"

"They're gone. Just like that. The house is completely empty, and the doors are padlocked." Josey sucked air and exhaled sharply before explaining the eviction notice and that a neighbor said the mother and the older girl had loaded the old car to the gills, and the three had driven away.

The night of the big fight, he had walked out leaving behind the twenty-five hundred dollars he'd earned. Still, it seemed Leah had been unable to hold off eviction, and a court order had come through. That meant she must be looking for cheap housing.

He realized if Leah intended to steal the girls away, she would have confiscated Grace's phone before she could let him know. While his fear ripped through his gut as though he had swallowed knotted barbed wire, he somehow managed to focus on what Josey had learned from the old noisy bitch next door. It was not his first time they had relied on her incessant snooping to help unravel Leah's wild schemes.

"What else did the old woman say?"

"Only that she saw three men loading furniture onto an old truck. The name on the truck wasn't a moving company but some salvage outfit, and she doesn't remember the name. Maybe we could check out salvage companies, see if they can tell us something that might help know where she's headed. There can't be that many of them."

"Yeah, call around. See what you can learn." But he didn't think they'd have any reason to care.

"Right, I'll get back to you if I discover anything worth knowing."

Daniel agreed that he'd see what he might learn from what they left behind. He didn't want to think about where Leah might go with the girls. Wherever she went, he prayed she had cash or credit enough to carry them until he could rescue his daughters.

Daniel searched among the items left on the sidewalk and found no clues to where or why; only what Leah had chosen to leave behind. He took a framed photo from the refuse and carefully removed the shattered glass, working the photo free from its bent frame. He sat on the curb, smoothing the creased photo of Leah, the girls, and himself, taken by a passing stranger on an afternoon they'd spent building an elaborate sandcastle. The occasion had been their only real vacation. Though Leah had refused to go surfing, he'd taught Grace to swim. Zoey had dug in the sand for fiddler crabs, giggling at their escape, and Leah had been the loving women he'd married and mother to the girls. He treasured that week as one of his family's happiest.

He separated the few remaining pieces of discarded furniture, planning to borrow Sam's truck to haul them away. He went into the backyard for the trash cans and filled them with the balance of the debris. He was unwilling to leave any part of their broken lives lying on the sidewalk.

He walked two doors down the street and rang the doorbell. The door opened, and he reminded Mrs. Patrick that he was Grace's dad.

"Yes, I know who you are. What do you want?" He knew her answer, but still he took a hard swallow and asked.

"If you don't mind, I would like a minute with Alice. It's about my missing daughter, Grace."

"No, you may not. She has nothing to say to you... and certainly not about your daughter."

"Then maybe you could ask her if she knows anything about where they might have gone?"

"I'm telling you she hasn't been in contact with your daughter. They are no longer friends." She paused but was unmoved. "Their move means they've taken that killer cat out of our neighborhood, thank God."

He nodded. "Sorry to have bothered you."

— 50 —

Grace

Grace studied the road signs, intent on memorizing their route. Otherwise, how would she direct Dad when she had a chance? They traveled east out of the city to I75 north. They had traveled for no more than an hour when Mom suddenly drove the car off the highway and into a rest stop. Mom chose a space among motorhomes and semis at the outer edge of the rest area.

"Okay, my darlings, here we are." She pointed to a cement table and benches painted industrial green.

Zoey looked about and frowned. "But we don't have a picnic."

Mom laughed and stepped to the rear of the car. She raised the trunk and began to plunder through the items they had loaded.

"Ah, here we are." She retrieved an open box of graham crackers and a container of black olives. "Come on, girls. Don't just sit there. We're having a picnic."

Mom carried the graham crackers and olives to the table for what she insisted was a nutritious snack. Returning to the Impala, Mom began emptying first the trunk and then the backseat, piling everything onto the ground. She directed Grace to sort the contents into three separate piles labeled *discards*, *maybes*, and *travel gear*. Mom's system made little sense to Grace, and when she messed up, Mom impatiently corrected her.

The trunk was to serve as storage for *maybes*, including three cook pots, tableware, a small carton of scented candles,

Mom's wooden treasure box, and a blue tarp. The wicker rocker remained lashed on the roof. One half of the backseat was for *travel gear*, and there they stacked two bed pillows, a double blanket, Mom's makeup case, and three changes of clothes for each of them, sorted by season. Flip-flops were for spring and summer, sneakers for fall and winter. When sorting and storing was completed, Mom instructed Grace to carry *discards* to a row of trash receptacles. Although Grace felt guilty for filling all four receptacles to overflowing, she disregarded the disapproving stares of other travelers and did as she was told.

Mom stepped back, a pleased expression on her sweaty face, though the Impala looked like an over-burdened pack mule.

"So, my darling girls, you are to think of our new life as a grand, long-delayed, mother-daughter adventure." Mom's strident laughter grated on Grace's nerves. More evidence that Mom had not made an actual plan. She wondered how Dad would find them when nothing about Mom's decisions made sense.

Zoey looked skeptical but joined Mom in celebrating, and Grace wished for a glimpse of what had put a smile on Mom's face. Mom told them to spread the one blanket on the grass beneath a nearby tree. Grace and Zoey spent the warmest part of a long afternoon sitting on the blanket, Zoey munching on the remaining stale graham crackers until she fell asleep.

Grace read and made study notes from the biology textbook she now believed was stolen, along with several others. She and Zoey had not withdrawn from school; they had simply disappeared. Leah removed the wicker rocker from its perch on the sedan's roof and spent most of the afternoon either frantically rocking or pacing the sidewalk, greeting anxious travelers who were bound for the bathrooms.

As the sun's fleeting colors faded, bats gave chase to swarms of mosquitoes. The number of travelers dwindled until there were only those who made hasty visits to the restrooms and snack machines before returning to their vehicles and driving away.

Mom handed Grace a towel and a sliver of bath soap and directed her and Zoey to go into the restroom to wash and dress in their pajamas. Leaving the bathroom, Grace spotted a uniformed man who watched her and Zoey as they returned to the car. Grace had pointed out a sign that prohibited travelers from staying overnight, but it had not mattered to Mom.

The uniformed man stood next to the open window of the Impala and spoke to Mom. His name tag read *Tom Trimble, Park Attendant*.

"Hello, Tom. It has been a lovely evening, don't you agree?" Mom smiled as though he had already forgiven their violation of the overnight parking rule.

Tom blinked hard, perhaps surprised at the sound of his name spoken in the musical lilt of Mom's voice. He blushed and glanced into the evening sky, though the security lighting had begun to come on.

"Yes Ma'am, you're right about that. We do get awful nice evenings this time of year. Though winter nights are nicer." Tom paused, and Grace sensed his dread.

"Well then, my daughters and I will need to return. Thank you for your kind invitation." Mom's smile, clearly aimed at disarming Tom Trimble, could have melted a glacier.

He appeared to gather his resolve.

"But, Ma'am, I'm awful sorry, but you can't stay here overnight. So, you just might want to go ahead and start looking for a... suitable motel for you and your girls."

"My, my, Tom, that's so sweet of you. But here suits us fine." Mom looked about as though reassessing the appeal. "It's very nice here."

"That's just it, Ma'am. Like I said, you can't stay overnight, and I've already allowed you some slack."

"Oh, but can't you make an exception? I'm too tired to move on. I need rest." Mom rubbed her temples, sinking a bit into the seat.

"Maybe I could, but the man relieving me at midnight won't. He's a hard ass." Tom blushed. "Excuse me. Your girls and all."

Mom sat looking into the gathering darkness as though she, too, searched for a better outcome.

— 51 —

Daniel

Dawn broke on the fourth day of Daniel's search for Leah in the parking lots of cheap motels along the off ramps north on I-75 without a glimpse of the Impala. He was unsure why he had chosen such an unlikely plan, beyond his near panic, and a wild notion that he might overtake them.

Nearing home, he stopped at a local joint where he knew he could find strong coffee for a price that matched his flat wallet. On the road he had slept and eaten little, permitting himself only brief stops to sleep for an hour or so, always waking anxious about time lost in his search.

He grabbed a coffee with the color and density of liquid tar and returned to his truck. He swigged scalding coffee while watching hurried customers as they came and went. He replayed memories of other mornings, when he and Leah had awakened to their shared desire for sex. Afterwards, he would leave her content and dozing while he showered and dressed for work, then woke Grace and Zoey with his off-key rendition of *wake-up, wake up you sleepyheads.*

He wiped his wet cheeks on his shirt sleeve and stared at the movement of traffic on the highway. Had Leah changed her mind, and were she and the girls returning home? But they no longer had a home. Would Leah humble herself and return to her sister's house where Josey's husband Robert would not welcome her and the girls? Or were Leah and their daughters truly homeless? His thoughts twisted his gut, and he rushed back into the restaurant's nasty bathroom.

Daniel returned to Tiny's old car and drove back onto the highway in the direction of his basement room. He would shower, dress, and report to his job. The leave he had taken without pay meant he would see a serious dent in his next bi-weekly paycheck. His long-time shitty credit had gotten even shittier, and he would need to raise cash to secure a rental unit for his family. But first, he had to find them. Rather than wishing for a miraculous sighting of the Impala among an endless stream of vehicles, he would need a better plan.

— 52 —

Daniel

Daniel knew nothing but trouble would come of going to the police for help. But Josey insisted, and she approached the local police to inquire about filing a missing persons report. Afterwards, she had called him in tears of frustration and anger.

"You were right not to go to the police. They're worthless." Her words were ground through clinched teeth.

"How's that? What'd they say?"

"They questioned me about proof that she had come to some harm, or that she didn't just leave because she wanted to. Otherwise, they have no reason to look for her." She paused. "I'm sorry, Daniel. There were more questions about you than Leah and the girls being missing."

"Right, and what'd you tell them?"

"That I was the one who'd first told you about her and girls."

"You think that satisfied them?" Daniel was sure he'd see a visit from the law.

"Lord, I wish I could say."

Daniel wanted to say something comforting to Josey, but he didn't have it in him.

There were four cities within an hour or two drive that were of sufficient size to have multiple programs for the homeless. But Daniel now realized that although Leah had always envisioned one grand adventure after another, she had, in the end, always sought the familiar. Daniel now believed that Leah and his daughters were somewhere within his reach. He would concentrate his searches on the county.

He and Josey began by dividing the city and its suburbs into geographic sectors. If Leah's illness had kept her from seeking employment, she was most likely out of cash, and would soon be out of credit, forcing her and the girls to seek free shelter and meals.

Josey researched city-wide want ads and temp agencies and made a list of shelters that ministered to women and their children. Daniel's days began at five a.m., at the shelter on his list for that day, in time for early morning release, and he was back again for evening intakes. He made a practice of sitting in the car, parked where he had a clear view of the entry, praying to catch sight of Leah and the girls.

Daniel bargained with Robert for more flexible hours that would allow him to leave the shop an hour early in the evening and to arrive an hour late the next morning, offering to work a ten-hour shift on Sundays.

Robert argued that he needed Daniel in the shop when customers dropped off and picked up their vehicles. Still, Daniel continued his routine, and as a consequence, Robert fired him. Daniel now depended on picking up odd jobs within the hours he could work, which meant he earned barely enough to avoid the very streets he searched.

He extended his search to the seediest bars and known homeless encampments, locations where the homeless gathered, questioning those who agreed to look at the family photo he carried. Women were among those who turned him away with anger-laced quips about whether the pretty woman and girls in the photo wanted to be found by the likes of him. After a markedly harsh rejection that questioned the sanity of any woman who would trade the street's dopamine life of sex and drugs for the pathetic likes of him, Daniel cut his hair, shaved his scraggly beard, and took regular baths.

When the school year started, Daniel called the girls' schools, inquiring about their attendance and details of any withdrawals, though they were questions he believed an attentive parent would have had no need to ask. He learned that school personnel were forbidden to release any information to him about his daughters, and that any attempt on his part to come onto school property would be viewed as trespassing.

Daniel approached the entrance to Sarah's condominium community and made an impulsive decision. He parked and sat waiting, and at his first glimpse of her, he slid down in the seat like a stalker and watched her through the side mirror. She carried a steaming cup in one hand, and an oversized purse hung from her shoulder. He grimaced at the thought that he had slept with a woman he did not know. He could not say as much as whether she was right or left-handed and wondered whether that was even something a man should have noticed beforehand.

Sarah was smartly dressed in tailored slacks of either navy blue or black, a lavender blouse, and heels. She set the cup on the roof of a late-model Honda CRV, placed the purse on the passenger seat and settled behind the wheel, her movements efficient and practiced. As she drove onto the street, Daniel watched the cup slide off the sunroof and puddle onto the street. He felt an odd sense of pleasure and considered, if he were to confess to having witnessed her small imperfection, whether they would share a comfortable laugh. Yet he was unsure why he came or what he had wanted to happen. What he knew was that he was a nearly broken man and felt alone in his grief.

— 53 —

Grace

Grace woke with her stomach cramping, and she wrapped her arms tightly about her middle, unsure whether her spasms resulted from needing to pee or her gnawing hunger. Her family's last meal was thin dollar tacos, eaten at noon yesterday. She and Zoey told each other about their dreams of food, but never when Mom was around. The time Mom overheard, she cried, and afterward she started leaving her and Zoey alone at night while she prowled the streets. Grace was more afraid for Mom than she was for her and Zoey alone in the Impala.

Grace searched the floorboard for the roll of toilet tissue she had stolen from the bathroom when they had last bought tacos. The nearest unlocked bathroom was ten blocks away, on a dark street she dared not walk alone. An unlocked bathroom was an oasis in a desert of doors locked against street dwellers. Mom's argument that these bathrooms were unsafe changed nothing in her and Zoey's anxieties in needing to go, nor did her periods stop because they were homeless. There was never money spent on anything but food. During her period, she made do with multiple layers of stashed-away napkins she took on the rare occasions when they had money enough to eat at fast food restaurants.

She was careful not to disturb Zoey, who slept on discarded chair cushions they had discovered while searching for cardboard to cover the Impala's windows. Mom had called their search a scavenger hunt and Zoey had gone about it in the way Mom sometimes referred to as Zoey's impish delight. It was not so much what she said but that she had smiled.

Grace was satisfied enough with the good of recycling other's waste, but the cast-offs they found on the streets and in the alleys were two-times or more used junk. Yet she and Zoey had found a thousand-piece puzzle in its original, undamaged box. Neither she nor Zoey took to heart Mom's excited talk about their taking a road trip so they might see first-hand the majestic Grand Canyon pictured on the puzzle box.

She and Zoey had sat on the rooftop of the Impala for a full day, assembling the puzzle pieces, only to have an unforeseen late afternoon thunderstorm chase them off the roof and into the Impala. From the car windows they watched rain-soaked puzzle pieces slide off the rooftop into the nearby flooded rain gutters.

"Rats, I guess this means we don't get the trip?" Zoey said.

"It means both the puzzle and trip are history."

"I'm keeping the box, cause I like the picture." Zoey had put the box on the dashboard, but Mom had yet to mention the road trip to the canyon.

Zoey moaned in her sleep, and Grace decided against getting her out to pee, though there was the risk of her wetting herself. Awakened, Zoey was bound to beg to be taken to Aunt Josey's, where there was food and saucers of milk for Jimmie. The cat, unlike her and Zoey, was born a street-savvy kitten and he had easily returned to scavenging a diet of scraps. Evenings after Zoey had fallen asleep, Grace returned Jimmie to his night prowls. Mornings, the cat sometimes returned with a dead mouse or an undetermined morsel.

Grace had desperately wanted to call Dad, but she dared not risk his arrest. Aunt Josey would come for them, but Mom hated Uncle Robert, and he hated her. She understood there was nothing smart about her and Zoey continuing to stay with Mom, but the memory of her mom's trembling body cuddled against hers, and her promise in that moment to never leave

Mom alone, trapped her. She prayed Dad would find them, and take them to their aunt's, so that she would not need to break her promise to Mom or spend another moment on the streets.

Grace squatted next to the back tire, wary of splattering her feet, and returned to the small measure of safety afforded them behind the Impala's locked doors. The car had been home for three weeks and in the beginning, the street odors of rotten food, unbathed bodies, and animal and human excretions had caused Grace to gag. But less so now that she was a part of the same squalidness.

Beyond the city's tallest buildings, in the direction Grace knew to be the path of the wide river, the pre-dawn sky was a vaporous glow of city lights. Grace remembered its contrast to the palette of splendid colors she had shared with her dad on their morning walks during the family's weekend beach vacation. Most vivid had been the play of early light across the wide expanse of sawgrass anchored in the pungent, brackish-scented marshes.

Grace left her backseat bed, squeezed from among the last of the belongings Mom had refused to discard even though they were worthless — without resale value even among those with so little. She climbed onto the car's rooftop and below her, up and down the street, human forms, encased in what they had against the night chill, filled vacant doorways and lay pressed against building fronts. Perhaps they too dreamed of better memories.

— 54 —

Grace

After two months of random movement throughout an area known on the streets as the *marginal kingdom*, a pattern of sorts had emerged. Mom had fashioned herself as a multitasking organizer, and her habit was to drive them each evening to a new, poorly lit location where they parked overnight. On the mornings that Mom felt up to facing the world, she cleaned herself up, out of the view of the curious, by using Grace and Zoey's own privacy invention: a discarded orange shower curtain they retrieved from a dumpster and stretched along a piece of twine hung between the two clothes hooks above the back doors. She and Zoey used the same curtain at night to shield them from the prying eyes of those they called street boogers.

Mom sometimes drove them to a big shopping mall where she sought work among the mall stores. Grace and Zoey remained in the Impala, and if they were questioned by those Mom called the *long noses*, Grace was to explain that they were Christian, and they were home schooled.

Zoey had argued against the designation as Christian, so Mom had allowed them to drop that part, but reemphasized *home schooled*. Afterwards, she and Zoey laughed. How were they home schooled when they were homeless? They decided that they were *car schooled*. On their next trip to the library, an excited Zoey declared their school mascot was an Impala: a large and graceful animal. In what she called an artistic choice, she drew Jimmie poised in a menacing crouch and placed the drawing on the car dash along with the Grand Canyon puzzle picture.

Mom stole a license plate from a Honda Accord and replaced the expired tag on the Impala, explaining that an expired plate on an old, parked car was a cop's wet dream. Weighing their odds of starting yet another argument, Grace acquiesced. Although she had braved an argument when she learned that Mom had sold her expired driver's license for ten dollars.

"God, Mom, moving around the city the way we do is dangerous enough. But without a driver's license, what if a cop pulls us over?"

"Oh Grace, my love, you worry too much. We're not technically homeless. I meant only to show compassion to a desperate woman." She had seemed to enjoy the fact that she had sold an expired license. Mom had shrugged off Grace's warnings as if there was nothing *improper* about how they lived.

Grace and Zoey attended regular schools only when Mom felt the Impala was sufficiently hidden from prying eyes to allow for longer stays. A stay of five weeks in a junkyard was the longest in any one place. Mom joked that the Impala fit in very nicely in the graveyard of junked vehicles; perfectly camouflaged and unlikely to raise suspicion. She consented to Grace and Zoey's enrollment only after declaring to the enrollment officer that her brilliant daughters were not to be thought of as homeless but as temporarily misplaced. The yard, occupying an entire city block, was surrounded by an eight-foot wooden fence, encircled by double strands of barbed wire, and a secured gate. Grace decided the heavy fortification was seriously overdone, given that the vehicles were junk and surely of no interest to anyone.

The owner of the junkyard withheld her name, for reasons of security, she said. Grace and Zoey referred to her as *yard boss*, though she stood only a few inches taller than Zoey. She cursed in a soft voice; her frequent profanity was a repetitive stream of *crap-damn-fuck*. Grace and Zoey hid and watched in admiration as beefy drivers wilted under her flaming tongue.

Mom got light work in the yard office, and they had honest money to buy better food and to purchase two outfits each for school. The use of the office washer and drier meant she and Zoey went to school in clean clothes.

Exploration among the junked vehicles became one of Grace and Zoey's favorite pastimes. In the center of the yard, they discovered several rows of bullet-riddled cars, vans, and boats. Gangster cars, Zoey had declared in a high-pitched voice. Behind the tall fence, their discovery felt both safe and mysterious.

Showers were three days a week at a nearby church-run mission where toiletries were free. An unexpected plus were the students from a vocational school who volunteered at the mission to give free haircuts. Grace's hair had grown longer than she had worn it since she was old enough to have a preference. She got an unintended cut she called a smoothy; short and flat on top. Zoey's curls were a wild brush heap, and she got a cut that looked as if the nervous student had used a bushhog, leaving her hair an even wilder heap.

Grace sat on the outdoor patio she had fashioned from the discarded backseat of a Kia. She was reading a book about clouds, not for school but for fun, when Mom stormed out of the office screaming that she and Zoey were to get their asses in the car.

Now? Why? Grace had wondered, although a knowing sense of doom settled about the certainty of the command. Mom slid behind the wheel, but multiple attempts to restart the motor only ground the battery down lower. Mom got out of the car, raised the hood, and stared angrily, as if that would frighten a dead battery into action. She slammed down the hood and calmly declared that their departure would be delayed.

She took her purse from the car and walked out the yard gate and onto the sidewalk toward Roy's Fix It shop. She shouted back to Grace, asking where the hell was their father when he could be of use. Mom's plan for the next phase of their lives extended no further than having Zoey steer while Grace and Mom pushed the Impala to Roy's, which was in the next block.

Their stay in the security of the junkyard had coincided with one of Mom's better times — until it had not. Without as much as an earned thank you to *yard boss*, they were back to Mom taking work, when available, at whatever pay was offered. Her employment at any one job often lasted no longer than a day or two. Her special talent for pissing off bosses and co-workers had only worsened.

— 55 —

Grace

Grace hated fitful nights when Mom did not sleep but left her and Zoey alone in the Impala, huddled against the prying eyes of gaunt faces pressed against the glass. She had heard stories of the evil done to women and children that were too depraved to repeat. Grace attempted to dispel her fears by telling herself that these desperate men thought the car was abandoned, and that they only sought its warmth. It saddened her that the street demanded she must distrust everyone.

The light from Mom's compact awakened Grace. Mom sat behind the steering wheel, her hair combed, and she had applied cheap makeup stolen from an all-night pharmacy. The makeup failed to hide the deep sadness in her dark eyes, nor did it hide her bruises and bloody split lip. Grace feared for her mom and pleaded with her to stay with her and Zoey. Grace offered to rub her mom's temples, for it sometimes helped her to sleep through her impulse to wander the streets and alleys.

"My darling girl, I want you to know that your mother was once someone." Mom blotted her lips on the back of her hand and snapped the ornate compact, a cherished gift from Mom's father on her sixteen birthday, shut. Grace noted that Mom's once meticulous makeup was smeared and showed clownish white around her eyes. But the time Grace dared to speak of her mother's misapplied makeup, Mom lashed out with the chilling declaration that in dark alleys, it was not a beautiful face that fed her and her sister. Sometimes, the food Grace put into her mouth after nights Mom wandered the streets caused Grace to gag.

Another evening, Leah spoke in a soft voice that she was going to look for something of value stolen from her. Her tone was one Grace associated with an episode of depression. Grace tried to persuade her that what she thought had been stolen had simply fallen from her pocket.

Leah said nothing but got out of the car and set out on her way, halting only to call back that Grace must lock the doors. Grace listened to the sound of her mom's heels striking the sidewalk until the long grey tentacles of fog swallowed her.

Mom returned just before daybreak, smelling of whiskey and a sour odor Grace chose to deny. Using baby wipes, Mom cleaned herself and dressed in cleaner jeans and her prettiest blouse. She shoved crumpled bills into her pocket and told Grace and Zoey to wipe their faces clean and comb their hair.

They walked eight blocks to get breakfast, and Leah insisted Grace and Zoey order the *Big Man's Special.* She ordered coffee and unbuttered toast for herself. Grace choked down her food while Zoey stuffed herself. Mom finished her toast, excused herself, and went into the bathroom.

The server approached the table and handed Grace a brown bag containing four buttered biscuits and extra sausage patties. She apologized and said the food came with their meal but that she had mistakenly shorted her and her sister. Grace thanked her and when she had stepped away, Grace gathered the tubs of milk and sugar packets, placing everything in her backpack. Though their bellies were full, their next meal was never far from her mind.

That same evening, Mom drove them to a squalid motel where the clerk glared, though he took the wadded bills Mom counted out and placed on the counter in exchange for a room key.

Grace and Zoey took long baths and washed their hair with one of the tiny bars of soap, and afterwards Mom took her turn. Grace washed their clothes in the bathtub with the last of the bath soap and hung them on the shower rod to dry. She set out food from her backpack and the vending machine and they watched tv while pretending to have an indoor picnic.

Mom sat in the middle of the bed and counted the remaining cash from her pocket; a total of fourteen dollars and ten cents. If they shopped at the discount store for peanut butter and bread, they had enough for two meals per day for two or three days.

Zoey marched around the room leaning backward with her belly extended. Mom's laughter was strained, and unspilt tears clouded her eyes, but she joined Zoey in a celebration of the good of the moment. Let the devil take tomorrow.

Grace got into bed smelling sweet from the soap, grateful she would sleep warm and safe behind a locked door. In her head, she tallied what they had spent and realized that Mom had brought back more money than she ever had. She lay wondering how dangerous it had been for Mom to acquire that much money. But then, she too pushed all thoughts from her mind and slept soundly.

– 56 –

Grace

On days Mom took work, she sometimes dropped Grace and Zoey off at the downtown Public Library. Mom's reminder that they were not to speak to anyone rung in Grace's ears, though Mom had laughed at the absurdity of a school officer who would look for truants in a library.

Grace and Zoey were free to prowl the fiction aisles, and Grace searched the science section for just the right books. Grace's favorite days were those Mom managed not to offend the boss, and she and Zoey had an entire day to read. She noticed her hunger less, though the growling of her stomach sometimes embarrassed her.

On their first full day at the library, nearing the time for Leah to return, Grace approached the check-out desk with two books she had chosen; for Zoey one of her favorites, about a young girl named Scout and her older brother Jem, who had a secretive neighbor named Boo, and for herself the book on star gazing. The librarian smiled and asked for her library card.

Grace offered her expired card and stepped back, anticipating her next move. When the card was rejected, Grace placed the books on the counter, thanked the woman for her assistance, and stepped away.

The kindness in the woman's voice was encouraging as she offered to renew the card. Grace wanted the books enough that she answered that her address information was still correct. Grace Danielle Killian did not just walk from the library with the curse of a habitual liar; she had given false information to acquire a public document, making herself a criminal.

— 57 —

Grace

Grace rolled her eyes at the absurdity of Mom's warning that she and Zoey were not to go near the crazy old woman who insisted on being addressed as *Ms.* Babe. The title was an act of resistance, she had said, a claim to her share of an ongoing struggle for women's liberation. Odd behaviors, including violent threats toward others, were studied traits Ms. Babe celebrated as her hard-earned *street brand*.

The times when Mom slept off a drunk or wandered off on her own, Grace and Zoey welcomed invitations to visit Ms. Babe in her encampment at the end of a closed alley, which she had named *Queendom*. She had constructed her paradise from scrap boards and tin, with a roof fashioned from a discarded sign that once advertised Coppertone sun lotions. Ms. Babe frequently spoke of her ideas for future renovations, showing Grace and Zoey detailed plans. She had lined the pathway that led to her castle with selected relics: colored bottles, broken pieces of garden pottery, and jars of wilted flowers rescued from the dumpster behind a local mom and pop business, Eloise's Flower Shop.

On their visits, Ms. Babe served Grace and Zoey hot chocolate in delicate unmatched cups and week-old banana bread she'd bargained from a kind baker. After teatime—her word, not theirs—she read from a battered copy of Walter Scott's *Ivanhoe: A Romance*, declaring it was her sons' favorite book. She had repeatedly shown her guests a wrinkled faded picture of her three young sons that she carried plastered between her sagging breasts. She would squint at the picture and point to each boy. Out of politeness, Grace and Zoey never asked, but waited patiently, hoping that on their next visit, the old woman would remember her sons' names.

Simon, a panhandler and sometimes friend of Ms. Babe, when he had a bottle of wine to share, carried an American flag and walked with the help of a cane. He wore dark glasses, though he admitted to not being blind. He claimed, in what he referred to as a *generalization*, that women were spurred to give by their belief that a ragged blind man was not to be blamed for his situation. Offering something of a disclaimer, Simon admitted that his conclusion about women's generosity was based entirely on anecdotal data and could not be considered the results of exhaustive research. Simon talked that way because he was once a college professor.

Zoey stopped beneath the ripped awning hanging over the doorway of a junk store; a place where all things discarded by those privileged to own more than they needed could be found. The third Monday of the month was large item pickup day in just such a neighborhood within walking distance of the Impala. Grace and Zoey scrounged for smaller items among the discards that they could carry or drag to the junk store. There, Grace bargained a few dollars for their loot from the foul-tempered but generous owner Zoey had nicknamed Mr. Good Grump.

"Why're you stopping? You know we don't have anything to sell," Grace called back to Zoey.

"I know. Just resting my feet." Zoey slipped her dirty feet out of her worn sneakers, removed her socks, riddled with holes, and wadded them into her pocket. She rested her bare feet on the cool sidewalk.

"I double hate holey socks. They make oozy blisters."

"Yeah, but we gotta keep going." Zoey's feet were a mess, but she and Zoey had spotted a school truant officer earlier in the week, and Zoey had argued that they should tell the officer they were truant because their mom was mental.

Across the street, a block away, the same school officer she and Zoey had seen before stepped through the door of a gun shop and onto the sidewalk.

"Oh shit, I ain't believing my eyes."

"What?"

"Hush, we gotta go, and now." Grace grabbed Zoey's hand and, against her resistance, dragged her sister and herself into the nearest alley.

Glaring, Zoey yelled, "Let me go," and pulled free of Grace's grip.

"Look, there, across the street. That's why."

"But why can't we do like I already said? We'd get free meals like the poor kids. That'd be good, right?"

"Yeah, but you know Mom would never agree to apply for anything free. And if we snitched on her, she'd be in a boatload of pain. Maybe she'd even do jail time. Is that what you want?"

"I'm no snitch. But I don't care anymore what happens to Mom."

"Are you hearing yourself?"

"Okay, but I'm borrowing Mr. Good Grump's phone and calling Dad. And you can't stop me."

"All right, go ahead, but remember Dad doesn't really have a place. And I won't come with you. Mom needs us and I promised to stay, no matter what. And unlike you, I'm keeping my word."

"But I never promised anything that dumb."

"Fine, not a snitch but a traitor, so go ahead. All you gotta do is walk across the street there."

Zoey sucked on her bottom lip and glared, and Grace feared her sister meant to call her bluff. She needed a different tactic to regain control.

"Aw, come on Zoey, make up your mind. I ain't hiding here in this stinking alley." The modest street dwellers used alleys when they tired of searching for bathrooms open to them.

"Alright, but can't we just sit somewhere and look homeless? Somebody might give us money for a dollar taco." Zoey had become obsessed with Simon's tale of what he called *working the guilt* of those who had more than what was fair.

Grace watched the officer, who joined the line of customers at a food truck. His back turned, she and Zoey rushed from the alley and around the nearest street corner. Their adrenaline carried them blocks away before Zoey's pace slowed, and she began to limp.

"How much farther do we gotta go?"

"I don't know. Until we find some place safe and green." Grace walked on, knowing that Zoey would spend the balance of the morning pouting, but that she would follow.

Grace guarded against her own confession that she desperately wanted to enroll in a quality high school that offered a selection of advanced classes taught by gifted teachers. But she was not naïve. Students attending these schools were largely drawn from neighborhoods of stately homes surrounded by meticulously manicured lawns and enclosed behind the exclusory boundaries of brick and iron fences.

They reached a narrow open stretch of grass beneath a large tree near an apartment building. Grace never wanted hard feelings between her and Zoey and thought that a story of Mom and baby Zoey might help to fix things between her and her sister. But Zoey covered her ears and yelled.

"No, stop, stop, stop! I hate your stupid stories! They're just lies to make Mom seem nice when she's not." Zoey turned her back to Grace and pulled a roll of white paper and her box of colored pens from her backpack and began to angrily deface a drawing of a pretty woman the likeness of Mom.

Hurt by the outburst, Grace said nothing to counter Zoey but opened her library book on geometry, one of the advanced classes she had planned to enroll in this fall. She wished for the luxury of Zoey's displaced anger.

They sat without speaking in a studied attitude of belonging, and no one questioned their right to be there. Until Zoey surprised Grace with the return of her excitement.

"I got it! What we can do to make money!"

"And what is that?" Grace did not want to start another row about Mom's rule about begging.

"We'll sell my drawings."

Grace frowned. "You mean to sell drawings to those no better off than us? That's crazy talk. And if they did buy a drawing, where would they hang them?"

Zoey blinked hard. Her sudden rush of enthusiasm appeared to take a nosedive, but just as quickly, she said, "But it's easy."

"Oh yeah, which part?"

"We'll go where buyers say they care about homeless kids."

"And that's where?"

"The library. Besides, arty people go to the library."

Zoey gathered her drawings and pens, placed them back into her backpack, and abruptly stood and walked in the direction of the downtown library. This time, it was Grace who followed.

On reaching the library, they sat in the shade of the building and waited for the person Zoey described as her best shot. Grace assumed Zoey meant to rely on her intuition to identify the one most susceptible to her con. Still, she asked how Zoey would know.

"Mister Simon has his way and I have mine." Zoey's stance was noticeably similar to their mother's phases of hyperbolic confidence.

An elderly man cradling a stack of children's books under his arm, his car keys in his hand, approached. He nodded and continued on his way. Zoey got to her feet and chased after the man.

"Hi Mister, I know your grandkids love you 'cause you bring them books." Zoey put on her sweetest, pretty girl smile.

"Uh, hi. Yes, but are you lost?" He looked about and, and seeing no one, he grimaced. "Where are your parents? Surely you aren't out on your own."

His grimace reminded Grace of Aunt Josey's nastiness toward kids who came to her door offering pamphlets, as if their God and Jesus were somehow better than hers.

"Our mom lost her real job, and now we're homeless except for the Impala." Her giggle was, surprisingly, a bit weepy.

Grace saw in his frown the judgement underlining his sympathy. He mumbled something about being sorry she and her family were homeless. Yet he turned and hurried away.

"Come on, Zoey, we've gotta go."

"No, I want him to give me money for one of my drawings. He can put it on his fridge along with pictures of his grandkids'." Zoey's determination was driven by desperation. She caught up to the man for a second time and begged him to buy just one drawing.

"I'm sorry, but I do not approve of begging."

"No," Zoey screamed. "I'm not allowed to beg!" She began a loud and pathetic wailing, which attracted the attention of other patrons entering and leaving the library.

The man looked around, and his thin face turned red. He put his hand into his pocket, hastily withdrew a five-dollar bill, and thrust it at Zoey, who immediately stopped screaming and smiled.

"Thank you, thank you, but... that's not enough." Zoey tugged at the sleeve of the man's shirt.

"No, Zoey, stop." Embarrassed, Grace pushed Zoey aside and, apologizing to the man, she grabbed Zoey's hand and they fled.

Zoey was right that five dollars would not pay for two meals at a fast-food joint. But it was enough at the discount store for a jar of peanut butter and a loaf of bread. Zoey wanted jelly, but there wasn't enough.

It mattered less now whether Mom found work at good pay. They would not go hungry; she and Zoey would have a sandwich each for five days. Though even in her relief, Grace worried that Zoey's success in shaming the old man meant she would believe she had discovered her own winning scheme and would not want to stop.

The sleeping tiger that was her sister's willful determination burst into full force, though Grace warned Zoey the streets were much too dangerous for kid pranks. And who did she expect to open their wallets to her con of public humiliation? The streetwise inhabitants would view Zoey as just another gutter pup, seeking to squeeze from them what they did not have.

Still, Zoey beamed with confidence. She had a perfect plan that required nothing more of Grace than she walk the thirty blocks to an upscale food store. Grace refused, but Zoey was hell-on-wheels when she did not get her way, and threatened to go alone.

Grace sat on a bench outside the store and watched Zoey approach two older women exiting the store with an overflowing shopping cart. Zoey approached, calling "trick or treat" with the eagerness of a younger kid. The woman pushing the cart barely slowed, but the second woman placed her hand on the retreating woman's sleeve, signaling for her to stop.

Zoey smiled and repeated her request.

"Oh, aren't you just the cutest... dressed in your... your homeless costume." Zoey had blackened her two front teeth and was wearing one of Ms. Babe's moth-eaten sweaters that hung off Zoey's shoulders almost to her knees.

"Yes, of course." The woman began sorting through the contents of the cart, Grace supposed for Halloween candy. But even Grace was ill-prepared for Zoey's brazenness.

"Please, may I have money instead of candy? Mom says it's bad for my teeth." Zoey grinned big, showing her blackened teeth. The poor woman winced.

"Jesus, Irene. Can't you see the kid's conning you?" Other shoppers slowed and stared, but most scurried past the two women. Zoey looked puzzled and perhaps she, too, was unprepared for the second woman's anger.

"But how was I to know?" The woman sounded wounded, and Grace was embarrassed for her, and that Zoey had played on the woman's emotions.

"What's the difference? Go on. Give her something, if that's what you intend." The woman pushed the cart into the walkway and didn't look back.

"Oh, honey, I'm so sorry... you're homeless... and your mother's right." She retrieved her wallet from her purse, handed Zoey a ten-dollar-bill, then turned and rushed to catch up to the disgruntled woman pushing the cart.

Grace and Zoey left the fast-food place and although they had eaten their fill, their long walk back to the Impala was strained. Zoey said nothing more than Jimmie would be happy for the scraps she had wrapped and tucked into her pocket.

The streets had fostered in her and Zoey an instinct for survival, and swindling a naïve rich woman out of ten dollars to satisfy their hunger felt neither right nor wrong, merely opportunistic. Grace felt increasingly trapped between what she and Zoey had become and her steadfast promise to Mom that she would never leave her. Mom showed few signs of getting better and hers and Zoey's futures were only becoming grimmer. If only Dad would somehow locate them. There was little chance of such an occurrence outside of a miracle, and Grace was not a believer.

— 58 —

Daniel

After an hour's drive from Bailey Cove, Daniel parked on the street opposite the Hopkins Street shelter, where he had previously failed in his appeal for information about Leah and his girls. Despite the odds of being turned away again, he approached the heavily fortified metal door. He rang and waited.

A woman's harried voice came to Daniel through a scratchy speaker, and he stepped closer. He knew he would need to be quick but persuasive.

"Evening, ma'am. I'm here to ask about my missing wife and our two daughters."

"Sir, we're closed." Her tone harbored the suspicion he had come to expect. Her reply was not about hours, which were clearly posted. Rather, it delivered the message that their doors were closed to men, all men, asking about missing wives or families. He had been turned down so many times his hope was hardened, but he was determined to never give up.

"Yes ma'am, but I'd thought you might at least take a look at this picture and tell me if you remember seeing either this woman or these girls?" He pressed the picture of Leah and the girls to the peephole. "Leah, my wife, is likely thin now, dark hair and eyes. Grace, my oldest, is tall, and some say built like me. Zoey, the younger, is nothing like me; pretty with blonde curly hair."

"Sir, any response to your questions..."

She paused, and he believed he heard something in her hesitancy.

"... would violate our security policy and the women's privacy." He got the part about protection from abusive husbands and fathers, but he was neither.

"Please, Ma'am, Leah's on strict medication. And I worry she can't afford her refill... and she could... die."

"No, I'm... sorry." The peephole closed, and he heard its latch slide into place.

Daniel stood on the wind-swept sidewalk with nothing from which to fashion hope other than the woman's slight hesitation, suggesting that she may have recognized Leah, or one or both of the girls. He would continue to return to Hopkins during morning release and early evening intake, and should they show, he would be there, waiting to take them home.

— 59 —

Grace

Grace believed it was the emotional tug of Christmas Eve and its memories that had finally broken their mom's resistance to joining the lengthy line of women and children outside the building that housed the Hopkins Street Shelter. Grace and Zoey anchored their place in line while Mom chattered incessantly to the others who were waiting. But after a day of surviving the streets, exhausted mothers and their streetwise kids ignored Leah and turned away in cold numbness.

Grace glanced toward the guard at the shelter door, who the women called *Big Devil*, and back at her mom. Leah was up in the face of a much larger woman who pushed back against Mom's intrusion. Grace bit down on her bottom lip and pressed her back against the building's rough wall. Zoey squatted at Grace's feet, as though she too feared a repeat of the first evening they came here, when Mom's acting out had gotten them turned away to spend another cold and hungry night huddled in the Impala.

"Crazy fucking cunt!" the woman yelled. Her angry outburst was met with guttural moans among those waiting in line, desperate that there be no delays in opening the shelter door.

A flurry of flailing fists ensued, and Mom caught a hard blow above her left eye, causing her to stagger back, stumble, and fall hard onto the sidewalk. The bigger woman was on Mom before she could regain her feet and she lay curled on the sidewalk. No one dared to move to help Mom; instead, they struggled to hold their hard-earned positions in the collapsing line.

Grace watched as the guard drew his over-sized night stick and rushed from the entryway. He ran along the line of frightened women and children, pushing those who were slow to obey his command that they hug the wall. He slugged the big woman with such force she bounced onto the curb in a huge lump of agony.

Mom pushed up from the ground in a burst of profanity and struggled against the man's strong grip, landing only a glancing blow to his shoulder. He slapped her so hard across her face that she slid down the wall like a tossed bundle of rags. Blood poured from her busted lip and nose.

"Mom, Mom!" Grace screamed, breaking from the line, Zoey behind her. But a strong arm reached and encircled both girls, pulling them back. Grace struggled against their captor, a woman with shoulders as broad as Daniel's.

— 60 —

Jordan

Officer Jordan McCall pulled to a stop in front of an establishment she would be unwilling to risk entering without her weapon. She, like other coffeeholics, came here for the absolute best and cheapest coffee in the city; coffee strong enough to sober a drunk and to keep a cop's eyes open straight through a double shift.

"God, Butch Girl, someday your coffee habit's gonna eat your gut," Nikki, her partner riding shotgun, teased.

"Take your point, but figure a rotted gut beats the hell out of a chest full of hot lead complements of the fucker I failed to see through sagging eyelids."

"Well, if that means I'll never need to call that sweet wife of yours, then okay, I'm a convert to the benefits of coffee."

"Does that mean I should bring you a hit of that doctored wakey juice you drink? There's always your pretty husband and pit bulls to be considered."

"Go on with your mess." Nikki's imitation of a southern accent sucked.

The dispatcher squawked out a 10-10 fight in progress, at 1780 Hopkins Street. Nikki responded with a 10-4, and Jordan pulled the patrol car back onto the street, speeding toward the city's largest shelter for women and children, which was frequently over-crowded, especially on nights when temperatures dropped into the thirties. They were south of the Mason-Dixon, but they still got their share of cold nights in December.

"Damn, but you'd think a bunch of bottom-feeding women might just pass on trying to kill each other."

Jordan scoffed at her partner. "Thought by now you would've learned better."

"Yeah, it's just that I want to believe we women are less violent."

It was a nice sentiment, but eleven years on the job had taught Jordan differently. Still, among the dispossessed she had witnessed amazing acts of generosity. Nikki might still be naïve, but Jordan preferred to ride with a cop still looking for the better acts of humanity. She had ridden with far too many of the other type.

— 61 —

Grace

The woman whispered, "Hush and stand still." The stranger's hot breath caught between her mouth and Grace's ear. Still, Grace struggled against the woman's powerful grip.

"Let go, she's our mom."

"Not tonight, she ain't," the woman whispered. "Where she's headed, you can't do her no good."

"No, she needs me. I know what to do to make her better." Grace pushed back against the stranger. She had heard stories about women who kidnapped young girls into sex slavery.

"Trust me, girl. You don't want nothing to do with child protective services. They took my Chester and I ain't seen my baby since." The pain in the woman's voice was real and Grace shuddered, remembering Mom's warning of the horrors should she and Zoey be separated. Grace stood quietly, and the woman let up on her hold.

Mom sat beneath the glare of a streetlight, her forehead resting in her blood-smeared palms. Grace decided the worst of the blood came from her busted lip and nose. The guard had turned his attention away from Mom and the other woman who lay motionless where she had fallen. He moved up and down the line and shouted more threats, demanding that everyone stay back against the wall.

A patrol car slid to a quick stop, strobe lights flashing, and two officers rushed from the car. The guard taunted, "Shit, I do believe it's the city's finest."

The taller cop with short, cropped hair glared and ordered him to move away. She squatted next to the woman and took a studied look at her injuries.

She stood and spoke through gritted teeth. "You fucking monster. You damn near busted her skull." She called to the second police officer to radio for medical assistance.

"Oh yeah? Was I supposed to let the big ape tear the head of the crazy bitch?" He sneered and pointed to Leah. "It's not the first time that one has started a ruckus. Bitch is crazier than a bedbug. She belongs in the loony bin."

"Ain't nobody asked you, so shut your mouth and stay the hell out of my way."

His withering glare radiated contempt, but he stepped back. An ambulance arrived, and after the EMTs quickly assessed the woman's injury, they placed her on a stretcher and loaded her into the ambulance. The paramedic team leader called to the officer he called Jordan.

"Want I should load that one there? She's pretty bruised up. Minor lacerations, but we've stopped the bleeding and cleaned her up. She'll wake in the morning feeling as worthless as elephant crap, but she'll heal."

"No thanks, Danny, we'll take it from here."

Danny motioned to the driver, and they climbed back into the ambulance and sped away.

The second officer walked over to Leah, leaned, and spoke to her. But Leah seemed not to have heard the officer over the confusion that was likely echoing in her head. The officer leaned closer and spoke a second time.

Leah moaned and swung wildly, but the officer grabbed her arm and flipped her face down, pulled her arms tightly against her back, and cuffed her. The officer dragged Leah to her feet and walked her to the patrol car.

Grace called out to the officer, wanting to explain that her mom's fight was likely with *underground invaders,* and not with the officer. But the stranger's rough hand muffled her, warning her to think about her and her sister.

Accepting that she couldn't help Mom, and afraid of child protective services, Grace stood quietly.

The woman let go and whispered, "You go with this woman." She spoke to a panicky, middle-aged woman as she gently pushed both girls toward her. "Take these here girls through that door there and keep them close."

"No, no, no puedo. Soy temporal," the frightened woman pleaded.

"Speak American, fool, unless you want a long bus ride back to Mexico or wherever you came from. That damn cracker there ain't about to believe these two are with me." Her tone softened, but her black eyes never lost their fierceness. She nodded toward the guard, who had returned to the shelter entrance, out of the worst of the howling wind.

Grace did not understand Spanish, but she recognized the look of terror etched in the woman's brown face. Still, her and Zoey's only chance of getting past the entrance checkpoint without being marked as unaccompanied children rested with the woman's willingness.

The second officer, who had placed Mom in the patrol car, walked over to the cop the EMT had called Jordan.

"If you're thinking one of them will talk, forget it. Hell, those poor souls will be back here tomorrow night, grateful not to have been raped or their kids stolen into sex trafficking."

Officer Jordan nodded. "Yeah, they're mostly fucked all right. But I'll ask just the same. One of these days, I'm nailing that sociopath to a cross."

Jordan walked the line calling, "All right, ladies, who's going to step up and tell me how that woman got her head split? So, let's not let the soup cool."

A veil of silence descended over the women. Even their babies were hushed. Not a single set of parted lips among them. Their dull eyes looked elsewhere, long mindful that survival trumped decency.

Officer Jordan reached the trembling brown woman and stopped. "These two yours?"

The woman nodded; her eyes cast downward.

The officer turned to Grace.

"Did you see what happened here? What can you tell me about her?" She pointed toward the patrol car.

Grace glanced at the brown woman, weighing the consequences to her and Zoey should the woman be exposed as a liar. She chose silence, rather than openly denying her mom, and all the wrong that had taken place.

The officer squinted at the woman and back at Grace as though making up her mind about what she was seeing. She asked the woman her name.

"Shelia... umm... Garcia." Her accent was heavy, and she continued to avoid eye contact with the officer.

"Shelia Garcia, look at me."

The frightened woman lifted her face.

"You got some identification? Maybe a driver's license, social security card or something with your name printed on it?"

The woman shook her head.

"I see. And if I should leave these girls with you and walk away from here tonight, will I find you and these kids here tomorrow morning?" The officer's sternness caused Zoey to move closer to Grace.

"Sí, sí," the tearful woman answered.

"Good, because otherwise I'll issue an Amber alert right after I've notified ICE." She leaned in close, topping the terrified woman by a foot.

Shelia Garcia crossed herself and swore profusely. The officer put her notepad back into her pocket and signaled the second cop. The two turned their backs, but Grace overheard.

"What the fuck are you doing? Both of them are lying like rugs. We've got to notify child protective services. Otherwise, the sergeant will be up our asses with a flagpole. Add that to you just lying to that poor woman. You know fucking well we aren't going to notify those ICE outlaws."

"Yep, for a fact."

The second officer stepped away, turned back, and said to Officer Jordan, "Any harm comes to those two girls, and I promise I'll not lie to protect your stupid ass."

"Fair enough. Just need until tomorrow morning." Officer Jordan turned back to Shelia Garcia. "Here." She pointed to the sidewalk. "Seven o'clock sharp or I promise you the worst day of your life."

The two officers got into the patrol car and Grace watched as the car pulled away, Mom stumped in the back seat. Scared of what would happen to their mom, Grace understood Shelia Garcia stood between her and Zoey, and a frosty night alone.

— 62 —

Jordan

Jordan glanced back toward the two girls, reasonably certain that they were the daughters of the woman slouched in the cage. Jordan remembered the woman from an earlier auto accident. The one who had insisted she notify her dead father. All the more reason she had decided not to unload her at the precinct jail. The night jailer was a Nazi who got off on tormenting women prisoners.

Jordan made a sudden hard left onto Spruce Street and Nikki exhaled sharply.

"All right, genius, you gonna tell me what the hell *we're* up to?"

"That one doesn't belong in jail. Figure to drop her at Harbor House. They've got a nurse there and maybe she'll agree to stay long enough to at least sober up."

"She's a raging nut case alright." Nikki lowered her voice. "But I'm thinking she's hyped on crystal or something else just as mind bending."

"Could be, but I'm not so sure. I'm thinking maybe some kind of wacky mental episode. Granted, it's hard to tell one from the other."

"Okay, but, girlfriend, the stunt you pulled back there, leaving those girls with an illegal? What if ICE beats you back? God only knows what could happen. We don't want that on our plate."

"You'd be right on that. But tell me you want to ship them off to endure the miseries of foster care." She knew she would have only overnight to determine an alternative to social services. Time to search her duty reports for names associated with the auto accident. Maybe call Anna, ask her to do the same.

Jordan had an emotional pit about kids, especially girls, though boys suffered on the streets as well. She felt if she had a second crack at the older girl, she might get a name; a decent father or a relative who'd agree to take the girls until their Mom got herself into treatment. Give herself and her kids at least a fighting chance.

Jordan had spent time in juvenile detention for physically assaulting her mother's murderer; her brutal stepfather who hid behind his police shield and was never charged for his crime. She had gone from juvie to an eleven-month stint on the streets as a runaway teenager. There, she had teamed up with two other homeless girls; one pretty, one not so much. The three had called themselves the *Thorny Roses*, and while their hunger had kept them sharp, they had schooled each other on the necessity for hyper-vigilance and the appeals that worked on the sympathies of the good hearted.

Hers was an awareness that had served her over the harrowing months she had known homelessness as a runaway lesbian. Though the Thorny Roses had watched each other's backs, Jordan was the sole survivor of the streets' pitfalls: sex trafficking, gangs, guns, drugs, alcohol, depression, rape, pregnancy, STD, suicide, and murder. Why had she survived, and not sweet Juniper or tormented Delores, teenage lovers forced from their homes by their families' blind piety? It was the cruelties Jordan witnessed that had stoked her anger, her defiance, her readiness to fight to the death anyone who sought to do her harm. In her more honest moments, she believed she had survived to bear witness to her stepfather's just reward.

"I know you've got your personal grievances, but what happens with kids in foster care isn't always despicable."

"And you know this how?" Jordan's tone was sharper than she intended.

"Okay, I'll give you the streets, but bad shit happens to rich girls, and they get hurt, too."

"I do take your point. But what's done is done."

Jordan falsified her duty log, excluding any reference to the two girls or their mother, reporting only the poor soul delivered to the one hospital in the city that accepted patients who could not pay.

— 63 —

Grace

The shelter door swung open, and women and their older children clutched their belongings with cold-stiffened fingers while mothers prodded their bone-weary younger children forward. Shelia Garcia placed a hand on Grace's shoulder and Grace gave Zoey a gentle push.

"Gotta pretend she's our mom."

The guard glanced in their direction, then looked away, and Grace was relieved. She picked up the bag that held her overdue library books, Zoey's pens and remaining drawing pad, and their few clothes, and joined the shuffle toward the open door and its promise of warmth. The scent of the hot meal she had dreamed of made Grace dizzy. She rubbed her hand across her damp cheek, although she didn't recall crying.

Grace searched for the woman who had helped them among those who were crowded into the large open room filled with multiple rows of single cots. Upon spotting the woman near the exit door, Grace directed Shelia Garcia and Zoey in the woman's direction.

"Excuse me, but is it okay if we sleep near you?" The woman stared at Grace as if she had never seen her before.

"Look here, child, what happened out there was just that. Ain't I already failed my boy, Chester? I ain't got nothing left for y'all." She turned her back to Grace, bent, and stashed a large garbage bag beneath a cot.

"Uh...." The unexpected rejection stung. "Right, sorry I bothered you." Grace turned away, surprised by the dwindling number of choices now available for three cots together.

"Hey, girl," the woman called to Sheila Garcia. "I'm talking to you, and them two. Come back over here, but understand it's just for the night. Daylight comes and you're on your own." Most of the woman's harshness had softened, and she pointed out nearby cots.

"Uh, thank you, and I promise we won't be any trouble." The woman grunted and said nothing more.

Grace and Zoey were making their way across the packed room when Grace heard her name called. A woman she recognized as a shelter volunteer whispered, "Honey, where's your mom? She's not with you?"

"No, the policewoman took her away," Zoey blurted. "Does that mean we can't stay?"

"I won't tell, but you'll need to move through the line quickly and stay close to that woman." She nodded across the room to where Shelia Garcia waited.

Grace thanked the volunteer and scurried Zoey away.

"Is she a Christian?"

"Maybe, but you need to keep your mouth shut." Grace squeezed Zoey's shoulder. "We're not allowed here alone. So, unless you want us back on the street, you'll keep quiet."

Grace and Zoey joined the shuffle of mothers and their kids along the steaming food service line and the promise of a full belly. Mom had argued that she and Zoey were not like the other children with their failed mothers. She was a successful professional with the certainty of a promising future, and they were simply enduring a temporary setback. Whatever Mom wished to believe about their situation, their hunger was no different from that of any woman or kid in the line stretched before them. Grace accepted the miracle of turkey and dressing, mashed potatoes and gravy, hot bread, and pumpkin pie.

After they had eaten all their stomachs would hold, there were hot showers that steamed away their deepest chills;

showers that came with gift packets of sweet-smelling soap, tubes of shampoo, toothpaste, and toothbrushes. Afterward, she and Zoey dressed in the clean clothes they had selected from among stacks of donated clothing. Grace had chosen a pair of sweats and a plaid flannel shirt, and they were each given a pair of packaged socks. Zoey had picked a pretty blue jumper with white leggings that Grace could not talk her out of for something more practical. But Zoey was always about the moment.

The room's warmth, her hunger satisfied, and the nearness of the big woman comforted Grace, and she drifted into a rare deep sleep. Absent were her fearful awakenings to the images of prowling men, their gaunt faces pressed against the Impala's windows.

Shelia Garcia hurried Zoey to finish her oatmeal, whispering that her work was a far walk, and that she must not be late. Grace stuffed her remaining hard bread in her pocket and poured Zoey's cooled oatmeal into a paper cup before they followed Shelia Garcia through the door and onto the sidewalk. The rush of chilly air took Grace's breath.

"Come on, we've gotta find Jimmie. He's scared without me." Zoey attempted to pull Grace in the direction Mom had parked the Impala.

"Later, but first we're calling Dad." He would come for her and Zoey and would find the police report of Mom's arrest that would say where they could find her. Grace meant to stop the first person she saw and beg to use their phone. She, alone, could not care for herself and Zoey. If it was not moved regularly, the Impala was not safe from impoundment. She had keys but did not know how to drive.

— 64 —

Grace

Leah sat slumped on the curb, and upon seeing Grace and Zoey, she slowly got to her feet and called out to her daughters. Her face was swollen, a shiner beneath her right eye.

"There are my precious girls." She embraced first Zoey and then Grace, cooing their names in a sing-song rhythm as she had when they were babies.

"Mom, we were afraid. Grace said we should call Dad. Umm... to help find you." Their secret now in the wind, Zoey did not dare look at Grace.

"Oh, I know, my sweet. I, too, worried I'd lost you forever. But I'm here now and I have good news." Tears streamed down Leah's face and if she had fully grasped Grace's intention regarding their dad, she did not let on. Instead, she pointed to Shelia Garcia and snarled.

"And you? Are you with child services, here to steal my children?" Leah's agitation was immediate.

"No, no, she's our pretend mom," Zoey answered.

"Please... I only wait for the big police officer. Then I go."

Grace hurriedly explained Shelia Garcia's part in her and Zoey avoiding the choice of either returning to the Impala alone or being reported as unaccompanied minors.

A late model truck braked hard and stopped at the curb. The tall cop from last night, now wearing jeans and a jacket, hurried onto the sidewalk. Shelia Garcia moaned and began pleading not to be sent back. But the cop's attention was on Leah.

"What the hell are you doing here? I told you I'd come back for you."

Leah glared and flipped her hand in scornful dismissal. The police officer frowned, and for the first time looked toward Shelia Garcia.

"You kept your word, and you'll have no trouble from me."

The officer watched the woman as she fled, and Grace believed she saw a brief pained expression on the cop's face. It reminded her of the unexpectedly caring way the librarian had looked at her.

In a calmer voice, the officer spoke to Grace. "Tell me your names?"

Not sure she had a choice, Grace hesitated, but answered.

"Okay, good. I'm Officer Jordan McCall. How old are you, Grace?"

"I'm fifteen. My sister is nine. I'm sorry I lied to you before. I was afraid," Grace said.

"Yeah, here on these streets, lying has its place." Grace noted that Officer Jordan's eyes were Dad's blue color. She remembered he had once said blue eyes can't lie; but he had lied.

"Do you want me to contact a family member?" Officer McCall's forehead gathered, and her earlier intensity returned. "Tell me. And I can make it happen."

"Please, Grace, I don't want to stay with Mom anymore," Zoey whispered.

"Stop this immediately. It's police brutality. You have no legal right to question my daughter." Mom attempted and failed to step between Grace and the officer, though Grace saw she had the presence of mind not to touch the officer.

Grace wondered if the officer knew about Dad's restraining order and, if so, would she still have offered to contact him?

Grace believed that even in the wrong, the law had always taken Mom's side over his.

"Now dear, you must tell the nice officer the truth." Leah's demeanor had changed abruptly but neither she nor the officer were fooled.

Lying was familiar, yet Grace hated that her lie forced her to choose between their parents, rather than what she knew to be best for her and Zoey. The truth was Mom would not survive the streets alone.

"My sister and I... want to go with our mom. But maybe you could...." For a moment, Grace had foolishly thought to ask the officer how she might learn the fate of the woman who had helped them and her missing son, Chester.

"Grace, darling, you must not further impose on the officer's duties."

"What would you have me do?" the officer asked, leaning in closer, shielding Grace from her mom.

"Uh, nothing, really, we're... okay." Grace had awoken to find the woman's cot empty, and regretted that she had not thanked her. She had not even learned her name; she knew nothing of the woman other than her kindness.

The officer paused, her searching gaze focused on Grace, and there was something in her earnestness that caused Grace to decide that the officer knew things about her unwillingness to speak truthfully. The officer returned to her truck and drove away, and Grace slipped the card she had given her deep inside her pocket.

Mom suggested that instead of returning to the Impala right away that they should spend the morning reading in the heated library. They were among the first patrons to arrive, and there was the added treat of orange juice, muffins, and hot coffee. When she and Zoey had washed their faces and hands and brushed their teeth in the library restroom, they took what Mom insisted was a polite share of juice and two muffins while Mom had only coffee.

Leaving the warmth of the library, they braced for the first impact of the chilly wind and hurried along the street. Mom jabbered on about having met a nice man who had greeted her as she left the facility where she's spent the night and offered to buy her breakfast. Afterwards, he gave her a ride to the shelter. He had been so impressed with her that he offered her a good-paying job with free housing and a managerial title. They would leave for their new home first thing tomorrow.

Grace wanted to be optimistic, but Mom often saw more in a vague promise than truth supported, especially offers that fed her craving for recognition and reward. She considered the card in her pocket and wondered what calling the cop might mean. It would likely result in unwanted consequences for their mom, so she settled on going along with Mom's newest illusion of grand success.

When they reached the street where they had left the Impala, Mom began hurling profanities as she ran toward the empty space where the Impala had been parked. Grace and Zoey joined Mom in a search along the street, but the car was nowhere in sight. The bit of safety they had known was no longer theirs.

– 65 –

Grace

When Mom had worn herself out pacing and swearing that some gestapo cop falsely claimed the Impala had been abandoned, she sat exhausted on the curb, knees pulled to her chest, her forehead resting on her folded arms. Mom had not noticed Ms. Babe's approach and Grace wanted her to offer them overnight sleeping in the castle, warmed by a small Sterno stove.

"About that old car. I saw who took it."

"You nasty old witch. Was it you who ratted? Got our home hauled away?" Mom stood shaking her fist and screaming more profanities.

Ms. Babe glared with instant fury that silenced even Mom's ranting.

"Murderer, yes, but I ain't no snitch." She handed Mom a folded scrap of paper and walked away in the glowing arrogance of her street legend.

Mom stared at the paper and placed it in her pocket. She ran into the center of the busy street, looking first in one direction and then the other before shouting for Grace and Zoey to follow her. Grace hesitated, knowing that following Mom into the gathering darkness was worse than a masked scavenger hunt with no clues and no prizes at the end.

"No, no, no! I'm not leaving Jimmie!" Zoey screamed.

Ms. Babe stopped at the entrance to the Queendom and looked back at Zoey, now squatted on the sidewalk. "Girly, that wild thing you're so crazy about is right there." She pointed at a cardboard box.

Zoey lifted the top flap and squealed with relief. A crazed Jimmie jumped into Zoey's arms, and she kissed the cat repeatedly between spitting cat fur and shrieking. She tucked the freaked cat inside her over-sized red coat that had likely been a dog bed in a prior life. Zoey did not mind the doggy-smell, though being stuffed inside its folds surely unnerved the cat.

Grace was oddly struck by the adage that cats were graced with nine lives, and that there was no way of knowing how many more lives Jimmie had coming. But Mom's wild quest to rescue the Impala was certain to draw down Jimmie's account along with theirs. Still, she urged Zoey forward to catch up to Mom, who had walked on alone.

"Is Ms. Babe really a murderer?" Zoey whispered.

Grace didn't know, but whether she was or not, she prayed that her street legacy held against those who might think of harming an old woman. Simon once said Ms. Babe carried a Saturday night special in her garter belt. Grace was unfamiliar with such a belt and decided the old man had said *guarder*, which would have made sense.

— 66 —

Leah

Overhead, the night sky was a vast orange halo of light pollution, and the atypical deep south freeze had continued to wrap Leah and her daughters in its icy grip. Their breaths hung in the frosted air like cartoon word bubbles and, ignoring Grace's insistence that they turn back for the shelter, Leah plodded on, leaving Grace to coax an exhausted Zoey to keep up.

Beyond the open field where she and her girls now cowered, belly-down, amongst dried weed stalks, unsettling flashes of bright light swept across the vacant field from a ribbon of late-night motorists, and they pressed their weariness tighter to the ground.

Zoey moaned in her sleep, unnerving Leah, and she placed a trembling hand over her daughter's weather-cracked lips, meaning only to stifle her dream-whimpers. Too weary to mount more than a weak resistance, Zoey's eyes stretched wide above Leah's cold hand.

"Mom, stop. You're scaring her. We've got to find shelter out of the wind." Grace's desperate pleading bristled with contempt for all that was insane about their huddling in a frozen field. Or any other place that wasn't warm and safe.

Leah's chest constricted with pain, and she pressed Zoey against her breasts, singing a broken promise her father had sung: *Hush little baby don't say a word. Poppa's gonna buy you a mockingbird. If that mockingbird won't sing, Pappa's gonna buy you a diamond ring.*

Zoey burrowed into the damp folds of Leah's overcoat, seeking warmth and nourishment she did not have to give. She rested her chin lightly on her daughter's mop of clammy, disheveled curls, embracing the sweet return of a memory not wholly caught up in her spiraling madness. The fragile memory crystallized in an moment of clarity.

A younger Zoey sat patiently while Leah brushed tangles from her daughter's canary-yellow hair. When Zoey's locks lay subdued under her tender persistence, she gathered a handful of curls and tied them with a bright ribbon. Zoey's reflection in her grandmother's heirloom hand mirror. Their delightful burst of giggles. Color? What color? Ribbon of memory? Was it not a ribbon, but the frayed sash of her sexy negligee? Emerald-green, she thought. Yes, and Zoey's beautiful father, whose name shall remain forever locked in secrecy, had declared her radiant. Their brilliance together had paled, leaving only Zoey's beauty to remind her.

"Mom, my stomach hurts," Zoey whimpered, her pursed lips like the searching beak of a blind hatchling.

Leah shook Zoey. "You remember. I know you do, for I had carried your wee tininess inside me. Sassy red, he'd said. He was laughing. Yes, red, it was. You know how I hated green." Leah hated that her precious memory was turned to stone. She roughly released Zoey into Grace's arms. Got onto her knees and stared.

Ahead, thirty yards or more, a dilapidated building with a ridiculous string of red and green seasonal lights hanging above its one window, facing the street. Leah loathed its poorly scrawled, hand-painted sign: *Big Al's Wrecker Service.* It matched the name the old witch had scrawled on the scrap of paper.

"No, Mom, please. Can't we call someone?" Grace fingered the small card in her pocket. If not Dad or Aunt Josey, then the police officer who had given her the card.

Leah ignored Grace, welcoming a surge of purest clarity. Her mission was vivid, pulsating in its ultimate promise. She crawled forward, careful to avoid human and animal feces, shattered glass, condoms, broken hypodermic needles, and discarded tins of cheap, counterfeit meats. Pausing, she watched the corner traffic light repeatedly flashing from green to yellow to red, until the colors became indiscernible one from the other.

A sudden burst of light from the building prompted Leah to stare back toward the girls. Neither seeing nor hearing approaching vehicles, Leah wiggled her jeans down over her bony hips and squatted. Urine gushed warm, burning her inner thighs, and it smelled of the vaginal infection she worried she may have contracted. She patted the ground around her in search of a scrap of paper, anything she might use to relieve the stinging.

Righting her multiple layers of oversized clothing, she moved to the outer-most edge of the corner streetlight's reach. A door she believed to be the entrance to the small office attached to the bigger shop pushed open, and *he* stepped into the glaring light. His bulk filled the narrow doorway, and her scent memory was of their rancid body odors that clung like a second skin, their rotten breath smelling of cheap wine and stale tobacco. His heavily tattooed forearm flaunted the stricken face of a woman burned into his flesh. Leah's shame was so complete, she imagined her anguish sucking the last life-sustenance from the marrow of her bones. She imagined their bodies hung from stout trees.

From somewhere behind her, she heard what she thought was Grace calling her name, and she strained to pierce the veil of silence. But what she had heard was the wind rustling dead grass stalks, and not her daughter. Determined, she moved beyond any retreat, and stood fully exposed.

$$- 67 -$$

Daniel

There o'clock Christmas morning, Daniel stood beneath the dim light above Sarah's front door. After a second ring and no answer, he turned away in both disappointment and relief.

Behind him, the door opened the width of its chain, and he turned back. The door closed and reopened, and Sarah stood in its opening, looking startled. She gathered her robe tighter about her and glanced into the brightly lit parking area. Maybe she searched for something that might help to explain his unlikely presence.

"Daniel, what on earth?" Her breath seemed to catch in her throat.

"I know it's late. And it's wrong that I've come." He was prepared for her to turn him away, but she stepped aside.

"It's okay that you're here. Come in out of the cold."

As he stepped into the warmth, her hand slightly brushed his, and her touch was so perfect his own neediness besieged him.

"Oh god, Daniel. You must be freezing. And you're... so thin. When did you last eat?"

Through her eyes, he saw that his clothes hung on his frame in the disheveled fashion of the wretched souls among whom he searched. Yet, he told himself her expression was kindness, absent of pity.

"Uh, breakfast, I think." Or was that yesterday? He was no longer sure. Time was an unbroken chain of failure and pain.

"Come into the kitchen and I'll get coffee going and make you an early breakfast."

Daniel followed Sarah into her bright kitchen, and she invited him to sit at the counter while she took eggs and cheese from the fridge. At the far end of the counter, a large calico sat alertly on its haunches and refused to look his way, though he felt the cat's harsh judgement. His mother had kept cats, sometimes four or five, and he had never tried to make friends. If that was what one did with cats. Was that why his referring to the calico as nice seemed to amuse Sarah?

"He isn't my cat. He'll stay only as long as it pleases him."

The cat, as though on cue, rolled on to a haunch, a hind leg raised, and ran a sandpaper tongue over his privates. Though he and Sarah shared but a fleeting nervous laugh, Daniel felt a moment of lightness that he had not felt since retrieving the photo he now carried at all times from its broken frame.

Sarah turned back to preparing food, and Daniel began to slowly unreel his story: showing up at her door demanded that he tell her as much of his truth as he dared.

"I want you to know that I can't find my wife and girls. I've looked everywhere. It's as if the earth opened up and swallowed them."

And he didn't stop until he had entrusted her with all the fear and guilt bottled up inside him: Leah's recurring illness that had required repeated hospitalizations. His and Leah's strange dance of a failed marriage. His jail time and court order that denied him contact with her and their daughters. His fears that his wife and daughters were homeless. The possibility that an episode of Leah's illness had left the girls to survive on their own wit.

Sarah listened intently but asked nothing more from him. She set before him a cheese omelet, a toasted English muffin, and a second cup of steaming coffee, then took the seat next to him. When he had eaten what he could manage and said all that he knew to say, he stood and took his jacket from the back of the stool. He thanked Sarah with an awkwardness he felt stinging his cheeks and turned to leave.

Sarah walked with him to the door and there she laid a warm hand on his arm. His wounded heart had wished to remain faithful to Leah, but Daniel surrendered to his loneliness. He turned back to embrace Sarah, and their closeness aroused him, and she invited him to share her bed.

Their lovemaking was nothing like before: hurried and driven by sex alone. It was slower, even tentative to start, though in their shared climax she had called his name and he hers with a passion he had not expected. He drew her closer and attempted to speak, perhaps of his gratitude. But she, wiser than he, had gently quieted him.

A Career in Motel Management
Winter 2019

– 68 –

Grace

There was a roar as the Impala burst forth from the rear of the squatty building, Mom at the wheel. She sped toward the street, then braked hard, as if she suddenly remembered Grace and Zoey waiting in the open field. She lowered the passenger window and leaned across the seat, shouting for her and Zoey to hurry.

Grace pulled Zoey to her feet, and half-carried, half dragged her to the car. She dumped Zoey onto the back seat before jumping in behind her. Mom giggled and drove onto the street as if they were escaping some wrong, but what, exactly, Grace was unsure. Only that it felt dangerous, if not illegal.

"Merry Christmas, my darlings." Mom laughed wildly, waving a short iron pipe.

"Mom, what'd you do?" Grace shouted over the roar of the Impala's engine, the heater blasting warm air, and the radio blaring Christmas music.

Mom shouted back. "What? Haven't you heard of stand your ground?"

"Oh, God... you killed someone?"

"No, no, the wicked man only sleeps." Mom giggled.

Although she was certain that she had not yet heard the worst of Mom's deeds, tears of relief streamed down Grace's cheeks.

Mom drove them to a twenty-four-hour super Walmart and parked among late holiday shoppers. Mom's surprise gift: a hubcap filled with candy bars, nuts, crackers, chips, and Zoey's favorite jellybeans. Grace and Zoey set about stuffing themselves and Zoey fed Jimmie cheese curls she declared were his very favorite.

Grace did not want to spoil the good of the moment with the truth of how Mom had rescued the Impala. An acceptable version of her own took shape; one in which she gave Mom the strength and cunning of a superwoman in an alternate reality where assault and theft in repelling the evil deeds of men were not crimes.

Leah filled the gas tank using money Grace was sure she did not have before and drove onto the northbound I-75 ramp. Mom said nothing about where they were going, but Grace was relieved that she was not drinking nor recklessly weaving in and out of high-speed interstate traffic. They drove for over an hour, mostly in silence, before Zoey set aside her drawing pad and stared ahead.

"Mom, when are we going to be there? I gotta pee bad." She squeezed her palms between her legs and frowned. Mom was clearly irritated but agreed to a bathroom break. She pulled into the next rest area, demanding that Grace and Zoey hurry and return to the car without delay.

Four hours or so later, they exited I-75 onto I-10 west and Mom, who had remained mostly silent, began to jabber about her newest career opportunity in motel management. She would earn a good salary and they would once again enjoy the benefits of a stable and respectable life. Grace momentarily settled on the notion that whatever lay ahead could not possibly be worse than their months on the city's streets.

Mom took a folded scrap of paper from her pocket and studied the hand-drawn map. She left the interstate at the next exit and passed among a small cluster of buildings, including a Wendy's, and two service stations. For the next thirty minutes, they drove along a lightly traveled state road where there was nothing to see but overgrown fields broken by a scattering of small frame houses and mobile homes set back off the highway on small parcels.

Ahead, Grace could see what looked like a failed housing development of roughly twelve houses, with more unoccupied than occupied. The surrounding countryside bore an intense sense of gloom and the high-traffic tourist destination motel of Mom's story appeared nowhere except in her delusion.

Mom slowed and eagerly pointed out a stripped billboard for rent, then turned onto a side road and into a crumbling asphalt parking lot.

"Here we are... our new home." Mom's earlier excitement was decidedly subdued, yet she attempted to put on a good face.

Everything about the concrete, two-story stack of twelve rooms, bearing the name *Motel Mount Pleasant,* mirrored its deteriorating parking lot and screamed out to any sensible person to drive away. The lush winter-landscaped grounds and sparking blue pool Mom had spoken glowingly of were, in fact, sadly overgrown boxwoods surrounding a drained, plastic-lined hole in the ground. The pool bottom was covered in sand, weeds, and scattered beer cans, with a few sun-faded plastic chairs scattered about the pool's edge. The playground was nothing more than a rusted swing set, located in a washed-out dirt pit.

The royal palms Mom had described as towering beauties gently swaying in a balmy breeze, were nowhere in sight, nor was any other variety of trees. The building and grounds, which occupied a narrow strip of barren land that appeared to have been clear cut, stood as a mockery of what Leah had heralded as a tropical paradise.

"But there's no water. And where's the playground?" Zoey's plaintive voice reeked of her disappointment at the absence of the fully equipped playground and a sparking pool where Mom had boasted she would meet kids her age and make new friends.

"Temporary, my love. Come spring, the playground will be expanded with new equipment, and the pool filled."

"But Mom, you said...."

"Hush now, you aren't to fret. Now that I'm in charge. You'll see."

It was a characteristic offering from the realm of Mom's inventiveness in the presence of their newest reality in all its bleakness. Mount Pleasant was a fraud in both name and character.

Mom pulled the Impala into a space near a one-story structure attached to the two-story building by a narrow breezeway. A sign identified the separate building as the motel office.

"We are to live there, behind door one." Mom giggled as if she had made a joke and that there were prizes behind the mystery door. "You girls start unloading while I check in with the failed manager. Be advised, now that I am in control, identified shortcomings will be remedied immediately. You'll see."

"Uh, yeah Mom, but shouldn't we wait until you're sure this is the place?" If Aunt Josey's God gave a damn, Mom would return with new directions to the place of her imagination.

"Good grief, Grace. We've arrived. Here will be... grand."

"But... what about school? What about advanced classes?"

College had hinged on earning a scholarship, but now, even graduating high school with her age-group had been delayed.

"You two will start afresh after Christmas break. The schools here are excellent."

Mom knew nothing of the schools other than what she was likely told by the same liar who had sold her a job in *paradise*. Who was this stranger who had hired Mom to manage a motel in hell? One that had a flashing sign proclaiming *NO VACANCIES* and an empty parking lot.

A bone-thin, heavily tattooed woman stepped from Room 2 onto the walkway. Her hair, the color Mom had called purple passion, was piled on top of her head in the shape of a halo and sprayed as stiff as strands of wire. The overly cheerful woman peered in through the window and flashed her and Zoey a big smile, marred by decayed teeth. A sulking girl Grace guessed was about her age had followed the woman out of the room but had not as much as glanced their way.

"Hey, honey bunches. I'm Miss Juniper. And ain't y'all just the cutest." She called back to the disinterested girl. "Be nice, Angel Baby. Come say hello to our new neighbors."

The girl shrugged. "They ain't nothing to me," she replied, leaving Grace to question whether this starkly white woman was the mother of a daughter the color of rich caramel.

"I'm so sorry, honeys. Her rudeness is her own." The woman walked on, her behind swaying as if she pleaded to be noticed. In contrast, the girl's loose gait was one that invited all to kiss her big ass: an air that shouted she would change nothing of herself. She stood before a vending machine and fed it coins with a noticeable flare. Grace was drawn to the girl with equal amounts respect and caution.

Zoey squinted up at Grace and whispered, "The girl's mean. But the funny-looking lady's friendly, right?"

"Oh, yeah, I'm sure the lady's nice." Grace thought, but did not dare say, the woman looked like those on the streets who were "nice" for the right number of Washingtons. The thought of what Mom might do here terrified Grace.

"I like her hair," Zoey said, waving to the woman who had stopped at the door and looked back.

Mom had refreshed her makeup and left Grace and Zoey with a harsh reminder to unpack the car. She walked through the door the woman had entered and disappeared inside.

Grace considered just how much of their stuff would fit inside the room. She went to the door and slowly pushed it open. The stench of cigarettes, whiskey, and human odors took her breath. She backed off, leaving the door open, and took a seat on the walkway curb. Zoey joined her.

"Are we really going to live here?"

"God, Zoey. Don't start with your dumb questions. We're here, aren't we? If it makes you feel better, tell yourself whatever you want."

"I think we're staying. And you're mean. Cause you're mad at Mom."

"So, give yourself an A for rational deduction."

Zoey squinted with a confused expression.

"Okay, I'm sorry." Grace encircled Zoey's shoulders, but she could not bring herself to voice the usual lie about their being okay. Here they would no longer have Ms. Babe or books from the public library to make things better. Dad was far away, and Grace didn't have a phone.

– 69 –

Grace

Leah worked nights alone and was free to drink as long as she remained sober enough to perform her duties, which were unclear to Grace. Night hours required Leah to sleep days until time to meet Zoey at her afternoon bus drop. Supper was at one of the two fast-food joints located twenty miles away at the interstate exchange. Then straight back to the motel for Leah to catch her last nap before reporting to work around nine. Grace and Zoey were alone for the balance of the night.

The schools Grace and Zoey had entered at mid-term was a complete drag for both of them. There was no advanced placement math or science and Grace attended boring classes with redneck, brain-dead, glue-sniffing boys, and girls vying for these boys' attention. Even the few girls who were serious students with plans to attend the local community colleges were pressed to give it up to these same boys. The school's sports program included boys' football and baseball, and both boys' and girls' basketball. Entering school at mid-term meant Grace had arrived after basketball season.

There was no one among the students that Grace wanted to know other than the girl whose mother had called Angel Baby. She was, as Grace had expected, clearly not an angel. Rather, she was scary tough, smart, and wise to every con known. The rednecks talked their racist trash behind Angel Baby's back, but never to her face. In a gun-at-school incident, Grace wanted to stand next to the fearless girl. She had planned ways of talking to her, but Angel Baby always walked away as if she were determined that they would remain strangers.

Zoey fared worse; routinely given additional unchallenging worksheets to complete while her classmates struggled to finish their first. When Zoey grew bored, she acted out in class and on the playground. Her behavior bewildered her unimaginative but kind teacher, who sent notes home, attempting to convince Mom to come to the school for a parent-teacher conference. Yet, without further inducement, Zoey returned to being the quiet, obedient star student, and the notes stopped. Grace believed Zoey had simply given up on attracting Mom's attention and had begrudgingly settled for long days of agonizing boredom.

The high school library was small, but Grace was excited to accept a non-paying librarian's student assistant job for an hour before and after classes. She did so with a plan to use one of the school's three computers to contact their dad through her cousin Jenny's social media, only to learn that the computers were locked away for safe-keeping, awaiting the long-sought availability of regional internet service.

On one return trip to the motel after supper, Grace attempted to persuade their mom that she and Zoey did not feel safe alone at night. She was careful to avoid the kind of confrontation that had occurred earlier when Mom had slept through the time to meet Zoey after school and Zoey had walked a stretch of the state road alone.

Grace arrived back at the motel from her afternoon hour at the library to find Mom and Zoey sitting in a shallow pool of filthy water. Hand in hand, the two ran from the muddy water pooling around their ankles, just as they had on family trips to the coast. Leah called Grace to join them.

"Your sister and I are constructing an impregnable mud castle." Mom dropped onto her knees, gathered a handful of mud, and attempted to shape it into a castle wall before water from the hose they had dropped into the pool washed the mud away. Zoey joined her in this losing game.

Mom's laughter faded as the castle washed over her bare feet and she fell onto her back at the bottom of the pool. She lay there peacefully, staring into a cloudless sky, and began to sing a song about raindrops falling on her head. Mom knew the lyrics to countless songs that could easily lead to hysterical sobs or joyful laughter.

Zoey looked to where Grace sat in one of the remaining pool chairs and shrugged before joining Mom. Jimmie watched from a safe distance and Grace wondered what the wise cat had unraveled of Mom's descent into an even deeper state of madness. Her illness had no timetable, only its certainty.

— 70 —

Grace

During the three months they had been at Motel Mount Pleasant, the flashing neon sign had continued to read *No Vacancies*, although the steady traffic of men to and from the second floor that began on their first night had continued. When Grace dared to question her mother about her growing suspicion that Fat Joseph was trafficking in sex on the second floor, Leah responded with outrage, accusing Grace of making up stories.

But what Grace had witnessed between Fat Joseph and the one she identified as *the thin man* was real. On Mondays, Fat Joseph came out of the room he shared with Ms. Juniper and Angel Baby to stand next to the man's car and pass a green bag through the open window.

Grace reluctantly came to accept that what she witnessed meant their mother's job placed her inadvertently in the role of Fat Joseph's money collector. Although Leah's job did not require her to break legs but merely collect, Grace feared for her mother's legal jeopardy.

A deeper fear, accompanied by shame at her mom's apparent criminal involvement, took hold with the predawn arrival of a white cargo van. She watched as the driver hurried to the back of the van and hustled three cowering girls through the rear door. Grace judged all three girls as minors, the youngest girl no older than her. Ms. Juniper hurried from the office and handed the man an envelope. He got back into the van and sped away, and Ms. Juniper rushed the girls up the outside stairs and into a room on the second floor.

Grace watched for the reappearance of the girls, but there was no sign of them until the morning of the sixth day after their arrival, when the same driver angrily forced one of the three girls, sobbing, back into the white van. After what appeared to be a grudging exchange with Ms. Juniper, he climbed back into the van and sped away toward the interstate.

Grace gathered her courage and approached Angel Baby about the fate of the girls upstairs.

The big girl scoffed and walked away, calling back over her shoulder, "Fuck girl, I hear you're smart. So how come you've just now figured out this hell hole ain't nothing like Six Flags?" Her contempt could be measured by her biting laugh.

"Wait, Angel Baby." Grace's cheeks burned with a flush of embarrassment. "I'll have you know I'm not stupid."

"Ain't nobody called you stupid. But you'd think by now you'd know enough to call me by my true name. And that's Luna Diaz."

"Okay, I will from now on. And I'm sorry." Grace had already felt stupid, but now she felt multiple stupid.

"Right, and you need to know that fat asshole is hers and those poor gals' pimp." She nodded toward the second floor. "He gets free fucks whenever. Like they're on some kind of apprenticeship and he's the master. Poor girls could have just as well stayed south of the border and had what they got here. Ain't right, but it's what they've got." She paused, and lowered her voice. "And if you're looking to start something where you figure to save those girls, maybe calling the local law, you need to understand that there's no law within fifty miles. And maybe you'll need to figure on leaving *her* behind and getting yourself and that pretty little sister gone from here. When you're prepared to do that, then you'll be able to leave this hellhole."

Grace stood slack-mouthed with the weight of Luna's words and her own gullibility. Her belief that she could somehow change the fate of the girls brought stinging tears to her eyes, and she turned away in despair. Still, she would learn what she could about her mother's role. Just how deep was she in?

Midnight arrived and Grace left Zoey sleeping. She crossed the narrow breezeway and hid in the shadows outside the motel office. She watched as money for a room key passed between Leah and a man Grace recognized as a regular. He crossed the breezeway within six feet of Grace and took the outside stairs to the second floor. She could no longer deny their mom's intentional or unintentional culpability in these crimes. Grace stepped out of the cover of darkness and into the office, her dread filling her throat so she felt she would suffocate.

Leah looked up from the computer screen. Her hand moved to clutch the front opening of her blouse. "Grace, why are you here?" Her words were only slightly slurred.

"Because we've got to... to leave this horrible place." Grace's words were not the ones she had practiced.

"Leave? What are you talking about? Where is your sister? You must go back. You don't belong here." Grace believed that what she saw was shame in the trembling of her mother's chin.

"That's what I've come to say. We... you, me, and Zoey... we don't belong here."

"No, stop your... meddling. Or you will condemn you and your sister to... foster care. Me... your mother... to... away. Is that what you want?"

"Away, yes, but foster care? What on earth are you talking about?"

Grace heard only bits of her mother's rant. Zoey, young and pretty... sweetly obedient... and she, a troubled teenager, destined to linger... never again to know a loving family.

"Mom, how can you do what you do?" Against her will, Grace had teared.

"Oh Grace, my love, your imagination has taken flight. You must go now, for we are fine here." Mom turned back to the computer as though harsh words had not passed between them.

Grace clutched her aching chest. She was helpless to save her mother from the certainty of arrest and imprisonment; a confinement Mom could not survive. Yet, Grace was more determined than ever to save herself and Zoey.

Grace eased her way back into their room and into bed next to Zoey.

"We're staying, right?" Zoey whispered. Her body was tense.

"For now, yes."

"But I'm scared."

Footsteps on the stairway echoed Grace's own fear and she drew her sister close.

Spring 2020
Chocolate Candy

− 71 −

Grace

The library job meant Grace walked the two miles between the motel and school before the morning bus ran, and again on her afternoon return. She did not mind the walk, and some days she ran the entire way. But she remained diligent, careful to leave the library before the baseball team's afternoon practice ended. She did so to avoid a repeat of her worst incident with three wretched dickheads.

The three boys had formed a circle around her, blocking her way, taunting her as one of Fat Joseph's whores in training and bragging that they could teach her plenty about how to please men. She made repeated attempts to break their grip but failed. The boys began pushing her from one to the next, each taking his turn at feeling her up. The leader, shorter than her, shouted for the others to trap her up against the gym wall. He tore at her shirt, and she bit him on the shoulder hard enough to draw blood. He yelled in pain and let go of her. She rammed her knee into his balls, and he dropped to his knees. The other two boys stood slack-mouthed and slowly backed away. Grace ran and did not look back, but as she reached the front of the gym, she heard a familiar voice.

"Hey, tough girl. If you're going my way, I just might decide to tag along."

"You... you saw that fucking shit back there?" Grace's heart raced and she was unsure whether she was angrier at Luna or the three fuckwads.

"Uh huh, I surely did."

"Then why didn't you do something?"

"From where I stood, it looked like you settled things just fine."

Odd, Grace thought later, that she and Luna had erupted in laughter; a shared celebration of mutual respect for girl strength; owning and protecting one's body.

The spring day was unseasonably hot and humid, as if Mother Nature had a grudge to settle with her selfish earthly inhabitants. Grace's tee was plastered to her sweat-sour body and the hot asphalt burned through the thin soles of her shoes, forcing her to walk in fresh patches of sandspurs beside the roadway.

Ahead at the motel, Luna slouched in one of the two webbed chairs at the pool. Grace thought maybe she too harbored the notion of cooling off in an actual pool of cool water. Luna had begun to show Grace a friendlier attitude, and she respected the girl's steely cut, and understood that beneath all her toughness dwelled a fierce sense of loyalty. Grace wanted to earn that kind of respect; the promise of loyalty.

"Hey, why are you out here in this heat? AC busted again?" Grace called ahead.

"Naw, machine's doing what it can against this hell." Luna squinted against the sun's white glare.

"Yeah, I'm sweating like a two-dollar... oh, shit, I'm sorry. Didn't mean nothing against...." The word "whore" was mean, but it was the way Luna referred to her mother when she was angry. Which was most of the time.

Luna was clearly enjoying Grace's embarrassment.

"Her life ain't no feather mattress for sure, and with Fat Joseph, she's got to do all the heavy lifting." Her tone lightened somewhat, but she didn't smile.

Uncomfortable with the idea that Luna spoke so easily of her mother's relationship with Fat Joseph, Grace turned away, focusing her attention for the moment on a lone brown dog trotting along the edge of the highway. The bag of bones dog stopped now and again for morsels of food torn from scattered food wrappers that littered the roadside.

Grace flopped down on the second chair. She stared across the empty tar road and watched heat rays that were like so many feathered dancers, wondering how Luna could be so honest about her mother and what she was. While referring to *her*, and never *Mother*. Maybe that was part of what happened when a kid gave up on a failed parent.

"Your Mom's not just a drunk. She's certifiable, ain't she?" There was no animus. Just honesty, and Grace no longer felt the need to lie.

"Yeah, but when she's on her meds and not drinking she's... better than you know her. There're times when she's good... even fun. And our dad gets to come home. Viewed from a distance, we passed for a normal family."

"This surely ain't one of them times, right?" Luna looked toward the road and Grace followed her gaze. The brown dog was a vanishing dot moving toward the empty horizon.

"No," Grace answered. "It's not. Maybe her worst."

"You still mean to save her?" Luna's smooth skin wrinkled at her temples in a way Grace took as deeply held doubt.

"You saying something's wrong with that?" Grace felt her heat rising.

"No, 'cause there are no shortcuts to knowing we can't save somebody. 'Specially one we keep wanting to love in the face

of all the bad shit they do." She paused. "If saving worked…
then we could cut short a whole lot of hurtful trying."

"You do know you ain't making a lot of sense." Grace
wanted Luna to be wrong.

"Yeah, and it's likely that you aren't ready to hear sensible."

Luna was right that she did not know what to think, but
she knew how to hope.

"What's this daddy of yours like? Looks like your mama's
running from something or somebody, and you two got
dragged along."

"No, Daniel's nothing like that. Mom lied and got a judge
to put a restraining order on him. But it's up now. And we're
not exactly running, but we're hiding from him and our aunt.
Mom brought us here all on her own."

"Daniel?" Luna squinted and tilted her head in a way that
called for more.

Grace shrugged. "Only because my sister has a different
daddy. He's a secret, though from who all I'm not sure."

Luna crossed her arms over her chest and exhaled slowly.

"Don't remember nothing about my daddy. *She* claims
I was just two when he last split. Said he was a pretty man.
What she knew of his parents was that my grandmother was
a mulatto and her husband an illegal, dark-skinned Mexican.
But it must have been the black that counted. She said it was
the reason he beat her whenever cracker shit happened."
Luna snorted through flared nostrils. "Joked that between the
beating and the loving, hardly left time for the black and blue
to heal."

Grace nodded, working to hide her gratitude that Daniel
was never mean like Luna's daddy.

"You still talk to this fine daddy of yours?"

"Don't have a phone anymore."

"What? The lowest redneck around here's got themselves
a phone."

"We've moved around a lot." Grace explained that she no longer had a paid cell phone account.

"Well shit, girl, if you ask me, that's bad messed up. It ain't safe around here." She took her phone from her pocket. "This fine phone's 'bout all I've ever got out of *her* nasty mess with *him*." Luna got to her feet. "And me, I ain't 'bout to do none of that mess she does. I'll slit that mad dog's throat first." Luna walked away, her laughter joyless.

— 72 —

Grace

On Grace's last day as student librarian, Ms. Pidgeon, the librarian, said pleasant things about her work and invited her to return next term, should her situation permit. Hearing praise felt good, but she wished the librarian had omitted the part about her *situation*. Was it naivety or willful self-deception to have ever thought she could keep such a secret? But the librarian had no way of knowing that Mom was drinking more heavily than ever. Just last week, Mom had again failed to meet Zoey at the bus drop and had left her frightened sister to walk to the motel on her own, only to find the door locked. Unable to rouse Mom from her drunken stupor, Zoey sat outside on the curb, waiting for an hour alone.

Grace approached the motel and what she saw ahead terrified her. Zoey sat across Fat Joseph's knees, eating a fast-melting chocolate bar.

Zoey looked up and, seeing Grace, smiled and waved.

Grace ran across the parking lot, imagining all the horrors that could have befallen her sister, her burning hatred for Fat Joseph so intense, he seemed aflame.

"Zoey, get down, now! What the hell are you thinking?" Grace grabbed Zoey's upper arm and shook her hard.

"What'd I do?" Zoey pleaded her innocence, at once breaking Grace's heart and horrifying her.

Glaring at Fat Joseph, Grace screamed into his sweaty face, "Don't you ever touch my sister again!"

"Ah now, big sister. It's just a candy bar." He looked at Zoey in a way that caused Grace's blood to boil, and she understood the impulse to kill.

Zoey's hand in hers, Grace banged on the room door and shouted until Mom staggered to the door.

"Good God, Grace. I'm sleeping here. What's all the damn fuss about?"

Mom stared at Zoey's face, and the chocolate melting in her hand. She spotted Fat Joseph walking into the next room, and he looked back at her like Jimmie toying with a mouse before closing the door behind him.

In that moment, it was as though Mom was entirely lucid. She picked up the chair he had been sitting in and repeatedly banged it against the door, screaming profanities and threats. She swore that if he ever came near either of her daughters, she would knife him in his sleep. Emotionally drained, her knees buckled, and she slumped against the wall.

Zoey was now screaming, her hands pressed against her ears, and Mom was blithering regrets through her wretched sobbing. Grace stood as though in the midst of a flaming pit of hellfire, yet her heartbeat slowed to a calmer rhythm of terror as she realized what she must do now.

— 73 —

Grace

Grace watched for Luna to come from the room next door. When she did, she slammed the door behind her, went straight to the vending machine and fed it quarters, retrieving two candy bars. Grace had learned to measure Luna's anger by the number of candy bars she withdrew.

Grace called, and at the sound of her name, Luna turned and saw her.

"Hey girl, you want some of this shit?" She held out the last of the loose quarters in her palm. "That damn fool still pays me to disappear. Like he thought I'd want to stay and watch." Her jaw was set hard. Her eyes were icy hot with fury.

She unwrapped the first candy bar and bit into it with vengeance. "I ain't got no fucking idea why she ain't slit his throat." She studied Grace. "But we both know that ain't why you're here."

"Right, I mean no. I need to use your phone. I've gotta call my dad." Grace glanced toward the office where Mom was distracted, lambasting a defenseless FedEx driver, who likely sped back to his employer and quit.

"So, it finally took that candy bar, right?"

Grace nodded, fighting back tears. Crying made her feel especially weak.

"Funny, ain't it, how something as sweet as chocolate can trap the innocent. Open the eyes of others." Luna took the phone from her pocket and handed it to Grace. "I'll take my business elsewhere. Maybe there." She pointed to the office as the delivery man hurried toward the door. She winked and strolled into the office.

Grace walked into the bright sunlight and stared in the direction of the interstate.

"Dad… it's me. Please come right away and get me and Zoey."

He repeated her name between gulps of air, and they each openly sobbed. When she had given him directions, he asked, and she answered.

"No, Mom doesn't know. And Dad, please hurry." She worried that if Mom were to learn of her call, she would panic and attempt to outrun his arrival.

She walked back to where Luna now waited on the breezeway.

"He coming? Your daddy, I mean?"

"Yes, and Zoey can't know," Grace answered between hiccups.

"That's good, and I promise there ain't nothing happening to y'all before then."

Despite a lifetime of broken promises, Grace knew in her gut that she could trust Luna. She took a deep breath, and together they walked away from the office and took seats in the remaining two chairs near the sand pit.

"Here, don't you want your phone back?" Grace laughed between sobs that caught in her throat.

"Sure as shit, girl. Me and this phone, we ain't parting." Luna smiled and for the first time Grace could remember, she felt someone was looking out for her. She handed her the phone and said what she'd imagined never saying. "I think I love you, Luna Garcia."

"Oh yeah? You sure you ain't just being grateful?"

"That, too," Grace answered and when Luna smiled, Grace felt something pass between them; a deeper feeling new to her, but welcome.

— 74 —

Josey

Through her narrow kitchen window, Josey watched an angry sky grow more ominous with the approach of an afternoon thunderstorm. She paused from scrubbing potatoes to watch a lone magnolia leaf twist in a gust of wind and rip from its mooring, left to float aimlessly to the ground.

Since her sister and nieces' disappearance more than a year ago, much of Josey's existence had drifted between hopeless days and restless nights. She rose in the predawn hours, in advance of her duties as wife and mother, to resume her computer search for clues to where Leah and her nieces might be found. But everywhere she looked had proven to be a dead end. They had simply vanished beyond the reach of her repeated searches.

Daniel's obsessive returns to the Hopkins Street Shelter and its sprawling neighborhood had failed to bear fruit, until his chance meeting with an old street woman who claimed to have known a strange woman and her two daughters, whom she described as well-mannered guests. But the mother had taken the girls away in search of an old car. Daniel returned a second time, wishing to learn more about Leah and the girls, but he was told by a sad man who wore dark glasses and used a cane that the woman Daniel sought was dead. The tearful man offered only that he had found her dead, the faded photo of two young boys clutched in her hand. Simon confessed to having never believed that the photo was of her sons but was only a discarded photo Ms. Babe had claimed as her own. Neither Josey nor Daniel had known the woman, yet her loss had felt in an odd way like their one connection to Leah and the girls had been severed.

A flash of lightning delivered a loud thunderclap, rattling the windowpane, and rain fell in solid sheets. Josey watched as rainwater puddled in bare spots across the back lawn and was reminded of Leah's childhood fear of drowning, even in a thunderstorm. She had sought refuge in the darkness of a bedroom closet until Josey persuaded her that it was safe to come out.

Since losing his family, Daniel had grown even thinner, with sunken cheeks and hollow eyes. Josey worried that he dwelled inside his grief and was becoming more of an apparition of himself than real. The odd jobs at which he worked were physically demanding and made more difficult by little or no sleep. He missed meals or picked up unhealthy fast foods, most often eaten during nightly searches that frequently stretched into the early mornings. He went days without showering, his uncut hair curled over his collar, and never seemed to have clean clothes.

Although Daniel had to no measurable degree lessened his quest to find Leah and their daughters, Josey had recently noticed subtle changes for the better in Daniel's overall wellbeing. He remained skin and bones, but his weight loss had abated. He had cut his hair, his personal hygiene returned to normal, and his clothes were regularly washed. His overall appearance was that of a man wishing to please a woman.

Josey's religious teaching told her that adultery was a mortal sin, but she vacillated on just how harshly to judge Daniel's betrayal, if her suspicion was correct. Her poor sister was a serial adulterer who had conceived a child Daniel had welcomed and loved as his own. Though, as she had often said to her quarreling kids, two wrongs never make a right.

Perhaps what she truly felt was her own guilt over longing for something more than the emptiness she felt in surrendering her own dreams to those of her husband and family. Three children in the first seven years of her and Robert's marriage meant her ambition to become a nurse had been set aside for a future time that had yet to arrive.

Josey drained the boiled potatoes, added butter and seasoning to make mashed potatoes. Glancing at the clock hanging from the wall above the stove, she checked the meatloaf, estimating the time she had to herself before Robert came through the door, expecting her to have supper waiting. Other than its sentimental value, her mother's clock was an inheritance much too ordinary to be more than an object of obsolescence. She had come to think of the clock as a reflection of her own dated role as mother and wife.

Her cell pinged, but in her haste to finish preparing supper, she let Daniel's call go to voicemail, pausing only to consider that his calling at this hour was unusual. He normally waited until later, when her household had settled. But second thoughts about returning his call were overridden by the sound of Robert's truck. Any minute now, the silence she had welcomed would be replaced by her husband and their three explosive teenagers bounding through the front door.

The last of the food was on the table and everyone was settled when the doorbell sounded. The kids looked to Robert, who forbade them to have friends call or stop by during the supper hour, ironically arguing in favor of uninterrupted family time.

"Everyone stay right where you are," he demanded.

Josey remembered Daniel's unanswered phone call, and despite Robert's hard glare, she sent Jake to answer the door.

Jake called back that Uncle Daniel was at the door and that he was asking for her.

"What the hell!" Robert shouted. "Tell him to turn that rattletrap truck around and hit the road. He's not wanted around here."

"Don't you dare." Josey pushed up from the table and hurried to the door.

"I called earlier. I can't wait any longer." Daniel's eyes were blood-red and swollen.

Josey felt faint. "Merciful Jesus, Daniel. Tell me what's happened."

"Grace." He wiped his tears on the sleeve of his shirt.

Robert came from the kitchen, glared at Daniel, and yelled a stream of profanity Josey ignored. Purse in hand, she followed Daniel to his idling truck and never looked back.

— 75 —

Grace

Leah came into the room where her daughters sat on their neatly made bed. Zoey clutched Jimmie, and Grace held the two long over-due library books she planned to return in the hope of reactivating her library card. They had stuffed their few clothes and personal items into a plastic bag that lay on the floor at their feet. Grace reached for Zoey's hand; their readiness stamped on their drawn faces, their bodies tense.

Leah stepped around the bag and sat on the bed opposite the two girls. She folded trembling hands tightly in her lap. "And tell me, my darlings, where do you two think you're going without your mother?"

Leah's disposition was hurt, rather than the outrage Grace had prepared herself to resist. Feeling herself swayed by her mother's familiar aggrieved tone, Grace blurted out before she lost her courage.

"Mom... Dad's coming for us. This is a dangerous place." Her voice was barely more than a whisper and her words were not those she had rehearsed. She jammed her clammy hands into her armpits.

Leah scanned the breadth of the room, as though she was seeing its squalor for the first time, and she smiled. "You're so right. We must paint... cheerful colors. And, yes, new matching bedspreads. Maybe add a more comfortable side chair." She paused as if she imagined the transformation in all its promised pleasantness.

"Yes, we can make it beautiful again. I'm sure it was once, so why not now?"

"Mom, please. It's not just the room. It's everything. We have to go now, before it's too late." Her effort to conceal her distress with determination was a rubber band stretched to its limit.

"God, Grace, you are so like your unimaginative father. You'll see that I am right. All will be... better." Leah's voice was raspy, and her dismissal frightened Grace.

"Please... Mom. I know how hard you've tried, and it's not your fault. But you have to know Fat Joseph forces young girls into prostitution." In her mind, Grace had forever exempted Luna from all that was wrong with the second floor.

"That has nothing to do with us. We are safe here. He promised."

"No, Mom, we were safer on the streets." Grace fought back her panic. "This time won't be like before. We'll know what to expect."

"No, Grace! You promised! Dad is coming for us!" Zoey hugged Jimmie so close the cat yowled.

Mom turned to Grace, her expression pensive. "And you... you would do that for me?"

"Yes, I swear." Grace's heart ached at the thought of betraying her dad, but she would live with her guilt if only Mom could be persuaded.

"Yes, of course you and your sister must go." Leah stood and took the bag of clothes from the floor, opened the door, and set it outside on the walkway. She turned and said, "Wait outside for your father."

"But Mom...."

"There will be no more talk. You two must go now, before my madness returns." Leah crossed her arms over her breasts and her body slumped. Grace remembered the same sense of vulnerability when her mom had stood before her naked and frightened, and Grace had dressed her and comforted her as though she were a child. Was her mother frightened by her illness yet somehow reconciled to its inevitability?

Her sister's hand in hers, Grace stepped from the room and onto the walkway. Behind them, she heard the sound of the lock. Grace fingered the room key she had slipped into her pocket. A second door opened, and Grace and Zoey turned toward the sound.

"Hey, though I'd keep y'all company." A baseball bat rested on Luna's broad shoulder. "That's if you don't mind." Her face glistened in the weak light. She carried a blanket in her hand.

The three waited on the breezeway where oncoming traffic was visible for a long way out, and among them there was little need for talk. A late afternoon shower had turned the night air into a perfect dome of humidity, yet the refreshing scent of overgrown grasses filled the air.

Zoey grew tired and slept on the folded blanket, her head and shoulders resting on the bag of clothes.

Grace slipped her hand into Luna's.

An approaching set of headlights shone from the state highway, and they watched a vehicle slow as it approached the motel road sign. Grace's heart pounded from an overwhelming sense of both guilt and relief.

— 76 —

Daniel

Daniel spotted the hotel sign and cried out, "There!" He pulled off the state road onto what was no more than a rough right-of-way that led to the motel. Its dim, sputtering neon sign and near-empty parking lot caused his stomach gases to lurch into his throat.

Josey slid to the edge of the seat, her hands braced against the dash, and she swore. "Holy shit, what kind of place is this? It looks like hell's back door."

Daniel saw the squatty building for what it was, and he felt the dread of Leah, entrenched, watching him from one of the twelve rooms. He wanted the girls in the truck and away before Leah could summon the local cops, crying that he intended to kidnap *her* daughters.

Grace, Zoey, and another girl were caught in the bright glow of headlights and Grace and Zoey ran toward the truck as it slowed. Daniel felt his heart would explode as he jumped from the truck. He and his girls embraced. Their pounding hearts were once more in rhythm with his, and it was as though his months of horror, waking in a cold sweat, terrified that he would never hold them again, evaporated. Josey stood next to the truck, sobbing so hard she was speechless, and Daniel reluctantly released the girls into her embrace.

Grace resisted his efforts to guide her toward the truck and instead pulled free.

"I won't leave Mom. She's sick. She could die if we leave her here alone."

"Grace, please let me get you and Zoey to safety first. And then I swear I'll come back for your mom." No matter how much pain he'd suffered, he would not leave Leah here sick and alone.

"You and Aunt Josey take Zoey. I'll wait here with Mom until you come back."

"No, Grace, we're going to leave this hell together."

Josey spoke to Daniel. "Put Zoey and that damn cat and the girl's stuff in your truck. When you have, come back. I'll need your help, but I want you to wait outside the door. Grace, you come with me."

Josey did not knock but used Grace's key to unlock the door. She stepped into the room, Grace behind her, and gagged at the smell of urine and whiskey. An empty bottle lay next to Leah's wasted body, and she was drawn into a fetal position. She did not move at the sound of their entry.

"Oh God, please. Is she unconscious?" Josey bent over Leah and crooned the way she might to one of her children. "Leah, sweetheart, it's me, baby." She checked Leah for a pulse while repeatedly whispering her name. "Leah, I've come to take you home. Come with me now and we'll make all this go away."

Leah did not respond.

"Grace, do you know if she took something with that whiskey?"

"No Ma'am. I think she's just drunk."

"You think? But can you find out?"

"Maybe. The woman she gets stuff from lives next door."

"Then go ask her now."

Grace returned and reported that Mom had not gotten drugs from Ms. Juniper in the last two days. Leah moaned and stirred slightly but did not open her eyes.

"I've lost my babies. I must find them." Her face was awash in fresh tears.

Josey cradled Leah in her arms and spoke softly against her ear. "Oh honey, your babies aren't lost. Come with me and I'll take you to them."

"I can no longer care for them. You must take them away with you."

Josey attempted to help Leah sit, but she slumped back on the bed. Josey called for Daniel, who was waiting outside the door, as instructed. She told Grace to gather what was left of Leah's things and put them in the truck.

Josey cleaned Leah up a bit and when she had done what she could, she wrapped her in a nasty top sheet from the other bed. Daniel lifted Leah into his arms, carried her from the room, and placed her on the back seat of the Impala. Her head rested on Grace's lap and Josey handed Grace the ice bucket from the room and two damp towels, warning her that the road motion was likely to make her mother sick.

Daniel took the tire iron from the Impala, walked to the room next door, and pounded on the door until a girl opened it. A quick look told him that the man he meant to beat within an inch of his sorry life was likely hiding in the bathroom.

"Go on and get him out here or I'm coming in." His anger was so intense it blinded him.

"Mister, he ain't due back until morning. But if you'll leave me that iron, I promise I'll do us both a favor. Catch him in his sleep and take pleasure in scattering his fucking brains. What do you say? Deal?"

Daniel studied her and knew she had her own reasons for wanting the man dead, but she was no more a killer than he was.

"You're right. If you want, we've got room for one more."

"No, I thank you, but I've got my own way of leaving."

Grace looked back at the horror they were leaving behind and saw Luna standing on the breezeway. Grace lowered the window and called to her, but she did not return her wave. Maybe Luna's survival rested on her distrust of what she believed was fleeting human sentiment. Still, Grace swore she would someday come back for her.

Josey drove the Impala onto the interstate, and Daniel followed closely behind. He felt a keen sense of relief from what had been his fear that someone would attempt to prevent their escape. He had no idea just how deeply Leah was embedded in the evil he had witnessed back at that motel. He breathed deeply, exhaled slowly, and relaxed his grip on the steering wheel. He looked over at Zoey who had, for her, remained too quiet.

"You okay, partner?" He forced a smile.

"Why couldn't Mom stay back there?"

"What do you mean? Your mom's real sick. She needs us to take care of her. That's what families do."

"But I don't want to be her family. I'm scared. And I don't want to stay with her."

"I know back there had to be scary. But Mom always gets better, and things get easier,"

"That's what you always say, but it's a lie." She turned away from him and stared out the window as an empty landscape framed the window.

"I know it can feel that way...."

She continued to stare out the window, and he did not have the heart to continue.

– 77 –

Grace

Despite Robert's angry protest, Josey had made room for Leah and the girls to crowd in with her family of five. Although no one pretended to be happy with what was referred to as the *temporary situation*, which was well into its third month, everyone, with the exception of Robert and Jake, worked at getting along. Leah had gotten sober and was back on the expensive meds Daniel had thus far managed to purchase. When Leah was well enough to hold down temporary employment and earn money, she contributed toward her and the girl's portion of the household expenses. Leah and Daniel's joint earnings were not enough to afford a place of their own.

Grace felt that even in the mounting chaos that was her family's situation, there was much to like about windows without plywood covers, neighbors who did not gawk, and two good meals a day that Aunt Josey always prepared and served on time. Grace no longer needed to wash smelly bed linens. The house smelled the way Grace thought of as normal, except for Jake's dumb boy farting, stinky sneakers, and Zoey forgetting to empty Jimmy's litter box.

Grace and Zoey had the luxury of clean clothes daily, and they shared an air mattress Grace inflated and placed on the floor at night, deflated and put away in the morning. Their cousins Lucy and Jenny had no choice but to share their bedroom. The best part of their living with her aunt was that Grace slept unafraid through the night, and Aunt Josey helped with encouraging Mom to stay on her meds. It meant she and Mom argued less.

Grace enrolled in her cousin's school, which offered advanced classes, though Grace had accepted her dream of studying marine biology on an academic scholarship would demand she work harder than ever, plus a miracle. Her enrollment while living at the motel had meant easy top grades but her current GPA was in the toilet. Still, she was determined to earn high grades in advanced classes. A quiet space to study in a household of eight with limited rules was a challenge.

Although Mom had not sought to renew the restraining order, she still refused to let Dad visit, so he met Grace and Zoey at a park near Aunt Josey's weekly grocery shopping route. They talked about their new schools, and when he remembered, he asked if she was making new friends. The fact that she and her cousins were in different classes meant that Grace came in contact with none of their friends. Zoey was enrolled in her final year in elementary school.

Grace often thought of Luna and felt the sting of her loss in a way she had not expected. The cell phone number she had committed to memory was no longer in service. The letter she sent to the motel address came back stamped return to sender. The scribbled note across the unopened envelope read: *gone no forwarding address*. Grace had put the returned letter into the tin box she kept hidden in the outdoor shed, along with her meager savings from money she earned weeding a neighbor's flower beds and walking her old dog. In the event of future homelessness, she did not want to be caught penniless.

In the first month after they moved in with Aunt Josey, Dad had continued to press Grace with questions about Mom's sobriety and whether she was staying on her meds. He sometimes spoke of their chances of reuniting as a family. But now he mostly asked about Mom's state of mind and said less about plans for their getting back together.

Aunt Josey continued to defend Mom against Uncle Robert, but she could not hold out forever against his determination to be rid of the three of them. Just now, from the utility room where Grace was folding laundry, she overheard his latest threat coming from the kitchen.

"Mark my word, she'll piss away even the jobs she gets now, such as that are. And I ain't picking up the tab. I didn't marry the weird bitch. Your saintly Daniel did."

"Robert, please, can't you at least see she's trying. And Daniel's doing all he can to earn extra money so they can afford a place of their own."

"Word is he's shacked up with some rich whore. And I bet he ain't looking hard."

"Daniel would never do such a thing. He loves Leah and those girls. He's proven it over and over again."

"What is it with you two, anyway?"

A chair scraped across the kitchen linoleum, the back door slammed, and as the roar of his truck faded in the distance, his fury remained in the air. Grace believed Robert's lie was leftover bitterness about Dad quitting his job at Uncle Robert's shop. And Aunt Josey was right; Dad would never be unfaithful to Mom or leave her and Zoey, though Grace felt the fate of her family, and her own future, would be forever fraught with uncertainty.

— 78 —

Grace

Mom burst into the girls' shared bedroom and announced that tomorrow they would take a day trip to the beach. Mom took her phone from her pocket and handed it to Grace.

"Call your father. I know you girls have missed him. Tell him he's invited. Oh, and he's to drive us."

On the third ring he answered, his voice tense. "Grace, what a... surprise. Are you and Zoey okay? You have a phone?"

"No, but Mom is here and said I should tell you that you're invited to the beach with us tomorrow, and she wants you to drive."

"Uh, the beach... tomorrow. Yeah, right... that would be... great. But are you sure?" Grace believed she heard a woman's voice in the background and decided that she had interrupted him on a job. Mom's sudden change of heart, while welcome, was a bit nerve-wracking. Neither she nor Dad wanted to be hurt by Mom going back on her word.

"Okay, baby, if you're sure... it's... great." They settled on a time for him to pick them up. Grace apologized if she had gotten him in trouble with his customer. But he had already left the call.

Mom motioned for Grace to return her phone. Though Mom was totally wrong to not allow her a phone, Grace dared not risk a fuss. Not now anyway.

"And how did your father seem?" Her lips were pressed together in a slight grimace and Grace wanted to reassure her.

"Excited. Real happy. Surprised, I think. But happy." She blushed. To her ear, her gushing never sounded earnest.

Still, Mom smiled broadly. "Now, the three of us must have new swimsuits. We leave in ten minutes."

Grace was encouraged that Mom wanted to look her best, now that Dad was coming, but a shopping spree created the risk of a repeat of their past misadventures. A wrong outcome could undermine Mom's present mood and torpedo the day.

Zoey, who had said nothing thus far, sighed deeply. "Is that forever?"

Grace shrugged. "With Mom, there is no forever."

Grace was just as unsure about Mom's sudden change of heart, and she dared not wish for much, though a day at the beach might become a first step in Mom allowing Dad back into the family. If so, maybe it wasn't too much to believe that they might leave Aunt Josey's for a place of their own.

— 79 —

Grace

Grace woke Sunday morning to the sound of rain, her disappointment so intense she shuddered. Her anguish was made worse by the fact she had no sensible target for how she felt. Shitty luck was just that, and there was nothing to do but accept her fate.

Zoey, who had insisted on sleeping in her new bathing suit, opened her eyes and moaned. "Oh no, Aunt Josey's God is hateful." Her pouty lower lip matched Grace's mood.

"Yeah, well, blaming God is crazy talk." Grace flung back the covers and went to the window. Her view of the nearest streetlight was nearly obliterated by the rain.

The sound of hurried footsteps approached along the hallway, and the bedroom door flew open. Mom stood in the doorway wearing her new yellow swimsuit. She had begun to put back on a bit of weight, and she looked good. She called for Grace and Zoey to get up and get dressed.

"But Mom...."

"Yes, it's raining here, but not there. And I have that on good authority." She handed Grace her phone. "Call your father, then grab your beach bags and pack plenty of sunscreen." She then reminded them to wear their raincoats over their suits. She laughed, and maybe it was her own foolishness that amused her.

Grace took the phone from Mom's hand and checked the weather. The radar showed nothing but rain along the west coast from Cedar Key to Naples. Still, Grace stepped into the next room and made the call.

"Dad," she whispered. "Mom says we're going to ignore the rain."

"Uh, what the... oh, shit." Then he muttered something about the sky falling. His voice sounded as though he scraped clogged gravel from his throat. And before he could ask, she answered that they were fine. Mom said he was still to come for them.

"Give me a minute... and I'm on my way." There was an indistinct sound. Maybe a second muted voice, as though he held his hand over the speaker. Or maybe he dropped his phone. Dad often slept overnight in his truck.

— 80 —

Daniel

The thunderstorm left a refreshed landscape in its wake and Daniel considered the miracle of nature; its suddenness of mood, power, and unmatched beauty. Despite the awkwardness of their initial greeting, he had wrapped himself in the good he felt in Leah's unusually quiet presence and the girls' chatter of anticipation.

At Zoey's inevitable chanting of *are we there yet* when he slowed the truck and eased onto the beach roadway, Daniel glanced across at Leah and she smiled. Granted, it was no longer the smile he once cherished, but his memories of their early years were strong.

Daniel had brought a red beach umbrella and ice chest filled with water and juice, and they joined an unbroken line of multi-colored umbrellas and tents stretched along the water's edge. Waves at high tide broke along the shoreline. Leah and Zoey, hand in hand, made a game of outrunning the breaking surf. Grace followed Daniel into the water, and when he stood armpit deep, she climbed onto his broad shoulders. Holding her nose against the sting of saltwater, she repeatedly jumped from his shoulders into the breaking waves. When they tired, she joined Leah and Zoey, who were digging in the wet sand, searching for coquina clams.

Daniel stood knee-deep in the breaking surf and motioned for Leah to join him in a swim, but she shook her head and wrapped her arms about her torso as she backed away. Daniel leaned forward, his hands resting on his knees, before turning to Zoey, who eagerly splashed into the surf. Grace sat with Leah on the blanket and watched him swim with Zoey.

After a morning of diving, swimming, and digging for clams that in the end Leah freed from the bucket of water, everyone was starving. For lunch, they choose an outdoor café named Fanny's Boathouse Grill.

— 81 —

Ellie

Ellie scanned the green waters of the bay to where it met the blue-grey depths of the ocean, and beyond. A covey of tiny sanderlings scurried along the shoreline in search of morsels of food washed ashore by incoming waves. Ellie reached and took Jordan's hand in hers and smiled.

"What makes you smile?" Jordan asked, glancing in the direction of a parade of scampering fiddler crabs.

"You. Our being here, surrounded by such beauty, always makes me smile." She squeezed Jordan's hand and leaned into her shoulder. Jordan reached and put an arm around Ellie's shoulders and drew her closer. Ellie felt the promising sensation of forever; its safety and a level of contentment she had never known before Jordan.

Ellie looked at Jordan, pleasure in her broad grin. "And what are you thinking?"

"That maybe we should turn for home? I'm thinking the bedsheets may have cooled."

Ellie laughed. "Ah, yes, there's that in due time, but first, you did promise me lunch."

"I do believe you mean to hold me to my promise."

Ellie thought of her and Jordan's six-year marriage as a period of deep emotional growth: a time in which she had unraveled some of her more disappointing and painful earlier relationship choices. Her brief marriage to Wallace, a man she found pleasing enough, had started badly and their short, two-year marriage never rebounded. Their divorce was amicable, and in retrospect, she believed she may have loved him, and he her, but never in the way she came to know her and Jordan's abiding love.

They reached the southern tip of the island, known to locals as the place of sunbaked tourists and weekend spoilers, and as expected, it was crowded with loud beachgoers. They selected a table beneath the outdoor canopy.

Neither she nor Jordan needed to see a menu. They would have their standard orders of medium-sized shrimp, battered and deep-fried, Jordan's with a basket of hot, deep-fried hushpuppies, and both with Fanny's garden-fresh house salad. Gloria, co-owner with her husband and in-a-pinch waiter, glanced their way, waved, and gave a welcoming thumbs up.

A young girl, maybe ten or eleven, with a mass of bright curls, approached and without a word to Jordan, stared at Ellie, and it was clear from her ease that she recognized Ellie.

She squinted at Jordan and frowned. "I know you. You were nice to my mom when she got in trouble with the boss at the shelter. Mom doesn't like you, but my sister and I do."

Jordan smiled. "Thanks, and that's okay about your mom. I'm not mad at her."

Zoey nodded, letting out a slow breath, seeming relieved.

Ellie realized with a jolt where she had first seen the child. She was equally stunned that her connection to Leah had unexpectedly resurfaced, and in Jordan's presence. Ellie's nagging uneasiness regarding her decision to euthanatize the two dogs had dulled after her discovery of the erroneous records of the dogs' deaths. But Jordan was certain to ask how she knew Zoey.

Ellie looked for Leah among the restaurant patrons, but she was nowhere to be seen. She was poised to suggest that Zoey return to her parents when a tall slender man wearing dated swim trunks and a stained *Save the Earth* tee approached the table. He apologized for his daughter's intrusion and introduced himself as Daniel, Zoey's dad.

"Your daughter is a pleasure," Ellie said, and introduced herself and Jordan.

Daniel nodded to Jordan, and then quickly turned his attention back to Ellie.

Ellie noticed the slight change in Jordan's demeanor that she recognized as Jordan's cop sensibility; a memory or connection to a name, place, or event. Did Jordan know Daniel, and if so, was she also at least acquainted with Leah? But how exactly, and to what extent? Daniel swallowed hard and his nervousness was evident. It appeared that he either knew nothing of her and Leah's secret or if he did, he chose, though awkwardly, discretion.

Ellie cleared her throat, surprised by her own awkwardness.

Zoey pointed toward an empty table and frowned. "Where did Mom and Grace go?"

"Maybe they've gone for the ice cream you like so much." He smiled at Zoey and thanked Ellie and Jordan for their patience.

As they walked away, Zoey looked back and waved.

"My, that was an odd encounter. I had no idea you were acquainted with Zoey... her sister and their mother," Ellie said.

"Yes, it was strange."

Gloria came with their food and Ellie was grateful that the conversation certain to be forthcoming had been delayed. She wanted Jordan's sudden silence to simply mean that she was enjoying her food.

The low tide favored the brown pelicans, gulls, and blue herons gathered on an emerged sandbar to feast on sea creatures trapped between the sandbar and shoreline. The pleasant tidal event she and Jordan routinely enjoyed was, for Ellie, now marred by her dread of having to answer Jordan's inevitable questions. Still, she asked, "How do you know Zoey and her mother?"

Jordan sighed. "I've had two encounters with Leah Killian. Neither good, I'm afraid."

"Really, and when was that? I'm sure you never mentioned Leah or her daughters before now."

"An accident some time back. Remember, I told you that the driver, who I learned later was Leah Killian, was transported to the county hospital's psych ward. Leah had instructed me to notify her dead father of the accident."

"Oh, yes, I remember the incident, but I'm sure you didn't identify Leah by name or mention her daughters."

"I wouldn't have mentioned her name; I was on duty."

"And the other encounter?"

Jordan explained the Hopkins Street fight and admitted to breaking protocol by transporting Leah Killian to a local clinic rather than arresting and jailing her. She included her encounter the next morning with the older girl in Leah's presence. She omitted falsifying her duty record.

"How do you know Killian and her daughters?"

"My involvement is more complicated. Perhaps even illegal."

"Illegal? What are you saying?"

Ellie explained her encounter with Leah and her frightened daughters at the shelter, and her own role in euthanizing the two dogs, leaving nothing unsaid.

"I think a big part of why I remained silent was my fear that if you knew I was responsible for the dogs' deaths, that you, as a police officer, would need to report what you knew could be a crime."

"Have you had contact with Killian since?"

"No, none before today. And it appears she did not even tell her husband."

Jordan nodded. "Maybe, but a shared secret with Leah Killian has got to be risky."

"I know," Ellie said. "And my keeping a secret from you was a mistake. I'm deeply sorry, and you must do that you're drawn to do regarding what I've told you."

"What, if anything, do you know about the Director's actions, shelter records or anything that could tie you to her and the dogs' disappearance?"

Ellie told her what she found in the shelter's records.

"Hmm, that's odd. Let me check if there's a report of stolen dogs matching their description. If they were never reported as stolen, then I am unaware of a crime." Jordan reached and took Ellie's hand. "Next time you're tempted to do good for stolen dogs, which is a crime, please talk with me first."

"I promise." Tears of relief welled up in Ellie's eyes, and they entered the beach path for home.

– 82 –

Daniel

The return trip to the city was subdued. Grace and Zoey, exhausted from the day, dozed in the back seat and Leah had grown quiet. Daniel glanced over at her, but she had turned toward the last light of day as it slipped away. He hoped the day's reprieve from their bitterness would not be lost in her melancholy. Wishing to have misread her silence, he dared to probe her mood.

"A penny for your thoughts." His awkwardness embarrassed him, but in all their time together, he had always been anxious about her long silences.

"I was thinking that you might like to... see more of the girls. They miss you."

"Ah, yes, yes... I've wanted that for so long...."

"Oh, no... not like before for you and me. But more days like today." It seemed she also misunderstood his response.

"And Daniel... is it okay that I cannot promise... more of myself?"

"Yes, it's okay," he whispered.

She slid across the seat and rested her head against his shoulder. Her hand resting on his upper thigh sent a warm erotic shiver through his body, though it was not sex he wanted from her. He felt a sense of clarity between them that was new. It was the thing he had always wanted, that she had been unable to give.

Ahead, a swirling circle of light cut a passage through patches of fog, and overhead a reticent moon showed itself. He kissed her lightly on her head and her damp hair smelled of salt and sunlight.

Fresh Paint
Winter 2020

– 83 –

Daniel

Daniel took the two flights of stairs down to the ground floor and inserted a card bearing Leah's name into the tarnished brass holder. He glanced at the names of other apartment occupants, wanting there to be other families, especially those with kids Zoey's age. Making friends was hard for her, while Grace needed only to raise her hand in class or step onto a basketball court to be noticed.

The one-bedroom apartment with a sleeper sofa had been in only slightly better condition than the motel room where he had found the girls living with their mom, but the landlord had agreed to his offer to paint the apartment throughout in exchange for a reduction in the move-in deposit. Fresh paint had helped to brighten up the space and covered the harsh nicotine odor. He had borrowed a buddy's carpet cleaner and had lessened the odors and stains on the worn carpet, though its worst stains remained. He had rearranged the furniture to cover the most noticeable ones. Sam had scrubbed down the kitchen cabinets and rehung the sagging cabinet doors with new hinges.

For two weeks, he and Sam had worked late into the night and were nearing the end of Daniel's goal to make the apartment move-in ready. Leah and the girls would have a place of their own. Zoey's newly constructed elementary school was six blocks away, but Grace would need transportation to the high school. Still, neither would be required to change schools. In case of an emergency, Josey was a ten-minute drive away.

A weary Sam stopped painting baseboards, stood, and straightened his sore back before slumping into the apartment's one comfortable chair. Daniel stopped rolling the final coat of paint and sat in one of the kitchen chairs. Sam took Daniel's offer of one of the two remaining beers.

"What the hell are we doing here man, except breaking our backs for a bet only slightly better than one of us dating Jennifer Lopez?"

"What're you asking? You know fucking well what I'm doing here, and you're here as God's little helper. What else do you need to know?"

"Okay, for sure I'm here of my own accord. But your notion that she's gonna agree to live here with the kids is tricky shit. And if I'm reading you right, you're still thinking about a future of some sort with Miss Banker." Sam took a hard pull on the beer.

"Fuck you Sam. You're no damn mind reader. And if you're ready to leave, the door is there."

"Hmm. I'll stay a bit longer. Finish those baseboards." He drained the last of the beer, pushed up from the chair and picked up the paintbrush.

Daniel had done all of this against Sam's advice that he would be smart to talk with Leah and the girls first about the move, the apartment building, and the neighborhood. But Daniel had bet on Leah and the girls wanting to get out of Josey's chaotic household enough to agree.

Daniel had paid the move-in deposit and first month's rent, using all of his savings, made possible by his newly acquired full-time employment in a reputable auto dealer's shop at good wages, plus his earnings from odd jobs. If his luck held, he'd earn enough to cover monthly rent and utilities for Leah and the girls. He looked forward to offering Grace and Zoey a small allowance.

Daniel's newfound confidence was bolstered not by logic but his feelings. His conversation with Leah on their drive back from the beach had felt to him like a promise in the making, and the apartment could change everything for the better for him and the girls. Since the beach trip, he and the girls had enjoyed three Friday night outings. And he had taken Leah's ease as an undeclared invitation back into Grace and Zoey's daily lives. The work he and Sam had done on preparing the apartment had further reinforced Daniel's hope that Grace and Zoey would soon know a stable home life; one he could provide.

— 84 —

Daniel

Despite his mounting anxiety as Friday arrived, Daniel took Leah's agreement to join him and the girls for the evening as a good omen. He showered and dressed in good jeans and a freshly laundered sports tee. On leaving the building, he noticed for the first time the fresh graffiti, or what some spoke of as street art, scrawled on the building wall. He remembered the rainbow-colored walkway Leah had painted, and he wondered if it was possible for her to see a new promise in what he had to offer her and the girls.

Daniel called ahead and at the sound of Grace's voice, his spirit was lifted. "Hey gal, you ladies ready for a special outing?" He grimaced at the carnival barker quality of his tone.

"Ugh, Dad. And yeah, you're so fricking amazing at picking movies. Anything's gotta be an uptick."

"Ah, come on, give your old man a break." He had mistakenly assumed *Terminator*, part something or another, was a movie all kids liked. Grace had minced few words in labelling it a male fantasy flick, proven by the fact that he had loved it and she had hated it. He had barely saved the moment by agreeing that future movies would be chosen by her and Zoey. It was never about any movie, but their company.

"So, let's have a clue about the evening," Grace teased.

"Nope, it remains a tightly guarded secret." The more he hyped the evening, the more nervous he became.

"God, Dad, you're so weird you're scary sometimes."

He smiled, relishing what he thought of as a relaxed teenager jawing with a dad she trusted.

"Uh... do you know if...." He hesitated. "If... your mom's still up for the evening?"

"Uh, yeah, I think so. Why're you asking? Did she say something?" There was a familiar tension in their exchange, and he wished he had not asked.

"No, just wondered, that's all." He told her his ETA was ten minutes, joking that formal attire was not required. Grace pretended to be disappointed, and they shared an easy laugh.

He was unsure about the last time he had seen Grace wearing anything he considered "girly dressed up". He thought it might have been when she wore a dress to the funeral service for his mom, held at the small Catholic church his mom had faithfully attended. Grace would have been ten, he thought, and it would have been around the same time Leah had stopped choosing Grace's clothes. Grace still favored worn, boy-cut jeans, sports team tees, hoodies, and sneakers. She claimed her jock attire kept her geekiness at abeyance. Then, Grace was cleverer than him in recognizing the multiple rewards of a more subtle approach.

He admitted to puzzling from time to time on Grace's apparent lack of interest in boys. She declared that boys her age were gross, immature, and stupid. Daniel was certain that at Grace's age he and his buddies had fit her definition. Still, he expected the time would come when Grace would want *the talk* about boys and sex: a conversation he thought better suited to her mom. But he would need to be ready should Leah be unavailable to Grace.

Daniel pulled into the driveway behind Robert's truck and smiled at the sight of Zoey running toward him as he hurried out of the truck.

"Mom's coming, mom's coming," Zoey called ahead, and Daniel worried that her high-pitched, sing-song voice signaled her own tension. She jumped into his outstretched arms and kissed both his cheeks. "That's Italian kissing. But I know we're Irish, right?"

"Yeah, but I think your mom's family may have some Italian. Besides, an international flair is good."

She giggled. "Guess what?"

"You want pizza and soft ice cream?"

"Yes, and Mom's wearing a new skirt and a pretty blouse."

Daniel told himself to stay calm, Leah was coming, and he was prepared. Grace followed Zoey, and after a big hug, she and Zoey got into the back seat and the three waited for Leah.

Daniel drove Leah and the girls into the neighborhood, and for the first time he saw what he believed Leah must see: rows of aging single homes with heavily barred windows. Homes that displayed hand-written signage offering rooms for rent, cheap. A few young kids played in small yards behind chain link fencing, where old women sat on narrow porches in what he knew was a sentinel role. A mix of small businesses were situated among the rows of apartment buildings.

The neighborhood park Daniel had imagined the girls enjoying was dominated by muscular teenage boys with manly upper bodies, stripped to their lean hip joints. Smitten girls, some as young as Zoey, enticed boys to perform amazing feats above the rim. He had grown up in just such a neighborhood and these were the same talented boys, but of a darker hue, that he had admired for their prowess on and off the football fields and basketball courts. Self-assured but careless, boys like himself, destined to betray their natural talents by poor performances in the classroom. He knew their futures, for it had been his; a young man's unschooled, fast and loose crash into manhood.

Grace and Zoey had stoped their excited chatter and sat stiffly in response to the mounting tension in the truck cab. Daniel believed that anything he might offer in defense of the neighborhood Leah would turn into proof that there was nothing promising in bringing her and their daughters here.

Daniel parked and got out of the truck. He stood on the sidewalk, his sweating hands rammed in his pockets, and invited Leah first, and then the girls, to come with him and to have a look at their new apartment. But Leah's gaze was not on him. She was looking at an old man approaching with three young girls. Daniel turned toward the man and they exchanged hesitant nods.

"My God, Daniel, are you blind? Those girls need an escort to walk home. Is that what you've planned for our daughters?"

Daniel felt his despair building, along with anger at Leah's hypocrisy. How could she judge this situation so harshly, after exposing Grace and Zoey to the workings of a whorehouse and her pimp boss? Why could she not see a granddad walking his granddaughters home from school? Or maybe to his place, where the girls stayed with their grandparents until a parent came for them. But he had learned the bitter lesson that confronting Leah would only make matters worse.

Zoey whispered, "I think their granddad looks nice."

"Hold still before she totally blows," Grace whispered back.

"Look, maybe the neighborhood's a bit worn, but the apartment is nothing like you think. And I promise you'll be surprised if you just come upstairs and have a look. That's all I'm asking." Every dime of his savings had been spent on the move-in deposit and what it had taken to fix up the place. If not here, then how could he safeguard his girls against Leah's next crazy scheme?

Leah stared ahead, her arms folded across her chest like a petulant child, and Daniel turned to Grace and Zoey. "Come on girls. I think your mom intends to wait here while we take a look."

Daniel stepped back to the truck and passed the keys through the window, dropping them onto the driver's seat. He was not sure what she meant to do, but right then he could not muster the will to care.

"Zoey, it's okay if you stay with Mom. But I'm going with Dad." Grace reached for the door handle.

"Go, go with him. Both of you. I no longer care what you do." Leah squared her shoulders, but without her usual show of force.

Zoey whispered, "I'm coming with you." She slid off the seat, and she and Grace stood next to Daniel.

Leah moved behind the steering wheel, started the engine, and the truck burst forth onto the street. Zoey slipped her hand into Daniel's and he and the girls watched the truck until it had disappeared from sight before they turned toward the entrance to the building.

– 85 –

Daniel

The man they saw earlier exited the building, and as he drew nearer, he offered Daniel directions to the nearest bus stop, four blocks beyond the park. He remarked on its convenience but added, "Down in here, it hardly ever runs on time."

Daniel thanked him and the man resumed walking.

"She'll come back, right?" Zoey asked, her body rocking back and forth with what was clearly anxiety.

"Don't think so. But don't worry, we'll get a ride," Daniel answered.

Zoey looked up, "Mom's gonna be sorry she didn't believe you." Daniel heard a bit of payback in her tone.

Daniel placed a hand on Zoey's shoulder and smiled. "From your lips to God's ears."

The three entered the building and Daniel dismissed its noticeable scent of aging: layers of peeled paint, lingering smells of unfamiliar foods, and wood decay.

He challenged the girls to a race up the three flights of stairs and played jumping the gun. But Grace twisted around him and stood at the top, looking down at him and Zoey, who was trailing.

"Whew, Dad. You need more exercise." Grace smiled for the first time.

He unlocked the door with the tarnished key he had received, along with a receipt for twelve hundred dollars, and stepped back for the girls to enter. The scent of new paint lingered, but the room was fresh and clean. Grace and Zoey stood in the center of the room that doubled as an all-purpose room and a kitchen, separated by a counter.

"There would have been your mom's bedroom. You two would have needed to share the sofa bed. And the bath is there." He braced himself for their reaction, and when they were slow to respond, he added, "What do you think, a nice picture on the wall here? Maybe pretty curtains in the front window?"

Zoey responded with, "Yes, and we can put up my drawings!"

The bedroom window looked directly onto the brick wall of the adjacent building, and Daniel thought sarcastically that there would have been no need for Leah's demand that the window be covered with plywood.

"I like it, and now we can leave Aunt Josey's, right?" Zoey's smile slowly faded with his hesitation.

"I would've liked that...." He paused. "What I meant to say is I'm happy you... and your sister like the place. But... now that your mom has refused...."

"But why can't we stay here with you? You promised when you got a place we could."

He placed his hand on Zoey's bouncy curls, and she shied away.

"I don't think that would work out... my job and all." His breath caught in his throat at the sight of Grace's reddened face.

"God, Dad, go on and say whatever you want about what Mom will and won't do. But you've given up on us as a family. You had no intention of living here with us! It was your way of dumping me and Zoey and not betraying your image of yourself as a *good dad!* You're no different than Mom! Come on Zoey, we're on our own." Grace turned toward the door.

Zoey stared at her sister and then at him. She dropped onto the floor in a squat, her hands covering her eyes, and she sobbed.

"Jesus, Grace... please." Daniel stood next to Zoey and pleaded with her to stop crying so he could explain. Grace turned back to Zoey, leaned, and spoke quietly to her until she stood and took a seat on the sofa bed.

"Okay, explain, and this time the truth." Grace sat next to Zoey.

"I never told your mom about any part of this before tonight. Nothing. The whole thing started after our trip to the beach. And if I could believe that better things were possible between me and your mom, I'd want this place, or any place, for all of us. But that changes nothing between me and the two of you. I am first, and always, your dad."

"You can forget being with me and Zoey. Everything's fucked now. She won't let us see you anymore. Is that what you wanted?"

"Grace, please, I never intended anything like what happened." But he had always known anything was possible with Leah.

"Right, Dad, you and Mom just blunder into you own shit-making. And never own any part of its stench." Grace sank deeper into the sofa and Daniel pulled a chair from the table, drew it close and waited.

"Can we still go? I'm hungry." Zoey rubbed her red eyes and sniffed.

Daniel was grateful that Zoey's stomach ruled her heart. He took his phone from his pocket. "Hey, man. Me and the girls could use a ride. Yeah, the same, and can you hurry?"

On their way out of the building, Daniel stopped and removed the name card he'd made for the residence's holder.

Grace stood apart from Daniel and Zoey as they awaited Sam's arrival.

– 86 –

Leah

Leah told no one that she no longer expected calls from the temp agency that had last employed her. She still rose early and stood before the bathroom mirror to study her reflection, terrified that her flimsy outer layer would betray her masquerade.

Leah stripped naked, and only when she had lingered long enough to soak away a measure of her anxiety did she step from the tub. She stared at the swirling suction of water circling the drain as a certain sign of her hygienic purification. Its passing left her slightly less weighted by the things she found disgusting about herself. She meticulously applied the proper amount of makeup for the workplace and dressed in office causal; tan slacks and a pale blue blouse that revealed the American beauty rose bud tattoo that adorned the fullness of her breasts.

At the sound of children being hurried from the house, Leah went into the over-heated kitchen and sat at the cluttered table. Her sister was standing at the sink, her wide feet thrust into pink terry cloth slippers, her ankles swollen. Beneath the hem of her loose-fitting housedress, her stout legs were the color of skimmed milk and crisscrossed with an intricate routing of blue veins. Leah envisioned a complex circuitry converging in a massive gridlock at her crotch. Odd that she was once envious of her sister, believing that their mother had favored Josey's plainness over her prettiness. Mother had resented her husband's preference for Leah's company to the exclusion of their elder daughter. But although her father had showered her with affection and attention, Leah had not always wanted such attention. After all, it was he who had passed along his bitter root to sprout in silence. Its earliest buds appeared in her teens and had burst into full bloom after Zoey's birth, a condition that was initially passed off as normal hormonal changes, common after the birth of a child.

"Aren't you running late?"

Leah ignored her sister, for she hated her nosiness. After all, she was an adult, and not one of Josey's lazy children.

On the table, heavily buttered white bread, lumpy oatmeal, and bitter coffee awaited her.

"Just black coffee and unbuttered toast for me, please."

"Leah, honey, you need to eat more." Josey sighed and filled Leah's cup. "And stop taking Robert's newspaper. He'll want the sports page with his coffee. And I'm in no mood for your drama or his bitching."

How could she expected to search the employment section on her ride into the city center without the paper? Even though it was highly improbable that she would find a suitable position. Hiring her at her skill level was not an act of simply filling a vacancy. Positions at her level were either groomed from within or more broadly sought through the services of expert headhunters. Pity that she was no longer a highly sought-after candidate.

Leah ran a finger between the burnt outer wall of the toast and its softer inside. Touching it to her lips, she imagined an accumulation of crumbs residing inside the walls of the toaster, busily spawning a roach infestation. She put the bread back onto the plate and took a sip of the too-strong coffee Robert demanded, declaring that when she bought the coffee, she could have it the way she liked.

Josey crossed the kitchen, her slippers flapping against her crusty heels, and yelled a first call to Robert. She returned and cracked four eggs into a bowl. Robert was an ignorant man with no interests other than sports and what he called his "ruling the roost", as though when he crowed, the entire household clucked their glowing approval. He had fathered children he rarely noticed except to criticize, nor did he properly appreciate his wife. Though Daniel often failed as a husband and provider, he was an attentive father.

"I'll need your share of the grocery money before weekend shopping."

At the sound of Robert's approach, Josey dumped the whipped eggs into a hot skillet and Leah gathered her purse and notebook and left quietly through the front door, Robert's precious newspaper tucked under her arm.

The Messenger
Spring 2021

– 87 –

Leah

The city bus inched along in heavy morning traffic and Leah felt as though she was trapped inside the bowels of a giant slug that slithered across the city, emitting clouds of noxious gases. The bus stopped, and Leah joined those exiting onto a street corner far removed from the corporate wealth and power of the the midtown business district. She hurried toward her favorite used bookstore, the heels of her pumps striking with a business-like sharpness. She avoided the gazes of ragged panhandlers, for she was not part of them. These men and women were yesterday's news, pushed aimlessly about the streets by oily gusts of stifling air.

She would spend the day in the quiet confines of the bookstore, breathing in mold trapped between the pages of thousands of devalued books, sharing with them the humiliation of rejection. Running her fingertips along tattered spines, she would savor the sweet sensation of touch, the tightness of her chest would ease, and her unspilt tears would be swallowed whole.

Entering the store, she was startled by the approach of a stranger who demanded to know how she had gotten in. Leah stared at the boy-man she took to be either a rude customer or possibly an imposter, for she knew most of the store's regular patrons and no one tended to customers other than dear old Mr. Darden, the proprietor.

"What do you mean? I am a regular. And who are you?" She glanced about the store, surprised by the owner's failure to intervene on her behalf. "You need only to inquire of Mister Hemingway." She giggled at the joke she shared with the sweet old man.

"Look, lady, I don't know any Hemingway, but the store is closed." He pointed toward a sign on the opposite side of the door. The stranger spoke with the emphatic tone of an adulterer who had skillfully lied to a peeved wife.

"Nonsense." Leah turned and walked toward the rows of inexplicably empty shelves. "Oh, no, this can't be. What did you do to these books?"

"Look, ma'am, the old man died and his son in Boston sold the inventory to a bookstore in Atlanta. What's left is going into the dumpster out back." He stepped forward, cupped her elbow in a firm grip, and led her out the door.

"No, take your hands off me." She twisted free of his grip. "What's happening here is wrong. This is their home."

"Good God, lady. If you want, you can come back tomorrow when I'm done here and plunder through the dumpster. Take what books you want." Those were his final words before he walked back through the door and locked it behind him.

Leah hurried eight blocks to a dilapidated storage facility and, using the last of her credit, rented a small storage unit and a hand truck. She would rescue as many of the endangered books as possible.

– 88 –

Leah

Fading light began to distort the shapes of the city's tallest buildings as patrons rushed into and out of the city's main library, the curious pausing to stare before moving on. Leah cared nothing for their misguided judgments, born of their ignorant bias as to which literature should be deemed morally unfit to be read publicly from the steps of the city's grand library. Leah had read aloud the most erotic scenes from a book she had selected from her collection of rescued books, although her audience had yet to fully form. Leah concluded her reading with a professional snap of the book and promised more sexually explicit scenes from her favorite, *Beauty and the Trumpian Toad*, by an obscure author of immense talent.

Her sole listener stepped forward. The poor woman possessed a single, fang-like tooth, her breath so vile Leah leaned away and breathed through her mouth. The woman stepped closer and spoke to Leah in a soft, yet confident, voice.

"My brave sister from the universe of the tortured, I come bearing you, and you alone, a message of healing."

"I apologize, but I must go now. You are welcome to return tomorrow." Leah set about gathering her scattered books.

"Watch and believe," the woman said. She waved her thin arms over her head, hands clasped, and spun in tight circles; faster and faster, her presence more an apparition than real. Leah shielded her eyes against the woman's new brilliance as a miraculous transformation unfolded.

The old woman's soiled and ragged street garments were remade into a wedding gown of glowing purity. A youthful smile formed on her rose petal lips, showing a mouth of perfectly formed white teeth. Her golden hair flowed loosely to her slim waist, and her deep blue eyes were translucent. Leah stared at her own reflection in their glow, and her image, too, was transformed to that of her youthful prettiness. Leah dropped onto her knees and kissed the hem of the woman's garment.

"Rise, Sister of the Chosen, and hear the Good News. I am not the Good News, but its humble messenger, bringing word of the magical healing powers of the ancient Whooping Crane."

The Messenger reversed her spin, and the wretched street woman reappeared. Leah watched as the woman limped down the steps. Upon reaching the sidewalk, she drew a thin shawl about her narrow shoulders and vanished into a shroud of emptiness.

The Messenger had filled Leah with purpose, and she continued to flush her daily doses of the mind-destroying chemicals down the toilet, in order to maintain her superb new high. She returned daily to the public library, and although there was no sign of Her return, Leah's faith remained strong. The Messenger's promise of the magical healing powers of the whooping crane solidified with every enlightenment gained from her research of the ancient texts. At closing hour, Leah's legs felt dead, and her feet were swollen, her eyes bloodshot. Yet the sheer wonder and heft of all her new knowledge inspired her daily return.

At the library's closing, Leah gathered her research binders and exited the building, lingering beneath the library's portico. Overhead, a weak half-moon kept her company as she waited, long after the other library patrons had departed, and she was alone. The Messenger was nowhere to be seen, yet Leah felt Her spiritual presence, and she took a seat on a nearby stone bench and continued to wait.

– 89 –

Jordan

Five hours into a graveyard shift, Officer Jordan McCall spit on her index finger and rubbed her eyes. Ahead, she spotted a lone woman hurrying along the sidewalk. She wore a blouse and tailored slacks, unusual for women who frequented these streets late at night. The woman turned toward the sound of the patrol car, her terror caught briefly in the headlights, and she ran, stumbling and falling onto the sidewalk.

Jordan pulled the cruiser to the curb and paused to take note of any potentially threating movement on the street that might explain the woman's panic. Seeing nothing out of the ordinary, she exited the patrol car and, after identifying herself, slowly approached the woman. The woman struggled to regain her feet, and failing her attempt, she groaned and dropped back onto the sidewalk.

"Are you going to shoot me?" Leah raised her hands above her head, the heel of her hand bleeding.

"No, I'm not going to shoot you." Jordan stepped back, giving the frightened woman time to calm herself.

"You... you're a woman. I thought you...." The woman sounded relieved.

"No ma'am, I'm one hundred percent woman." It was not Jordan's first, nor by far her worst, insult.

"Now that you know I'm not going to shoot you, you figure on sitting there until someone you'd rather trust comes along? Like, say, the big dude rounding the corner, there?" She nodded toward the man who had just stepped into the weak circle of light from the dim streetlight.

Upon seeing the patrol car's flashing light bar, the white, middle aged, would-be drug customer retreated. Jordan spotted the dealer crouched in the shadows. She shone her flashlight into the alley opening, and the streetwise boy suffered his loss and smartly hauled ass.

Another criminal served by the force's limited staffing. Had her rookie partner been riding shotgun, she would have insisted on running the perp down and cuffing him. She was new to figuring out when to chase or not. The boy was low on the food chain and if some zealot judge enrolled him in one of the corporate prisons, the kid's sweet ass would become fresh meat, guaranteeing he'd return as either a hardened criminal or emotional cripple into one of the city's long-neglected communities.

Jordan took the woman's outstretched hand and pulled her to her feet. Seeing her face in better light, Jordan remembered her from a street fight at the Hopkins Street Shelter, but if the woman recognized her, there was no indication in her response. Jordan had wondered about the two girls who had refused her help until she had seen the younger one at the restaurant. From the way the woman was now dressed, her fortunes had somehow changed, and from her encounter with the girl and her father, it appeared that had extended to the kids. But that didn't explain her being alone on the street at this hour.

"Officer, please tell me which way is home. I seem to have missed my bus." Leah glanced toward the intersection of West Vine and 68th Street.

"That would depend on where you live. And yes, I'd say you did. The last bus ran over an hour ago."

"For an officer, you seem to suffer from limited recall. But never mind, I have specific directions home from the City

Library." Leah hastily retrieved the six binders that were scattered on the sidewalk and, clasping them tightly to her chest, she stepped closer.

"I sense in you deep wounds that can be healed only by the magical powers of the whooping cranes. I know this, for I am among the Chosen yet to receive redemption."

What the hell? What was she going to do with this woman?

The woman laughed at what must have been the shocked expression on her face. "Oh, I do apologize for causing confusion. You Christian zealots are taught to embrace falsehoods."

Half a block away, Jordan heard the drunken laughter of three males who had spilled onto the sidewalk from one of the street's seedy bars.

"Do you want to rape me?"

"No. I do not." Shit, she had to get this nut case safely off the street before any number of situations could escalate.

"Okay, then you may give me a ride." The woman went directly to the car and jerked on the handle of the locked door.

She turned back and said, "Well, are you coming or not?"

Twenty minutes later, Jordan pulled the patrol car to a stop in front of an address on the north side of the city. The woman sat upright and slid toward the door.

"FYI alert, Officer Jordan McCall. You may write Leah Killian in your little brainy notepad."

"And before you go, perhaps Leah Killian has a driver's license?"

"No, that's ludicrous. I was not operating a vehicle when you delayed me. Therefore, I could not have broken any of your silly traffic laws." She laughed brightly. "Unless falling on a public sidewalk is now a crime."

Sleep deprivation and mounting impatience with Killian's antics pounded a steady drumbeat against Jordan's temples. She was determined to avoid setting off yet another rant from this woman. Still, she ran the name Leah Killian through the DMV database for any outstanding arrest warrants. Killian had an expired driver's license, but was clean except for having racked up fifteen unpaid parking citations.

Jordan escorted Killian to the house, where a woman with blood-shot eyes and swollen face opened the door and exclaimed her relief. She embraced Killian the way a mother would welcome home a lost child. A long-legged girl stood in the shadows of a narrow hallway with one palm pressed to her mouth as if she smothered a cry. Jordan recognized her as the older of the two girls at the shelter; the one she had given her card.

"Dear God, Officer, thank you for bringing her home. I was so worried." The woman paused, dabbing at her wet cheeks. "I would have looked for her, but I was afraid to leave the children alone. My husband is a sound sleeper." Jordan detected an intense sense of guilt and maybe the sister lied to cover what she felt remained a family secret.

"I'm going to need your full name." Jordan wrote the sister's name, address, and relationship on her notepad.

"Will any harm come to her?" She glanced over her shoulder before whispering, "You might have noticed Leah... can make unintended trouble for herself... her girls."

A teenage boy lying on the couch snorted his rancor and flipped onto his opposite side, his back to them.

Jordan nodded. "Your sister committed no crimes that I'm aware of. But you might want to settle her outstanding parking tickets."

"Yes, right away, and thank you, officer. You are kind." Josey Pierce's weariness showed in her overall haggard demeanor.

"The girl there a moment ago...?"

"Oh, yes, my niece, Grace. Why do you ask?"

"No reason." She had no legal right nor responsibility to inquire about the girl.

Jordan turned eastward into a blood-red sunrise and fought back her worrisome premonition that she has not seen the last of Leah Killian or her daughters.

— 90 —

Leah

The frantic bugling of a lone surviving whooping crane reverberated in Leah's head and an unknown force expanded the room walls like an accordion. Exploding glass pushed inward and the room filled with dead and dying cranes. She stood in shards of crushed glass and the blood of the dead birds oozed between her bare toes. Her mind seized with the cruelty of human-caused devastation: famine, genocide, and hordes of the displaced and dispossessed who roamed the barren earth. Oil spills flooded the oceans and the last sea turtles choked. Giant redwoods, wildflowers and seed grasses were no more than memories. How few had stood against the ending. A grieving Mother Nature turned away in horror, her tears flooding the earth. The ark of perpetuity lay splintered at the foot of Mt. Everest, the deeply saddened planet's one remaining island of refuge.

Leah stumbled to the doorway of the room Grace and Zoey shared with their cousins, her fists pressed against her ears, and she sobbed uncontrollably.

"Oh God, Mom. What's wrong?" Grace's panic seemed caught in her throat, her voice trembling, as though she had woken from her own nightmare, rather than Leah's.

"You and Zoey must come with me," Leah shouted, her damp gown plastered to the backs of her legs. "We shall bring death to those who would slaughter the innocent."

"Mom, Mom, please. You're scaring everyone." Lucy and Jenny were huddled together and stared helplessly at their aunt.

"Come, we must go before the cover of darkness erupts into light." Leah took Grace's hand and pulled her toward the door.

"Mom... please. No one died. Look, we're all here."

"Oh Grace, must you also be a denier?" Leah let go of Grace's hand and grabbed her stomach, leaned and vomited.

"For fuck's sake, get her crazy ass out of here!" Jenny shouted, before burying her face in her pillow.

Josey's looming presence filled the room, and she shouted, "What is this?" She looked at Leah with alarm. Grace pretended it was she who had been sick, and her mother was tending to her. She would get forgiveness for waking the entire household. They would clean the mess from the carpet, and everything could go back to the appearance of normal.

"No, no, it's just a nightmare." Grace grabbed her yesterday's dirty tee, knelt, gagging, and began wiping vomit from the carpet.

Josey ordered Grace to stop and everyone else to grab pillows and bed down on the living room floor. Jenny complained that the worn carpet didn't smell much better, but she did as she was told. Jenny and Lucy, along with Zoey, who was sobbing, stepped around Leah's vomit and escaped into the narrow hall.

Josey sent Grace for carpet cleaner, rags, and spray, and Grace set about cleaning the mess her mom had made. She worried that it was the bigger mess she could not fix.

— 91 —

Josey

Josey led Leah into the bathroom and started a warm bath. She removed Leah's gown that smelled of blood and vomit. The blood was real; her period had come in the night with a rage of its own.

"Please, Josey, I promise I'm not crazy." Her sister's small voice was the one Josey remembered from countless nights she had risen to tend her nightmares. It had seemed to Josey that each was more real to Leah than the last.

"The cranes called, but I was too late to save them. What must I do?" Leah clutched Josey's hand. "They were my last hope."

"Oh, baby, you've got to stop obsessing over those birds. And trust God to look after His own creatures."

"No, no, your God has failed. Greed and evil politicians are ravaging Mother Nature."

"But please, just for now, can we agree to trust that your... special birds... are wiser than those who would destroy them? That they're safe. And they are going to be fine."

Leah smiled. "Yes, they'll wait for me."

Josey pressed her hand against her aching back and guided Leah into the tub.

"May I have a blue bubble bath?" A childish giggle escaped Leah's lips. Their shared childhood memories of mountains of blue suds were overridden by the muted bickering of five kids sorting out how to occupy a crowded floor. And dear God, Josey would soon bring yet another child into this cobbled-together household. How much was bearable before the strain was too much?

— 92 —

Grace

Mom had rejoined those she referred to as the *hordes of aimless small humans* who moved quietly through their uninspiring existence, working four mornings a week at a branch of the public library. She insisted she was ingesting her full daily regimen of drugs.

Despite Uncle Robert's constant complaint that Mom was not paying her fair share, Aunt Josey could still be counted upon to turn a blind eye and to praise her sister's daily recommitment to stay on her medications and her six weeks of steady employment. Despite Aunt Josey's praise, Grace worried that her mom was not taking her full doses and viewed her sudden burst of new-found energy troubling.

In an angry outburst at her mom's reluctant admission that yes, she was pregnant, Jenny had yelled that the little fucker should be put up for adoption. *What were you thinking?* Jenny screamed.

Aunt Josey said nothing in response to Jenny's outburst. Maybe she felt there was nothing useful to be said.

"God, Mom, if it's not too late, there's abortion." Jenny was crying now.

"Baby, you know I could never consider that. I'll have this baby and love it like I love each of you."

Grace followed her cousin out of the house and onto a patch of weedy grass behind the rusted shed. For a time, they sat in silence until Grace asked Jenny if her sister felt the same about their mom's pregnancy.

Jenny snorted. "Lucy's even worse. Her brilliant escape plan is to spread her legs for *loser boy*. She believes he'll marry his knocked-up girlfriend and take her out of this loony bin." Jenny paused and in a calmer voice she added, "Even if loser boy wanted to marry my sister, how is a nineteen-year-old high school dropout planning to support a wife and kid on what he earns bagging groceries part-time and hustling lawn service jobs?

"It's not that I don't get that we're all trapped rats. Paying big-time for our parents' selfish choices."

"Yeah, I get living with Mom and her... nutty ways makes everything a thousand times harder on everyone." It sometimes felt as if the screams of its angry dwellers were enough to explode the walls of the house.

"Yeah, it's her fucking craziness, all right. Just knowing she's bound to do something even crazier than the last time." Jenny paused. "But it's my parents, too." Jenny's voice trailed off, and she pulled at a sandspur before adding, "It's enough that he's a sexist asshole. But I think Mom's afraid of him. And her pregnancy couldn't have been her choice. What if he forced her?" Jenny fought back tears with the sheer strength of her anger.

Grace wished for Luna's wise ways of making Jenny's truth about her parents less painful. But she didn't have Luna's way with hard truths. Grace wanted to locate Luna, but nothing she had done to locate her—letters, phone calls, internet searches— had provided a single clue. It was as though Luna had simply disappeared.

"You want to get high? I got some shit stashed there." Jenny nodded toward the shed.

Grace shrugged. "No, I don't think so." And they left it at that.

Garden Party
Fall 2021

– 93 –

Leah

When Leah finished her shift at the library, the mild weather invited her to walk the twenty blocks to Josey's rather than wait for the next bus. Block after block, Leah's newfound energy surged as her heart pumped warm rich blood to her legs, and she lengthened her stride.

Reaching Josey's, she unlocked the kitchen door, her body exploding with even greater energy. In room after room, her repeated greeting ricocheted through the empty house, until she remembered Sundays meant compulsory church attendance for everyone but her and Robert. Her obedient sister reacted negatively to Leah's refusal to join them and warned of God's disapproval. Leah was certain God himself was bored with churches and did not attend regularly. Nor did God pray to himself for that which he could not grant.

She returned to the kitchen and decided to surprise the kids with freshly baked oatmeal raisin cookies when they returned from a grueling morning of tedium. She set about gathering ingredients: flour, oatmeal, brown sugar, baking soda, eggs, and milk. After mixing these ingredients, she discovered there was no vanilla extract, so she substituted colorful paprika.

Oh no! She had failed to find raisins. She tossed the giant bowl of batter into the sink and collapsed onto a kitchen chair in disappointment. Until she hit upon a perfect raisin substitute. Her mission saved, she retrieved the glob from the sink and stirred in finely chopped prunes.

The kitchen radio blared, and Leah sang along while she dabbed tablespoons of dough onto large cookie sheets. She placed the first three batches on racks to cool and laid out the last of the cookies on the washer and dryer. She surveyed the open containers of ingredients set about on kitchen chairs. The mixing bowl, cookie sheets, and utensils were piled in the sink to overflowing. But it would be best if she left the cleanup for later and cut the lawn first, a chore Josey complained was among Jake's many failures.

Leah went into the cluttered garage, gassed up the lawn mower, and cut both the front and back patches of grass. Finished with her outside chores, she showered and dressed in her snug, bright yellow bikini. She took little time to distress over the extra weight across her stomach and hips but celebrated the increased size of her breasts. A hand under each breast, she lifted, held firmly, and pointed her nipples at her image in the mirror. She let go and her breasts crashed. She repeatedly lifted and let go, and with each drop, she giggled.

Now that she had cut her prescribed daily doses in half, she didn't need to worry long term about her extra weight. She celebrated her ability to concentrate longer on her research now that she needed less sleep. Alone at night, in the privacy behind her closed door, she worked into early morning. She was regaining her true self, not the drugged zombie of her own horror movie. She ran a quick comb through her hair, loudly exclaiming to the beautiful woman reflected in the full-length mirror, *Come now, you have a party to host.*

But what was a party without balloons? It was much too late to drive to the store to purchase balloons, but she had a clever idea. She rushed into the bathroom her sister and brother-in-law shared and searched the wall cabinet, beneath the sink cabinets, and finally their bedside table, where she located an unopened package of condoms.

"Hmm," Leah giggled, imagining the celebratory use of a product no longer needed by her sister. She stuffed the packet into her overflowing beach bag and rushed into the garage in search of a spool of twine. She ran a line from a porch post across the front lawn and secured it to the streetlight post. Inflating each condom, she secured them to the line of twine. Standing back, she admired her stroke of genius at saving the party.

She took wobbly lawn chairs from the back patio, Robert's battery powered radio from the garage, and out of consideration for selfish Robert, took only five beers from the six-pack he horded in the fridge. She placed the beers on ice in a cooler, set up the sprinkler in the center of the yard, and stood back, assessing her meticulous preparation. Nothing left to do but await her guests' arrival. She opened a beer and sat, her anticipation of a fun time spinning through her thoughts like an electric jolt.

— 94 —

Grace

Ahead, a near-naked woman danced a lewd circle beneath the spray of a lawn sprinkler. Bright sunlight created brilliant flashes of rainbow colors. The dancer wore a yellow bikini, her breasts exposed, and she waved to the startled passengers aboard the minivan as the driver slowed and pulled the vehicle into the driveway. Grace Killian closed her eyes, denying all she saw; her mind split from her body.

The woman waved to a gaggle of jeering boys who left their game of driveway basketball next door and stood gaping. The woman called out that there were homemade cookies and fresh milk. A boy called back with vulgar gesturing that she could forget the cookies; he'd have some of that fresh nipple.

A red-faced man slid his truck to a skidding stop and exited, raising his fist in anger at the jeering boys, who retreated, only to gather again on an adjacent driveway. The man called to the pregnant woman who had gotten out of the minivan and demanded that she stop chasing the bikini-clad woman.

In the hysteria of the moment, the three drenched adults became a slapstick routine, something the girl's teacher had presented as an art form known as tragicomedy. But she did not know whether to laugh or cry. A small hand clutched tightly, she and the younger girl responding to the man's frightening order to go inside. The smaller girl slipped on the wet, freshly cut grass and fell. Her church dress and best shoes were covered in mud. Her face was streaked with snot, tears, and muddy water.

Grace's frozen mind began to thaw, and she was overwhelmed with shame. The mad woman was not another kid's public humiliation, but hers. Grace pulled Zoey to her feet, and, captured by the scene playing out before them, the two stood as if rooted to the ground.

Aunt Josey, now breathless, stopped chasing Leah and bent forward, a hand supporting her belly. She called to Robert to back off, for he only made matters worse. Leah, her expression that of a child, laughed and ran back toward Josey. She attempted to engage in playful tussling that caused Josey to lose her balance and fall to the ground.

Aunt Josey moaned, grabbed her swollen belly in both hands, and rolled onto her side, knees drawn. Leah stood transfixed and stared down at Josey, who had stopped moving. Robert swore and roughly pushed Leah aside. He bent over Aunt Josey, but before he had gotten her to her feet, Leah screamed and sprang onto his back. She pounded him with her fists until he grabbed her by the hair and threw her onto the ground.

Josey regained her feet, calling for Grace to get a blanket from the house, and she quickly retrieved one from the sofa. Uncle Robert tossed the blanket over Mom as though he was capturing a wild animal with snarling teeth. Kicking and screaming, she accused him of kidnapping; still he managed to lift her onto his shoulder. He carried her inside the house and into what had been Jake's bedroom and her aunt followed, locking the door behind them.

A locked door did nothing to silence Leah's raging accusations of kidnapping, and now rape, while the kids huddled together in the living room, each caught up in their own version of what had transpired and what measure of humiliation they were to bear.

"Your crazy bitch Momma has fucked up my life!" Jake shouted, pushing Grace hard against the wall.

"Back off, bully boy." Jenny pushed herself into the space between Jake and Grace, who struggled to gain her balance.

"I could score a thousand fucking points a game and nothing would change." Near tears, he turned and stomped from the room. His heels striking his anger, he shouted back that he could never return to school.

"Oh, fine. You're piss-poor at sports. And you'll never make any team." Jenny snarled.

"All right, I hate his shit, but he's right. After this, our friends will avoid us. And laugh behind our backs." Lucy collapsed onto the sofa, a pillow hugged to her chest.

"For sure you're never making cheerleader." Jenny shrugged. "But what are friends for if not to abandon you? Still, going after Grace is nothing but lame. Be the same as going after Dad for...."

"Yeah, yeah, I get it, but Mom's never going to kick her out, is she? And nothing's ever going to change." Lucy had lost most of her earlier spite, but her words still rang true.

"God, Lucy, I'm no fucking shrink. How am I supposed to know?"

Robert emerged from the bedroom wearing dry clothes, got into his truck, and sped away. Sundays also meant a customary barrel of takeout fried chicken with all the sides—Robert's one noble notion of sparing his wife the duty of preparing one of their twenty-one weekly meals.

Aunt Josey called Grace to the door and whispered, "Go call your daddy. Tell him I said he's got to do what we talked about and do it now."

"Uh, what if he's working?" Grace had not found the nerve to tell her aunt that she believed her dad may have moved in with someone. She didn't want to acknowledge, even to herself, her fear that he might not come.

"Grace, go and do as I said. And tell Jenny to bring me an ice pack and a change of clothes." It was the first time Grace had noticed smeared blood from a gash at her aunt's damp hairline.

— 95 —

Jordan

Jordan had completed a rare 7 to 3 stint and was anticipating an afternoon with Ellie. As she exited through the precinct's main door, a tall slender man dressed in paint-spattered jeans and a hoody called to her and hurried across the boulevard toward her.

"Officer, I'm Daniel Killian, and we met… with my daughter, Zoey, at the beach restaurant."

"Right, I remember." Daniel Killian had chosen to omit their earlier encounter on the street near his house, when she had decided that he was no threat to his family.

Daniel Killian hastened to add that he was not there entirely on official police business but on more of a personal appeal concerning his daughters.

"If you could just hear me out. And should you decide it's nothing you want any part of, I won't blame you."

"Alright, but this is gonna need to be quick."

Why did she feel as if she was somehow connected to this sad man, his insane wife, and especially their neglected daughters? Even now, her first reaction was an emotional consideration of the girls and their safety. Had their mother's illness forced them back onto the streets? Was he here to ask for her help in locating his lost family? If not, then what could he possibly want from her? She accepted the cup of steaming black coffee he offered and agreed to hear him out.

"Thank you, officer, and I will be quick." His stark grimness remained, and he apologized for his awkwardness in approaching her as he had, confessing that he had gone inside to ask how he could find her, but was not comfortable waiting in a police station. She took this to be his backward acknowledgement of their first encounter.

"Yeah, they told me someone had asked for me but didn't give his name." She followed him across the street to a public bench.

"Ah, I don't know just how much you know… or may have guessed… about my wife's… condition. But her illness recently took a down-hill trajectory." He paused and she said nothing. He stared off across the park toward the busy street.

Jordan was far more concerned with information about the girls and their safety than fresh details of their mother's mental illness. The incident at Hopkins and additional encounters with his wife told her all she needed to know about adverse consequences for the girls' welfare. Still, she sipped the cooling coffee and listened while he recounted his desperate, year-long search and then the horrific physical and emotional trauma to which her illness had subjected their daughters. About Grace's desperate call, and his and his sister-in-law's rescue of Leah and the girls from a dangerous situation.

Jordan did not ask for details about the parties involved or their location, suspecting his wife's role in the motel operations he described were more criminal than he admitted. Child abuse and endangerment were obvious.

"Leah got better and held down a job until yesterday, but in her current state, she has caused unintentional physical harm to her pregnant sister. That's what we, I, need from you."

"Christ man, you don't need me to arrest your wife on an assault charge. All you've got to do is cross the street and file a complaint." She got up to leave.

"No, I'll never agree to having my wife arrested. She needs professional care. I know you helped her before, after the Hopkins Street fight." He pulled a wrinkled business card from his pocket. "You gave my daughter your card, and she held onto it."

Jordan stopped and looked at the card in his hand.

"I've got to have help getting her admitted against her will to the county clinic until I can make an appeal to a judge."

"You meant to Baker Act her? And you think as a police officer I can transport her and have her admitted short term against her will?"

He nodded.

"Do you understand that what you're asking is a much more complicated decision?"

"No, I don't know details. I just know what I have to do." He had grown more tense.

"What's her physical state?"

"Just now she's heavily sedated, according to her sister, Josey."

"How's she likely to react when the drugs wear off? Your best guess."

"She'll no doubt put up a fight against going to the clinic."

"So, you need her transported as early as possible, right?"

He added that he had spoken with admissions personnel at the County Mental Health clinic, and confirmed they had a bed for her.

"Good, that's the first step."

She instructed Daniel to wait until she returned to duty and called him. He was then to call the station and request a police escort and transportation for his wife, who was experiencing a mental episode.

"They'll want to know her behavior and you need to answer 'erratic'. They'll want to know if she poses a danger to herself or anyone else. Answer that you don't know but fear she might; leave out all details about her act toward her sister. Don't speak about any previous conversation with me."

When Jordan and Daniel parted, Jordan went back into the station and into the office of her desk sergeant. She needed to make sure she caught the call.

— 96 —

Grace

Grace followed her aunt into the kitchen, cringing at the sight of the mess Mom had left.

"I know it's awful, but I've got this. You're not to turn a hand." Grace wanted to correct even a small part of the upheaval her mom had created.

Josey picked up one of Leah's forgotten cookies, nibbled at an edge, and spit it into her palm, crying out *Sweet Jesus* in a prayerful cadence.

"In her entire life, the poor child never turned out a decent batch of cookies, no matter how hard she tried." She stared at Grace with such pain in her eyes, then suddenly burst into unrestrained laughter. She began feverishly tossing cookies into a garbage bag, and Grace, spurred into action, joined her aunt.

Together, Josey and Grace heaved the bulging garbage bag into the outside container. Afterwards, Josey took a seat in the one remaining patio chair and Grace settled on the edge of the patio, her feet resting on the freshly cut grass.

"At least the yard looks decent, if you overlook the weeds." Josey let go of a stifled whimper and pulled a wrinkled tissue from her pocket, dabbing at her eyes.

"Mom will want to see me," Grace said with far more certainty than she felt.

"Honey, your mom is in no shape to see anyone. She's out cold and I pray it'll hold 'til your dad has time to take care of things."

"What things? What're you two planning? Is it about him wanting the officer's card? She left that card for me and Zoey. It was never about using it against Mom."

"Honey, it's not like that."

"What then?"

"Why don't we wait for your dad? He'll explain better."

"No, he's no good with the truth when it comes to Mom."

Her aunt began to cry but said nothing more.

— 97 —

Grace

Daniel approached through the kitchen and stood just inside the patio door. Josey brushed away her tears, sighed deeply, and pushed up from the chair. He stepped aside and as Josey passed through into the kitchen, stepped out onto the patio and sat in the chair she had occupied. His breathing came hard, as if he were being chased, and he asked between shallow breaths about her and Zoey.

"We're plenty scared, but did you see Mom just now?" Grace wanted him to say that their mom was going to be okay after a good long rest. That was how he usually spoke of Mom's recovery.

"Looked in on her. She's still heavily sedated." He sighed.

"Then you need to take her back to the neighborhood clinic. The doctor there will prescribe more meds, and afterwards Mom always gets better."

Daniel moved from the chair and took a seat next to Grace, who had remained on the patio floor, and put his arm around her shoulders.

"Do you remember Officer McCall tried to get your mom help after the street fight at Hopkins, but she didn't stay for an evaluation?"

"Yes, but what has she got to do with what you and I know is best for Mom? Besides, Mom has never stayed anywhere but with us."

"This time is different. Officer McCall has agreed to transport Leah to the County Mental Health Clinic. And if your mom refuses treatment, the officer can admit her for a staff evaluation. Then they can hold her there until I can go before a judge to ask that your mom stay for treatment against her will."

"But did you forget there's no insurance to pay for all that?"

"Sold my dad's old tools to a collector on the internet. It's enough for a start. And you're right, it will be a struggle, but where she's going, they'll extend credit based on my ability to pay."

Grace felt as though her chest had ripped open under the weight of a lifetime of lies. She whispered into his chest, "Dad, will she ever forgive us for breaking our promise?"

"I can't really say. But if this helps her to get better, maybe she'll understand and even come to accept that what we're doing was always out of love."

At the sound of two vehicles approaching, Grace slipped her hand in his, and together they walked toward the sound of their deed.

— 98 —

Grace

During the drive to the County Mental Health Clinic, Aunt Josey had spoken easily of her plans for Leah's homecoming meal, including her famous homemade double chocolate cake. Now she stared at the building, her breath labored.

"There, I think, fourth floor, with barred windows."

Grace squinted into the bright sunlight and wondered whether patients housed on the uppermost floor behind barred windows differed from those on the lower three floors. The good thing was that Mom had stayed for four weeks of treatment; her longest stay ever. Grace desperately wanted to believe her mom's new faith in therapy had erased her strange obsession with the healing powers of whooping cranes.

"I'd like to think Leah has enjoyed looking down on these neat beds of colorful flowers." She paused. "I've always believed beauty and order made her happy." For a moment, the tight muscles in her aunt's round face relaxed. "She once talked about having an English-style garden and opening an upscale café, serving fancy ladies what she called *high tea*." Josey shook her head and briefly smiled. "For her, one good idea was never enough."

On her first day of kindergarten, when Grace had been afraid, Mom had bent and picked a small purple flower that grew in a sidewalk crack and pinned it in Grace's hair. She had kissed her cheek and said Mother Nature meant the brave little flower for her. And that she need not be afraid while wearing it. Grace had pressed the flower and carried it with her until she was no longer afraid.

"I'm not sure what we should expect. Still, I think it's safe to say Leah will be much calmer. Easier on herself and those who love her and are willing to care for her."

They entered the hospital lobby and were directed to take seats in the waiting area until they were called to see the discharge nurse. Josey and Grace joined others who wore similar expressions of both hopefulness and dread. A young man got up and moved across the semi-circle of chairs, permitting Josey and Grace to have seats together.

Grace stole glances at the man who sat stiffly, his back pressed up tightly against the chair back. He stared across the lobby at the sound of the elevator doors opening. At what appeared to be a letdown, he tugged at the too-short sleeves of his suit coat. Grace felt a measure of familiarity with the stranger's awkwardness, remembering that her dad had worn a suit coat and tie only on their Christmas and birthday visits to Granny Sybil, and then at her funeral.

When a pleasant staff member crossed the lobby and called to Aunt Josey, it was as if the room sighed in unison. In moments of anxiety, delays were better than facing their fears.

"And you, my dear, are to remain here."

Grace settled into what she knew would be a hard wait.

The woman came for others, but not the man in the ill-fitting coat, until they were the only two left with their worries.

"Your mom?" The man leaned and asked in a low voice.

Grace had never acknowledged her mother's illness to anyone other than Luna, and certainly not to a stranger. Still, she did not want her silence to be taken as rudeness.

"Sorry... I didn't mean...." He blushed and stared at his scuffed shoes. "It hurt really bad the first time my wife refused to see me. But she's much better now. And I'm here to take her home."

"I'm... uh... yes. My aunt and I are here to take... my mom.... home. Four weeks now." She felt a flush of relief like nothing she had experienced, other than stepping into the warmth of the main library after a night spent freezing in the Impala.

He nodded. "That's really good." He responded to a text message and slipped his phone back into the pocket of his coat.

"That was my mother. She's looking after our two girls and our new baby boy. I'm hoping their mom... is soon well enough for our family to be together." He stood, a hand in his pocket, and jingled loose change. "Going for a Pepsi. Do you want one? Maybe crackers? We're both missing lunch, so how 'bout it?"

"Yes, thanks. I'd like peanut butter. If you've got enough... change, I mean."

"You got it." He walked away toward the vending machines.

There was something reassuring in the man's openness, and oddly enough, she cared what he might think if he knew she had coached her little sister in perfecting a look of innocence and using it to distract a cashier while Grace filled her pockets with snack foods. She would run from the store to hide in the clutter of the nearest alley until Zoey's shorter legs had caught up.

She and Zoey had quickly learned which storekeepers willingly looked away, and which Zoey insisted were *mean*. Grace had no hesitation in stealing from those who were only concerned about their meager losses and punishing street kids for their hunger. She came to accept that the rules of the street cared little for her ambivalence regarding thievery. A moment of doubt carried a host of dire consequences. She was a gifted runner, and that was her one advantage.

Aunt Josey stepped off the elevator, crossed the lobby, and dropped heavily onto the chair next to Grace. She was breathing hard through her mouth, mumbling that the baby was taking her oxygen. When she'd caught her breath, she explained that Leah had refused to leave with her, though her discharge was mandatory.

Nothing made sense. Even if Mom was still angry with Dad and Aunt Josey, where did she intend to go? She wasn't sure her dad still had even the basement room, and surely Mom did not intend that they return to the streets. The woman from behind the desk crossed the lobby, and Grace held her breath.

The man she had spoken to came to his feet and hurried to the elevator. The door opened, and he and Grace exchanged waves. The door closed and just like that, the person Grace had spoken honestly to about her mom was lost to her.

Road Trip
Fall 2021

– 99 –

Daniel

Daniel stood on the small deck amid pots of fragrant herbs. He turned the steaks on the grill and poured a second shot of bourbon, watching as tall, vertically developing thunderheads moved inland. He thought of these moments as private reprieves from the prevailing chaos of his real life. Though these too-prefect moments carried their own guilt, as if they were stolen from his daughters.

Sarah's suspicious tom cat, which was sprawled on the railing, had continued to watch him with an absorption the cat might have used for stalking prey.

Although he had agreed to move in with Sarah, Daniel needed time to sort through the multiple ambiguities of their situation, and they had yet to set a date. But he felt tonight might signal a decision.

He struggled with thoughts of how to explain his decision to Grace and Zoey. He remembered his own bewilderment and lasting anger at his parents' divorce. Whatever he decided to say, he could not change the fact of his selfishness, nor his unfaithfulness to their mother.

He removed the steaks from over the flaming coals and stepped from the patio into the kitchen. Sarah had placed candles, and the mixed bouquet of flowers he had picked up from the supermarket, on the table, and she bent to remove roasted vegetables from the oven. She turned to him, smiled, and pushed her brown hair from her face. He set the steaks down on the stovetop and pulled her into his arms, and their warm, deep kiss left him with a disturbing mix of gratitude, arousal, and guilt. From the counter, his cell vibrated, and Daniel stared at the phone spinning in circles on the countertop but made no move to answer.

"Daniel?" Sarah said, her voice strained.

He released Sarah and picked up his phone.

"Leah. Jesus, yes, I hear you." Daniel imagined the relief he would feel if he could place his hand over Leah's mouth and smother her repeated screams.

Daniel stepped back onto the patio, the sky darker now, and glanced back into the brightly lit kitchen. The candles were no longer glowing, and he wanted that to be the result of a rising breeze through the open door.

"Stop yelling and tell me what it is you want."

"Did Josey not tell you I am not allowed to leave on my own? You put me here, so now you must come to take me away."

He willed himself to set aside the angry urgency in her voice.

"Uh, it's late, Leah. Why not stay overnight? I'll come for you early tomorrow." He had delayed returning Josey's earlier call and now needed time to reaffirm their agreement regarding Leah's release. And he wanted somehow to regain the evening with Sarah, but feared it was already lost.

"No, there is no bed for me here." Leah paused to catch her breath. "You must come now, and we must talk about our girls' futures."

Their future—tonight? What could she be plotting?

He agreed to come for her, and yes, right away. He would speak with Josey and give her a heads up before arriving with Leah.

Sarah came back into the kitchen and began placing the food into storage containers, although rare steaks could not be saved and reheated as rare.

"I've agreed to drive Leah to her sister's. I'm not sure how long settling her in might take. Just that it's never easy. It's about what's safe for my girls. And that means I can't say if I'm talking about hours, days, even weeks."

He paused, and Sarah reached and took his hand in hers.

"Daniel, I am trying to put myself in your... situation... but you must know how difficult it is for me. And I can't say how I'll feel about our future should you choose to remain your wife's forever caregiver. But, for now, do whatever you must."

Daniel stepped through the door into a downpour and pulled his jacket collar up, undeterred by an act of Mother Nature. He would soon learn the full weight of Leah's demands, but for now he knew only dread.

— 100 —

Daniel

Daniel held his raincoat over Leah against what remained of the passing thunderstorm as they picked a less-puddled path to his truck. Leah's body pressed against his was intensely familiar and altogether unsettling. He helped a notably weaker Leah into the truck, shook out the wet raincoat, and tossed it onto the back seat. He started up the engine and drove away, neither he nor Leah looking back.

They had not gone far before Leah said, "A healing rain should come gently and do no harm." Her voice was so soft Daniel barely made out her words over the sound of the truck's tires on the wet pavement. He decided she meant the downed blossoms from crape myrtle trees that grew in the wide median.

As they drove, Leah's silence deepened, and Daniel failed to engage her with small bits of news about the girls. Leah remained unresponsive, her silence so intense Daniel lowered the truck window, welcoming the street noises and cool, wet air.

He tightened his grip on the steering wheel and drove on, replaying his conversation with an infuriated Josey. He had offered no defense for his delay in returning her phone call, which meant less time for her to make a new plan for Leah's arrival. He had asked Josey not to tell the girls just yet and she agreed, enlisting Lucy's boyfriend, Jerome, to drive the entire gang to some kid place filled with loud noises. Daniel had forgotten that it was Robert's poker night; too much alcohol and too many losing hands guaranteed he would return home in a foul mood. While Josey was willing to have Leah and the girls stay on, Robert would almost certainly make such an arrangement hell for Josey, and surely for Leah and the girls.

Approaching the intersection, Daniel steered the truck into the eastbound lane and Leah suddenly sat erect, frantically pointing in the opposite direction.

"No, stop." She glanced about as if she were searching for a familiar landmark. "I'm never going back to that despicable place."

Daniel believed Leah was confused and perhaps feared he was returning her to the clinic. Over her loud protest, he made the turn and moved along with the east-bound traffic, while attempting to reassure her he would turn around as soon as he found a suitable place.

"Don't you have that... apartment? I want you to take me there and bring my girls to me tonight."

"No, of course I don't have the apartment. You didn't want to live there." Had Leah forgotten that it was she who had sped away, leaving him and the girls stranded?

"If not there, then where do you live?" Her tone was incredulous.

"Couch crashing, you might say. Now and then I've slept in my truck." His lie stuck along with the heavy mucus that had built in his throat.

"No matter. I'm coming with you." Leah pushed back against the seat, her resolve unyielding.

At the risk of arousing her further, Daniel felt forced to respond. "You need to return to Josey's until I can arrange something more permanent." Now that he was staying most nights with Sarah, he had given less time to finding a place Leah would approve of.

"Stop this instant and let me out!" Leah screamed as she removed her seat belt and threw her shoulder against the locked door.

"Okay, okay, I'm stopping, but for god sakes, stop." He braked hard, barely avoiding a rear-end collision, and pulled into a near-empty parking lot. He shut down the engine and turned to Leah, who appeared to have regained a degree of restraint.

"Daniel, I do not intend for us to fight. What I want is someplace private so we may talk about our daughters' futures and our own." Leah's tone held a slight hint of compromise, though she didn't look at him but stared ahead.

Memories of the midnight rescue of Grace and Zoey from the vile motel flashed through Daniel's thoughts, and he agreed to take her to the basement room. If he were to have any chance of impacting Leah's plan for their daughters, he would first need to hear her out.

"Okay, I'll take you where I sometimes stay."

She looked across at him and gestured her agreement.

— 101 —

Leah

The dark basement room smelled of mold, nicotine, oily sweat, bourbon, and to her surprise, cannabis. Perhaps the cannabis was Sam's and not Daniel's. She had never bothered to get to know Sam, though he was Daniel's best friend.

Leah sat on the rumpled bed, Daniel across from her in the room's lone chair. His shoulders slouched, and his muscular forearms rested on his bony knees. He had spoken little on the drive here, and when he had, he did so cautiously, evidencing his distrust of her in matters related to their daughters, and her past transgressions.

"Our daughters are well?" she asked.

"Yes, and they've... we've missed you." He rubbed at his left forearm as was his habit whenever he wished to withhold the whole truth. He had unnecessarily troubled himself. Her concern was entirely for Grace and Zoey, and not the woman Daniel believed was a secret.

"Good, I am glad," she replied.

"Uh, and you do seem more... at ease. Better... I mean." He looked not at her, but at the gritty cement floor.

"Oh yes, Daniel. I am that, and so much more." Leah had expected more of Daniel's enduring optimism, not the hesitant man who pushed back in the chair and said nothing more.

Oh Daniel, her sweet Daniel, his loss, his pain, his fears prevented him from joining her in what was her moment of endorphin overload; hours stolen from the pain of her madness. She leaned into the emotional space that separated them and sought to vanquish his fears.

His forehead gathered and he squinted, as if he prepared himself for an emotional blow.

She took his rough hands between her palms. "Do you remember the snowy February evening when you and I surrendered our beautiful infant Grace into the whole of the universe?"

A proud Daniel had cradled a swaddled baby Grace to his chest and beckoned her to follow him into the chilly night. The air was weighted with a refreshing scent, and the bare branches of trees were giant arms reaching to embrace the radiance of the starry sky. They had watched as a shooting star burnt its path across the sky. And Daniel had spoken of the universe making way for its brightest new star: Grace Danielle Killian. They had held each other; baby Grace warm and safe cradled between them, and in that moment, above all others, she had loved him as love was intended.

"Of course. I remember. Leah, what we had was good. And now that you're... better, and I have a job with good pay, maybe you, me, and our girls... we can try... to be a family again." His face had lost some of its earlier starkness and he seemed to have mistaken her whimsical recollection of a beautiful memory as a sign she believed they might recapture the youthful fantasy of eternal love. A fantasy neither of them now believed.

"Daniel, please...."

"No, it's possible. I've changed. My new job means we can afford for me to attend night classes. I'll learn a new trade. You'll get even better and return to your job. And we'll rent a small but nice house while we save for a down payment on the house you've always wanted. You can make Saturday morning blueberry pancakes with funny faces. And I can have pancakes drowned in Tupelo honey. Like all the times before, you'll get better, and we can again be a happy family."

"No, Daniel. That was never our life. Ours was an elaborate fabrication built upon lie after lie, presented as truth. And now my desire is that your life, and that of our precious daughters, must change. You and they must have lives built upon truth and not deceit."

"God, Leah, what are you saying? Do you imagine that I will ever again permit you to take Grace and Zoey...?"

"No, no, I swear," she interrupted. "I understand your fear that I will again deliver them into a hell of my own making. I ask only that you agree to care for our daughters and that they are never returned to my sister's."

"But you've always said...."

"My fears were not only for your failures, but also for my own. Now, we must each forgive the other, and work together so that our daughters may have a chance at better lives."

Leah was flushed with a rare emotion she thought lost to her, and she whispered, "Now, come and lie with me for the good moments you and I have shared."

He removed his boots and lay down next to her. She felt his damp, tearful breath on her neck, and she took his hand in hers and drew his arm to encircle her waist, urging him to move closer until her back rested firmly against his heaving chest.

His tense body relaxed, and the room's darkness wrapped around them.

— 102 —

Grace

Aunt Josey came into the bedroom to instruct Grace and Zoey to dress for school, but their dad had called to say he was coming for them. Their aunt's voice was soggy, and she brushed tears from her cheek, not wanting the girls to see.

"Why Dad? Where's Mom? Does that mean she's with him?" Grace struggled to make sense of what she had heard. Yesterday, Mom's refusal to come here with her and Aunt Josey had made no sense, and now felt even more unsettling.

"Lord, hon, I wish I could tell you. Then we'd both know. We'll just need to wait for answers." The despairing slump of her aunt's shoulders convinced Grace that she was not holding back due to some notion of sparing her and Zoey.

In light of these new concerns, Grace set aside her worries about missing a major geometry test; one she had prepared to ace. But when had her and Zoey's lives not been pitched upside down by one parent or the other? Still, they had rarely been in concert. Something big was in the works, and Mom needed Dad's help to make it happen.

Grace stood at the rain-fogged window watching her envious cousins board the school bus. Zoey, fully dressed, sat on the unmade air mattress, untangling her knotted shoelaces.

"I'm scared," Zoey said.

Grace sat next to her sister.

"Aw, come on. We've got each other, don't we? And there's Aunt Josey and now maybe Dad." Grace had not forgotten their mom's threat to put them up for adoption and that she and Zoey would be separated.

Zoey squinted at Grace. "But Dad won't stay. He never does."

— 103 —

Daniel

Daniel parked on the street and suggested that the girls wait in the truck while he summoned their mom. He stood with one foot on the ground but turned back at the unusual high-pitched tenor of Grace's voice.

"Mom came here... with you... you were together?" Daniel felt Grace's mounting ire and he understood that she sought answers; not so much about her parents' on-again off-again, mostly destructive relationship, but rather what it might portend for her and Zoey.

"Yes, last night your mom demanded I bring her here. She also insisted that I wait until now to bring you girls to meet her." He paused, but when Grace said nothing more, he walked onto the path that led him to the basement door.

Daniel entered the basement room and found it cold and empty. The impressions of his and Leah's bodies on the sagging mattress was the one sign that they had slept there. He took out his phone and realized the number Leah had called from last evening was the clinic's and not her own. He searched the room to discover that she had not left a note to tell where he and the girls should go next. He hoped Leah had left word with Miss Belle.

Daniel entered the over-warm kitchen that smelled of ginger and sought answers from Miss Belle. She told him that soon after his departure, a woman who said she was his wife had driven away in the old car that had been parked near his basement room.

Daniel struggled to set aside his sense of betrayal and focus on how he was to safeguard the girls until he could unravel Leah's actual intentions for Grace and Zoey.

He explained to Miss Belle his need to secure immediate housing for the girls and asked if she might have a vacant efficiency unit he could rent while he searched for suitable housing in the girls' current school district. He counted on the kind woman's fondness for the girls she had shown since their first short stay.

"Oh my, Daniel, had I only known three days ago. I'm sorry, but I have nothing to offer." She clenched her fist, and for the first time he noticed her severely crippled arthritic fingers. "But what I will do is make the rental unit available to you and the girls until the new tenant is scheduled to move in on the first of the month. I know it's only five days, but would that help?"

With those words, Daniel went from deflation to a deep sigh of relief. He hugged the kind woman and whispered, "You're an angel and I thank you with all my sinful heart."

"Goodness," she said, giggling. "Let me wrap up some of this warm gingerbread for the three of you."

Daniel returned to the truck, where the girls waited anxiously.

"Where's Mom? She's not coming?" Zoey asked with what he thought was a mix of sadness and maybe relief.

He explained about their mom driving away earlier.

"Didn't you... phone her? Ask her where we should go now?" Grace's voice was stilted, halting, as if she knew to dread his answer.

"Your mom blocked my calls when she arrived at the clinic. I had not heard from her until last evening, when she called from a clinic phone."

"Did you even try to see her while she was there?" Grace's tone was accusatory.

"Yes, but she refused to see me." He had made three trips to the clinic, and each time she had turned him away. After her final rejection, he sat for a time in his truck, convinced that Leah never intended to forgive him for having admitted her against her will.

"That was convenient, I'm sure." Grace took out her phone and muttered under her breath.

"Wait, I don't understand." She tried a second and a third time, her anxiety mounting with each failed attempt to connect.

"What's wrong?" Zoey grimaced.

"Mom has blocked my number. But why me?" Grace asked with a fixed stare, her shoulders slumped.

"But what does that mean?" Zoey stared first at Grace, and then at him.

"I'm sorry, but I don't know." He explained that Leah had said nothing last evening that led him to think she had a plan other than that they would not return to Josey's. He had believed Leah's refusal to leave the clinic with Josey and Grace was entirely about Josey's part in Leah's forced admission. Still, he turned to Grace.

"What do you think it might mean?"

"Christ Dad, you're asking me? I'm no better at reading Mom's whacked mind than you. And no, I don't have a damn clue." Grace's hard gaze broke off, and she turned away. He was sure that had she let go of her anger, her tears would have spilled forth.

"Right, and I'm sorry. But I'm as baffled as you two. And until we've had word from your mom, I'm not sure about our next move."

"Can you please just take us to school like normal? I don't want a scary day worrying about Mom taking us away." Zoey squeezed her hands into tight fists.

"Don't worry. You're staying with me. Your mom gave her word." He dared not lie, but reached and drew Zoey into a hug. Over the top of her head, Daniel looked to Grace, but his own need for reassurance was not met.

— 104 —

Daniel

Rather than wait for Sam in the overcrowded office building where they had agreed to meet, Daniel had decided to wait near the employee's parking area. Sam had a cushy job as a residential building inspector with the county permitting department that afforded him some flexibility in setting his own work schedule.

Earlier, Daniel had called into the shop, hoping to have his absence without prior notice forgiven. He told the office manager that he was at the hospital with his mom who was undergoing emergency surgery. He wasn't sure a gallbladder rupture was a medical condition requiring surgery, but who would actually believe his true circumstance?

"Hey, what's so urgent that it won't keep 'til beers at O'Lary's?" Sam asked, getting out of the county's sedan.

"It's about the kids."

"Fuck. Don't tell me she's run off with them again?"

"No, it's not like that. The girls are safe for the moment."

The two leaned on the car's hood, the engine pinging as it cooled, while Daniel explained his strange evening with Leah. Her welcome but disarming promise to place the girls with him on the condition that he never returned them to Josey's care.

"I think she may have left town, without as much as a good-bye to the girls," Daniel admitted.

"Okay, okay... her leaving's not good, I know. But the girls' staying is good, right?" Sam's hesitancy registered his own doubt about the girls' future safety.

"Yes, and no. But now I need to find a place for me and the girls to live."

"But aren't you still moving in with Sarah?"

"Don't think that'll work. Not now, with two kids and a forever-pissed stray cat. Space is limited in her apartment... and Sarah's never really been around the noise and messiness of kids. It's way too much to spring on her."

"Okay, but what woman claiming to love you won't help out a man and his kids in a tight?"

"You don't get it...." Daniel felt unfairly squeezed.

"What? That if you were to ask, she'd say no? Is that it?"

"Fuck you, mommy's boy. And what do you think you know about it?"

"Enough to know I'd never agree to move in with some woman who refused to help me out in a tight."

Sam's words bit hard and true, and Daniel set off toward the visitor's parking lot where he had left his truck.

"Jesus, Daniel, hold the fuck up. I know you didn't come here for advice on women, so why did you come?"

Daniel stopped and turned back. "No, I came to ask if you'd get the girls today after school and drive them to your mom's. I don't need to lose my job just now."

"Dumb ass, all you had to do was ask straight away for once."

"Right, and I'm sorry about the name calling."

— 105 —

Grace

Grace sat alone on a beach towel just beyond the reach of an incoming tide, and she glanced over her shoulder at Dad and Zoey, who trudged through the sand toward a beach vendor's stand. They were going to bring back a lunch of chili dogs, chips, and sodas.

Dad had planned the trip to the beach as a surprise for her and Zoey so that they might set aside their worries that there was no word from Mom and enjoy a day of fun. Dad had unsuccessfully searched for Mom among bars and cheap motels she had frequented during her previous disappearances. He had returned only to report that neither bartenders nor desk attendants at the motels had done more than pretend to look at the worn photo he had shown them.

Dad had finally aborted his search to focus on the more pressing matter of securing housing, and found an efficiency unit located above an elderly man's weathered garage. The unit came with a refrigerator and a stove with two of its four burners actually working. The balance of the furnishings included a rented kitchen table with four straight chairs and a sofa with a pullout bed for her and Zoey.

Dad slept on a folding single bed he had borrowed, along with a tv, from a friend. Miss Belle offered from her own kitchen a set of three cook pots, a frying pan, and a set of mismatched dishes. She and Zoey had saved takeout plastic spoons and forks.

The place was worn and cheap, but the good thing was neither she nor Zoey had needed to change schools. Dad now drove them to school, and Sam picked them up after school and dropped them off at his mom's because Dad feared that Mom might steal her and Zoey away. But what would safeguard against Mom arriving at their schools, demanding that they leave with her? It had happened before, and there was nothing and no one who could prevent the same from reoccurring.

Grace looked in the direction Dad and Zoey had gone and noticed a tall woman running along the shoreline. She ran with an effortlessness that distinguished her from labored weekend runners. Grace recognized the runner as Officer Jordan McCall. She slowed and stopped, then walked closer and called out to Grace.

"Hey, are you alone?" The officer looked about as if searching for an answer to her own question.

"No, just waiting 'til my dad and sister bring back lunch." Grace felt awkward sitting in her presence, so she stood, her arms folded across her front.

"I thought you might have waved me on my way. Given that our last time must have been really hard for you."

"Right, it was, but Dad explained that he'd gone to you, asking for your help."

"I'm glad there's no hard feelings."

"No ma'am, uh, Officer McCall."

"Mind if I rest a minute there with you?" Grace noted that the officer wasn't breathing hard and her request seemed more than she'd said. Grace offered half of the beach towel and though she was pleased, she was unsure what conversation she might have with a police officer.

She decided on the one thing they appeared to have in common.

"Uh, I run sprints for quickness and endurance in prep for basketball. And... and I just like running. If I lived some place like this, I think I'd run every day." Grace stopped short of saying that Dad now ran with her because he was worried the new neighborhood was unsafe for her running alone.

"Yeah, I run daily, with few exceptions. Training for my job and for the sheer pleasure."

Grace nodded. "Me too, but not as much as I'd like." Dad did not have the time or energy to run as often as she wanted.

"You and your family come to the beach often?"

"Pretty much never, 'cause dad works most weekends to make extra money. So, we don't get to come as much as I'd... we'd like."

"I live a mile or so in that direction with my wife, Ellie." She seemed to pause and maybe measure Grace's reaction to *wife*.

"That's gotta be special... uh, waking up every morning at the beach." Grace did not feel it would be smart to let on that her mom had told her the name of the vet after their chance meeting at the beach restaurant, and had admitted for the first time that Ellie had helped Mom save Mary and Beauty from a horrible death. She could not know how much Officer McCall knew about her wife and Mom's big secret.

"I best go before I completely cool down." Jordan stood, brushing sand from the back of her shorts. "And I'd like it if you'd called me Jordan. Officer feels a little stiff."

"Yeah, I'd really like that..." She wanted the sound of Jordan's name to come out of her mouth, but it was too much.

Jordan smiled and turned to leave, and Grace stood.

"My mom's missing again. And I think my dad has given up on looking for her. I'm worried she can't take care of herself."

Jordan turned. "I'm sorry. I'd hoped she'd...."

"Oh, she did... stay, I mean. For a while."

"How was it that she left? Circumstances, I mean."

Grace recounted what little she knew of her mom's disappearance.

"Your dad was the last person to talk to her?" Jordan's facial muscles tightened around her drawn mouth. The air around them suddenly felt heavier.

"Yes... and no. My parents spent the night together before she left. But Miss Belle saw Mom last. Not to talk to her, but to see her get into the Impala and drive away. And that was it."

"I wish I could help, but unless there's a reason to suspect that she left under threat, then there's really nothing I can offer as a police officer."

"I think he might look for her if my sister and I had some place safe."

"Safe? You're not with your aunt?"

"Not anymore." Grace explained her mother's threatening objections.

Jordan nodded. "I see."

"Do you think my sister and I could stay weekends with you for a while, so our dad could go look for our mom?" The sheer boldness of Grace's exposure to rejection roared in her ears over the sound of the surf, and she felt as though her knees would collapse beneath her.

Ellie intended to do what she knew to make Grace and Zoey welcome on what was their third consecutive weekend visit, though regrettably she did not enjoy Jordan's ease with either girl. An unexpected change in Jordan's duty roster meant the weekend would not be the exciting one the girls had eagerly anticipated. Tomorrow's kayaking trip was now out of the question. Ellie did not possess the skills nor the will to assume full responsibility for two beginners.

Daniel and the girls had arrived at her office for the scheduled exchange nearly two hours late, delaying their arrival home. An unpredicted thunderstorm had cancelled the bonfire and hot dogs on the beach. Ellie instead hurriedly prepared a dinner heavily dependent upon last evening's takeout potato salad, oven roasted wieners, and frozen mixed vegetables. Grace ate only sparingly, and in an angry outburst, Zoey refused.

"These aren't real hot dogs. And Dad never makes us eat putrid vegetables." Zoey pushed her plate aside.

While impressed with the insolent twelve-year-old child's vocabulary, Ellie struggled to know how to respond. Her initial response was a weak offer to plan their next meals with fewer vegetables, but that vegetables were healthy. To which Zoey faked a loud gag.

"I get you're disappointed, but we're saving beach hot dogs until Jordan can join us."

"I wish she was here instead of just you." Zoey's cheeks glowed with her defiance.

Grace glared at her sister. "Come on Zoey. You're being a butt. None of this is Ellie's fault."

Ellie's patience was running thin. "You do eat peanut butter, right?" Her tone was more strident than she intended. Zoey nodded sheepishly.

"Fine. So, help yourself. I'm going for my evening walk on the beach. You're welcome to come or stay."

"Mind if I come along? I've never walked on the beach after a thunderstorm." Grace took her and Ellie's plates into the kitchen and turned on the garbage disposal.

"Yes, of course you're welcome."

"Wait for me," Zoey called, her hastily prepared sandwich clutched in her hand. Peanut butter dripped onto the floor and Ellie looked away, pretending not to notice.

Watching the girls, Ellie remembered another evening on the beach. That evening, a southeasterly wind was blowing across the bay and ominous rain clouds were building offshore. The shoreline breeze stirred the pit of embers from her small fire, releasing floating sparks like flitting dragonflies into the gathering darkness. Jordan had called earlier, explaining her delay as an unexpected shift change.

Ellie had watched as Molly, her neighbor's live-in nanny, called to her young charges, Marcus and Todd. The boys left the water and stood shivering in the sudden cool air. Molly stooped and wrapped a dry towel around each boy. Ellie had rarely seen either parent with the boys, though she had occasionally shared brief exchanges with Molly while the boys played.

The boys raced along the path that led to the sprawling house perched above and Ellie smiled at the boy's playful scuffle to be first to reach the summit, marveling at the abundance of boy energy. Ellie, on an impulse she had not entirely understood, had invited ten-year-old Marcus to join her on one of her afternoon strolls. Marcus had taken it on himself to extend her invitation to subsequent walks. Marcus had proved to be delightfully curious about the natural setting and her family pioneers, and he was unusually sensitive to the feelings of others.

On one of their walks, Marcus asked if she had ever been a mom. Though puzzled by his implied notion that motherhood was somehow tentative, she answered that she was not, nor had she ever been, a mom. He slipped his warm hand into hers and, smiling, offered that he thought she would make a good mom. She said in return that he was sweet to have said as much. It was not until later that she learned Marcus's mother lived with her new husband in Vancouver, BC, and that he and Todd visited her only at Christmas. Their mom liked playing Mrs. Santa, he said, and she and her new husband had no children.

Ellie had suppressed her earlier desires for motherhood, and at 39, she was past the age she felt comfortable at the thought of childbearing. Adoption for two workaholic moms was out of the question. She did not want a child of hers and Jordan's to ever feel the way Marcus had implied.

Marcus came more often for walks, and he sometimes brought her perfectly shaped shells and rare flowers from his mother's greenhouse, which was tended, he said, by an indifferent gardener. She felt Marcus had, perhaps unintentionally, shared his feelings about his mother's absence. Ellie came to accept that Marcus sought her out because he was lonely, and perhaps he thought she was too. Ellie found herself looking forward to Marcus' visits. When Marcus' family unexpectedly moved to Colorado, she returned to her solitary walks, and had missed Marcus' presence and their conversations.

Thunder clouds were rapidly moving inland as she, Grace and Zoey walked the beach in a path of moonlight. Grace commented on the view of the night sky; its brightness. She told of nights when she had lain on the rooftop of the Impala, wishing for such a beautiful sky.

"It was as if the stars had disappeared and there was only darkness," Grace said.

Ellie's heart tightened in an ache of sadness, and although she was deeply moved by the girls' plight, she dared not speak of other such nights in the girls' future. Temporary was just that.

On their return, Ellie suggested popcorn and a movie. Zoey was allowed to select the movie, and though Grace complained about having watched the movie multiple times, she, too, seemed agreeable to placating her sister. Perhaps she too was unwilling to risk another outburst.

After the girls had retired to their bedrooms, Ellie returned to the kitchen, poured herself a glass of wine, and went onto the deck. But not even the sound of the gentle waves licking the shoreline eased her growing doubts.

She replayed an earlier exchange between her and Jordan in which Ellie had reluctantly consented to Jordan's persistent pleas for deepening their relationship with Grace and Zoey. It was not what had been said, but rather the troubling lack of clarity as to the meaning of a *more involved* relationship.

She wondered what part of Jordan's commitment to Grace and Zoey was motivated by guilt at the loss of two young friends to the horrors of the streets. Was she somehow seeking redemption for acts of cruelty against these two? Acts that Jordan could not have possibly prevented? Ellie reasoned that if she asked, Jordan would be unable or unwilling to answer.

Ellie left the deck desperate for sleep, but as she passed Grace's bedroom, she paused. Zoey and the testy cat whose name Ellie had forgotten slept curled into the curve of Grace's back. Memories of moments spent with young Marcus flooded back and Ellie left the bedroom doors ajar should either Grace or Zoey awaken during the night and need her.

— 107 —

Daniel

Daniel watched as Jordan entered the door to the coffee shop and was relieved that she had changed out of her uniform. A cop in uniform attracted attention while a tall woman wearing jeans did not. He stood and extended his hand, thanking her for agreeing to meet. Her hand was cool against his sweaty palm.

He pushed the steaming cup of coffee across the table and mumbled something about remembering she took her coffee black. They sat, and she nodded and put the cup to her lips.

"Tell me, Daniel, why are we here?" She pushed back against the seat as though she meant to distance herself from any notion that her presence required small talk.

"Right. I'm sure the girls told you that we've had no word from their mom."

She nodded. "Has that changed somehow?"

"Yes, just yesterday, after I dropped the girls off at the vet clinic for a ride to your place. Leah called collect from Duval County. She wouldn't say why or for who, but she wanted me to wire bail money before a scheduled court hearing."

She glanced at him and then turned away, as if some sudden movement or sound had attracted her attention. Maybe her reaction had nothing to do with what he'd said, but a cop's keen alertness to her surroundings. He couldn't be sure, but he believed what he saw in her eyes was wariness.

"And I know you understand what bottoming out means for someone like Leah. And... I'm thinking about going up there to find out if she's being held in jail. But, like I said, she didn't say the bail money was for her. It's not like her to risk me knowing where she is. Unless she wants me to come for her."

She held his gaze and leaned forward, her forearms resting on the table.

"And if you're chasing after what may very well be your wife's ghost, then you can't look after Grace and Zoey. Is your plan to return them to their aunt?"

"No. Leah threatened to steal the girls away before allowing them to return to her sister's. And although she could be in jail, I won't take that chance."

"You want me and Ellie to care for them while you're gone, is that right?"

Her frankness should not have surprised him, but it did, and every word he had rehearsed left his brain. Still, he understood that Grace was his connection with Jordan, and he meant to use that connection to strengthen his appeal.

"That's what Grace wants, and Zoey must stay with her sister. Since her birth, those two have been joined at the hip. There's no separating them. Not that I've ever thought... to do anything like that."

"Right, but I need to know what *you* want."

"I... agree with Grace. But like you once said, you're a cop and not a social worker. Still, I've noticed after weekends with you and Miss Ellie, the girls are calmer. Eager for their next visit." He had spent those weekends with Sarah and looked forward in much the same way.

"And how long do you intend to be gone?"

"With Leah, I can never say what she might require of me."

A server came with a pot of hot coffee, and both he and Jordan pushed their empty cups forward. She refilled their cups and moved on to the next customers.

"If Ellie and I were to agree to take the girls, there would be conditions. Starting with the fact that neither of us would agree to some shitty arrangement that resulted in those girls ricocheting from one household to another on your or your wife's whims. Second, a change of schools would be required. Are Grace and Zoey agreeable to that?"

"Yeah. After the hell they've known with me and their mom, that kind of ongoing shakeup would be real bad for them. And as far as changing schools is concerned, they're fine. Zoey is always smarter than any kid in her class and Grace is all about advanced classes and good grades. Earning her way into a good college is what she lives for."

Jordan squinted, and he felt she knew he lied. He had not spoken to either girl about their willingness to change schools.

"I'll talk with Ellie, and you and I will talk again. Understand that any decision will be a joint decision. We can't be good for the girls if there's friction between Ellie and me."

"I get it, and that's the way it should be." He blushed, and his awkwardness spoke to his lack of experience with joint marital decisions.

"In case you do decide to take on the responsibility of looking after my girls...." He drew a labored breath and looked into her eyes. "I need to be clear that I am their father, and I'll never agree to give up my girls to anyone... or for anyone."

She held his gaze, and if she felt his pain and fear at the thought of losing Grace and Zoey, her training and experience had surely taught her that even a well-intended man could turn dangerous when cornered.

She stood to leave and placed a ten on the table. As she headed for the door, she turned slightly and said, "That was some really weak coffee."

He stood watching as her truck pulled through a caution light and disappeared into heavy traffic. He would say nothing to Grace of his conversation with Jordan, for he wished to spare her any disappointment.

— 108 —

Ellie

After what seemed a thousand rings, the groggy voice of Lilly, her attorney and best friend, streamed a litany of profanities.

"What the fucking fuck? It's dark damn two o'clock in the morning."

"Lilly, it's me. I'm sure Jordan has lost her... her senses."

"For Christ sakes, she's a fucking cop and whatever crime she's committed...."

"No, Lilly, please, you've got to hear me out. I'm absolutely terrified."

"What the hell are you rattling on about?"

"I, we... Jordan and I... have consented to becoming... *Co-Moms on demand.*" Ellie didn't have a proper word for what she feared.

"Okay, listen, Jordan's working nights and that always makes you a bit squirrely. And you're drunk. So, for my sake if not yours, take a couple of Xanax. Get into bed and call me in the morning... because I know you two are too damn smart to agree to do what I just heard you say."

Lilly's further non-legal advice as a friend was that if what Ellie was saying was true, then Jordan was "bat-shit crazy", and Ellie was to demand that Jordan recant any verbal agreement she might have made and the two were to decline any and all further contact with the children in question or their mad parents.

Lilly's words were much too harsh. Still, Ellie worried that Jordan was so caught up in the emotional tragedy of Grace and Zoey's lives, that she had failed to consider, in legal terms, her proposal that Grace and Zoey be placed in their care in the absence of their mother and with the consent of their father. What legal or emotional jeopardy was hidden in their handshake agreement? One truth had emerged; her and Jordan's orderly world would be turned upside down in multiple ways that neither could possibly imagine.

Ellie and Jordan stood on the sidewalk in front of Lilly's office and watched as Daniel drove away in search of Leah.

During Ellie's frantic midnight call, Lilly had reluctantly agreed to prepare a standard, boiler-plate agreement, although she warned that any legal agreement she produced could not protect the two against inevitable heartbreak at the future loss of the girls.

She had assembled the three parties in her office and explained that the agreement granted Jordan and Ellie *temporary custodial* status. As they signed the agreement, Ellie had understood that the word *temporary* meant that she and Jordan would assume the responsibility and expense of caring for the girls but have no clear legal grounds to affect any ultimate outcome on behalf of Grace and Zoey. The agreement had done little more than limit their personal liability against any future lawsuits.

— 109 —

Ellie

Although the girls had made several weekend visits prior to coming to reside full-time, the four had remained strangers in many ways. Everyone was called upon to cope with new roles that carried unclear expectations and the resulting anxieties. Grace and Zoey were confronted with adjusting to a home that both Ellie and Jordan adored for its isolation and natural beauty, while Zoey had exclaimed that they might just as well have landed on Mars. Ellie was stung by Zoey's sentiment, though she had heard similar remarks from friends and co-workers. Lillie had expressed disbelief that the two were happy to live without fast-food delivery.

Ellie continued to be mystified as to how she and Jordan were to respond to the demands of a resentful and outspoken pre-teen. If she was not acting out, Zoey talked non-stop. And there was the belligerent cat, Jimmie.

Ellie had prepared pasta to serve with homemade sauce from her Italian grandmother's cherished recipe. She hoped that a meal without vegetables could persuade Zoey that there was something edible other than frozen chicken nuggets and French fries.

Zoey came into the kitchen, wearing her familiar defiant expression. She took one look at the steaming pot of pasta and burst into a shrill scream.

"No, I don't want that. Mom always got us pizza on Fridays."

Grace scoffed at Zoey but waited for Ellie's response.

"I'm sorry you're disappointed. I thought you would like spaghetti for a change." Ellie felt her face stinging, and her own screams were barely under control.

"Why are you keeping me away from my aunt's? I don't like it here."

Grace spoke up. "Ah, come on Zoey. Stop with your freaking bullshit. You like pasta. Besides, I'm starved. So you need to sit down."

"No, you're siding with her against Mom." Zoey's twisted face was now even more defiant. It was as though she could not get control of her emotions.

"I'm calling Dad."

"No, you aren't, and I'm siding with my empty stomach. Everything smells great. So cut out the freak show."

"I hate you. You're a traitor." Zoey screamed and ran from the house.

Ellie was prepared to go after Zoey, though she was totally baffled and had no idea what she might say.

"She won't go far," Grace offered.

"But... shouldn't I go after her? Try to reason with her?"

"Nope, she never listens when she's angry." Ellie heard something in Grace's tone she hadn't heard before; a welcome arm around the shoulder.

The door swung open, and Jordan stood in the doorway, staring toward the path to the beach.

"Hey, wasn't that Zoey I saw just now?"

"Yeah, I'll go after her when she's had time to cool down," Grace answered.

"Right. Something smells great. And I'm starved." Jordan locked away her weapon and badge. Afterwards, she stepped into the kitchen and kissed Ellie, who was filling a plate with steaming food. "Hey kid, you ready for me to run you into the ground?" Jordan teased.

"That'll be the day." Grace pumped her arm and grinned.

Jordan and Grace ate seconds and offered numerous compliments for both Grandmother's sauce and Ellie's effort while pretending not to notice Zoey's reappearance on the deck. When hunger overcame her stubbornness, Zoey came back into the house, took her place at the counter, and ate without further complaint.

Ellie offered up thanks to her long-departed grandmother, who had taken her and her older sister in during their parents' bitter and protracted divorce. She remembered her resentment toward her grandmother, which had sprung from her confusion over loyalties to her parents and acceptance of her grandmother's stricter rules. Zoey was likely experiencing similar feelings. Maybe that was where she and Zoey would start a new conversation.

After a particularly difficult day for Ellie that had ended with an unsuccessful emergency surgery to save a drop-off—a feral cat that had suffered a hit and run—she and the girls had gotten a late start for home. In the car, Grace had incessantly fumed, and Zoey had demanded to know why she had let the cat die.

Grace asserted with frustration that she had been robbed of the grade she deserved on a lengthy biology project by her teacher, who she declared held a bias against any solution that suggested his fixed conclusions were subject to even the slightest review.

"It's faulty science. Arrogant and narrow-minded," Grace exclaimed.

"Oh no, you failed," Zoey shouted from the back seat.

"God no, that's lame. I got an A minus." Grace crossed her arms in defiance.

"Arrogant? I see. And narrow-minded?" Ellie replied with a restrained chuckle.

"Okay, I get the sarcasm. But if I earned an A, I should have been graded that way."

Grace typically spoke admiringly of the same teacher, and her present response may have resulted from a handwritten note that read: "I expect the absolute best from you."

Changed into shorts and a tee, Ellie stepped barefoot onto the deck and contentedly breathed in the salt air. She watched a lone figure moving with the elegance and rhythm of sheer joy. Grace ran daily, rain or shine, and she no longer returned with her face smeared in what Ellie had despairingly thought was a mix of sweat and tears. Now she returned with her face flushed and sweaty, but clear-eyed and relaxed.

Grace ran onto the deck, breathing hard. "Is that pizza I smell?"

"It's Friday night. What else." They laughed as the oven timer buzzed.

Ellie marveled at the volatility of teenage emotions. Yet she found it difficult to discern Grace's emotional state because she, not unlike Jordan, was more self-contained. Consequently, Ellie did not fully understand the source of Grace's recent antagonism toward her dad, and there was no sign that her refusal to speak with Daniel had abated.

Ellie, too, was uncomfortable with Daniel's insistence that she intercede with Grace on his behalf. During Daniel's last call, he had reminded her of her and Jordan's sworn agreement to allow him visits with his daughters. Ellie had explained to him that she wished to avoid any perception of divided loyalty that might jeopardize her evolving relationship with Grace. He was welcome to visit but only at Grace's invitation. She had avoided a conversation with Jordan, concerned that Jordan's adage, *confront a problem head-on,* could result in further antagonism between herself and Daniel.

— 110 —

Grace

It had taken Grace weeks to finally sleep through the night. She had clutched her phone in her hand, fearful that she would miss a late-night or early morning call from their mom. After a month and no calls, Grace had stopped listening to her phone at night. The noises of the city streets she thought would forever be in her worst dreams were replaced by the peaceful sounds of the gentle surf and the musical calls of the Whip-poor-wills. The harsh squawk of the Night Herons foraging for food for their young in the mudflats on low tides.

The high school she now attended had a smaller student enrollment but was new, and the science department's offerings included a full range of advanced placement classes. Grace had persuaded herself that earning her way back into these courses could still give her a decent shot at earning a scholarship to a second-tier college. But she would always need a backup plan and, although basketball was not her first choice, her overall GPA was still not where she believed it sould be and it was likely her better option.

Grace joined the varsity basketball team near mid-season and her first game with her new team was against a perennial top district contender. Her team was beaten like a drum. Although her teammates lacked the skills to win, the young coach was eager to improve player skills and instill a winning attitude. Grace easily became the team's top scorer and rebounder, and although the team simply did not have the talent, the players worked hard at improving.

Losing was never easy, but somehow it stung less. Maybe the difference came with the fact that other parts of her life were calmer, more predictable, and far less complicated. Jordan and Ellie attended games together when Jordan's duty schedule permitted, and Ellie, who knew nothing about game strategy or rules, attended all home games. She and Jordan were invited to sit in the section reserved for team parents.

Grace peered into Zoey's bedroom, where she was reading aloud from one of her many favorite books, *Call of the Wild*, to a dozing Jimmie. Zoey had been delighted to discover Ellie's collection of novels, and at Ellie's invitation, she set about reading. Grace was sure Zoey had read the same book during their many visits to the library while they were homeless. Zoey would have been seven or eight then.

Grace sat on the bed next to Zoey, who reached her arms around Grace, resting her head against Grace's chest. "Do you think Mom means to come back for us?"

"Umm, I can't say, but I think she just might. What do you think?" Grace pulled Zoey closer, and Zoey smacked Grace on the cheek, giggling the way she had as a little kid when some new idea had excited her.

"Thought you were too old for that kind of kid stuff." Grace pretended to wipe the spittle from her cheek.

"I miss Mom, but it's okay that you, me, and Jimmie are rescues. And that Jordan and Ellie are like the John Thornton character. I'm writing my own story about us, but I'm not ready for you to read it." Zoey had long ago stopped asking Grace for stories about Mom and baby Zoey.

"I know I'll love your story." Grace wanted Zoey's stories to be happy, adventurous ones, and Grace dared not speak of her fears that Mom could show up any day or night. That she might cajole or frighten her and Zoey into agreeing to follow her into some other hell-on-earth scheme born of her illness.

Zoey's smile wavered. "I've decided I like it here with Jordan and Ellie. It's... umm... easier."

Grace squeezed Zoey's warm hand. "Yeah, and easy is good."

"So, why are you staying mad at Dad? Cause I really don't want to anymore."

"My *why* is... well, complicated. But you're old enough to decide for yourself." Zoey's forehead gathered, and it occurred to Grace that she and Zoey had faced adversities together and that Zoey's awareness of her independence was new to her.

Grace got into bed but lay awake long after the familiar sounds of the household had quieted. Grace accepted that understanding Mom's decision in its entirety was impossible and the family's familiar excuses had never been anything but lies. Mom had simply followed yet another all-consuming delusion brought about by her illness.

More crushing for Grace was her lingering question as to why Dad had stopped looking for Mom and was rumored to have moved in with a woman neither she nor Zoey had met. Had he chosen this woman over her and Zoey? Grace cared nothing about her aunt's religious judgement of Dad's infidelity. Rather, her condemnation was based on his betrayal, that he had bargained her and Zoey away to Jordan and Ellie in favor of *her*. How could she ever forgive him? Though Zoey was right and she, too, was weary of her anger.

— 111 —

Grace

Grace woke before the day's first light and pulled on running shorts and a tee, quietly leaving an otherwise sleeping household. She ran comfortably toward the first mile marker and turned back. Her mind was made up to finally do what she had most dreaded. Reaching the beach in front of the cottage, she took her phone from her pocket and removed the block from his number.

"Dad, it's me." Grace had only a vague notion of what she now expected from an exchange with her dad. Nor did she know how she would handle failure.

"Oh my God, Grace I've..."

"No, Dad." She interrupted. "I'll go first."

"Uh, alright." His willing acceptance deepened her uncertainty. Neither she nor he had experience with honesty, and she now realized that what she most sought was shared candor between them.

"Dad, are you looking for Mom?"

He reiterated what Grace already knew about his earlier failed attempts and his response to Mom's urgent phone call that he wire bail money to Jacksonville. But offered nothing more specific than his disappointment that when he arrived there, she was not there waiting for him and, as far as he could discern, had never been in custody.

"I'm sorry, and I understand why you might lose hope. But, Dad, if you're no longer looking, why are Zoey and I still here with Jordan and Ellie?"

"When I first agreed for you and Zoey to go to Ms. Jordan and Ms. Ellie's, I was still convinced that if you girls stayed with me, your mom would never be persuaded that I alone could keep you safe, teach you what you need to know about being successful, and she would return and steal you away. I could never let that happen."

"That was then, but what about now? What has changed?" A long silence followed, and the air around Grace stopped moving, and she felt her lungs might collapse. She wanted him to tell her whether or not the rumored woman existed. Maybe tell her the woman's name, and most of all, whether he had shared with her anything about his daughters or his volatile wife. Though Grace asked herself if she possessed the will to hear a truthful response, should he offer as much.

"Grace. Grace," he repeated. "Are you still there?" His voice was a panicked scream, and she assured him she was there.

"Thank God," he exclaimed, "I thought I'd lost you again."

Grace recalled her desperate phone call the morning following her parents' big fight, and her near paralyzing fear that she and Zoey would be alone, without him in their lives. She had been wholly unprepared to hear the truth then, but now was different.

"Grace, please forgive me. I should have told you and Zoey much earlier... about Sarah and me. At first, I was ashamed of my unfaithfulness to your mom, and afraid that you would believe Sarah was the reason I stopped looking for Leah. And that is not the whole truth."

"Then what is, Dad?"

"I started accepting after Jacksonville that her disappearance isn't like all the other times." He hesitated before continuing. "I now believe your mom doesn't want to be returned to us, and I accept that you and Zoey are better off with two kind and smart women than you would be with me. And I swear that's the whole of what I know to be true."

"Do you know yet what you want from... Sarah?" It was difficult to think of Sarah as real, but speaking her name aloud felt like a start.

"Not entirely, no. First, I need to know if I am capable of letting your mom go."

Grace had no answer, and welcomed their silence, but was comforted by the sound of his steady breathing. And maybe that was the source of her strength, which enabled her to ask whether he believed Mom would ever seek them out.

"I thought she was far more likely to call you and Zoey than me."

"After a time, I stopped expecting Mom to call."

"We shouldn't give up on her. You know how she likes... surprises."

Grace knew he held even less hope than she did. Still, she remembered Mom's Saturday morning breakfasts of pancakes, Dad's jars of honey, and their last trip to the beach. She had chosen to set aside her and Zoey's frightening late-night escape to the park, weird speeches delivered atop a kitchen chair, and the notorious front lawn party.

"Grace, I'm not sure it was right, but I asked Ellie if I could visit you and Zoey."

"And what'd she say?"

"That any visit was your and Zoey's call."

"I'd like it if we continued to talk. But I'd like to wait on a visit." Grace was pleased with Ellie's answer. It showed her respect. The kind one adult gives another.

"Right. I understand." He sounded disappointed, even hurt, but once lost, trust is hard to get back. Rushing could spoil any future they might have.

— 112 —

Grace

Grace walked to the mailbox on the highway, imaging how it would feel to finally glimpse a part of her future. She had received five athletic recruitment letters of interest, though nothing solid. Each program had detailed the merits of their university's athletic facilities, team histories, and academic programs. Follow-up phone conversations with assistant coaches had yielded invitations for her to schedule a campus visit. Grace had celebrated each with relief while she anxiously awaited a scholarship offer from the university of her first choice. If not a scholarship, then an award from one of several academic grants for the study of marine biology for which she had applied.

She reached into the mailbox and extracted a lone, official-looking envelope addressed to *Ms. Grace D Killian.* Her fear of rejection overrode her excitement, and with a trembling hand she gently removed the envelope from the box. Read over and over again the return address and her name printed on the envelope. Wishing to calm her fears, Grace slipped the envelope into her jean pocket and walked back along the oyster shell path toward the tranquility of the blue-green waters. Reaching the narrow strip of coastal shore at high tide, Grace sat on the wet sand, her feet in the surf, and pulled the envelope from her pocket.

— 113 —

Grace

Grace stayed up late reviewing her research notes, especially those gleaned from a series of articles published online detailing Green County law enforcement's largest-ever bust of a drug and sex trafficking ring. The investigation had yielded eighteen members of a widespread criminal enterprise, including Joseph ("Big Joseph") Lamar Light, Florence Louise Griner, and others involved in what the reporter called *The Mount Pleasant Operation.*

Grace had scoured other articles, searching for any references to ongoing investigations that might hold clues to whether her mother had been named as a person of interest. Would Big Joseph or the woman named in the formal accusation, who Grace believed to be Luna's mother, give up Mom to the authorities? Grace had continued to follow online the reports and so far, Mom's name had not appeared.

In the first article Grace had read, there was a reference to seven female minors believed to have been immigrants illegally transported into the country, held against their will, and forced into sex work. As minors, their names had been withheld, and the girls were placed under the supervision of the state's division of children and family services until they could be delivered to the proper agency of authority within Homeland Security.

Grace had only known of six girls ever delivered by the Spanish-speaking man in the battered white van. Was the report simply incorrect in having named a seventh girl? Grace agonized over the possibility that the seventh girl was Luna, and that she was deported along with the other six.

Still, Grace clung to her belief that Luna was too smart to be drawn into the fate of the other six girls. Luna had been so determined to never become her mother that she had threatened to slit Big Joseph's throat.

Grace meant to be prepared for her conversation with Jordan. She turned off her computer and desk lamp, only to lie awake in the darkness with her memories of Luna: how she had felt safe in her presence.

Grace's slim thread of hope rested with Jordan's last text message.

— 114 —

Jordan

Jordan entered the bar and scanned its customers, and there was not a recognizable cop among the other patrons. Nikki had picked a bar filled with stockbrokers and money managers. Nikki sat at a table up front, and Jordan was grateful she did not need to make her way through the bar. It was clear a brash dyke cop did not belong there.

"Hey," Nikki said, and smiled. "Pull up a chair, partner."

Jordan looked around the bar with its over-stuffed chairs and lounges, and high class, skimpily clad women. "Damn, girl, just because I'm buying. I know a place where there's better-looking women, and beers are way cheaper."

"Right, but do you see other cops with big ears and loose tongues?"

Nikki smiled, and Jordan realized anew just how much she had missed her. Jordan took a seat and ordered for the two of them. With their second drink, Jordan invited Nikki to share what she had learned.

"Court records on the disposition of the seventh, and unnamed, girl are sealed, of course, because she's a minor. You'd need a court order to break the seal. You don't have that, and I can't fabricate just cause."

"Damn, I was wishing against reason for something to take back to Grace."

"Yeah, but you've got to admit *Luna Diaz* isn't much to work with. There's too much secrecy among locals who might have leads. And like I said, there's the bigger issue of her being a minor."

"According to Grace, Griner is the name of the woman who claimed the seventh girl was her daughter."

Nikki frowned. "Yeah, I'd say so. If there's anything to what I learned from a talkative cop who was on the scene when the motel bunch were taken down. She claimed to have overheard Griner claim the seventh girl was an American citizen and her name was Luna Diaz."

"Did she mention whether or not a father had presented himself?"

"No, but it makes sense that the girl was placed in the foster care system if efforts were made to locate the father and they failed. Or they located him, and he refused."

"Still, there are school records."

"Sealed too."

"Yeah, I get that... privacy and all."

"Yeah, and as you know many of these kids are among the most vulnerable in the fucking universe."

"What are the chances of reaching the mother? Wouldn't she know where her kid is?"

"That may depend on if the kid had wanted to make contact. Though she is a minor, and if she's in the system, she may not have gotten a say in the matter."

"Damn, I hate to go back empty-handed."

"I know, but I'll stay on it for a while longer." Nikki agreed to approach the reporter who had written a series of newspaper stories on the chance she would be willing to divulge anything she had learned from Griner, such as where Luna Diaz might have been relocated after the arrests.

Jordan spotted Grace waiting on the deck and hurried to meet her.

"Hey, tell me, please, did you learn anything from your friend the detective?"

"Yeah, but first, why don't we go for a short walk down on the beach?" Jordan removed her shoes and rolled the cuffs of her pants, and she and Grace walked a short way before Grace pressed Jordan to tell what she had learned.

"I'm afraid it wasn't much." Jordan reported to Grace what Nikki had told her.

Grace recalled that Luna had once referred to her father as a *Mex-mix*, and she had refused the school's effort to force her into any one identity. She had argued that race was not even a thing, and that the world's population was nothing more than an opportunistic mix of mongrels.

Grace was disappointed but welcomed Nikki's willingness to dig further into Luna's whereabouts.

The Magical Whooping Crane
Spring 2022

— 115 —

Leah

The highway had stretched before Leah like a ribbon of mercy, beckoning with the obsessiveness of a new lover. The scent of decaying wild grasses and brine stirred from the tidal mudflats as an early spring morning rose to meet her, gently whispering her name, and she pushed the dutiful Impala harder. The roar of its engine powered her forward in her struggle to outpace her madness.

Over the months of her healing pilgrimage, Leah had known moments of amazing clarity; unmarked days during which she had taken employment at bottom-rated motels. She showered in vacant rooms, washed her clothes in lavatories, and ate scraps of food left behind in guest refrigerators. She had performed eight-to-ten-hour shifts of mindless tasks, wary of the briefest contact with those who shared the works' drudgery: worn women like herself whom she thought of as black and blue; runners all, with their own tightly held secrets.

She had spent her meager earnings on street drugs when she failed to persuade a late-night pharmacist to refill her legal but expired prescription. When her greater need came near the end of the month, she bought Percocet from street vets she nicknamed Generals, who sacrificed their own pain meds to buy food, their monthly disability checks long since spent. On the days she was paid, Leah would buy gasoline and motor oil for the road-weary Impala, and alcohol for herself. Occasionally she bought meals at off-interstate dinners, though she largely survived on cheap canned meats and over-ripe bananas.

Now, she knew only desperate days and nights, and had stopped showing up for anything except bargaining sex in exchange for either drugs or cheap wines. With every act of bargaining, her fragile being, her very soul, had plummeted further into the abyss.

Leah woke with a warm midday sun in her face, a golden fairness of day that brought tears of longing to her eyes. Beautiful memories of radiant happy days when she had taken Gracie to the park while beautiful Zoey had yet floated peacefully inside her. These moments were her gifts as she, with the fear of a snarling dog, had managed to hold her raging illness at bay. Those moments of sweetness were now no more than pictures left out in the rain, and whose loss made her want to pass from this realm into the one promised her.

Leah's first attempt at sitting upright failed, and she struggled a second before pushing open the car door and standing alongside the Impala. Empty wine bottles were scattered about on the ground and Leah did not want to remember their price to her battered psyche. A fit of dry heaves ripped through her empty gut, and the stench of her breath gagged her. She wiped her mouth on the soiled blanket stolen from someone who needed it far less than she.

Startled by a distant sound, she leaned heavily on the Impala for support, and somehow managed to stay upright. What she heard was not a human or animal threat, but Mary frolicking with a Monarch butterfly in a field of tall grasses punctuated by colorful patches of milkweed. Mary and her new playmate invited Leah to join in their antics.

In the pleasantness of the moment, Leah's mind seemed to split, and she gloried in all things good: past and future. The images she saw were no longer those of shame, but ones of pride, filled with the promise of seeds cast upon fertile soil. Ahead lay the victory she had been promised by the messenger: *"Rise, Sister of the Chosen, and hear the Good News. I am not the Good News, but its humble messenger, bringing Word of the magical healing powers of the ancient Whooping Crane."*

Taking nothing from the Impala, Leah called to Mary and her new friend, and the three set off across the grassy field.

— 116 —

Moses

Moses caught sight of a lone woman walking along the edge of the road. Although such an occurrence was not uncommon, he was an inquisitive man, and pondered what circumstance might explain her walking alone in the mid-day heat. He recalled seeing an old Impala, three or four miles back, parked beyond an open field beneath a sweeping live oak. Might this woman have fallen victim to some random mechanical failure?

The woman stopped and stooped, as if she coaxed a small child to follow, but there was no one other than her. He slowed his truck to a crawl so as not to frighten her, and drawing alongside, he called to her. The woman put her head down and walked on. She feared a rapist, maybe? For she clearly possessed little of what might interest a would-be thief. He was neither a rapist nor a thief, but how was she to know?

Leah walked on, ignoring the would-be intruder, while sorting through her jumbled thoughts. Had her wounded Daniel surrendered his readiness to love another and come for her in an act of duty? Wondering, she stopped and turned to face the craggy old man behind the plaintive voice that was not Daniel.

"Ma'am, I can't know where you might be headed. But if I did, I just might be going that way myself." He stopped the truck, reached across the seat, and pushed open the door, inviting her in.

The silly old man's confusion as to his destination, though mildly perplexing, was none of her concern. Mary, to Leah's surprise, left her side and leaped onto the truck seat, settling next to the stranger. The Monarch sat on the tip of Mary's nose, excitement showing in the rhythmic beat of her wings.

"Name's Moses, ma'am." He softly chuckled, as though his name was something of a joke. "I'm nothing like the Bible Moses. Meaning to say, I ain't led a single soul any place they weren't already headed."

Not a joke, for his eyes held sadness, not glee.

"Would you know the place where I'm to meet the whooping cranes? They're expecting me. I've kept them waiting much too long."

"I do," he answered softly.

"Will you take me there?"

"Yes, I'll take you when I've made a delivery to an old, wounded friend. He doesn't live far from here."

Leah studied Mary's calm demeanor and was reassured. She whispered to Mary, and not to the man, "Then I'll go with him."

Leah got into the truck next to Mary and she and the stranger rode in silence before he asked, "About this place you seek...?" He did not turn to her in a manner of inviting shared discourse, but added, "Somewhat strange you would be going that way, and I happened to come along like I did."

He paused. "Susie, my sweet wife, gone eight years ago this day, spoke of that place as 'enchanted'. One of 'healing that only the goddesses of nature could have dreamt with such perfection,'" he said.

For a fleeting moment, the man, Moses, whom Leah now considered by name, studied her with intensity. He blinked hard and his haggard face held all that was fathomable about a lonely man's compromise with grief. Leah turned away, not daring to risk knowing more of his pain. He was a kindred soul to her wounded Daniel. Still, Leah had nothing of comfort to offer either.

Her own years of madness and pain had left her hollow, a hull of womanhood, rendering her incapable of human compassion. Still, she would stay with the man who answered to the name Moses. She tried and failed to recall such a character from her childhood book of Bible stories.

— 117 —

Leah

Approaching a narrow bridge over a meandering body of cypress-stained water, Moses pulled the truck to a stop on the shoulder of the road and got out. He took a large cloth bag from the truck bed and walked toward a bellow unlike any scream of desperation Leah had ever heard, the creature's cry echoing through the trees, scattering songbirds and waterfowl alike.

Moses returned and tossed the empty sack in the truck bed and slid behind the wheel.

He turned the truck about and started back in the direction they came before he said, "Methuselah back there is said to be somewhere around one hundred years or more, according to my kin longest in these parts. Don't know if that's true or not, but I've taken to bringing him roadkill whenever I find it. And danged if he don't come up when I call him to me." He laughed with surprising joy.

Leah had never known a man who fed an alligator for no reason other than it made him laugh. How was it that this broken man was destined to speak of her will? She did not know, for the workings of fate would always remain a mystery.

After a mile or so, they left the coastal highway for a narrow, paved roadway. Overhead, splashes of filtered sunlight penetrated the tunnel-like overhang of centuries-old oaks and less magnificent trees. Moses pointed out lovely yellow spring foliage unfamiliar to her that he named a native of Florida; yellow maple. The red maple lent its vibrant red flowering, together with the vividness of flowering redbud and dogwood. Wild grasses, palmetto, and cattail framed the wet edges of the roadway. Beyond the common sand pine were stands of rare longleaf pine. Nature's surviving gift stood towering, and it gently swayed to the ancient rhythm of time.

They left the stands of hardwoods, pines, and flowering trees and bushes to continue along a narrow finger of slightly elevated land bordered by shallow lagoons that reflected the brilliance of sunlight, and beyond, the serenity of the wider bay. Its vast expanse stretched to join the Gulf of Mexico.

Leah's soul lifted, and her spirit interlaced with the message: *Sister of the chosen. Receiver of the ancient gift of magical healing.* A youthful Mary turned her massive head, eyes shining, and Leah reached an arm about her friend's strong shoulders.

At the end of an oyster shell road, they approached staggered rows of barriers. Moses slowed the truck and pulled to a stop a short distance from the barriers. He explained that, for the protection of the cranes, the public was not permitted beyond this point. They had to wait there for a chance at spotting cranes in flight, although in March their chances were slight. The independent cranes had begun to respond to nature's pull for them to return to their northern feeding and breeding grounds.

"Yes, I understand that I am late, but they now know that I am here." Did this simple man not understand that she was no ordinary public? The birds were expecting her. "Are there those whose job it is to stop me?"

"Yes, there are spotters, and they know we are here. Should we move closer, they'll send wildlife officers."

"I see." Leah and Mary got out of the truck, and Leah shaded her eyes and looked back along the empty road. She knelt next to Mary and whispered. "I must go now."

Leah stood and walked to the barriers, squeezed between two of the wooden posts, and walked to the water's edge, scanning the distant horizon. On the far side of a shallow lagoon was a magnificent male crane who stood five feet tall, and although his mate lifted skyward, the male waited.

Moses had gotten out of the truck and walked toward the barrier, where he stopped and watched.

Leah turned to the good man who had delivered her here. "My name is Leah."

He inhaled deeply, his shoulders raised, and exhaled slowly.

Leah stepped into the water. When she stood knee-deep, she turned back and called, "You may tell them the truth of what you witness."

"But I am not good with words."

Leah smiled, turned, and waded deeper into the water and she was unafraid, for John Wayne bobbed on ahead of her. From the direction of the road, she heard the roar of the departing yellow dragon. Her daughters' shining faces were framed in its window, and they smiled and returned her waves.

From the far side of the estuary where she first spotted the splendid crane, it again called to her, and she surrendered all her fears and slipped beneath the surface of the warm water to lie on its sandy bottom. Cradled by the water's rhythmic motion, Leah embraced its solace; its gift of silence. From above, a shadow fell across the smooth surface, and the magnificent Healer tipped its massive wing. Leah's spirit was lifted into flight, and she too soared above clouds fashioned from whipped cream.

— 118 —

Moses

Moses left the island highway and drove onto an oyster shell lane where he stopped, the truck engine idling, and took an envelope from his shirt pocket. At the end of the lane, there was a weather-beaten, shingle-sided beach cottage, and Sam had said on Saturdays, he had a good chance of finding Daniel Killian there.

Moses' journey to keep this promise to Leah had begun a week after he had carried her from the water and sat cradling her to his chest in an effort to drive the chill from her limp body. The wildlife boys had come too late to stop her, and had stood staring across the shimmering water as though there were signs to be had. At some point, the two agreed the situation was out of their hands and that Paramore, the local sheriff, should be notified.

The county coroner, a local dentist, arrived on the scene. He crouched over her body, playing a part he had fashioned from television shows. When he was done, Leah was delivered to the county morgue and Moses was arrested and placed in jail, where he spent five days. Chester Paramore was convinced that this time he would convict Moses of murder.

Paramore had concluded that the unidentified woman was the victim of kidnapping, rape and murder. Moses Yancy had picked up the victim, an unidentified homeless woman, for sex, and at her refusal he had drowned her in a fit of rage. Moses had continued to repeat his own accounting of events, and after five days, a qualified coroner out of Tallahassee found no evidence of sexual assault. He declared the cause of death as drowning, while intimating suicide.

Moses' search of the abandoned Impala resulted in the discovery of an expired auto registration for Daniel Killian, with an address. Moses slipped the registration into his pocket for future reference, removed the license plate, gathered Leah's few possessions from the vehicle. He loaded the wine and whiskey bottles into his truck to dump on his way out of town. Then he set about wiping down the car for fingerprints in an attempt to slow efforts by the locals, should they locate the Impala, to identify Leah before he could find the man he decided was her husband. Maybe there were children, extended family, and friends who would want to know what he had witnessed.

Moses was well on his way out of town when he remembered that in his haste, he had forgotten to put out extra dry food for his fifteen regular visitors. Though the mob had been feral since birth and knew how to look after themselves, he still regretted having failed to fill the feeders. Number Twelve had a young litter hidden in the woods and healthy kittens needed their mom to have better than she got scrounging for scraps. He returned to put out the food, which was the reason for his late afternoon arrival.

Moses arrived in Bailey Cove and drove directly to the address printed on the expired vehicle registration. A name other than Killian appeared on the freshly painted mailbox. Still, he repeatedly rang the doorbell on the slim chance that whoever lived there now might know Daniel Killian's whereabouts, or if not, perhaps what kind of work he did. No one answered the door.

He stepped back onto the oddly painted walkway, and though he could not explain why, the faded rainbow colors left him with a strange sense that Leah had had a hand in its creation. He stood on the sidewalk and scanned the near-empty street for anyone he might ask about the family who had once lived in the yellow house with brightly colored drapes hanging in the front window.

A next-door neighbor was curt in her response, quick to declare that the dad and girls were okay, but that the mother was certifiable. Her story was familiar, for he and Susie had moved more times than he wanted to recall. The best part was the neighbor's notion that the man must have been some kind of auto mechanic, for he was always cluttering his driveway with old vehicles. She had hated the loud engine roars that frightened her parrot, Luther. Moses had thanked her and felt it was a useful clue.

His spirits low, Moses drove out of the neighborhood, thinking that if he were to deliver Leah's message, he needed a new plan. Spotting what he decided was a working-class bar, he reasoned that getting out from behind the wheel and downing a few beers would help him think clearer. He wished he knew something about computers and searching for missing persons. But he'd never owned a computer.

He walked into the bar, which was mostly empty, and ordered a Bud on tap from a huge man wearing what he thought was a lady's frilly pink blouse the size of a pup tent. Beer in hand, he noted a customer sitting alone who wore the uncomfortable silence of a man passing empty time. Unexpectedly, the man invited Moses to join him, declaring that he had been stood up and was damn tired of talking excuses to himself.

After several beers and an hour of rambling talk, against all odds, Moses found he had spent an evening drinking with Sam, who declared himself Daniel's best buddy. Moses thought of his Susie and Leah, strangers who shared a belief in the power of whooping cranes to bestow miracles. Maybe his luck was somehow a part of an extended miracle. Yet he was not a believer in miracles; Jesus, cranes or otherwise. He would stick with the old adage that sometimes even a blind hog lucked up on an acorn.

He bid Sam and the big man behind the bar, whose pink blouse had begun to look perfectly normal, a good evening, bought a couple of hamburgers, and drove to a cheap motel where he slept off the beers.

The beach cottage was as Sam had described, and Moses pulled the truck to a stop next to a late model Jeep. Moses stood next to the truck looking up at a girl with a mat of blonde curls who squinted down at him from a second story deck and waved.

"Afternoon to you too, young lady. I'm Moses, and I was told by a nice man named Sam that I might find Daniel Killian here."

The girl smiled widely in recognition and though he was a man of cautious hope, Moses exhaled sharply, allowing himself to believe that his search for Leah's family was nearing an end.

"I'm Zoey, and Daniel is my dad. He lives in the city with Sarah, but he's coming here for supper." She added that he should wait until Ellie was out of the shower.

Moses slumped onto the tailgate of his truck and squeezed his eyes shut. Now that the act of delivering Leah's message was upon him, he thought about getting back into his truck and driving away, leaving the telling of Leah's story to the county deputy, who was sure to show up soon. But he heard a familiar voice say, *"You may tell them the truth of what you witness."*

A deeply tanned woman stepped through the cottage door and, from above, introduced herself as Ellie. "If you're a friend of Daniel's, please come on up and sit. We expect him later."

"Thank you, ma'am. The truth is, I don't know Daniel. But I met Sam, and he told me to come here. It's a mighty pretty place. A lot like back home, where we were truly hidden."

She looked puzzled and rightly so, he thought. "If it's okay with you, I'll wait here."

The drive, poor food, little sleep and hygiene, and a hangover had drained more sap from him than he had figured. A can of that mess the doctor insisted he stomach, and a quick snooze would do him some good.

"That will be fine. I'll call Daniel. Let him know you're here. Maybe move him along." She smiled. "Can I tell him your business?"

"Ah, on that, ma'am, I'd like to wait if I could. It's the sort of thing best delivered face to face." She nodded, and when she had arranged more deck chairs, she glanced down at him and went back inside the house.

Afterwards, the house was quiet, and Moses took a pillow from the cab and lay in the truck bed. He stared through the deep foliage of a giant oak and squeezed his eyes shut. Scene after scene of his brief but memorable time with Leah played against the backs of his eyelids like black and white newsreels in the old movie theaters of his youth. The mysteries of metaphysics were far beyond his humble grasp, but again he asked himself, had those two desperate souls, his Susie and Leah, somehow known each other.

Leah had somehow known that he would come to understand the meaning of her choice, and that of his sweet Susie, for himself. He would offer peace to her loved ones as Leah had gifted him, for he now knew that she and his Susie had each, in the absence of hope, willed themselves good deaths.

He would deliver the same truth to Leah's family, for she had chosen him as her messenger.

— 119 —

Moses

A slim bearded man Moses took to be Daniel got out of a battered truck and looked toward the deck, where Moses had joined Ellie. Daniel was physically fit, neither young nor old, his bearing that of a man in conflict with his soul. He stepped quickly around to the passenger door and took a fair-haired boy from the arms of a woman who got out, then reached back for the squirming child. She balanced him astride her round hip in the manner of mothers since Eve's firstborn, Cain. Together, the two walked onto the deck.

"I'm Daniel, sir. Sam said that you have come to tell me, uh, us, something important about my wife." He looked beyond Moses, the messenger, to the sorrow he likely already felt.

"I'm Moses, Daniel." The younger man's grip was firm. His large hand was calloused and there was grease under his nails. He was like the men Moses had known for his entire life.

"And this is Josey, Leah's sister, and Josey's son, Casey."

Moses took the woman's extended hand. "Pleased, ma'am." He paused. "And your fine boy there." He smiled, despite the awakening of an old sense of loss, for Susie had never wanted their child.

Josey nodded with little of a mother's pride, though she was likely drained of any emotion other than sadness. Perhaps she, too, was prepared to hear the worst. Both Daniel and Josey hugged Ellie before taking the chairs she offered. Daniel asked about Grace and Zoey.

"Grace has gone for what I suspect will be a long run. No offense to you, sir, but I don't think she wants to hear about her mother from anyone other than Daniel." Ellie's slight smile for Daniel was warm.

Daniel nodded. "And Zoey?"

"In her room, for now, and I would like for Josey to come with me when we have heard Moses." Ellie glanced at Josey, who nodded her acceptance.

The child whimpered and his mother shifted him about to rest against her shoulder. A thumb in his mouth, he closed his eyes and settled.

"Moses, thank you for coming. Now, please tell us about Leah...." Daniel choked back tears and wrapped his long arms tightly around his middle and leaned forward.

"I asked her what I should say, and she answered that I should tell you the truth of what I witnessed."

Moses told how he had met Leah and driven her to the place she sought. That she had waded into the water unafraid and had slipped beneath its surface and was no more. How he had taken her from the water and carried her onshore, where he had waited with her until the authorities took her away. How he had withheld information about the abandoned Impala from the authorities and how he had known to look for Daniel. He finished with Sam's part in last evening's conversation and his arrival here.

"I must confess that I carry a certain burden for making no effort to stop her from going into the water. And that you may rightly hold that against me."

Daniel lifted his bowed head, his face stricken, and he spoke softly, not to Moses, but as though he meant his prayerful words for his lost love alone. The women embraced, shedding fresh tears Daniel seemed to no longer have. Instead, he stared along the narrow strip of sand toward a distant runner as she pounded her grief into the warm sand.

Daniel lifted his gaze to Moses. "No one here is a stranger to one's own burden, nor do we find fault with you, only gratitude.

Where do I go and who do I see about bringing my wife's remains home?"

Moses answered directly.

"Again, I thank you for coming. For bringing the word she wanted us to know... and for having honored her."

"Did she happen to mention me?" Josey asked through her tears, and she squeezed the stirring child closer. Young Casey reached a chubby hand to touch her wet cheek. Ellie placed a hand on Josey's and Moses read no animosity in either woman.

"No ma'am, she spoke of no one. But our time together was brief."

Ellie stood and reached a hand to Josey. Together, they would tell Zoey of her mother's death.

— 120 —

Grace and Daniel

Grace bent forward, her long tanned arms hanging at her side, her breath coming in painful gasps. When her heart rate had returned to normal, she sat on the sand. Behind her on the pathway, she heard the crunching sound of her dad's approach.

Not wishing to intrude on his daughter's grief, Daniel paused and stood quietly without speaking.

Grace reached and patted the space next to her and he sat, their shoulders nearly touching, and it was as though he understood that his touch would have been too much for either she or he to bear. The two sat for a time without speaking.

The sun, like a giant orange ball, appeared to pause astride the earth's gentle contour, its fleeting colors disappearing as if caught in a closed fist with the same caution he had taught her to hold and release fireflies. Twilight came with the dexterity of a pickpocket, robbing the imposing seascape of its familiar details.

"The stranger? Why has he come?"

"To bring word of your mom. Of her passing." His voice was hoarse; filled with emotion.

"I felt her presence just now and I knew. Was she alone at the end?"

"No, the good man whose name is Moses was with her. He said she smiled and stepped into the water, and he thought she was unafraid."

"Had he known her?"

"No, just for a day. But somehow he knew her; her illness. And that was what drew him to her. Maybe her to him."

Grace shivered with an odd sense of familiar energy stirring, reminding her that Mom had once said that *the mystery of death was no more knowable than that of life.*

Grace's eyes filled with tears, and she slipped into her father's embrace, and they held each other. She whispered into his shoulder, "Where do we go to make arrangements to bring her home?"

"We'll leave tomorrow for a small coastal town near Tallahassee. We can receive her body there and transport her for cremation. And when it's returned to us, Moses has agreed to show us the place he drove her. There, we will surrender her ashes."

"Zoey, Aunt Josey, Jordan and Ellie." She paused. "And Sarah."

He looked away with an unfocused gaze before turning back to her.

"You sure?"

"Yes, and Zoey has said as much." Grace felt the tightness that had encased her heart ripped loose and she too, was set free.

His eyes cleared; a sense of a burden lifted. They sat for a time longer without either speaking, likely each absorbing in their own way the reality of their loss and how their lives were to move forward.

"I was just thinking about how proud your mom was of you and Zoey. The promise she held for each of you." His eyes brightened and the earlier tightness around his eyes had relaxed.

"Is it okay that Zoey stays here with Jordan and Ellie when I leave for the university?" Grace had just yesterday received a letter awarding her a four-year grant to study marine biology at one of the state's major universities. "Zoey has made friends, and you were right about here with Jordan and Ellie being best for both me and Zoey."

"I know, and you're not to worry about Zoey."

"What about you? Are you going to be okay?"

"In time, I think," he said.

"Is Sarah willing to wait for your heart to heal?"

"Yes, I believe so."

Her hand in his, they walked toward the voices of those gathered on the deck. Among them was the man who told of her mother's passing, though her mother's narrative would remain hers alone. Grace required nothing more. What remained was her gratitude to a kind stranger. Odd, she thought, that Moses was his name.

— Epilogue —

An excited assistant coach ran onto the floor, whistle blaring. The team's highly touted first-year center with skin the color of creamy caramel came onto the court, brimming with the confidence of an African lioness. Her thighs were jackhammers, and she spouted a fiery brand of smack.

"Yo, walk-on brainy girly. Your bitch momma still crackass crazy?"

"No, yours still whoring?"

"Naw, she got prison and Jesus turned her, and she quit the trade. Strange talk from a bro whose best woman was rumored to be a whore herself." The big woman grinned.

"Goddess help me, but I'm fuckin' crazy about your blasphemous ass," Grace whispered.

Their bodies engaged, bumping, measuring, and inviting, with a familiarity more sensual than competitive.

The big woman laughed with her own brand of sarcasm, and Grace heard an echo from their past: *Oh, yeah? You sure you ain't just being grateful?*

Acknowledgements

In the course of creating a fictional family beleaguered by mental illness and homelessness, I consulted with numerous mental health and law enforcement professionals, all of whom were generous with their time and expertise. There were many private conversations, consultations, and thoughtful discussions with people whose names I will not share, but you know who you are, and you have my undying gratitude.

I am most grateful for the support of my fellow writers. To Darlyn Kuhn, Jim Carpenter, Vicki Weaver, Rosemary Porto, and Gail Dixon who read early versions of the manuscript and offered valuable feedback, thank you for the most unselfish gift one writer can give another.

There are many parts to putting together a book, and I am grateful for everyone who lent their talents and expertise. My editor and publisher, Joan Leggitt, was with me through every revision and idea for revision. Bob O'Lary did an outstanding photo shoot to produce the image on the front cover. And Elizabeth Babski was, as always, talented, skilled, and above all, patient in putting together the final cover.

To Dorothy Allison and Connie May, I am most grateful for having met you all those years ago, and having your encouragement to carry with me throughout my writing journey.

And finally, to my dad, Charlie Spears, for all the stories he told on the back porch, and for showing me the power of story.

About the Author

Pat Spears is the author of three novels and numerous short stories. Her stories have appeared in numerous journals, and anthologies. She is a sixth generation Floridian and lives in Tallahassee, Florida with her partner, two dogs and a rabbit.

Also by Pat Spears:

It's Not Like I Knew Her

Jodie Taylor's childhood is filled with loss, abuse, chronic disappointment, and an instinctive awareness that her desire for women will forever make her an outcast. At 18, she flees her home town in rural north Florida and arrives in racially charged Selma, Alabama in 1956 as a penniless fugitive. She finds work in a café that is frequented by racist night riders and, with an eye on the door, she hunkers down behind a wall of lies and half-truths. Her self-imposed silence with the family she left behind is broken when a crisis sets Jodie on a backward journey. As she struggles to reconcile her past with the present, she begins the inward journey she must take to truly find her home.

Dream Chaser

Jesse McKnight wakes to find that his wife has vanished with only a vague note declaring that she has done so in search of "something better." Her departure thrusts Jesse into the role of reluctant single parent, and his clumsy attempts to bridge years of emotional absence only further alienate his three children. It's his daughter Katie's dream of owning a horse, coupled with his own desire for redemption, that leads him to purchase, sight unseen from a brutal owner, a mustang mare. The mare has been removed from the only place she's ever known. Jesse has managed to hold onto his home but almost nothing else. When their lives intersect, they become each other's best hope for regaining what they've lost.

For more information, plus a look at some of Pat's short fiction, visit her website: www.patspears.com

www.ingramcontent.com/pod-product-compliance
Lightning Source LLC
Chambersburg PA
CBHW051003210726

48287CB00004B/1353